新制多益
聽力考題完全戰略

模擬真實考試情境，完全掌握最新常考句型和聽力題材！
題型分門別類，解析詳盡透澈，輕鬆掌握解題技巧！
最短時間最大效果，三步驟一眼就懂，
最直觀的多益學習書！

STEP 1

Don't Panic!
題型暖身

∨

STEP 2

Comprehension
命題分析

∨

STEP 3

Practice
實戰應用

MP3

作者：Ki Taek Lee
譯者：彭尊聖／沈家淩
審訂：Helen Yeh

Perfect Learning for the TOEIC Listening Comprehension!

新制多益
聽力 考題完全戰略

BASIC

Perfect Learning for the TOEIC Listening Comprehension!

作者：Ki Taek Lee
譯者：彭尊聖／沈家凌
審訂：Helen Yeh

在英語評鑑考試中，多益是最有效、也是最值得信賴的考試。特別是從 2018 年 3 月開始，增加了「整合型試題」，這類題型光靠背誦和解題技巧，是無法完全攻破的。在聽力的「整合型試題」中，例如「詢問對話者意圖」，考生一定要理解前後對話才能選出正確答案。另外在閱讀部分，以往應試舊制多益，只要看文章的一部分就能解題，新多益則融合了各式型態的文章來出題，也增加了許多「整合型試題」，例如「理解文章大意」題型，考生要看過全篇文章、知道文章的脈絡後才能答題，還有在正確位置放入句子的「文意填空」。另外，閱讀的文章類型也出現變化，包括詢問即時通訊軟體的訊息、網路聊天室、三篇閱讀等。

本系列套書對新多益類型做了深層的分析，為了讓應試者能一眼看懂新多益試題，各單元（Part）也收錄了各類試題的詳細解說以及解題戰略。

聽力部分，Part 1 和 Part 2 的試題比重，較舊制降低許多，但選項句子的長度稍微增加了，句子的難度也有變難的傾向。Part 3 的簡短對話，大致會出對話者的意圖、三人對話，還有各式圖表資料同時出現的「整合型試題」。另外，Part 4 的簡短獨白在主題上沒有很大的變動，但是題型相當活用且具挑戰性，例如會問談話中的某特定句子，在整個對話中意涵為何，也會出附帶各式圖表資料的整合型試題。

閱讀部分改變也很多，因為會出現各式各樣的文章與試題，所以對考生來說，這是準備考試時感到最困難的部分。以 Part 7 單篇閱讀而言，共 10 篇 29 題；雙篇閱讀共兩篇，多（三）篇閱讀共三篇，雙篇閱讀與多篇閱讀共 25 題。本書擺脫了舊制多益題型及文章類型，將閱讀分成單篇閱讀、雙篇閱讀、多篇閱讀，在呈現文章模式的同時，還有系統地說明了文章特徵、試題類型及戰略，讓應試者一眼就能看懂文章的特徵和試題類型，並收錄了幫助考生容易解題的詳盡分析。

《新制多益聽力考題完全戰略 Basic 》一書的架構與內容，期望讓應試者能在最短的時間，獲得最大的成果。為了幫助應試者熟悉新多益，本書大量收錄了新多益的試題。

期望各位考生，能獲得最大的學習效果，迎戰新制多益。

作者　Ki Taek Lee 李基宅

Contents

目錄

Part 3 ▶ 簡短對話

Part 4 ▶ 簡短獨白

本書的結構與特色

① 考生一開始接觸多益聽力感到困難,因為只想熟記解題技巧,想靠解題技巧來解題,但平日仍須大量練習聽英文。

② 本書的單元安排為將新多益聽力測驗中,Part 1、2、3、4 常出的試題按題目類型分門別類。

③ 透過有系統的訓練,培養讀者能真正聽懂英文句子,理解句子含意的實力。

▶ 綜上所述,各個單元最先出現的是題型綜覽和學習戰略區,使讀者一目了然測驗重點。

Parts Overview
題型綜覽

幫助多益考生剛開始研習該單元時,先透過例題,掌握一定要熟知的事項。因為是綜覽整個單元,所以請先試著無負擔地掃視,一面掌握多益試題的出題類型。該單元的題型全都學完後,再從頭瀏覽一遍,就能更信心十足地面對多益考試了。

學習戰略及試題類型
揭示各單元的學習方向

因為考生對多益完全陌生,所以開始學習前,本書整理試題的型式與學習重點,幫助考生理解吸收,並集合能得高分的常見句型,以及常考的試題模式,方便讀者集中練習。考生若剛開始因不熟而擔心害怕的話,可以學習了解該單元後,再熟讀常見句型與試題模式,作個完美的結束。

▶ 每章先出現「題型暖身」和「命題分析」的區塊,透過階段式的訓練,不僅能充分理解,還能徹底提升考生的實力。

題型暖身
從簡單的試題開始

讓多益應試者,在介紹該單元各類型試題前,能無負擔地先理解題目,培養對題目的熟悉度,自然而然培養出信心。

命題分析
仔細看清試題

為了讓考生在作答各類型試題的過程中，更容易掌握答題重點，本書用方框標示可能出現的考點，或條列式整理出題方向，並作了條理清晰的說明。

實戰應用
解模擬試題

為了能確認學習成果，請考生透過「實戰應用」和 Mini Test 等，試著作答不同程度的模擬試題。

Actual Test
結束

讓考生作答真正符合多益試題水準的模擬試題，掌握自己的強項和弱點，不足處再學習補強。

這樣追上多益

多益是什麼？

多益（TOEIC, Test of English for International Communication）是美國教育測驗服務社（ETS: Educational Testing Service），為測定非英語母語人士，在商業上及國際上使用英語的流暢程度，而開發出的考試。重點放在會話溝通能力上，評斷在日常生活中，尤其是和商業相關的狀況下，實際使用英語的能力。

多益的結構

從 2018 年 3 月開始，多益考試有了下列的改變。

結構	Part	舊制多益		2018 新制多益		限制時間	分數
		各 Part 內容	題數	各 Part 內容	題數		
聽力測驗	1	照片描述	10	照片描述	6	45 分	495 分
	2	應答問題	30	應答問題	25		
	3	簡短對話	30 3 題 ×10 組	簡短對話	39 3 題 ×10 組		
	4	簡短讀白	30 3 題 ×10 組	簡短讀白	30 3 題 ×10 組		
閱讀測驗	5	單句填空 （文法／字彙）	40	單句填空 （文法／字彙）	30	75 分	495 分
	6	段落填空	12 4 題 ×3 篇	段落填空	16 4 題 ×4 篇		
	7	單篇閱讀 （9 篇）	28	單篇閱讀 （10 篇）	29		
		雙篇閱讀 （4 篇）	20	雙篇閱讀 （2 篇） 三篇閱讀 （3 篇）	25		
Total		7 Parts	200	7 Parts	200	120 分	990 分

這樣追上多益聽力測驗

從 2018 年 3 月開始改制的多益測驗，聽力測驗的題數仍然是 100 題，不過各單元的題數不同了，同時 Part 3 和 Part 4 增加了新類型的試題。

PART 1
- 看照片聽四個選項，從四個選項中，選出最符合照片內容的描述。
- 題型不變，但題數減為 6 題。

PART 2
- 聽問句和三個回答該問句的選項，從三個選項中，選出與問題最為符合的答案。
- 題型不變，題數減為 25 題。

PART 3
- 聽對話，並閱讀試題本上的問題和四個選項，從四個選項中，選出一個最符合對話內容的答案。每一個簡短對話會出 3 道題。
- 增加了新的試題類型，題數增加為 39 題。

新類型

❶ 增加了 3 個人的對話。

❷ 增加須參考**圖表、表格等資料**才能解題的試題。圖表、表格等資料會出現在試題本上。

❸ 增加**推測對話者某一句對話之意圖**的試題。

PART 4
- 聽各式各樣簡短獨白（廣播宣布、廣告、新聞報導、天氣預報、演説、電話留言等），並閱讀試題本上的問題和四個選項，在四個選項中，選出一個最符合談話內容的答案。每一個簡短獨白會出 3 道題。
- 增加了新的試題類型，題數仍是 30 題，沒有變動。

新類型

❶ 增加須參考**圖表、表格、略圖等資料**才能答題的試題。圖表、表格等資料會出現在試題本上。

❷ 增加**推測對話者某一句對話之意圖**的試題。

★ 請參考多益台灣區官方網站（http://www.toeic.com.tw），詳細閱讀注意事項，並看一下試題內容。

PART
1

Part 1 是測驗描述照片能力的單元。出題型式為：看 1 張照片，在四個選項中，選出一個最符合照片內容的適當描述。選項大部分是由一個主詞與一個動詞構成的短句，所以是比較簡單的單元。不過，句子雖然簡短，發音上讓人混淆的情形滿多的，所以要熟悉各式發音。Part 1 一共會出 6 道題，除了美式發音外，也會出現英式發音、澳式發音等各式發音及重音。

Example 1   ∩ 001

(A) A woman is dialing the phone.
(B) A woman is looking for her friend.
(C) A woman is looking out the window.
(D) A woman is calling her friend.

▶ 一面看著試題本上的照片，一面聽 (A)、(B)、(C)、(D) 四個選項，選項與題目均不會印在試題本上，全都要用聽的。

1. D

Part 1 題型綜覽

- **概要**：試題型式為，在四個選項中，選出一個最符合照片內容的適當描述。
- **照片類型**：出現 1 個人的照片／出現 2 個以上人數的照片／人物和事物的複合照片／事物及背景的照片。
- **Part 1 句子的時態**：多出現現在式、現在進行式、現在完成式；句子的語態多出現主動、被動、進行被動等。

新制多益核心要點

- 10 題變成 6 題，題數減少。
- 人物照片、事物及背景照片等既有的照片題型，出題數量平均。

新制多益準備策略

- 要熟悉描述各類照片時，時常會使用的字彙和片語，並掌握核心關鍵字。
- 要事先掌握會誤導應試者答錯的陷阱（完全不同的動作描寫／聯想字彙／類似發音字彙）。
- 除了用**現在進行式**描述基本動作，描述事物或背景時常會使用**被動語態**，例如：**進行被動語態／現在完成被動**等動詞的語態和時態。
- 要練習利用**錯誤答案刪除法**來找出正確答案的技巧。
- 在播放錄音選項前，先看一下照片。

解題技巧

- 在正式考題約 1 分鐘的考試說明（Directions）與例題（Example）時，先大略看一下所有照片，之後想一下會聽到怎樣描述它們的句子。
- 只有提到照片中出現的內容，才會是正確答案；想像的內容絕對不會是正確答案。
- 要區分是 1 人照片、2 人以上照片、人物和事物的複合照片，還是事物及背景照片；平常要以主題為單位，熟記常出現的句子。

試題類型

❶ 表動作時，常使用的句型

- **1 人或 2 人以上的照片**，會考這樣的句型：

  ➡ 句子的時態是**現在進行式**，表示「主詞正在做……中」。

  ➡ 偶爾和事物一起出現的話，用**現在進行被動語態**（being ＋ p.p.），表示「主詞正在被……中」。

  ➡ There 句型中，常會出現：「There ＋ be 動詞＋主詞＋ V-ing」的句型，表示「有正在做……的人」。

❷ 表狀態時，常使用的句型

- **事物或背景照片，或人加上事物背景的照片**，一般會考這樣的句型：

  ➡ 「主詞＋ be 動詞＋介系詞片語」，表示「主詞在……（某處）」或「There ＋ be 動詞＋主詞＋介系詞片語」的句型，表示「主詞處於……的狀態。」

- 若主要是**事物或背景照片**，會考這樣的句型：

  ➡ 「主詞＋ be 動詞＋ p.p. ＋介系詞片語」，表示「主詞被……著。」或「主詞處於被……的狀態。」

❸ 發音（其他英語系國家發音：英國、澳洲、加拿大）

- 以英國發音或澳洲發音來唸選項的話，學生多半會覺得比較困難。所以要另外學習它們的發音差異（本教材為了能比較各式發音，用了三種發音來錄音）。此外，平時將各主題的單字、句子，反覆聆聽並大聲地跟著唸出來，會很有幫助。

- 試題時常利用類似發音字讓考生產生混淆，所以平時要熟悉類似發音字。要特別注意，類似發音字的陷阱常出現在最後一個選項中。

❹ 類似發音字

● **同音異義字**

例 •mail/male   •sea/see   •site/sight/cite   •son/sun
•blue/blew   •meat/meet   •pills/peels

● **容易混淆的發音**

例 •letter/ladder   •here/near   •poor/pour
•caught/coat   •light/right   •late/rate
•alive/arrive   •face/phase/faith   •tire/tile
•directly/directory   •throwing/slowing   •farm/form
•waiting/weighing   •docks/ducks

❺ 例外的試題

● 因為是人物照片，所以會集中注意力聽人物動作的描述，但有時正確答案也會是**描述狀態或背景**的選項。因此，即使是上述的例外題，也不要緊張，一邊仔細觀察照片，事先想一下例外的答案會是什麼。答案一般都會出現在較後面的選項。

以1人為中心的照片

1 題型暖身

看照片，熟悉描述照片的句子。 🎧 002

1

The woman **is checking** the time.

女子正在看時間。

2

She**'s wearing** a coat.

她穿著一件大衣。

3

A man **is holding** a tie.

男子手拿著一條領帶。

1

Chapter

01

以
1
人
為
中
心
的
照
片

4

She**'s working** in a laboratory.

她正在實驗室裡工作。

5

She**'s using** some lab equipment.

她正在使用實驗設備。

6

A man **is holding** some paperwork in one hand.

男子正用單手拿著一些文件。

Part 1 的照片，可以分作出現人的照片和沒有出現人的照片。來具體了解一下，會出現怎樣類型的照片吧。

1 人照片

❶ 以 1 人為中心的照片

- 以一個人為中心的照片，選項中的主詞大多是人，而且時常會以**現在進行式**呈現。
- 如果主詞都一樣，就要特別注意聽**動詞**的部分，是否有關鍵動作的單字。
- 錯誤選項常利用照片中的事物形成錯誤的答案。
- 錯誤選項也常提到照片中沒有出現的事物。

❷ 1 人複合照片

- 以照片中出現的一個人和他周邊的事物為焦點的照片。時常會以**現在進行式**、**被動語態**、**進行被動語態**呈現。
- 要同時注意事物的動作、事物的狀態及位置。
- 錯誤選項常將人和事物的關係描述錯誤。

聽錄音，選出最符合照片內容的描述。🎧 003

(A)　(B)　(C)　(D)

STEP 2　確認正確答案及翻譯和解說。

(A) A wastebasket is being emptied.	(A) 字紙簍正被清空。
(B) Some trash has been left on the floor.	(B) 地板上留了些垃圾。
(C) A file cabinet is being unlocked.	(C) 檔案櫃正被打開。
(D) Some office supplies have been placed in a box.	(D) 盒子裡放了一些辦公用品。

正確答案

(B) Some trash has been left on the floor.

字彙

wastebasket 字紙簍　　empty (v.) 清空
office supply 辦公用品

解說

要看照片人與物的狀況，才能解題。因為 (A) 的 empty 這動作，並沒有在照片中出現，所以是錯誤答案。(D) 提到的盒子也沒有在照片中出現。(B) 提到照片中出現的垃圾，且句子以現在完成被動語態，表示「……被留了下來」，可知「有些垃圾留在地板上」，所以正確答案是選項 (B)。

The man is holding a pen with his left hand.

The man is sitting in a chair.

A telephone is on the desk.

Some trash has been left on the floor.

STEP 4 重複聽幾遍錄音，並填寫下列空格。🎧 004

(A) The man _____.

(B) A telephone _____.

(C) The man _____.

(D) Some trash _____.

3 實戰應用

STEP 1　聽錄音，選出最符合照片內容的描述。∩ 005

(A)　(B)　(C)　(D)

STEP 2　確認正確答案及翻譯和解說。

(A) The woman is lighting some candles.	(A) 女子正在點蠟燭。
(B) The woman is filling a vase with water.	(B) 女子正往花瓶裡裝水。
(C) The woman is arranging some flowers.	(C) 女子正在插花。
(D) The woman is clearing the plates.	(D) 女子正在清理碗盤。

正確答案

(C) The woman is arranging some flowers.

字彙

light 點亮；點燃　　arrange 整理；安排

解說

在現在進行式的動詞中，挑選一個和照片動作一致的選項。light 當動詞使用時是「點燃；點亮」的意思，照片中並沒有點燃的動作，所以 (A) 是錯的。另外，女子並沒有在擦盤子，所以和照片所顯示的情形不同，所以 (D) 也是錯的。(B) 也是錯的，因為照片並沒有出現裝水的動作。正確答案是 (C)，圖中女子正在插花 (arranging flowers)。

(A)　(B)　(C)　(D)

STEP 2　確認正確答案及翻譯和解說。

(A) He's writing on a piece of paper.	(A) 他正在一張紙上寫字。
(B) He's looking at a document.	(B) 他正在看一份文件。
(C) He's polishing a window.	(C) 他正在擦窗戶。
(D) He's leaning against a wall.	(D) 他正倚靠在牆上。

正確答案

(B) He's looking at a document.

字彙

a piece of paper 一張紙

解說

男子站在窗戶前面，兩隻手撐著桌子，站在桌子後面看一份文件。掌握了正確的人和物的關係以及人物動作，就能馬上知道 (A)、(C)、(D) 不會是正確答案了。正確答案是 (B)。

4 Part 1 常見句型

01	The woman is talking on the phone. 女子正在講電話。
02	The man is working on a computer. 男子正在用電腦。
03	The man is wearing a suit. 男子穿著一套西裝。
04	She's reading a newspaper. 她正在看報紙。
05	She's copying a document. 她正在影印一份文件。
06	He's using a keyboard. 他正在使用鍵盤。
07	The woman is tasting the soup. 女子正在品嚐湯。
08	The woman is arranging food on the table. 女子正在餐桌上擺放食物。
09	The woman is reaching out to pick up the fruit. 女子正把手伸出去撿水果。
10	He is paying for his groceries. 他正付錢購買食品雜貨。
11	She is making the bed. 她正在鋪床。
12	He's mopping the floor. 他正在拖地板。
13	The woman is ordering her meal. 女子正在點餐。
14	The waiter is taking her order. 服務生正在幫她點餐。
15	The woman is holding up a dress. 女子正拿起一套洋裝。
16	The woman is resting her chin on her hand. 女子正用手撐著下巴。
17	The woman is putting fuel in the vehicle. 女子正在給車子加油。
18	The woman is looking at her reflection in the mirror. 女子正在照鏡子。
19	The waiter is setting the table. 服務生正在擺餐桌。
20	The man is leaning against a handrail. 男子正倚靠在扶手上。

Chapter 01

聽錄音，選出最符合照片內容的描述。 ∩ 007

1.

Ⓐ　Ⓑ　Ⓒ　Ⓓ

2.

Ⓐ　Ⓑ　Ⓒ　Ⓓ

3.

Ⓐ　Ⓑ　Ⓒ　Ⓓ

4.

Ⓐ　Ⓑ　Ⓒ　Ⓓ

5.

Ⓐ　Ⓑ　Ⓒ　Ⓓ

6.

Ⓐ　Ⓑ　Ⓒ　Ⓓ

Chapter *02* 以 **2** 人以上為中心的照片

1 題型暖身

看照片，熟悉描述照片的句子。🎧 008

1

The people **are looking** at some paperwork.

兩人正看著一堆文件。

2

They'**re walking** together in a row.

他們正並肩走路。

3

Both of the men **are wearing** protective gear.

兩個人都穿戴防護裝備。

4

They're looking at a monitor.

他們正看著電腦螢幕。

5

The wall **is lined** with windows.

牆上裝著一排窗戶。

6

The people **are seated** side by side.

兩人並肩坐著。

2 命題分析

2 人以上照片

❶ 以 **2** 人以上為中心的照片

- 以多人為焦點的照片,選項的主詞會使用**複數代名詞**或**單數代名詞**。

- 要集中注意力聽**全都的主詞和動詞**。

- **共同的動作**或**相互間施與受**的動作很可能是正確的答案。

- 錯誤答案常把人物彼此的動作説反了,或把個別人物的狀況説成是全部的狀況。

❷ 2 人與事物的複合照片

- 選項中,主詞可能是人或事物,這種混合的情況也時常出現,這時人們的**共同動作**,以及照片中的**事物的狀態**很可能是正確的答案。

- 要快速掌握照片中人們的共同動作,或是事物的狀態。

- 請注意,錯誤選項時常會用**兩人都正在做某動作**或**其中一人正在做某動作**形成答題陷阱。

- 要留意錯誤選項常利用照片裡的事物做成錯誤的答案。

聽錄音，選出最符合照片內容的描述。🎧 009

(A) (B) (C) (D)

STEP 2 確認正確答案及翻譯和解說。

(A) The men are protecting their ears with earmuffs.	(A) 兩人都戴上耳罩保護耳朵。
(B) The men are facing each other.	(B) 兩個人面對著面。
(C) One of the men is cutting boards into pieces.	(C) 其中一名男子正把木板分切成塊。
(D) One of the men is packing lumber into a crate.	(D) 其中一名男子正把木材裝箱。

正確答案

(B) The men are facing each other.

字彙

earmuff 耳罩　　face (v.) 面向　　pack 包裝　　lumber 木材

解說

兩個人都沒戴耳罩，因此 (A) 說戴著 earmuff 是錯誤答案。(D) 的 lumber 是類似 timber，可做為建造建築物或製作家具的木材，而受詞是否為建造木材還是家具木材，從照片中無法確認，且看不出裝箱的動作，所以 (D) 是錯誤答案。選項 (B) 的 face 當動詞使用時表「面對面」，(B) 正確說出了兩個人的狀態，所以是正確答案。

STEP 3　看照片，熟悉描述照片的句子。

The man on the left is wearing glasses.

Sunglasses are on top of the man's head.

The men are facing each other.

The man on the left is holding a package.

STEP 4　重複聽幾遍錄音，並填寫下列空格。∩ 010

(A) The man _____.

(B) Sunglasses _____.

(C) The men _____.

(D) The man _____.

STEP 1 聽錄音，選出最符合照片內容的描述。 🎧 011

(A)　(B)　(C)　(D)

STEP 2 確認正確答案及翻譯和解說。

(A) The people are greeting each other.	(A) 這兩個人在打招呼。
(B) The woman is passing a pen to the man.	(B) 女子正遞給男子一枝筆。
(C) The man is taking notes on a laptop.	(C) 男子正在手提電腦上做筆記。
(D) The people are looking at the same document.	(D) 這兩個人正看著同一份文件。

正確答案

(D) The people are looking at the same document.

字彙

take notes 做筆記

解說

(A) 和 (B) 描述的動作，照片中並沒有出現。(C) 的主詞和動詞，和照片中的 man 和 taking notes 一致，但可以看出不是在筆電上做筆記，是在一般的記事本上做筆記，所以 (C) 是錯誤答案。選項 (D) 是正確答案，因為可以透過兩人的視線，確定兩人正在看同一份文件。

STEP 1　聽錄音，選出最符合照片內容的描述。 012

(A)　(B)　(C)　(D)

STEP 2　確認正確答案及翻譯和解說。

(A) Some of the people are standing side by side.	(A) 有些人肩並肩站著。
(B) One of the men is pointing at a chart.	(B) 其中一名男子正指著圖表。
(C) A presenter is showing a video.	(C) 報告人正在播放影片。
(D) Some people are seated on the bench.	(D) 有些人坐在長凳上。

正確答案

(B) One of the men is pointing at a chart.

字彙

side by side 肩並肩地　　presenter 報告人

解說

照片出現了好幾個人，仔細地觀察人們的動作和位置，就能解題。因為人們大多數都是坐著，所以 (A) 是錯誤答案。(D) 也是錯誤的，因為大家都坐在大桌前。(C) 的主詞 a presenter 可以用來說明照片中站著的那位男士，但是他讓大家看的不是影片，所以也不能選。正確答案是選項 (B)。

01	The man is speaking to the woman. 男子正對著女子說話。
02	Two women are shopping in a shopping mall. 兩名女子正在購物中心內購物。
03	All of them are wearing glasses. 所有的人都戴著眼鏡。
04	They are preparing some food in the kitchen. 他們正在廚房準備食物。
05	They are having dinner together. 他們正一同享用晚餐。
06	They are talking to each other. 他們正在聊天。
07	The girl and baby are swimming in the river. 女孩和小寶寶正在河裡游泳。
08	One of the men is wearing glasses. 其中一名男子戴著眼鏡。
09	They are watching television. 他們正在看電視。
10	The doctor is examining the patient. 醫生正在為病患做檢查。
11	They are walking in a garden. 他們正在花園裡散步。
12	They are eating their dessert. 他們正在品嚐甜點。
13	The women are chatting in the cafeteria. 女人們正在自助餐廳內聊天。
14	They are gesturing as they talk. 他們邊說話邊做手勢。
15	The men are all wearing hats. 這些男子都戴著帽子。
16	The barber is trimming the customer's hair. 理髮師正在幫顧客理髮。
17	The workers are sharing the office space. 這群員工共用一個辦公區域。
18	The two men are sitting next to each other. 這兩名男子相鄰而坐。
19	One man is explaining something to the other. 一名男子正對另一個人做解釋。
20	They are giving a concert. 他們正在舉辦音樂會。

聽錄音，選出最符合照片內容的描述。🎧 013

1.

Ⓐ Ⓑ Ⓒ Ⓓ

2.

Ⓐ Ⓑ Ⓒ Ⓓ

3.

Ⓐ Ⓑ Ⓒ Ⓓ

4.

Ⓐ Ⓑ Ⓒ Ⓓ

5.

Ⓐ Ⓑ Ⓒ Ⓓ

6.

Ⓐ Ⓑ Ⓒ Ⓓ

1 題型暖身

看照片，熟悉描述照片的句子。∩ 014

1

A man **is using** public transportation.

男子正搭乘大眾運輸工具。

2

Musicians **are giving** a performance outdoors.

音樂家正在戶外演出。

3

Lights **are suspended** from the ceiling.

電燈自天花板懸掛著。

4

A cart **is being** pulled by a horse.

馬車正被馬拉著。

5

Some people **are walking** outdoors.

有些人正在戶外行走。

6

Both of the women **are wearing** hard hats.

兩名女子都戴著頭盔。

事物及風景照片——掌握狀態及位置更勝於動作

❶ 近距離照片（事物照片）

「近距離照片」是指很靠近某個事物所拍攝的照片。主要會考的選項句型，也就是和事物主詞搭配使用的有：**現在簡單式**或**被動語態，表事物位置關係的介系詞片語**也常出現。

- 要最先掌握特寫事物間的位置關係。
- 要注意用錯誤人稱作主詞的答案。
- 要注意錯誤答案會用「進行被動語態（being + p.p.）」來表達錯誤的動作。
- 因為字彙和片語的難度較高，所以常考的字彙和片語要事先背熟。

❷ 遠距離照片（背景照片）

比起特定事物照片，這種照片要掌握整個照片的一般特徵。主要考點是選項中的主詞，也就是表**場所或事物的字彙**；表**位置關係的介系詞片語**，也時常會考。

- 照片中的一般性事實很可能是正確的答案。
- 要留意錯誤答案會出現照片中沒有的事物或人物。
- 要注意錯誤答案會用「進行被動語態（being + p.p.）」來表達錯誤的動作。

STEP 1　聽錄音，選出最符合照片內容的描述。🎧 015

(A)　(B)　(C)　(D)

STEP 2　確認正確答案及翻譯和解說。

(A) A woman is passing a pair of scissors to a man.	(A) 女子正把剪刀遞給男子。
(B) A man is hanging a mirror in a hair salon.	(B) 美髮沙龍裡，男子正在掛一面鏡子。
(C) Some people are having their hair cut.	(C) 有些人正在理髮。
(D) A worker is showing the customers to their seats.	(D) 一名員工正在幫顧客帶位。

正確答案

(C) Some people are having their hair cut.

字彙

have someone's hair cut 理髮
show someone to his/her seat 帶位

解說

解題要領是：快速掌握各選項所陳述的是否為事實。照片中呈現的場景是美髮沙龍，所以要選擇最符合這場景的選項。(A) 的主詞是 a woman，和照片一致，但是並沒有將一把剪刀（a pair of scissors）遞給男子的動作，所以是錯誤答案。(B) 也是，主詞 a man 並沒有掛鏡子的動作，所以也不能選。(D) 的動作也沒有出現在照片中，因此正確答案是 (C)。

看照片，熟悉描述照片的句子。

Some people are having their hair cut.

There are mirrors on the wall.

A male client is sitting on the left side of the shop.

A female client is looking at her reflection in the mirror.

STEP 4　重複聽幾遍錄音，並填寫下列空格。 🎧 016

(A) Some people _____.

(B) There are _____.

(C) A male _____.

(D) A female _____.

3 實戰應用

STEP 1　聽錄音，選出最符合照片內容的描述。∩ 017

(A)　(B)　(C)　(D)

STEP 2　確認正確答案及翻譯和解說。

(A) The woman is leaving the meeting room.	(A) 女子正要離開會議室。
(B) The man is holding a pen in one hand.	(B) 男子手裡握著一支筆。
(C) The woman is sipping coffee from a cup.	(C) 女子正在啜飲咖啡。
(D) The man is pointing at a chart.	(D) 男子正指著圖表。

正確答案

(B) The man is holding a pen in one hand.

字彙

sip 啜飲　　chart 圖表

解說

解題要領是：快速掌握照片的細節與人物動作。因為兩個人是坐著的，所以 (A) 的 leaving，是錯誤的動作。(C) 也是，沒有人在喝東西，所以也是錯誤動作。(D) 的主詞和動詞都正確，但是男子指的對象為何，無法從照片中確認，所以也不能選。正確答案是選項 (B)，它正確地描述了男子右手握著一支筆。

聽錄音，選出最符合照片內容的描述。 ∩ 018

(A) (B) (C) (D)

確認正確答案及翻譯和解說。

(A) The girl is resting her arm on the man's shoulder.	(A) 女孩正把手臂搭在一名男子肩上。
(B) One of the men is drawing a graph.	(B) 其中一名男子正在繪圖。
(C) A blueprint is being removed from the wall.	(C) 設計圖正從牆上被取下。
(D) The woman is taking paper from a printer.	(D) 女子正從印表機拿走文件。

正確答案

(A) The girl is resting her arm on the man's shoulder.

字彙

draw 繪圖　　blueprint 藍圖　　remove 移除

解說

draw a graph 是畫一張圖表的意思，但照片右邊男子的動作並不是在畫圖，所以 (B) 不能選。(C) 的敘述中，將男子一手扶著牆壁一手指著圖的動作，誤描述成在移除藍圖，所以動作也錯了。resting one's arms on 表示「將手臂靠在某物上方」，(A) 把小女孩用手環抱男子頸部的狀態，說成是把手臂放在男子肩上，這種說法也沒錯，所以正確答案是 (A)。

4 Part 1 常見句型

| 01 | The man is carrying some boxes. 男子正拿著一些盒子。 |

| 02 | The woman is putting gas in her car. 女子正在幫車子加油。 |

| 03 | The woman is holding a bowl in the kitchen. 女子在廚房裡捧著一個碗。 |

| 04 | The woman is holding a pen in her hand. 女子手裡正握著一支筆。 |

| 05 | The woman is holding a receiver to her ear. 女子正拿著聽筒聽電話。 |

| 06 | The man and his wife are holding their child's hands.
男子與妻子一同握著孩子的手。 |

| 07 | The man is holding a fishing pole at the edge of the water.
男子在水邊手持釣竿。 |

| 08 | The woman is holding the paper in the office.
辦公室裡，女子正手拿文件。 |

| 09 | The man is removing bread from the oven. 男子正從烤箱中取出麵包。 |

| 10 | They are admiring a painting. 他們正在欣賞畫作。 |

| 11 | They are looking at the same thing. 他們正看著同樣的東西。 |

| 12 | The woman is looking in a cabinet drawer. 女子正往櫥櫃抽屜裡面看。 |

| 13 | The woman is looking in a mirror. 女子正在照鏡子。 |

| 14 | The man is reviewing some documents. 男子正在審核一些文件。 |

| 15 | The woman is pointing to an image on the computer screen.
女子正指著電腦螢幕上的影像。 |

| 16 | The woman is holding a camera up to her eye. 女子正把相機舉至眼前。 |

| 17 | The man is taking a picture with his camera. 男子正用相機拍照。 |

| 18 | The man is using a ladder to climb to the roof. 男子正用梯子爬上屋頂。 |

| 19 | The man is using a shovel to clean the snow. 男子正用鏟子清理積雪。 |

| 20 | The woman is using a public telephone. 女子正在使用公共電話。 |

聽錄音，選出最符合照片內容的描述。🎧 019

1.

Ⓐ Ⓑ Ⓒ Ⓓ

2.

Ⓐ Ⓑ Ⓒ Ⓓ

3.

Ⓐ Ⓑ Ⓒ Ⓓ

4.

Ⓐ Ⓑ Ⓒ Ⓓ

5.

Ⓐ Ⓑ Ⓒ Ⓓ

6.

Ⓐ Ⓑ Ⓒ Ⓓ

Chapter
04 事物及背景照片

1 題型暖身

看照片，熟悉描述照片的句子。∩ 020

1

A wheel **is leaning** against a tree.

車輪靠在樹旁。

2

The bicycles **are facing** the same direction.

腳踏車都面對同一方向。

3

Umbrellas **are shading** the tables.

遮陽傘為餐桌遮陽。

4

A roadway **is congested** with vehicles.

車道上車潮擁擠。

5

The tables **are covered** with cloths.

餐桌上鋪著桌布。

6

A railing **is casting** shadows on the ground.

欄杆在地面上投下影子。

2 命題分析

依常考的場所及狀況，來區分照片類型

❶ 辦公場所、作業場所的照片

在辦公場所和作業場所中，時常出現的地方有：辦公室、會議室、工地、工廠、實驗室等。

❷ 外部建築物照片

有機場、旅館、理髮廳、醫院、圖書館、書店、展覽場、表演廳等。

❸ 和家庭、住房有關的照片

有玄關、庭院、陽台等建築物外部照片，以及客廳、廚房、餐廳等室內照片。

❹ 休閒生活、戶外照片

有餐館、商店、戶外，以及和運動活動有關的照片。

❺ 移動狀態的照片

大眾交通工具的照片、汽車修理及停放的照片、公車轉運站或公車總站的照片、和人們移動有關的照片。

聽錄音，選出最符合照片內容的描述。🎧 021

(A) (B) (C) (D)

確認正確答案及翻譯和解說。

(A) The lamp on the nightstand has been turned off.	(A) 床頭櫃上的檯燈被關掉了。
(B) The sheets on the bed are being changed.	(B) 床上的床單正在被更換。
(C) Some flowers have been placed in a vase.	(C) 花瓶裡插了一些花。
(D) Food is being carried on a wooden tray.	(D) 食物放在木托盤上正被送進來。

正確答案

(C) Some flowers have been placed in a vase.

字彙

nightstand 床頭櫃　　vase 花瓶

解說

床頭櫃是 nightstand，選項 (A) 的 lamp 和 nightstand 都和照片中出現的物品一致，但因為 (A) 說 lamp 是關著的，所以錯了。(D) 很容易被誤認為是正確答案，它用 is being carried「現在進行被動語態」，表動作正在進行中，但照片中的東西並沒有正在被搬動，所以 (D) 也是錯的。正確答案是 (C)，它正確描述與花瓶相關的細節。

STEP 3 看照片，熟悉描述照片的句子。

Some flowers have been placed in a vase.

The lamp beside the bed is on.

A teapot is on the wooden tray.

A tray of food is laid on the bed.

STEP 4 重複聽幾遍錄音，並填寫下列空格。 🎧 022

(A) Some flowers _____.

(B) The lamp _____.

(C) A teapot _____.

(D) A tray _____.

STEP 1　聽錄音,選出最符合照片內容的描述。∩ 023

(A)　(B)　(C)　(D)

STEP 2　確認正確答案及翻譯和解說。

(A) Some equipment is in operation.	(A) 某設備正在運作。
(B) A construction sign is being posted.	(B) 施工標誌正被豎立起來。
(C) Some machinery has been left unattended.	(C) 某部機械被閒置著。
(D) Stones are being removed from a building site.	(D) 石頭正被運出建築工地。

正確答案

(C) Some machinery has been left unattended.

字彙

in operation 運轉中　　construction sign 施工標誌
unattended 無人看管的

解說

因為 in operation 表「正在使用、操作、運轉中」,所以 (A) 和照片中的狀況相反。(B) 的主詞是 a construction sign,它雖然出現在照片中,不過 is being posted 是正在被張貼、公告,表動作現在正在進行中,和照片中標誌已被豎立的狀況不符,所以不能選。(C) 的 left unattended 表「無人看管的」,東西就被放在那裡的狀態,和照片有機械設備,但不確定是否有人在使用的狀態一致,所以 (C) 是正確答案。

STEP 1　聽錄音，選出最符合照片內容的描述。∩ 024

(A)　(B)　(C)　(D)

STEP 2　確認正確答案及翻譯和解說。

(A) The door of the aircraft is open.	(A) 飛機的門是開著的。
(B) An airport is crowded with people.	(B) 機場裡擠滿了人。
(C) An airplane has taken off from the ground.	(C) 一架飛機已經起飛。
(D) Some passengers are getting off the plane.	(D) 一些旅客正在下飛機。

正確答案

(A) The door of the aircraft is open.

字彙

be crowded with 擠滿著　　take off 起飛

解說

因為照片中顯示的空間沒有擠滿人，所以 (B) 是錯的。(C) 用現在完成式，描述飛機已經起飛了，也是和照片相反的狀態。(D) 描述的是和照片有關的情況，但是照片中並沒有看到乘客下飛機（getting off the plane），所以也不對。(A) 正確描述了照片中飛機機門的狀態，所以是正確答案。

01	There are buildings near a lake. 湖附近有些建築物。
02	Buildings are reflected in the water. 水面映著建築物的倒影。
03	There are lights in the center of the room. 房間中央裝有電燈。
04	Lights are hanging from the ceiling. 電燈自天花板懸掛著。
05	There are many cars lining up along the road. 許多車輛沿著道路排成一行。
06	Most of the trees have lost their leaves. 大部分的樹木葉子都掉光了。
07	There are many books placed on the shelves. 書架上擺了許多書籍。
08	There are logs stacked next to the fireplace. 壁爐旁堆疊著木柴。
09	There's a table in front of the sofa. 沙發前有一張桌子。
10	There's a tablecloth on the table. 桌子上鋪著桌布。

Chapter 04

聽錄音，選出最符合照片內容的描述。🎧 025

1.

Ⓐ　Ⓑ　ⓒ　Ⓓ

2.

Ⓐ　Ⓑ　ⓒ　Ⓓ

3.

Ⓐ　Ⓑ　ⓒ　Ⓓ

4.

Ⓐ　Ⓑ　ⓒ　Ⓓ

5.

Ⓐ　Ⓑ　ⓒ　Ⓓ

6.

Ⓐ　Ⓑ　ⓒ　Ⓓ

聽錄音，選出最符合照片內容的描述。🎧 026

1.

Ⓐ Ⓑ Ⓒ Ⓓ

2.

Ⓐ Ⓑ Ⓒ Ⓓ

3.

Ⓐ Ⓑ Ⓒ Ⓓ

4.

Ⓐ Ⓑ Ⓒ Ⓓ

5.

Ⓐ Ⓑ Ⓒ Ⓓ

6.

Ⓐ Ⓑ Ⓒ Ⓓ

PART

2

應答問題

Part 2 共有 25 道題，出題型式為：聽問句，接著再聽三個選項，從三個選項中選一個與問題最為符合的回答。雖然問句和答句都是短句子，但因為都要用聽的，所以比起長句子，反而感覺更困難。

Part 2 題型相當多樣，錯誤答案常用類似發音字彙、意思容易混淆的字彙混淆考生。除了美式發音外，英式、澳式等各式發音也會出現；同一個題目，問句和答句也可能出現不同的口音。

Example 1 　　　　　　　　　　　　　　　　　　　　　　　🎧 027

Did you win the game last night?

(A) It is great.

(B) Yes, I did.

(C) The game is being delayed.

Example 2 　　　　　　　　　　　　　　　　　　　　　　　🎧 028

Why isn't the heater on?

(A) A cold winter day.

(B) It broke this morning.

(C) Yes, it's on.

▶ 問句和答句選項均不會印在試題本上，全都要用聽的。

1. B　2. B

Part 2 題型綜覽

- 聽問句，然後再聽三個選項，從三個選項中選一個最符合該問句的回答。
- 試題本上只會出現 (A)(B)(C)，問句和答句都要用聽的，所以要集中注意力聽。
- 問句提供的線索有限，且片語和慣用語相當多，所以答錯的可能性相當高。
- 問句和答句的內容，主要和辦公室人際互動、日常生活有關。
- 問句的類型有：WH 疑問句、Be 動詞與助動詞形成的一般疑問句、選擇疑問句、否定疑問句、附加問句、間接問句、建議與請求類的問句、敘述句等。

新制多益核心要點

- 試題數減少了，以前是 30 題，現在是 25 題。
- 沒有新的問句類型，各類問句題型出題數仍平均。
- 刪除了 Part 2 一開始要聽的例題（Example）。

新制多益準備策略

- 要注意聽**問句前半部的關鍵字**，因為問句的關鍵字大都在句子前半部，所以要聽清楚關鍵字，才能選出正確答案。
- 要熟記各類問句常考的答句模式。
- 固定的錯誤答案模式，在選項中時常出現，常見的錯誤答案模式有：
  (1) 利用**類似發音字**、**同義字**或**衍生字**形成的錯誤答案
  (2) 利用**聯想**形成的錯誤答案
  (3) 時態不一致的錯誤答案
  (4) 和問句無關的人稱的錯誤答案

解題技巧

- Yes/No question 不一定要用 Yes 或 No 來回答。實際上在會話中，也會用其他方式來表達贊成或反對。
- 類似發音的字會是正確答案的可能性很低。在多益考試中，問句的單字不會重複出現在選項中，也就是說正確的答句一定會經過改寫（paraphrase）。
- 選擇疑問句，就是出現 or 的問句，要聽者在兩個選擇中擇其一。回答時，在兩個中**選一個來回答**即可。不過隨著題目難度提高，選兩個或以其他方式來回答，也可能會是正確答案。
- 選項中如果有「還沒決定」、「不知道」、「讓我確認一下」等，這些會是正確答案的可能性相當高。（It's not decided yet. / I'll check it out. / Let me ask. / I'll find out. / I'm not sure. / Not that I'm aware of. / I wish I knew.）

Q **Who 疑問句**

1 題型暖身

STEP 1 聽錄音，選出與問題最為符合的回答。 🎧 029

Mark your answer. (A) (B) (C)

STEP 2 確認正確答案及翻譯和解說。

Who has been put in charge of selecting a new location?	誰被任命負責挑選新位址？
(A) Wow, I'm so proud of you. (B) Mr. Brown has. (C) The new location looks nice.	(A) 哇，我真以你為榮。 (B) 布朗先生。 (C) 新位址看起來不錯。

正確答案

(B) Mr. Brown has.

字彙

location 位置

解説

用 who 詢問誰負責選擇場地，因此只要選項含有人名，就有可能是正確答案，選項 (B) 提到人名布朗先生 (Mr. Brown)，所以正確答案是 (B)。

聽錄音，選出與問題最為符合的回答。 🎧 030

Mark your answer.　　　(A)　(B)　(C)

確認正確答案及翻譯和解說。

Who's drafting the quarterly sales report?	誰在草擬季度銷售報告？
(A) I heard Ben is. (B) When the report is finished. (C) The report is on the table.	(A) 聽說是班。 (B) 當報告完成的時候。 (C) 報告在桌上。

正確答案

(A) I heard Ben is.

字彙

quarterly 季度的

解說

用 who 詢問草擬報告的人是誰，所以正確答案是選項 (A)。

> **Who(se) 疑問句**
>
> - 題目以 who（誰）或 whose（誰的）起始的疑問句，找出一個最合適的答句。
> - 聽清楚 who 接下來的**助動詞**或**動詞**。
> - 含有**負責人的名字**、**專有名詞**、**部門名**、**職位名**等的選項，很有可能是正確答案。
> - 「Matthew from accounting . . .」、「The manager . . .」、「I have no idea.」等，也可能是正確答案。

STEP 1　聽錄音，選出與問題最為符合的回答。🎧 031

Mark your answer.　　　　　　　　(A)　(B)　(C)

STEP 2　確認正確答案及翻譯和解說。

Who will clean up the meeting room later this afternoon?	今天下午過後，誰會打掃會議室？
(A) It's down the street.	(A) 沿著這條街走下去就是。
(B) I lent it to John yesterday.	(B) 我昨天把它借給約翰了。
(C) I think that's April's job.	(C) 應該是艾波的工作。

正確答案

(C) I think that's April's job.

字彙

meeting room 會議室

解說

用 who 詢問誰會打掃會議室，選項 (B) 和 (C) 含有人名，有可能是正確答案，但 (B) 句意與問句內容不符，所以正確答案是選項 (C)。(A) 選項完全不符題意，所以不用考慮。

STEP 1 聽錄音，選出與問題最為符合的回答。∩ 032

Mark your answer.   (A) (B) (C)

STEP 2 確認正確答案及翻譯和解說。

Who will design the window display?	誰要設計這櫥窗的布置？
(A) That's Janet's area of expertise.	(A) 那是珍娜特擅長的領域。
(B) The new products are on display.	(B) 新產品正在展示中。
(C) A pane of glass.	(C) 一塊玻璃。

正確答案

(A) That's Janet's area of expertise.

字彙

design 設計　　window display 櫥窗布置
area of expertise 專長領域

解說

雖然問句的關鍵字是 who，也就是問「誰」，但選項的主詞和受詞都不是人，因此解題的重點就是要找出選項中，哪一個間接暗示出「會去設計的人或單位」。(A) 的 that 指的是問句中的「design the window display」，而且間接說出了那是珍娜特擅長的領域，暗示珍娜特會去做，所以 (A) 是正確答案。(B) 和 (C) 完全沒有暗示誰會設計櫥窗布置，所以不用考慮。

3 實戰應用

STEP 1 聽錄音，選出與問題最為符合的回答。🎧 033

Mark your answer.   (A)   (B)   (C)

STEP 2 重複聽幾遍錄音，並填寫下列空格。

_____ attend the _____?

(A) Yes, it's _____.

(B) On _____.

(C) _____ will.

STEP 3 確認正確答案及翻譯和解說。

Who will attend the annual conference?	誰會參加年度會議？
(A) Yes, it's finished.	(A) 沒錯，會議結束了。
(B) On Oak Street.	(B) 在橡木街上。
(C) Mr. Lee will.	(C) 李先生會。

正確答案

(C) Mr. Lee will.

字彙

annual 年度的   conference 會議

解說

用 who 詢問會出席年度會議的人是誰，所以正確答案是 (C)。

STEP 1 聽錄音，選出與問題最為符合的回答。🎧 034

Mark your answer.　　　　　　　(A)　(B)　(C)

STEP 2 重複聽幾遍錄音，並填寫下列空格。

_____ on the _____ concert

_____?

(A) _____ stage event _____.

(B) _____ went to _____.

(C) A band _____ like.

STEP 3 確認正確答案及翻譯和解說。

Who's playing on the main stage at the concert next week?	下週的演奏會上，誰將擔綱表演？
(A) The main stage event starts after 10 p.m.	(A) 要到十點過後，壓軸主秀才會開始。
(B) My father went to a concert once.	(B) 我父親曾去聽過一次音樂會。
(C) A band from Norway that I really like.	(C) 我超愛的一個來自挪威的樂團。

正確答案

（C）A band from Norway that I really like.

字彙

main stage 主舞台

解說

問句的關鍵字是 who，也就是問「誰」，所以選項若提到特定人物或多數人物（團體），很可能是正確答案。選項 (B) 的主詞 my father 是人，但是句子只說明 my father 去聽過一次音樂會，但下週表演的人不是 my father，所以與問句不符。選項 (C) 明確提到了一個 band（樂團），樂團可以是表演者，所以是正確答案。

② Where 疑問句

1 題型暖身

STEP 1 聽錄音，選出與問題最為符合的回答。🎧 035

Mark your answer.   (A)   (B)   (C)

STEP 2 確認正確答案及翻譯和解說。

Where is the closest post office?	最近的郵局在哪？
(A) Next week.	(A) 下個禮拜。
(B) Across from the bank.	(B) 在銀行的對面。
(C) The last package.	(C) 最後一個包裹。

正確答案

(B) Across from the bank.

字彙

post office 郵局

解說

本題是詢問場所的疑問句，(A) 只提到時間，所以絕不會是正確答案。正確答案是 (B)。(B) 不是具備主詞＋動詞的完整句，而是口語會使用的句子，所以只要將省略的主詞和 be 動詞（The closest post office is . . .）補上，意思就通了（最近的郵局，就在銀行的對面。），解題就容易了。

STEP 1 聽錄音，選出與問題最為符合的回答。🎧 036

Mark your answer.   (A) (B) (C)

STEP 2 確認正確答案及翻譯和解說。

Where can I park my bicycle?	哪裡可以讓我停放腳踏車？
(A) I didn't notice.	(A) 我沒有留意。
(B) Next to the entrance.	(B) 入口旁。
(C) A faulty part.	(C) 一個報廢零件。

正確答案

(B) Next to the entrance.

字彙

notice 留意；注意

解說

因為是詢問能停放腳踏車的場所，所以正確答案要直接或間接表示「跟停車場所」有關的訊息。選項 (C) 用不定冠詞 a 來指稱某個不特定的對象，也就是零件，和場所無關，所以是錯的。正確答案是選項 (B)，因為它表示出特定場所——入口旁，而省略的部分是 you can park your bicycle。

Where 疑問句

● 題目以 where（哪裡）起始的疑問句，找出一個最合適的答句。

● 聽清楚 where 接下來的**主詞**和**動詞**。

● where 疑問句的句型是「Where ＋助動詞＋主詞＋動詞……? 」或
「Where ＋ be 動詞＋主詞? 」。

● 出現特定**場所**、**地名**、**位置**等的**介系詞片語**，是正確答案的可能性很高。

STEP 1 聽錄音，選出與問題最為符合的回答。🎧 037

Mark your answer.　　　　　　(A)　(B)　(C)

STEP 2 確認正確答案及翻譯和解說。

Where does the shuttle bus drop off passengers?	接駁車會在哪裡放乘客下車？
(A) Yes, at seven o'clock.	(A) 沒錯，是七點。
(B) I'll drop by your office.	(B) 我會順道去你的公司。
(C) At the intersection of 8th and Young Streets.	(C) 在第八街與青年街的交叉路口。

正確答案

(C) At the intersection of 8th and Young Streets.

字彙

drop off（通常指用車輛）帶某人至某地
passenger 乘客　　intersection 交叉路口

解說

因為是詢問場所的問句，所以選項 (A) 回答肯定／否定的疑問句不會是正確答案。(B) 雖然出現了 your office（你的辦公室）這場所，但是主詞 I 和動詞 drop by 都和問句內容不符，所以也是錯的。選項 (C) 是正確答案，透過表場所的介系詞 at，具體說出了場所。

STEP 1 聽錄音，選出與問題最為符合的回答。🎧 038

Mark your answer. (A) (B) (C)

STEP 2 確認正確答案及翻譯和解說。

Where do you want me to sign the document?	你要我把名字簽在文件哪裡？
(A) The same time next week.	(A) 下週同一時間。
(B) On the dotted line.	(B) 簽在虛線上。
(C) Use a black pen.	(C) 請用黑筆。

正確答案

(B) On the dotted line.

字彙

dotted line 虛線

解說

sign（簽名），一般而言是在紙或文件上完成的動作，所以介系詞要用 on。因此選項 (B) 是正確的，它用 on 表達出簽名的位置。此外，dotted line（虛線），是由動詞 dot（在……加點）衍生出來的詞，這點要知道。

3 實戰應用

STEP 1 聽錄音，選出與問題最為符合的回答。🎧 039

Mark your answer.　　　　　　(A)　(B)　(C)

STEP 2 重複聽幾遍錄音，並填寫下列空格。

_____ should I _____ these _____?

(A) Let's _____ it together.

(B) On _____.

(C) Use a _____.

STEP 3 確認正確答案及翻譯和解說。

Where should I put these brochures?	我該把這些手冊放在哪裡？
(A) Let's read it together.	(A) 我們一起讀吧。
(B) On Janet's desk.	(B) 放在珍娜特的書桌上。
(C) Use a large font.	(C) 用大的字級。

正確答案

(B) On Janet's desk.

字彙

brochure 手冊

解說

因為是詢問要把手冊放（put）到何處的問句，所以要看各選項是否有介系詞，有介系詞的話，再看有沒有用對。選項 (B) 用 on 和可以放手冊的 desk（書桌）搭配，所以是正確答案。

STEP 1 聽錄音，選出與問題最為符合的回答。🎧 040

Mark your answer. (A) (B) (C)

STEP 2 重複聽幾遍錄音，並填寫下列空格。

_____ does Henry _____ go to _____ ?

(A) I think you should _____ him _____ .

(B) I worked at a _____ when I was _____ .

(C) I _____ Henry in _____ yesterday.

STEP 3 確認正確答案及翻譯和解說。

Where does Henry normally go to buy his suits? (A) I think you should ask him yourself. (B) I worked at a suit shop when I was younger. (C) I saw Henry in his suit yesterday.	亨利通常都到哪裡購買西裝？ (A) 我覺得你應該自己問他。 (B) 我年輕時在一家西裝店工作。 (C) 我昨天看到亨利穿著西裝。

正確答案

(A) I think you should ask him yourself.

字彙

suit 西裝

解說

一般詢問場所的問句，會用場所來回答，但是本題選項的主詞和受詞大多不是場所。因此這題要掌握各選項隱含的意思，選出銜接得最順的選項。被問的人並不是亨利本人，所以 (A) 建議問話者（you）直接去問亨利，這樣的回答很合理，所以是正確答案。(B) 雖然有 suit，且有表場所的 suit shop，但卻不是亨利買西裝的地方，所以不能選。

③ When 疑問句

STEP 1 聽錄音，選出與問題最為符合的回答。 ∩ 041

Mark your answer.　　　　　　　　(A)　(B)　(C)

STEP 2 確認正確答案及翻譯和解說。

When did this package arrive?	這個包裹何時送到的？
(A) Here is the address.	(A) 地址在這裡。
(B) A man wearing a uniform.	(B) 穿著制服的男子。
(C) This morning at 9:00.	(C) 今天早上九點。

正確答案

(C) This morning at 9:00.

字彙

package 包裹

解說

包裹已經送達，用 when 詢問這動作是何時發生的。選項 (C) 是正確答案，因為它回答了包裹送達的時間。

STEP 1 聽錄音，選出與問題最為符合的回答。∩ 042

Mark your answer.　　　　　　(A)　(B)　(C)

STEP 2 確認正確答案及翻譯和解說。

When is someone coming to install the projector?	何時會有人來安裝投影機？
(A) Restart the system.	(A) 重啟系統。
(B) Yes, he's tall.	(B) 是啊，他很高。
(C) Sometime this afternoon.	(C) 下午吧。

正確答案

(C) Sometime this afternoon.

字彙

install 安裝

解說

因為是詢問特定時間的問句，所以 (C) 是正確答案。詢問時間的問句，不能用 Yes 或 No 來回答，故選項 (B) 錯。(A) 的命令句，也不能回答詢問時間的問句。

> **When 疑問句**
>
> ● 題目以 when（何時）起始的疑問句，找出一個最合適的答句。
> ● 聽清楚 when 接下來的**主詞**和**動詞**。
> ● when 疑問句的句型是「When ＋**助動詞**＋**主詞**＋**動詞**……？」、
> 「When ＋ be **動詞**＋**主詞**？」或「When ＋ be **動詞**＋**主詞**＋ V-ing？」
> ● 和時間有關的**副詞**、**副詞片語**、**副詞子句**、**介系詞片語**，很可能是正確答案。
> ● 模糊的回答，例如「I'm not sure.」，有時也可能是正確答案。

STEP 1 聽錄音，選出與問題最為符合的回答。 ∩ 043

Mark your answer.　　　　　　　　(A)　(B)　(C)

STEP 2 確認正確答案及翻譯和解說。

When will the package arrive?	包裹何時會寄達？
(A) In the delivery truck.	(A) 在貨運卡車裡。
(B) I'll check the receipt.	(B) 我查一下收據。
(C) Sometime next week.	(C) 下週吧。

正確答案

(C) Sometime next week.

字彙

receipt 收據

解說

因為 when 是詢問時間的問句，所以表場所的選項 (A) 不會是正確答案。(B) 表達了主詞 I 將要做的行動，所以也和問句內容不符。正確答案是選項 (C)，它直接回答某一時間。(C) 是口語的句子，其省略的主詞與動詞是 the package will arrive。

STEP 1 聽錄音，選出與問題最為符合的回答。🎧 044

Mark your answer.　　　　　　　(A)　(B)　(C)

STEP 2 確認正確答案及翻譯和解說。

When will you finish the report?	你何時可以完成報告？
(A) Next to the printer.	(A) 在印表機旁邊。
(B) Before the end of the day.	(B) 今天下班前。
(C) The ship was in Port Vans.	(C) 船停在梵斯港。

正確答案

(B) Before the end of the day.

字彙

next to 緊鄰

解說

題目是很普通的 when 疑問句，詢問報告何時完成。(C) 的主詞 the ship，在問句中並沒有提到，且和問句的疑問副詞 when 一點關係也沒有，所以是錯誤答案。(A) 和 (B) 都是口語的句子，省略了主詞和動詞，所以將問句中的主詞和動詞接在前面，就能解題了。(A) 是回答詢問位置的答句，和本題不符。所以正確答案是 (B)。

STEP 1 聽錄音，選出與問題最為符合的回答。🎧045

Mark your answer.   (A)   (B)   (C)

STEP 2 重複聽幾遍錄音，並填寫下列空格。

_____ is Tammy _____ back to _____ ?

(A) Yes, she _____ in HR.

(B) I usually _____ before 8:30.

(C) Three months _____ she _____ .

STEP 3 確認正確答案及翻譯和解說。

When is Tammy coming back to work?	泰咪何時回來上班？
(A) Yes, she works in HR.	(A) 沒錯，她在人資部工作。
(B) I usually get to work before 8:30.	(B) 我通常在八點三十分前就到辦公室了。
(C) Three months after she has her baby.	(C) 在她生完小孩、休息三個月之後。

正確答案

(C) Three months after she has her baby.

字彙

HR: Human Resources 人力資源（部）   get to work 上班

解說

因為是詢問時間的 when 疑問句，所以 (B)、(C) 可以考慮。不過 (B) 講的人不是泰咪，是 I，而且講的時間是上班時間（**get to work**），所以不能選。而 (C) 提到了（現在正在待產的）泰咪回來上班的時間，所以是正確答案。

STEP 1 聽錄音，選出與問題最為符合的回答。∩ 046

Mark your answer.　　　　　　　　(A)　(B)　(C)

STEP 2 重複聽幾遍錄音，並填寫下列空格。

_____ do we _____ to _____ at the _____ ?

(A) Two hours before _____ .

(B) In _____ .

(C) He's _____ .

STEP 3 確認正確答案及翻譯和解說。

When do we need to arrive at the gate?	我們何時該到登機門？
(A) Two hours before departure.	(A) 出發前兩個小時。
(B) In Chicago.	(B) 在芝加哥。
(C) He's still alive.	(C) 他還活著。

正確答案

(A) Two hours before departure.

字彙

departure 出發

解說

因為題目是 when 起始的疑問句，也就是詢問時間，所以在聽選項時，要特別注意聽時間。(A) 明確表達了 departure（出發）的時間，所以是正確答案。(B) 用介系詞 in 表示發生某事的場所，和問句無關。(C) 的 he 和問句中提及的人和事也完全無關。

④ What 疑問句

1 題型暖身

STEP 1 聽錄音，選出與問題最為符合的回答。⌒ 047

Mark your answer.　　　　　　　(A)　(B)　(C)

STEP 2 確認正確答案及翻譯和解說。

What time will the movie finish?	電影何時播完？
(A) Buy three tickets.	(A) 買三張票。
(B) A famous director.	(B) 一位知名導演。
(C) At 9:30.	(C) 九點三十分。

正確答案

(C) At 9:30.

字彙

director 導演

解說

what time 是詢問時間的問句，所以選項 (C) 說出時間，是正確的答案。不過 time 除了表時間之外，也可以是一段時間，所以各式各樣表時間的說法都可能會是正確答案，這點要注意。由於本題詢問時間，(A) 的命令句和問句內容不符，(B) 提到導演，完全和時間無關。

STEP 1 聽錄音，選出與問題最為符合的回答。∩ 048

Mark your answer.   (A) (B) (C)

STEP 2 確認正確答案及翻譯和解説。

What day do you usually do the laundry?	你通常都在哪一天洗衣服？
(A) That'll be 45 dollars.	(A) 這樣總共是 45 美元。
(B) Usually on Sundays.	(B) 通常都在星期天。
(C) Before I leave the house.	(C) 在我出門前。

正確答案

(B) Usually on Sundays.

字彙

do the laundry 洗衣服

解説

以 what day 片語形成的疑問句，一般來説，正確的答案可能會提到「特定的某一天、時間或反覆出現的狀況」。(A) 的「that will be ＋金額」的句型，是站在結帳者的立場告知總金額，所以不會是正確答案。(C) 是特定狀況，但問句問的是 what day（特定的某一天），而且洗衣服一般來説不是一次性的，而是反覆會做的事，所以只簡單説「出門前」，意思也不通。因此選項 (B) 是正確答案，它用頻率副詞 usually 表達洗衣服這反覆性的狀況，是在星期天發生。

What 疑問句

- 題目以 what（什麼）起始的疑問句，找出一個最合適的答句。
- 聽清楚 what 接下來的**動詞**和**名詞**。
- what 如果後接動詞，和**動詞有關的訊息**，很可能是正確答案。
- what 若後接名詞，和**名詞有關的訊息**，或模糊的回答，很可能是正確答案。
  例：若用「What time . . . ?」來問，和時間有關的回答，就會是正確答案。

STEP 1 聽錄音，選出與問題最為符合的回答。🎧049

Mark your answer. (A) (B) (C)

STEP 2 確認正確答案及翻譯和解說。

What is the reason for this call?	這通電話來電的原因是？
(A) I need to finish lunch first before I call.	(A) 我要先吃完午餐再打電話。
(B) He had a good reason to call in sick.	(B) 他打電話請病假的理由充分。
(C) We would like to tell you about our new products.	(C) 我們想要跟你介紹我們的新產品。

正確答案

(C) We would like to tell you about our new products.

字彙

reason 理由　　call in sick 打電話請病假

解說

從句意上來看，說這問句的人，接到了行銷廣告的電話，於是問說：來電的目的是什麼。來電的人用表「負責行銷的」團體的 **we** 當主詞，並介紹他們推銷的商品，所以 (C) 是正確答案。(A) 回答說要先吃午飯再打電話，無法回答來電的理由。(B) 的 **call in sick** 和 **he**，和本問句毫無關係。

STEP 1 聽錄音，選出與問題最為符合的回答。 ∩ 050

Mark your answer. (A) (B) (C)

STEP 2 確認正確答案及翻譯和解說。

What's the best way to get across town during peak hour?	如何在交通尖峰時刻最快通過城鎮？
(A) Let's just grab dinner across town.	(A) 我們就在城那邊隨便買個晚餐吧。
(B) I had to drive home in peak hour last night.	(B) 昨晚我必須在交通尖峰時刻開車回家。
(C) Take West Bridge and go down 5th Avenue.	(C) 開上西橋後，沿著第五大道一直走。

正確答案

(C) Take West Bridge and go down 5th Avenue.

字彙

get across town 通過城鎮　　peak hour 交通尖峰時刻

解說

本題是詢問通過城鎮最快的方法，若選項有提供通過城鎮的捷徑，就是正確答案。(A) 建議說要 across town 去吃晚餐，但沒有提供如何 across town 的方法，所以不對。(B) 雖然提及 peak hour（尖峰時刻），但它用 I 說明昨天開車的狀況，這也不是方法。選項 (C) 用 take（走……路）起始的命令句，建議通過城鎮的方式，因此是正確答案。

聽錄音，選出與問題最為符合的回答。🎧 051

Mark your answer.   (A) (B) (C)

STEP 2 重複聽幾遍錄音，並填寫下列空格。

_____ did you _____ this _____?

(A) I'm _____ some time off _____ because
     of _____.

(B) Which _____ did you _____?

(C) I'm a little _____ about my _____.

STEP 3 確認正確答案及翻譯和解說。

What subjects did you choose this semester?	這個學期你選修了哪些課？
(A) I'm taking some time off from studying because of my job.	(A) 因為工作的關係，我部分時間就先暫停學習。
(B) Which facial cream did you choose?	(B) 你選哪一款面霜？
(C) I'm a little nervous about math.	(C) 數學讓我有點神經緊繃。

正確答案

(A) I'm taking some time off from studying because of my job.

字彙

subject 科目　　semester 學期　　take time off 暫時停止做某事

解說

詢問對方挑選了哪一些科目，可以知道問話者認為，回話者應該是已經選好了科目，一般而言，這是解題的關鍵，但本題難在選項 (A) 的 take some time off（暫時停止做某事），和提問者認為科目已經選好的認知不同，(A) 告知了沒有選擇科目的原因，所以是正確答案。(C) 雖然提到了科目，但焦點不在「選擇了什麼科目」，而是在「對該科目的感覺」，所以也不對。

STEP 1 聽錄音，選出與問題最為符合的回答。∩ 052

Mark your answer. (A) (B) (C)

STEP 2 重複聽幾遍錄音，並填寫下列空格。

_____ will Jenny _____ from _____ today?

(A) I had better _____ and _____.

(B) I _____ every day.

(C) I _____ my _____ playing _____ with Jenny.

STEP 3 確認正確答案及翻譯和解說。

What time will Jenny get back from work today?	珍妮今天何時下班回來？
(A) I had better call her and find out.	(A) 我最好打個電話問問。
(B) I work every day.	(B) 我每天都上班。
(C) I hurt my shoulder playing tennis with Jenny.	(C) 我跟珍妮打網球時，傷了肩膀。

正確答案

(A) I had better call her and find out.

字彙

find out 查明；弄清楚

解說

若選項直接表示特定的時間，告知珍妮下班回家的時間，一定會是正確答案。但本題三個選項主詞全都是 I，而且都沒提及特定時間。選項 (B) 和 (C) 和珍妮下班回家的時間，完全沒有關係，可以不用考慮。(A) 的 find out，是去弄清楚珍妮回來的時間，所以是正確答案。

⑤ Why 疑問句

STEP 1 聽錄音，選出與問題最為符合的回答。🎧 053

Mark your answer.   (A)   (B)   (C)

STEP 2 確認正確答案及翻譯和解說。

Why does Jacob want to sell his house?	雅各為何要賣掉他的房子？
(A) The garden is beautiful.	(A) 花園很漂亮。
(B) He's moving to Texas.	(B) 他要搬去德州。
(C) Yes, please stop by.	(C) 對，請順道過來一下。

正確答案

（B）He's moving to Texas.

字彙

garden 花園   stop by 順道拜訪

解說

因為本題是詢問原因的疑問句，所以回答「是」或者「不是」的選項 (C)，絕不會是正確答案。(A) 和 (B) 都是敘述句，(A) 說花園很漂亮，這不會是賣房子的原因，所以 (A) 也不對；(B) 說要搬到別的地方去，從句意上聯想，要搬到別的地方去，所以要賣掉原來居住的房子，這很合理，所以 (B) 是正確答案。

STEP 1 聽錄音，選出與問題最為符合的回答。∩ 054

Mark your answer.   (A) (B) (C)

STEP 2 確認正確答案及翻譯和解說。

Why is Ms. Zhang taking six months off?	為何張小姐要請假六個月？
(A) Because she is pregnant.	(A) 因為她懷孕了。
(B) No, she works part-time.	(B) 不，她是兼職員工。
(C) Actually, the light is on.	(C) 事實上，燈是開著的。

正確答案

(A) Because she is pregnant.

字彙

take time off 休假　　part-time 兼職的

解說

因為是詢問張小姐休假的原因，所以要有心理準備，可能會聽到各種原因。否定句 (B) 不會是正確答案。(C) 以 actually 起始句子，可以知道後面接的內容會跟問句的內容（發問者所知的內容）不同，但是燈光和張小姐休假完全無關，所以也不能選。(A) 直接以表原因的 because 起始句子，說明請假原因，並將主詞張小姐換成 she，所以是正確答案。

> **Why 疑問句**
>
> - 題目以 why（為何）起始的疑問句，找出一個最合適的回答。
> - 聽清楚 why 接下來的**主詞**和**動詞**。
> - why 疑問句的句型是「Why ＋助動詞＋主詞＋動詞……？」或
>   「Why ＋ be 動詞＋主詞……？」
> - 因為是詢問原因，所以含有表原因的**不定詞**（to ＋ V），或**說明原因的句子**，很可能是正確答案。

STEP 1 聽錄音，選出與問題最為符合的回答。 ∩ 055

Mark your answer.　　　　　　(A)　(B)　(C)

STEP 2 確認正確答案及翻譯和解說。

Why don't you enroll in a computer class?	你怎麼不報名上電腦課呢？
(A) Yes, Helen will play an important role.	(A) 是的，海倫將演出要角。
(B) The shop sells computer equipment.	(B) 這家店販售電腦設備。
(C) It's already past the sign-up deadline.	(C) 已經過了報名截止日期。

正確答案

(C) It's already past the sign-up deadline.

字彙

enroll 註冊　　role 角色　　sign-up 報名　　deadline 期限

解說

本題是詢問原因的問句，所以選項一定要說出「沒有報名電腦課的原因」，才會是正確答案。因此表回答肯定／否定問句的 **Yes/No** 選項 (A)，不會是正確答案。(B) 的主詞 the shop，不但無法掌握它是什麼，也不能成為原因。(C) 的 it 就是 computer class，也就是要報名上的課過了報名時間，所以是最合適的回答。

STEP 1 聽錄音，選出與問題最為符合的回答。🎧 056

Mark your answer.　　　　　　　(A)　(B)　(C)

STEP 2 確認正確答案及翻譯和解說。

Why don't you review the proposal?	你怎麼不審查一下提案呢？
(A) I think John should do that.	(A) 我以為是約翰的工作。
(B) You need to submit your proposal by Thursday.	(B) 你必須在星期四之前繳交提案。
(C) Because he didn't have an optimistic view.	(C) 因為他對此並不表示樂觀。

正確答案

(A) I think John should do that.

字彙

review 審查　　proposal 提案　　optimistic 樂觀的

解說

雖然是詢問原因的問句，但選項 (A) 是正確答案，它沒有直接說出原因，而是間接地提出意見——回答者認為這不是他的工作，選項 (A) 主詞和動詞都和問句不同，所以很容易被認為是錯誤答案，這點要注意。相反地，(B) 即使出現了問句中的 proposal，但卻是告知提案最後繳交的時間；而 (C)，主詞 he 不但不能代稱 proposal，所講的內容也和原因無關，所以也不是正確答案。

STEP 1　聽錄音，選出與問題最為符合的回答。🎧 057

Mark your answer.　　　　　　(A)　(B)　(C)

STEP 2　重複聽幾遍錄音，並填寫下列空格。

_____ is the _____ so full _____ ?

(A) Because there's a _____ in the _____ .

(B) I _____ a _____ for _____ .

(C) I _____ too much, so I _____ today.

STEP 3　確認正確答案及翻譯和解說。

Why is the subway so full today?	為什麼地鐵今天這麼擠？
(A) Because there's a big food festival in the city today.	(A) 因為今天市中心有一場盛大的美食嘉年華。
(B) I bought a subway sandwich for lunch.	(B) 我買了一個潛艇堡當午餐。
(C) I ate too much, so I feel full today.	(C) 我今天吃太多了，感覺好脹。

正確答案

(A) Because there's a big food festival in the city today.

字彙

subway 地鐵

解說

以 why 來詢問的問句，選項可能會出現各式各樣的回答。(A) 用表原因的連接詞 because 來起始句子，說出了地鐵人多的原因：正在舉辦一個美食嘉年華，所以 (A) 是正確答案。(B) 是重複題目用字 subway 的答題陷阱。

STEP 1 聽錄音，選出與問題最為符合的回答。∩ 058

Mark your answer. (A) (B) (C)

STEP 2 重複聽幾遍錄音，並填寫下列空格。

_____ does the _____ need another _____ ?

(A) The _____ is _____ to a staff member.

(B) I _____ the new _____ .

(C) I'm not sure, but _____ and requested one.

STEP 3 確認正確答案及翻譯和解說。

Why does the manager need another staff member?	為什麼經理需要另一名員工？
(A) The manager is talking to a staff member.	(A) 經理正在跟一名員工說話。
(B) I like the new staff member.	(B) 我喜歡那名新進員工。
(C) I'm not sure, but he called and requested one.	(C) 我也不清楚，他就是來電叫一個人過去。

正確答案

(C) I'm not sure, but he called and requested one.

字彙

staff member 員工　　request 要求

解說

因為問句詢問經理需要員工的原因，所以 (A) 雖然提到了經理與員工，但並沒有提到需要員工的原因，所以 (A) 不能選。(B) 不但主詞不同（the manager 不能用 I 來回答），也沒明確指出「需要的原因」。(C) 的 I'm not sure，表對問句所問的內容「並不太清楚」，多少都給了一個答案，所以可以是正確答案。

1 題型暖身

聽錄音，選出與問題最為符合的回答。🎧 059

Mark your answer.   (A) (B) (C)

確認正確答案及翻譯和解說。

How much will it cost to change my departure date?	如果我更改出發日期，我需要付多少錢？
(A) Proceed to Gate 7.	(A) 請到七號登機門。
(B) The personnel file is up-to-date.	(B) 人事資料是最新的。
(C) 40 dollars.	(C) 40 美元。

正確答案

(C) 40 dollars.

字彙

departure 出發   proceed to 前進到   personnel（公司）員工

解說

how 單獨當作疑問詞使用時，時常詢問程度或方法，但問句問的是 how much，也就是要花多少錢。選項 (C) 是正確答案，因為它直接表示出金額。另外要注意，有關金錢的問句，正確的答案通常都是直接回答金額。

STEP 1 聽錄音，選出與問題最為符合的回答。🎧 060

Mark your answer.   (A) (B) (C)

STEP 2 確認正確答案及翻譯和解說。

How do I get on the freeway?	我該如何上高速公路？
(A) Take this on-ramp.	(A) 走這條入口匝道。
(B) Until Friday.	(B) 直到星期五。
(C) The toll is free.	(C) 免收過路費。

正確答案

(A) Take this on-ramp.

字彙

freeway 高速公路　　on-ramp 入口匝道　　toll 過路費；通行費

解說

因為是詢問「該如何」上高速公路，所以正確答案會表示特定方式，或給詢問者忠告，因此答句會出現各種表方式或忠告的名詞和動詞，要熟悉這些名詞和動詞的用法。take 有很多種含意，和道路搭配使用，表「走……路」、「往……去」；和交通工具搭配使用，則表示「搭乘……」。on-ramp 是「入口匝道、車道入口」的意思，所以 (A) 是正確答案。(C) 的主詞 toll 不能表示方式。(B) 表時間的片語也不能表示方式。

How 疑問句

- 題目以 how（何時）起始的疑問句，常詢問方法、狀態、意見等，考生要找出一個最合適的答句。
- 聽清楚 how 接下來的**形容詞**或**副詞**或**動詞**。
- 若 how 後面接形容詞或副詞，和**該形容詞或副詞有關的回答**，很可能是正確的答案。
- 常見 how 起始的疑問句有：how soon（時間）、how long（期間）、how many（數量）、how much（價格）、how often（頻率）、how far（距離）等，how 後接形容詞或副詞的話，要翻譯成「多……」。
- 詢問狀態或意見的問句，含有**慣用語的選項**，很可能是正確的答案。
- I have no idea.（我不知道）等「不清楚」、「不知道」的回答，時常是正確答案。

STEP 1 聽錄音，選出與問題最為符合的回答。∩ 061

Mark your answer. (A) (B) (C)

STEP 2 確認正確答案及翻譯和解說。

How often do you have to clean the supply room?	你多久需要清理一次倉庫？
(A) Once every two weeks.	(A) 每兩個禮拜一次。
(B) Please leave the door open.	(B) 請讓門開著即可。
(C) In the meeting room.	(C) 在會議室。

正確答案

(A) Once every two weeks.

字彙

supply room 倉庫

透過 how often 可以知道,本題是詢問特定活動發生的頻率,答案就要
找提及該活動頻率的選項。(A) 的 once (in) every 是最常使用的表頻率
的片語,這點要記住。(C) 適合回答詢問特定場所的問句,所以是錯的。

STEP 1 聽錄音,選出與問題最為符合的回答。∩ 062

Mark your answer.   (A) (B) (C)

STEP 2 確認正確答案及翻譯和解說。

How do you know Greg Tate?	你是怎麼認識葛瑞‧塔特的?
(A) Surprisingly, there is no record of that.	(A) 奇怪,竟然沒有任何紀錄。
(B) For about a year.	(B) 大概一年了。
(C) We work in the same department.	(C) 我們在同一部門工作。

正確答案

(C) We work in the same department.

字彙

record 記錄

解說

用 how 疑問詞,詢問對方認識葛瑞‧塔特的緣由。因此,正確答案一定
要提到回答者和葛瑞‧塔特之間的關係。選項 (C) 是正確答案,它用 we
指稱回答者和葛瑞‧塔特,說明兩人是同部門同事。(B) 很容易被誤認
為是正確答案,但它表示「期間」,適合回答詢問「認識了多久」這樣的
問句。

聽錄音，選出與問題最為符合的回答。🎧 063

Mark your answer.　　　　　　(A)　(B)　(C)

STEP 2 重複聽幾遍錄音，並填寫下列空格。

_____ many _____ did you think we would _____ for

the _____ ?

(A) Joe _____ that 10 should be _____ .

(B) The _____ is _____ .

(C) Let's _____ the _____ at 9 p.m.

STEP 3 確認正確答案及翻譯和解說。

How many desks did you think we would need for the new office?	你覺得新的辦公室需要放幾張桌子？
(A) Joe said that 10 should be enough.	(A) 喬說十張桌子應該就夠了。
(B) The office is next door.	(B) 辦公室在隔壁。
(C) Let's pick the desks up at 9 p.m.	(C) 我們九點去載桌子。

正確答案

(A) Joe said that 10 should be enough.

字彙

next door 在隔壁

解說

因為是詢問需要多少張桌子，所以提到桌子或數目的選項，就可能是正確答案。問句中的動詞時態（did you think . . . ?），很容易造成混淆，但它只是純粹表示「（比現在稍早一點時）你認為需要幾個……？」。選項(A) 提及數目，也接續了這個話題，表示喬說了（said）桌子張數，而且動詞的時態也一致，所以是正確答案。

STEP 1 聽錄音，選出與問題最為符合的回答。🎧 064

Mark your answer.　　　　　(A)　(B)　(C)

STEP 2 重複聽幾遍錄音，並填寫下列空格。

_____ do I _____ for my _____ online?

(A) _____ your _____ for the _____ .

(B) Your _____ is not _____ .

(C) Go to our _____ and _____ the online form.

STEP 3 確認正確答案及翻譯和解說。

How do I apply for my identification card online?	我該如何在線上申辦身分證呢？
(A) Check your purse for the card.	(A) 在皮包裡找找看那張卡。
(B) Your identification card is not valid.	(B) 你的身分證失效了。
(C) Go to our website and fill out the online form.	(C) 去我們的網站填寫線上表格。

正確答案

(C) Go to our website and fill out the online form.

字彙

apply for 申請　　identification card 身分證　　valid 有效力的
form 表格

解說

這是詢問如何申請（apply）身分證的問句，(A) 說「在皮包裡找找看那張卡」，和申請無關。(B) 說身分證失效了，也沒說出申請的方式。正確答案是 (C)，回答方法的答句，時常會用命令句來回答，這點要記住。

Chapter 01

聽錄音，選出與問題最為符合的回答。並將您的答案標示在答案紙上。∩ 065

1. Mark your answer on your answer sheet.   Ⓐ Ⓑ Ⓒ

2. Mark your answer on your answer sheet.   Ⓐ Ⓑ Ⓒ

3. Mark your answer on your answer sheet.   Ⓐ Ⓑ Ⓒ

4. Mark your answer on your answer sheet.   Ⓐ Ⓑ Ⓒ

5. Mark your answer on your answer sheet.   Ⓐ Ⓑ Ⓒ

6. Mark your answer on your answer sheet.   Ⓐ Ⓑ Ⓒ

7. Mark your answer on your answer sheet.   Ⓐ Ⓑ Ⓒ

8. Mark your answer on your answer sheet.   Ⓐ Ⓑ Ⓒ

9. Mark your answer on your answer sheet.   Ⓐ Ⓑ Ⓒ

10. Mark your answer on your answer sheet.   Ⓐ Ⓑ Ⓒ

11. Mark your answer on your answer sheet.   Ⓐ Ⓑ Ⓒ

12. Mark your answer on your answer sheet.   Ⓐ Ⓑ Ⓒ

13. Mark your answer on your answer sheet.   Ⓐ Ⓑ Ⓒ

14. Mark your answer on your answer sheet.   Ⓐ Ⓑ Ⓒ

15. Mark your answer on your answer sheet.   Ⓐ Ⓑ Ⓒ

Chapter 02 Be 動詞疑問句

1 題型暖身

STEP 1 聽錄音，選出與問題最為符合的回答。∩ 066

Mark your answer. (A) (B) (C)

STEP 2 確認正確答案及翻譯和解說。

Is this the latest sales data?	這是最新的銷售數據嗎？
(A) You can find the date of the sale on this line here.	(A) 你可以在這一行字裡找到特賣會的日期。
(B) Last months' sales were great!	(B) 前幾個月的銷售成績很亮眼！
(C) Actually, it is most likely last month's.	(C) 事實上，它很有可能是上個月的。

正確答案

(C) Actually, it is most likely last month's.

字彙

latest 最新的

解說

說話者詢問這是不是最新的銷售數據（the latest sales data），(A) 利用 date 和 data 類似的發音形成錯誤答案，要注意。因為問句問的不是銷售的日期，所以 (A) 不能選。(B) 也不能選，因為題目問題和銷售業績無關。(C) 選項明確回答問句的問題，表明數據是上個月的 (last month's)，而非最新的銷售數據，是正確答案。

聽錄音，選出與問題最為符合的回答。♬ 067

Mark your answer.   (A) (B) (C)

確認正確答案及翻譯和解說。

Isn't she a famous actress?	她不是知名的女演員嗎？
(A) You could be right.	(A) 可能是喔。
(B) She is acting.	(B) 她在演戲。
(C) She is married to a famous actor.	(C) 她嫁給一位知名導演。

正確答案

(A) You could be right.

字彙

actress 女演員

解說

(B) 不適合回答本題，因為題目不是詢問那個女子正在做什麼。對話的情境是，兩個人（問話者和回答者）看到一個女子，兩人都認為那個女子是知名演員，選項 (A) 的 could be right，是「（意見）可能是對的」，也就是「贊成對方所說的」，因此正確答案是 (A)。

2 命題分析

> **Be 動詞疑問句**
>
> ● be 動詞疑問句是最常出現的問句,同時也是沒有特定正確答案的問句。
> ● be 動詞疑問句常詢問**物件的位置**或**存在與否**。
> ● 此類疑問句也常詢問主詞是否在做某事。
> ● 詢問**不久之後的未來**的問句,句型是:
>   「be +主詞+ going to +原形動詞⋯⋯?」。

STEP 1 聽錄音,選出與問題最為符合的回答。🎧 068

Mark your answer.　　　　　　(A)　(B)　(C)

STEP 2 確認正確答案及翻譯和解說。

Aren't these library books overdue?	這些圖書館的書該不是逾期未還吧?
(A) Charles Quinn is my favorite author.	(A) 查爾斯・昆恩是我最喜歡的作者。
(B) Yes, I keep forgetting to return them.	(B) 沒錯,我一直忘記要還書。
(C) She's a new librarian.	(C) 她是新來的圖書館員。

正確答案

(B) Yes, I keep forgetting to return them.

字彙

overdue 過期的　　librarian 圖書館員

解說

這是 be 動詞形成的否定疑問句,也就是詢問事物的狀態。(A) 適合用來回答「誰是你最喜愛的作家」。(C) 的主詞(she = librarian)和問句的主詞 these library books 不一致,所以不會是正確答案。(B) 的 yes 確認了問句中的逾期未還狀態(overdue),接著對此作出了解釋,所以是正確答案。

聽錄音，選出與問題最為符合的回答。🎧 069

Mark your answer. (A) (B) (C)

確認正確答案及翻譯和解說。

Is there any toner left in the printer?	印表機內還有碳粉嗎？
(A) I would assume.	(A) 應該有吧。
(B) If I were you, I would tone it down.	(B) 如果我是你，我會把色彩調淡一點。
(C) I'll be finished in a minute and then you can have it.	(C) 我會在一分鐘內完成，到時你就可以用了。

正確答案

(A) I would assume.

字彙

toner 碳粉　　tone (v.) 調色

解說

選項 (B) 是陷阱，它利用問句中的 toner 和 tone 的類似發音混淆考生。問句問碳粉（toner）還有沒有剩，而 (C) 適合用來回答「能不能使用印表機」，所以也不對。(A) 的回答最符合題意，是正確答案。

3 實戰應用

STEP 1 聽錄音，選出與問題最為符合的回答。🎧 070

Mark your answer.　　　　　　　(A)　(B)　(C)

STEP 2 重複聽幾遍錄音，並填寫下列空格。

Are you going to _____ the boss for a _____?

(A) Yes, I was going to _____ the _____ about my
　　　_____.

(B) It was my _____.

(C) I am _____ to the _____ later today.

STEP 3 確認正確答案及翻譯和解說。

Are you going to ask the boss for a raise?	你會去跟老闆要求加薪嗎？
(A) Yes, I was going to tell the boss about my raise.	(A) 沒錯，我之前是有打算跟老闆談談加薪的事。
(B) It was my plan.	(B) 是有這個計畫。
(C) I am going to the bank later today.	(C) 我今天晚一點會去銀行。

正確答案

(B) It was my plan.

字彙

raise (n.) 加薪

解說

問句的時態是未來式「are going to . . .」，而 (A) 的時態「was going to . . .」是過去式，所以錯了。(C) 的時態沒錯，但不是去找老闆而是去銀行，所以也不對。(B) 選項雖然是過去式，但表達的是「之前就有這個計畫」，故最為合適，是正確答案。

聽錄音，選出與問題最為符合的回答。∩ 071

Mark your answer.   (A) (B) (C)

STEP 2 重複聽幾遍錄音，並填寫下列空格。

Are you _____ anyone with you on the _____ ?

(A) Actually, I _____ to _____ .

(B) I'm going _____ to accounting about the _____ .

(C) I _____ so happy about _____ before.

STEP 3 確認正確答案及翻譯和解說。

Are you taking anyone with you on the business trip?	你出差時會帶人隨行嗎？
(A) Actually, I have never been to Vietnam.	(A) 事實上，我從沒去過越南。
(B) I'm going to talk to accounting about the possibility.	(B) 我正打算跟會計部討論此事的可行性。
(C) I have never been so happy about traveling before.	(C) 我以前從未如此熱愛旅行。

正確答案

(B) I'm going to talk to accounting about the possibility.

字彙

accounting 會計

解說

問句問的不是曾經去過哪裡，也沒有提到越南（**Vietnam**），而是詢問「出差有沒有同伴」，所以 (A) 完全答非所問。(C) 也是錯的，因為問句問的是 **business trip**（出差）不是 **trip**（旅行），而且 (C) 時態用是現在完成式，表以前曾經有過的經驗，不是未來式，所以也不對。正確答案是 (B)。

Chapter 03 Do 助動詞疑問句

1 題型暖身

STEP 1 聽錄音，選出與問題最為符合的回答。🎧 072

Mark your answer.　　　　　　　　　　(A)　(B)　(C)

STEP 2 確認正確答案及翻譯和解說。

Do you need assistance finding something? (A) Their findings are interesting. (B) Yes, I could use some help. (C) No, I'm not an assistant professor.	你需要人幫忙找什麼嗎？ (A) 他們的研究結果很有趣。 (B) 嗯，我需要一些幫助。 (C) 不，我不是助理教授。

正確答案

(B) Yes, I could use some help.

字彙

assistance 協助　　finding 研究結果

解說

問句的 finding 是分詞，表「找尋某物」，而 (A) 的 findings 是名詞，指「研究結果」，字雖然一樣，但意思不同，所以 (A) 是錯的。(C) 雖用 no 來回應問句，看似正確，但 no 之後的句子是告知自己的職位，這和問句所問的內容完全無關，所以也不對。(B) 用 yes 來回應問句，表同意需要幫忙，和問句所問一致，所以 (B) 是正確答案。

聽錄音，選出與問題最為符合的回答。🎧 073

Mark your answer.　　　　　　(A)　(B)　(C)

確認正確答案及翻譯和解說。

Do you think the speaker will arrive on time?	你覺得演講者會準時抵達嗎？
(A) Well, he still hasn't called.	(A) 嗯，他還沒來電話。
(B) Please take the bus.	(B) 請搭公車。
(C) They are already seated.	(C) 他們已經就坐。

正確答案

(A) Well, he still hasn't called.

字彙

speaker 演講者

解說

由於題目問「你認為……怎麼樣？」，所以會有很多種回答方式。一般而言，答句可以直接回答「是／不是」，然後說明自己的想法，也可以像 (A) 那樣，間接說出自己的意見。本題難在，問句中的單字並沒有出現在選項中，而要透過聯想和推測解題。選項 (A) 隱含的情境是「回答者不久前就開始等演講者，直到現在，他仍沒有打電話來」，要透過這樣的聯想，才能推測回答者認為講者「可能無法準時抵達」了，因此 (A) 正確。

2 命題分析

> **Do 助動詞疑問句**
>
> ● **Do** 助動詞疑問句：一般來說，是確認特定**事件是不是事實**的疑問句。要特別注意時態和人稱，要聽清楚是 Do、Does 還是 Did，才能正確解題。
>
> ● 選項提到**詢問的對象**，才是正確答案；提到主詞，未必是正確答案。

STEP 1　聽錄音，選出與問題最為符合的回答。🎧 074

Mark your answer. (A) (B) (C)

STEP 2　確認正確答案及翻譯和解說。

Do you want me to put this in the back seat or in the trunk?	你要我把這個放在後座還是後車廂？
(A) We met him in front of the building.	(A) 我們在大樓前碰見他。
(B) In the back seat.	(B) 放在後座。
(C) I'll be back right away.	(C) 我馬上回來。

正確答案

(B) In the back seat.

字彙

seat 座位

解說

題目問兩個位置中選哪一個，因為選項不僅會出現兩個位置，還會出現其他的選擇，所以聽選項時一定要聽到最後。選項 (B) 直接在兩個位置中選了後座（**back seat**），所以是正確答案。

聽錄音，選出與問題最為符合的回答。 ∩ 075

Mark your answer.　　　　　　　(A)　(B)　(C)

確認正確答案及翻譯和解說。

Didn't you hear that Julie had a baby girl?	你難道沒有聽說茱莉生了一個女兒？
(A) Here it is.	(A) 就在這。
(B) Thank you for your cooperation.	(B) 感謝您的配合。
(C) Yes, and I'm happy for her.	(C) 有啊，真替她開心。

正確答案

(C) Yes, and I'm happy for her.

字彙

have a baby girl 生了女兒　　　cooperation 合作
be happy for 為……感到開心

解說

問句為否定疑問句，要注意英文用 yes/no 來回答時，和問句本身是肯定還是否定完全無關，而是依回答者的回答來決定，回答者對該事表示肯定，就用 yes，對該事表示否定，就用 no。

遇到否定疑問句，翻譯時要注意，答句的 yes 要翻成「不」，no 要翻譯成「是」，剛好相反，例如：
Didn't you hear . . . ?（沒聽過……嗎？）
→ No, I didn't hear about it.（是的，沒聽過。）

回答者確認茱莉生了小孩這件事，所以說 yes，接著並說「真替她開心」，所以 (C) 是正確答案。(A) 和 (B) 都和生小孩無關，所以均為錯誤答案。

3 實戰應用

STEP 1 聽錄音,選出與問題最為符合的回答。∩ 076

Mark your answer.　　　　　(A)　(B)　(C)

STEP 2 重複聽幾遍錄音,並填寫下列空格。

Do you _____ a _____ or _____ size?

(A) Yes, I _____ it _____ good _____.

(B) I _____ a _____.

(C) I'll _____ the _____ near the _____.

STEP 3 確認正確答案及翻譯和解說。

Do you want a bigger or smaller size?	你要大一點還是小一點的尺寸?
(A) Yes, I think it looks good on me.	(A) 沒錯,我覺得我穿起來很好看。
(B) I prefer a looser fit.	(B) 我喜歡鬆一點。
(C) I'll post the want ad near the entrance.	(C) 我會在門口附近張貼徵人啟事。

正確答案

(B) I prefer a looser fit.

字彙

prefer 更喜歡　　want ad 徵人啟事

解說

問句要聽者在兩種尺寸中選一個,所以選項若提到兩種尺寸之一,或其他選擇,可能是正確答案。選項 (A) 用 yes/no 來回答 do 形成的疑問句看似正確,但它沒有提到選擇哪一個尺寸,所以不是正確答案。(C) 也不能選,因為徵才廣告和衣服尺寸大小無關。正確答案是 (B),雖然沒有直接表明選擇哪一個尺寸,不過它用 I 做主詞,並用動詞 prefer(更喜歡),間接說出了自己的選擇,所以 (B) 是最合適的選項。

聽錄音，選出與問題最為符合的回答。∩ 077

Mark your answer. (A) (B) (C)

STEP 2 重複聽幾遍錄音，並填寫下列空格。

Did you _____ the _____?

(A) Yes, it _____ thrilling.

(B) An _____ load.

(C) The _____ is close by.

STEP 3 確認正確答案及翻譯和解說。

Did you see the film trailer?	你看過電影預告片了嗎？
(A) Yes, it looks thrilling.	(A) 有啊，很驚悚。
(B) An oversized load.	(B) 裝太多了。
(C) The theater is close by.	(C) 電影院就在附近。

正確答案

（A) Yes, it looks thrilling.

字彙

trailer 預告片　　thrilling 毛骨悚然的　　oversized 尺寸過大的
load 裝載

解說

題目詢問是否曾看過電影預告片（film trailer），因此選項若表達看過／沒看過，或表達跟預告片有關的敘述句，都可能是正確答案。(C) 雖是和電影相關的敘述句，卻和有沒有看過 film trailer 無關，只是在說場地。(B) 的名詞 load（裝載）也和電影預告無關，所以也不正確。(A) 直接回答看過，並表達自己對預告片的意見，所以是正確答案。

Chapter 04 選擇疑問句

1 題型暖身

STEP 1 聽錄音，選出與問題最為符合的回答。 🎧 078

Mark your answer.　　　　　　(A)　(B)　(C)

STEP 2 確認正確答案及翻譯和解說。

Should we take the express train, or the cheaper option? (A) Let's get there as fast as possible. (B) She is waiting at the train station. (C) I'll send it by express mail.	我們該搭特快車，還是便宜一點的普通車？ (A) 我們越快抵達越好。 (B) 她正在火車站等候。 (C) 我會用限時郵件寄過去。

正確答案

(A) Let's get there as fast as possible.

字彙

express train 特快車　　as fast as possible 越快越好
express mail 限時郵件

解說

因為題目詢問該搭哪種火車，所以正確選項要直接或間接提到選擇的車種。問句是在「特快車」和「價錢更便宜的」（可以推斷是普通車）擇一。選項 (C) 雖然提到 express，但 express mail 是限時郵件，和問句內容完全無關，所以不能選。(B) 雖然提到和火車相關的火車站，但選項中的 she、以及她會在火車站等候和問句內容無關，所以也不對。正確答案是 (A)，它用 as fast as possible，表「越快到達那裡越好」，推測就是指「特快車」（express train）了。

聽錄音，選出與問題最為符合的回答。🎧 079

Mark your answer.   (A) (B) (C)

確認正確答案及翻譯和解說。

Should I make a phone call or visit the client in person?	我應該打電話給客戶，還是親自去拜訪？
(A) I'm sorry I couldn't answer your call.	(A) 抱歉我剛才無法接聽你的電話。
(B) We expanded our client base.	(B) 我們拓展了客層。
(C) Why don't you speak face to face?	(C) 何不當面會談？

正確答案

(C) Why don't you speak face to face?

字彙

in person 親自   expand 擴充   face to face 面對面

解說

因為問句是要聽者在兩個方式中選一個，所以要先找找看，選項是否直接或間接表達選哪一種方式。(A) 和問句完全無關，(B) 雖提到顧客層（client base），但它和問句無關，所以也不能選。(C) 雖然是疑問句，但這個反問提問者的「why don't you . . .」，間接用 face to face 表示選擇 visit in person，所以正確答案是 (C)。實際對話時，也常用疑問句反問當作回答，所以答題時更要小心。

2 命題分析

選擇疑問句

● 選擇疑問句是在兩個選擇中擇其一的問句。

● 一般而言，問句中都會出現 or，要注意聽 or 前後出現的名詞或片語。

● 由於是選擇疑問句，所以考生會認為要選其中一個，不過最近，**兩個都選**或**兩個都不選**，會是正確答案的情形也滿多的。

● 下列這些也可能會是正確答案：

I don't care. / Either is fine with me. / It doesn't matter.
I'll leave it to you. / It's up to you. / Whichever you like.

STEP 1 聽錄音，選出與問題最為符合的回答。∩ 080

Mark your answer.　　　　　　　(A)　(B)　(C)

STEP 2 確認正確答案及翻譯和解說。

Should I send the document by e-mail or regular mail?	文件資料要用電子郵件或是一般郵件寄送？
(A) The road is closed on a regular basis.	(A) 這條馬路會定期封閉。
(B) Please send him immediately.	(B) 請馬上寄給他。
(C) I'd prefer a paper copy.	(C) 我比較喜歡紙本。

正確答案

(C) I'd prefer a paper copy.

字彙

document 文件　　copy 影本

解説

問句的內容是在兩個寄件方式中擇其一，若選項直接或間接選擇其中之一的方式，或者表示出其他的選擇，很可能是正確答案。問句中的受詞「資料」（document），不能用 him 來代稱，所以 (B) 不能選。(A) 提到有關道路的情形，和問句無關，所以 (A) 也是錯的。正確答案是 (C)，它沒有直接表達回話者的選擇，而是回話者講到自己比較喜歡紙本，所以郵寄文件是正確答案，這種正確選項要特別注意。

聽錄音，選出與問題最為符合的回答。🎧 081

Mark your answer.　　　　　　(A)　(B)　(C)

確認正確答案及翻譯和解說。

Should we take the stairs or the elevator?	我們要爬樓梯還是搭電梯？
(A) I like this building.	(A) 我喜歡這棟大樓。
(B) I exercise on the step machine.	(B) 我在踏步機上運動。
(C) It's a long way up.	(C) 要爬很高耶。

正確答案

(C) It's a long way up.

字彙

exercise (v.) 運動

解說

問句內容是要在兩種方式中選擇一個，(A) 未提及兩種選擇，卻提出了對「建築物」的意見，所以不能選。(B) 的 step machine 和問句中的 stairs 很容易混淆，而且動詞 exercise，和回答者自己的運動習慣有關，和問句詢問爬樓梯還是搭電梯無關。(C) 說「要爬很高耶」，暗示了比較喜歡搭電梯，所以是正確答案。

3 實戰應用

STEP 1 聽錄音，選出與問題最為符合的回答。🎧 082

Mark your answer.　　　　　　(A)　(B)　(C)

STEP 2 重複聽幾遍錄音，並填寫下列空格。

Should I _____ the _____ or ask Ryan for _____?

(A) I _____ Ryan is _____.

(B) Ryan is _____.

(C) Ryan _____ to be a _____.

STEP 3 確認正確答案及翻譯和解說。

Should I call the technician or ask Ryan for help?	我應該叫技術人員來或是請萊恩幫忙？
(A) I think Ryan is on vacation.	(A) 我想萊恩應該在休假。
(B) Ryan is my friend.	(B) 萊恩是我朋友。
(C) Ryan wants to be a technician.	(C) 萊恩想當技術人員。

正確答案

(A) I think Ryan is on vacation.

字彙

technician 技術人員　　on vacation 休假中

解說

本題詢問該找誰幫忙，所以正確選項要直接或間接提到幫忙的人選，或提出第三種建議。(B) 和 (C) 雖然提到了人選之一的萊恩，但僅提到萊恩的狀態或願望，和問句「尋求幫助（call/ask for help）」目的不符，所以都不能選。正確答案是 (A)，它說萊恩休假中，間接暗示了「叫技術人員來」的選擇，這點要注意。

聽錄音，選出與問題最為符合的回答。∩ 083

Mark your answer.　　　　　　　　(A)　(B)　(C)

重複聽幾遍錄音，並填寫下列空格。

Would you _____ to get the _____ membership or the _____ one?

(A) I _____ a one-month _____.

(B) I _____ many membership _____.

(C) _____ is the _____ deal.

確認正確答案及翻譯和解說。

Would you like to get the three-month membership or the yearly one? (A) I have a one-month membership. (B) I have many membership cards. (C) Whichever is the better deal.	您想取得三個月的會員資格還是一年的會員資格？ (A) 我有一個月的會員資格。 (B) 我有許多會員卡。 (C) 比較划算的那一個。

正確答案

(C) Whichever is the better deal.

字彙

membership 會員資格　　better deal 較划算（較佳的）交易條件

解說

問句內容是請對方選一種會員資格，一般都是依據回答者的喜好做出選擇。(A) 和 (B) 僅說自己有會員資格或證，並沒有說比較喜歡哪一種會員資格。(C) 透過 whichever，表明了不管哪一種，喜歡較划算（better deal）的那一個，所以是正確答案。

Chapter 05 附加問句和敘述句

1 題型暖身

STEP 1　聽錄音，選出與問題最為符合的回答。∩ 084

Mark your answer.　　　　　　　　(A)　(B)　(C)

STEP 2　確認正確答案及翻譯和解說。

The new keyboards have been distributed to all the employees, haven't they? (A) They hired around 50 people. (B) Yes, we did that yesterday. (C) At the distribution center.	新的鍵盤都發給員工了吧？ (A) 他們大概僱了五十個人。 (B) 是的，我們昨天就發了。 (C) 在配送中心。

正確答案

(B) Yes, we did that yesterday.

字彙

distribute 分發　　hire 僱用　　distribution (n.) 分發

解說

附加問句，是助動詞或 be 動詞與代名詞組成的問句，放在直述句後面，用來尋求對方的確認。若直述句是肯定的，附加問句要用否定形式，若直述句是否定的，附加問句要用肯定形式。

附加問句也可看作是一種否定疑問句，例如：

The new keyboards have . . . , haven't they?

= Haven't the new keyboards (= they) been distributed?（否定疑問句）

(B) 的 yes 表肯定、確認分發鍵盤的動作已完成，然後又說明了分配的時間，所以是正確答案。(A) 與 (C) 完全沒提到是否分發鍵盤，所以是錯誤答案。

聽錄音，選出與問題最為符合的回答。∩ 085

Mark your answer. (A) (B) (C)

確認正確答案及翻譯和解說。

Thanks to the landscaper, the front lawn looks great.	多虧園藝設計師，前院的草坪漂亮極了。
(A) He's sketching a landscape.	(A) 他正替景觀畫草圖。
(B) I'm going to apply for a loan.	(B) 我打算申請貸款。
(C) It does, doesn't it?	(C) 確實是，不是嗎？

正確答案

(C) It does, doesn't it?

字彙

landscaper 園藝設計師   landscape 景觀
apply for a loan 申請貸款

解說

題目是描述 the front lawn 的敘述句。(A) 的主詞 he 可指稱 landscaper，但題目是說園藝設計師將草坪打理得很美，草坪是已經整理過的狀態，所以和園藝設計師正在畫景觀草圖的狀態不符，故 (A) 不能選。(B) 是利用 lawn 與 loan 的類似發音做成的錯誤答案。

(C) 的 it does 是 the front lawn looks great 的簡化（it = the front lawn; does = looks great），所以 (C) 是正確答案。要注意，附加問句除了尋求對方的確認外，也有強調的含意，因此 (C) 不是反問對方的附加問句，而是表同意及強調，故為正確答案。

2 命題分析

附加問句

附加問句，是為了獲得確認、同意或強調，而放在直述句後的短問句。

- 若直述句是肯定，附加問句要用否定形式來問，若直述句是否定的，附加問句要用肯定形式來問。
- 要注意的是，答句和附加問句是肯定或否定無關，答句的內容是肯定的，就用 yes 回答，答句的內容是否定的，就用 no 回答。
- 另外，用 yes/no 來回答時，後接句子的內容也要是一致的，例：

肯定回答

It's supposed to snow tomorrow, isn't it? ➡ Yes, it is.

否定回答

You are going to go to the concert, aren't you?
➡ No, I am not going to go.

敘述句

- 考試裡的敘述句，型態雖是敘述句，但其實是當作疑問句來使用。
- 因為沒有像 WH 的疑問詞，敘述句缺乏一眼就可看出的關鍵字，所以考生要**理解整個句子的內容**，才能找出正確答案，這是此題型比較困難的地方。
- 要正確掌握整個句子的**內容和語調**。
- 敘述句的題型，答案也可能是 yes/no 引導的答句。
- 用**疑問句反問**的回答，也可能是正確答案。

確認訊息

The manager said we're still short on staff.
➡ Let's hope that they hire enough staff next year.

表達不滿情緒

I didn't expect to see Mr. Peter here. ➡ Yes, I was surprised, too.

表達意見

I like to ski when it snows like this.
➡ Yeah! It's the perfect time to go skiing.

建議忠告

I need to inform you that it's going to rain tonight.
➡ I am going to bring an umbrella.

詢問

Excuse me. I'm looking for the nearest station.
➡ Turn right. You can't miss it.

聽錄音，選出與問題最為符合的回答。∩ 086

Mark your answer.　　　　　　　(A)　(B)　(C)

確認正確答案及翻譯和解說。

You already washed the car, didn't you?	你已經洗好車子了，是吧？
(A) Yes, I did it yesterday.	(A) 是，我昨天洗的。
(B) I'll wash the dishes soon.	(B) 我馬上就去洗碗。
(C) No, she already left.	(C) 不對，她已經走了。

正確答案

(A) Yes, I did it yesterday.

字彙

wash the dishes 洗碗

解說

該直述句＋附加問句可以改成否定疑問句：Didn't you already wash the car? 因此 (A) 和 (C) 以 yes 和 no 引導的答句，可以優先考慮，再看看後接句子的意思和問句是否相符。由 (A) 答句的動詞 did 和其受詞 it，可以推測 it 指涉某種活動，可以指稱 washed the car，所以 (A) 是正確答案。

(C) 說 no，看似跟洗車有關，但問句問的是你，跟她（she）已離開完全無關，所以不對。(B) 也一樣，問句問的是洗車，跟洗碗完全無關，所以也是錯誤答案。

STEP 1 聽錄音，選出與問題最為符合的回答。🎧 087

Mark your answer. (A) (B) (C)

STEP 2 確認正確答案及翻譯和解說。

My computer completely stopped working today.	我的電腦今天整個當掉。
(A) Computer programming is a useful skill.	(A) 電腦程式設計是個有用的技能。
(B) I'll send a technician immediately.	(B) 我馬上派技術人員過去。
(C) I saw him yesterday at the intersection.	(C) 我昨天在路口看見他。

正確答案

(B) I'll send a technician immediately.

字彙

technician 技術人員

解說

題目提到電腦當掉，從句意上來看，回答者若表達自己的意見或提供解決的方法，可能是正確答案。(A) 對 computer programming 提出了意見，但和「電腦當掉」毫無關係；(C) 的 him 指稱人，無法指稱題目的電腦。選項 (B) 是正確答案，因為它提出了解決方法。

STEP 1 聽錄音，選出與問題最為符合的回答。🎧 088

Mark your answer.   (A)   (B)   (C)

STEP 2 重複聽幾遍錄音，並填寫下列空格。

The _____ meet _____,
don't they?

(A) Yes, I have a _____ today.

(B) They _____ do.

(C) I'm _____ .

STEP 3 確認正確答案及翻譯和解說。

The Board of Directors meet on Wednesdays, don't they?	每星期三開董事會，不是嗎？
(A) Yes, I have a meeting today.	(A) 是的，今天有個會要開。
(B) They usually do.	(B) 通常是的。
(C) I'm bored.	(C) 無聊死了。

正確答案

(B) They usually do.

字彙

board 董事會；委員會

解說

(A) 是陷阱，它以 yes 引導句子，呼應了題目中的附加問句；且重複出現問句中的 meet，會讓人誤以為該選項為正確答案，但 I 不能代稱問句中的主詞「開會的人們」，所以不能選。(C) 是利用 board 和 bored 的相似發音，形成的錯誤答案，而且回答內容和問句完全無關，也不能選。正確答案是 (B)。

STEP 1　聽錄音，選出與問題最為符合的回答。🎧 089

Mark your answer.　　　　　　　　(A)　(B)　(C)

STEP 2　重複聽幾遍錄音，並填寫下列空格。

Let's ＿＿＿＿＿ to ＿＿＿＿＿ the ＿＿＿＿＿.

(A) It's not ＿＿＿＿＿.

(B) OK, I have ＿＿＿＿＿ this week.

(C) No, thanks, I already ＿＿＿＿＿.

STEP 3　確認正確答案及翻譯和解說。

Let's meet to discuss the merger. (A) It's not true. (B) OK, I have time this week. (C) No, thanks. I already tried.	我們碰個面討論併購案。 (A) 這不是真的。 (B) 好，我這個禮拜有時間。 (C) 不，謝了。我已經試過 　　了。

正確答案

(B) OK, I have time this week.

字彙

merger 併購

解說

用 Let's 引導的祈使句提議採取一個行動（meet），一般來說，都是用
肯定／否定句來回答。(A) 的 it，從文法上來看指的是 merger，但接著
卻說：「合併不是真的」，無法很順地連接「我們碰個面討論併購案」，所
以不能選。(B) 和 (C) 分別用 OK 與 no 表肯定／否定，不過 (C) 說「已
經試過了」，表示已經見過面了，這也和祈使句的「碰個面」無法連貫，
所以也不對。因此正確答案是 (B)。

聽錄音，選出與問題最為符合的回答。並將您的答案標示在答案紙上。⌒ 090

1. Mark your answer on your answer sheet.　　Ⓐ　Ⓑ　Ⓒ

2. Mark your answer on your answer sheet.　　Ⓐ　Ⓑ　Ⓒ

3. Mark your answer on your answer sheet.　　Ⓐ　Ⓑ　Ⓒ

4. Mark your answer on your answer sheet.　　Ⓐ　Ⓑ　Ⓒ

5. Mark your answer on your answer sheet.　　Ⓐ　Ⓑ　Ⓒ

6. Mark your answer on your answer sheet.　　Ⓐ　Ⓑ　Ⓒ

7. Mark your answer on your answer sheet.　　Ⓐ　Ⓑ　Ⓒ

8. Mark your answer on your answer sheet.　　Ⓐ　Ⓑ　Ⓒ

9. Mark your answer on your answer sheet.　　Ⓐ　Ⓑ　Ⓒ

10. Mark your answer on your answer sheet.　　Ⓐ　Ⓑ　Ⓒ

11. Mark your answer on your answer sheet.　　Ⓐ　Ⓑ　Ⓒ

12. Mark your answer on your answer sheet.　　Ⓐ　Ⓑ　Ⓒ

13. Mark your answer on your answer sheet.　　Ⓐ　Ⓑ　Ⓒ

14. Mark your answer on your answer sheet.　　Ⓐ　Ⓑ　Ⓒ

15. Mark your answer on your answer sheet.　　Ⓐ　Ⓑ　Ⓒ

16. Mark your answer on your answer sheet. Ⓐ Ⓑ Ⓒ

17. Mark your answer on your answer sheet. Ⓐ Ⓑ Ⓒ

18. Mark your answer on your answer sheet. Ⓐ Ⓑ Ⓒ

19. Mark your answer on your answer sheet. Ⓐ Ⓑ Ⓒ

20. Mark your answer on your answer sheet. Ⓐ Ⓑ Ⓒ

21. Mark your answer on your answer sheet. Ⓐ Ⓑ Ⓒ

22. Mark your answer on your answer sheet. Ⓐ Ⓑ Ⓒ

23. Mark your answer on your answer sheet. Ⓐ Ⓑ Ⓒ

24. Mark your answer on your answer sheet. Ⓐ Ⓑ Ⓒ

25. Mark your answer on your answer sheet. Ⓐ Ⓑ Ⓒ

PART

3

簡短對話

Part 3 是聽兩到三個人的對話，接著回答 3 題和對話有關的試題。因為對話是由比較長的句子組成，考生不但要掌握整個對話的來龍去脈，還要同時掌握細節，所以會感覺比較困難。Part 3 一共會出 39 題。

Example   🎧 091

Man:	Do you need a lift home?
Woman:	Isn't it a little out of your way?
Man:	Don't worry about it. I'm in no hurry to get home.
Woman:	Thanks. If you want to come in, I can make us dinner.

1. What is the woman concerned about?
  (A) The man is in a hurry to get home.
  (B) Her house is not on his way home.
  (C) She lives too far away.
  (D) His car is not in good condition.

2. What did the man offer?
  (A) To make dinner
  (B) To go on a date
  (C) To drive the woman home
  (D) To pick the woman up

3. What did the woman say she would do for the man?
  (A) Bake him some cookies
  (B) Cook him dinner
  (C) Drive him home
  (D) Give him money

1. B   2. C   3. B

▶ 先聽兩個人的對話，然後一邊看試題和選項 (A)、(B)、(C)、(D) 一面做答，選項與題目均會印在試題本上。

Part 3 題型綜覽

- **題型概要**：聽兩到三個人的對話，從 (A)、(B)、(C)、(D) 四個選項選出正確答案，每個對話共有 3 道試題。對話只會播放一次，**而且不會印在試題本上**，會聽到試題錄音，試題也會在試題本上出現；選項則沒有錄音，只出現在試題本上。
- **對話類型**：職場工作、公共場所或服務機關、日常生活相關
- **試題類型**：
  ➜ 有關**整個對話內容**的題目：**對話主題、對話目的、對話場所、人物**相關題型
  ➜ 有關**細節**的題目：**問題點或擔心點、原因或方法、找出核心訊息、未來可能採取的行動、建議或請求**

新多益核心要點

- 從 30 題增加到 39 題，全部共有 13 個對話，每一段對話會出 3 題。
- **新題型：**

（1）再次顯示部分對話內容，詢問**對話者說這句話的意圖為何**。

（2）題目圖表對應部分對話內容，考生須綜合分析後選出正確答案。

（3）新增了 3 個人的對話。

（4）一來一往的對話次數增加到 5 次以上。

新多益準備策略

Part 3 的考試說明（Directions）有 30 秒左右，要利用這段時間事先看一下這 39 道題。

1. 先將試題和選項 (A)、(B)、(C)、(D) 都看一遍。答題時，一面看試題本上的試題和選項，一面注意聽對話中和試題有關的部分。

2. Part 3 測試的主要目的，是看考生能否掌握對話的**核心內容及細節**。

3. 作答 Part 3 時，不要錯過**對話一開始的部分**，因為開始的部分會說出**對話的主題**。

4. 看試題時，要確認 WH **疑問字、主詞、動詞**等重要字。
   - 試題用的字彙，可能是對話中原來使用的字彙，也可能經過**改寫，用其他字彙來表現**。

5. 若試題中有 when、where、who、which、what、why、how 這些疑問字，要牢記對話中符合它們的訊息。

6. 新多益中，出現了 3 個人的對話，所以也要記住談話者的性別，及彼此間的關係。

7. **注意聽對話焦點的指標**：however、but、in fact、actually 等字，因為在**它們後面一定會出題**，是多益重要的考點。

8. 若在答案紙上標示出正確答案後，可以先閱讀下一道試題，爭取時間。

9. 推測類的題型，大部分能在**對話的最後面**得到線索。為什麼呢？因為對話末段，可以推測出對話結束後，**說話者或聽話者的行動或想法**。推測類試題多半會出現在 3 道試題的最後一題。

10. 數字、星期、時間，幾乎不會原封不動地出現在正確答案中，都要經過**計算或變更**，才會得出最後正確的答案。

11. 有關圖表的試題，**先看一下圖表訊息，再整合試題和選項後**，仔細聽對話的內容。

12. 多益考試的內容，是和**辦公室、公共場所**有關，會聽到兩到三位有男有女的職場同事的對話，所以平時要多練習、熟悉這類對話主題內容的聽力。

試題類型分析

① 詢問主題的類型

What are the speakers talking about? 說話者在談論什麼？

What is the conversation mainly about? 對話的主題是？

What are they discussing? 他們在討論什麼？

● 以上句子是最常考的問題形式。

● 試題的解題關鍵常出現在**第一句話中**。

高頻對話主題和關鍵字，整理如下：

① 報告或課程進行得如何？
  ⇨ report（報告）, result（結果）, deadline（截止日期）

② 銷售增加或銷售減少
  ⇨ sales（銷售）, increase（增加）, decrease（減少）

③ 檔案、文件夾或文件在哪裡？
  ⇨ file（檔案）, folder（文件夾）, document（文件）

④ 人事異動
  ⇨ promotion（升遷）

⑤ 出差或辦公室搬遷
  ⇨ business trip（出差）, reimbursement（報銷；核銷）, move（搬遷）

⑥ 經濟狀況
  ⇨ economic boom（經濟繁榮）, inflation（通貨膨脹）, depression（不景氣）
    recession（經濟衰退期）

⑦ 新產品
  ⇨ new products（新產品）, reaction（反應）

⑧ 健康與否
  ⇨ health care（健康照護）, regards（問候；致意）

⑨ 休假與福利
⇨ vacation（休假）, benefits（福利）

⑩ 表演活動或休閒活動
⇨ resort（度假勝地）, concert（音樂會）, performance（表演）, exhibition（展覽）

❷ 詢問細節的題型

Who are the speakers? 說話者的身分是？

What is the man's problem? 男子的問題是？

What does the man want to do? 男子想做什麼？

What does the man say about the new job? 男子提到新工作何事？

When does the man want to meet? 男子想要何時見面？

Why is the woman late for the meeting? 女子為何會議遲到？

Where does the man suggest holding the party? 男子建議在哪辦派對？

How will the woman order the products? 女子將如何訂購產品？

How does the woman get to the concert? 女子如何抵達音樂會？

● 細節題是常考的試題類型。
● 詢問細節的題型，主要會以 WH 疑問字來詢問，要注意聽對話中和 WH 疑問字相關的訊息。

會考細節的對話狀況

① 會議或約會的時間或場所
⇨ where（何地）, when（何時）, conference（大型會議）, meeting（會議）, appointment（約會；預約）

② 進度表的時間，或場地的變更，或時間的延後
⇨ when（何時）, where（何地）, behind schedule（進度落後）, late（晚的）, delay（延後）

③ 辦公室設備的使用方法或故障
　　⇨ how（如何）, doesn't work（無法運作）, out of order（故障）

④ 截止期限
　　⇨ can't meet the deadline （無法如期完成）

⑤ 適應新環境
　　⇨ recommendation（推薦）, apartment（公寓）, a good restaurant（一間好餐廳）

❸ 推測的類型

聽完整個對話後，推測某對話者會有何種行動，或針對某部分對話內容作推測。

(1) 聽整個對話作推測的題型

● 要注意聽**說話者的身分**，還有暗示**對話場所**的關鍵字。尤其是在新多益中，因為會聽到 5 句以上的長對話，或 3 個人對話，或聽到有關圖表的相關訊息等，相當複雜，所以要非常集中注意力聽。

● 要事先熟悉有關**身分**或**職位**的單字，對話中出現這類的字彙時，也要記下**對話者之間的關係**。

● 要事先背下來和**公共設施、工地、交通工具**等相關的字彙，對話中出現時，也要注意聽。

(2) 針對某部分對話內容作推測的題型

● 先要確認推測的對象是誰，然後集中注意力聽有關他／她的部分，以掌握訊息。

● 一定要根據**對話中提到的內容**，推論出正確答案。

● 對話的最後面部分，常是線索所在，因此更要集中注意力聽。

短的對話

① 和日常生活有關的內容

1 題型暖身

STEP 1 聽對話，選出與問題最為符合的回答。🎧 092

When did the woman order the fabric?
(A) Four days ago
(B) About one month ago
(C) She will place an order soon.
(D) She ordered the fabric from a small company.

STEP 2 確認正確答案及翻譯和解說。

M The fabric you ordered finally arrived.	男：妳訂的布料終於到了。
W It's about time. I placed the order almost four weeks ago.	女：也該到了。我差不多是四個禮拜前訂購的。
M The company said there was a mix-up with the orders.	男：布料公司說他們把訂單搞混了。

When did the woman order the fabric?	女子何時訂購布料？
(A) Four days ago	(A) 四天前
(B) About one month ago	(B) 約一個月以前
(C) She will place an order soon.	(C) 她很快就會訂購。
(D) She ordered the fabric from a small company.	(D) 她向一間小公司訂購布料。

正確答案

(B) About one month ago

字彙

fabric 布料；織物　　place an order 下訂單
mix-up（引起混淆的）錯誤

解說

place 當動詞表「訂購」，對話中的 placed the order almost four weeks ago 是「約四個禮拜前訂購」。選項 (B) 將四個禮拜前換成說一個月前也可以，所以是正確答案。選項 (C) 的時態是未來式，和題目時態不符。(D) 回答對方訂購布料的來源，答非所問，也不能選。

STEP 1 聽對話，選出與問題最為符合的回答。🎧 093

Which country has the woman never been to?
(A) Hong Kong
(B) Korea
(C) Japan
(D) Asia

STEP 2 確認正確答案及翻譯和解說。

W We're opening a new branch in Hong Kong next year, so I'll be gone for a few months.	女：我們明年將在香港開一家新的分公司，所以有幾個月我會待在那。
M Wow, it'll be your first time to Asia, right?	男：哇，這將是妳第一次前往亞洲，對吧？
W Actually, I've been to every country in Asia, except for Korea. This will be my third trip to Hong Kong.	女：事實上，除了韓國，亞洲的每一個國家我都去過了。這是我第三次前往香港。

Which country has the woman never been to?		女子從未去過哪一個國家？	
(A) Hong Kong	(C) Japan	(A) 香港	(C) 日本
(B) Korea	(D) Asia	(B) 韓國	(D) 亞洲

正確答案

(B) Korea

字彙

branch 分公司

解說

答案線索在女子說的倒數第二句話中。她用表經驗的現在完成式「have been to」，說明她所有亞洲國家都去過了，除了韓國以外，意思就是韓國沒去過，所以正確答案是選項 (B)。而明年要去的地方（開分公司的地方）是香港，注意不要弄混了。

- 短的對話，主要會聽到職場上男女兩個同事之間的對話。
- **對話內容主要是：**
  - ➡ 公司的業務
  - ➡ 和職位晉升、分派、轉任有關的人事內容
  - ➡ 和員工訓練、行銷、出差、辦公室搬遷及變更相關
  - ➡ 日常生活中的旅行或其他休閒活動
- **試題類型：**詢問這段對話的**目的**或**主題**、**細節**，還有**推測**等題型。
- **解題戰略：**
  - ➡ 主題或目的題型的線索，會在**對話一開始的地方**出現
  - ➡ 細節型的題目，注意聽對話中和**題目 WH 疑問詞**相關的內容
  - ➡ 推測題型，正確答案的線索通常在**對話的最後面**出現

STEP 1 聽對話，選出與問題最為符合的回答。∩ 094

1. What did the speakers just finish doing?
   (A) Decorating a counter
   (B) Repainting some doors
   (C) Installing an air conditioner
   (D) Repainting the walls

2. What benefit does the man mention?
   (A) More available storage space
   (B) Decreased maintenance costs
   (C) Improved atmosphere
   (D) Extended store hours

3. What will the woman probably do next?
   (A) Change the light bulbs
   (B) Prepare an order
   (C) Design a window display
   (D) Rearrange the furniture

STEP 2 確認正確答案及翻譯和解說。

W Hey, Jim. Thanks for helping me repaint the walls with this beautiful blue color. I should have done this a long time ago. It looks great!

M You're right, Jill. It really brightens the atmosphere of the store. I'm sure your customers will be satisfied with this change.

W Yeah, I think so, too. In addition, this change has really inspired me. I think I might try moving some tables and chairs around as well.

女：嘿，吉姆。謝謝你幫我用這美麗的藍色油漆重新粉刷牆壁。我早就該這麼做了。看起來真棒！

男：說的沒錯，吉兒。這樣做真的使店裡的氣氛都活躍起來。相信妳的顧客都會滿意這個改變。

女：是啊，我也這麼覺得。再說，這個改變也給了我靈感。我想我應該也會把幾張桌椅移動位置試試。

字彙

brighten 使活躍　　atmosphere 氣氛
be satisfied with 對……感到滿意　　inspire 激發靈感
air conditioner 空調

1. What did the speakers just finish doing?
   (A) Decorating a counter
   (B) Repainting some doors
   (C) Installing an air conditioner
   (D) Repainting the walls

1. 對話者才剛完成哪件事？
   (A) 裝飾櫃台
   (B) 重新漆門
   (C) 安裝空調
   (D) 重新粉刷牆壁

正確答案

(D) Repainting the walls

解說

女子因男子為她做了某件事，而向男子表示感謝，因為這件事的動詞是 repaint（重新粉刷），所以正確答案可能是 (B) 或 (D)，又因為被粉刷的是牆壁，所以正確答案是 (D)。(A) 無法從選項中確認，(C) 和對話無關，所以都不能選。

2. What benefit does the man mention?

(A) More available storage space

(B) Decreased maintenance costs

(C) Improved atmosphere

(D) Extended store hours

2. 男子提到什麼益處？

(A) 儲藏空間增加

(B) 維修支出減少

(C) 改善氣氛

(D) 延長營業時間

(C) Improved atmosphere

掌握題目中的 benefit 是什麼，就能立刻解題了。在裝潢上，重新粉刷牆壁是有益的，男子在女子感謝他之後提到了 brightens the atmosphere 和 customers will be satisfied，所以選項若包含這兩點，或提到其中一點，就會是正確答案，所以正確答案是 (C)。

(B) 和 (D) 都無法從對話中確認。最後女子提到想試著移動幾張桌椅，替店內增添更多變化，和 (A)「儲藏空間增加」目的不符，也不對。

3. What will the woman probably do next?

(A) Change the light bulbs

(B) Prepare an order

(C) Design a window display

(D) Rearrange the furniture

3. 接下來女子最有可能做什麼？

(A) 換燈泡

(B) 備餐

(C) 設計櫥窗展示

(D) 重新布置家具

(D) Rearrange the furniture

女子的最後一句話提到 moving some tables and chairs around，選項 (D) 將桌椅統稱為家具，並將 move around 換成 rearrange，所以選項 (D) 是正確答案。(A)、(B)、(C) 提到的事項，都無法在對話中確認。

4. What is the purpose of the woman's visit?
   (A) To get a refund
   (B) To purchase a device
   (C) To pick up an item
   (D) To order a part

5. What problem does the man mention?
   (A) A replacement part has not arrived yet.
   (B) An order has been canceled by mistake.
   (C) The store will be closed temporarily.
   (D) A repair fee has been charged incorrectly.

6. What does the man offer to do for the woman?
   (A) Deliver an item to her
   (B) Inform her when work is complete
   (C) Give her a discount
   (D) Refer her to another store

PART
3

Chapter
01

短的對話

W Hello. I came to retrieve the Blu-ray player that I brought in for repair last week. Could you please get it for me?	女：嗨，我上個禮拜送修一台藍光播放器，我是來取件的。可以請你幫我取來嗎？
M Actually, we still haven't finished repairing it. We had to order a special part from the supplier and it should arrive tomorrow. I'm sorry for the inconvenience.	男：事實上，我們還沒有修理完畢。我們必須向廠商訂購特殊零件，預計明天才會到。抱歉給您帶來不便。
W Oh, you should have told me. But I live nearby, so it's not a problem for me to stop by again. When do you think it will be finished?	女：喔，你應該及早告知的。但我住在附近，所以再過來一趟沒問題。何時會修好？
M Thank you for your understanding. I will finish it as soon as possible and call you so that you can come to pick it up. Would that be OK?	男：感謝您的體諒。我會盡快修好再去電請您取件。這樣可以嗎？

字彙

retrieve 取回　　repair (n.) 修理　　part 零件　　refund 退費
temporarily 暫時地　　discount 打折　　refer 轉介

4. What is the purpose of the woman's visit?	4.女子來訪的目的為何？
(A) To get a refund	(A) 要求退款
(B) To purchase a device	(B) 購買設備
(C) To pick up an item	(C) 拿東西
(D) To order a part	(D) 訂購零件

正確答案

(C) To pick up an item

解說

因為女子在對話開始，就提到來這裡的目的是 to retrieve the Blu-ray player，因此選項 (C)「拿東西（Blu-ray player）」是正確答案。

5. What problem does the man mention?
- (A) A replacement part has not arrived yet.
- (B) An order has been canceled by mistake.
- (C) The store will be closed temporarily.
- (D) A repair fee has been charged incorrectly.

5.男子提到發生什麼問題？
- (A) 替換的零件還沒送到。
- (B) 他誤把訂單取消了。
- (C) 商店將暫停營業。
- (D) 維修費收錯了。

正確答案

(A) A replacement part has not arrived yet.

解說

對話中出現了兩個問題，第一個是播放器還沒修理好，第二個是修理時需要的某特殊零件（special part）還沒送來。若選項中提到這兩個問題或其中一個，就是正確答案，正確答案是 (A)，對話中的「明天會送到」（should arrive tomorrow），在選項中換成了「還沒送到」（has not arrived yet），要注意正確答案常會改寫。

6. What does the man offer to do for the woman?
- (A) Deliver an item to her
- (B) Inform her when work is complete
- (C) Give her a discount
- (D) Refer her to another store

6.男子向女子提出什麼提議？
- (A) 寄送某物件
- (B) 修理完成後通知她
- (C) 給她打折
- (D) 把她轉介給另一家店

正確答案

(B) Inform her when work is complete

解說

先掌握各選項的動詞與受詞，就能很快解題了。對話中，男子並沒有跟女子說會配送，而是女子要自己取件（pick it up），也沒提到折扣和轉介（refer），所以 (A)、(C)、(D) 都不對。要熟悉片語 refer A to B 是「將 A 轉介給 B」的意思。正確答案是選項 (B)，它將男子說的「……盡快修好再去電請您取件」這句話中的去電（call），改成了通知（inform）。

聽對話，選出與問題最為符合的回答。🎧 096

1. Who is the man?
   (A) A reporter
   (B) An actor
   (C) An editor
   (D) A director

2. What does the woman say she would like to do?
   (A) Conduct an interview
   (B) Purchase tickets
   (C) Take a photograph
   (D) Get an autograph

3. What does the man say about the theater?
   (A) It is under construction.
   (B) It is closed on weekends.
   (C) It is the only one in town.
   (D) It is understaffed.

4. Where are the speakers?
   (A) In a computer lab
   (B) At a gym
   (C) At a training seminar
   (D) At an appliance shop

5. What does the woman ask the man for?
   (A) A combination code for his locker
   (B) A piece of identification
   (C) A membership fee payment
   (D) A computer password

6. What does the woman say she will get for the man?
   (A) A discount coupon
   (B) A brochure
   (C) A complimentary item
   (D) A map of the facilities

② 和上班有關的內容

1 題型暖身

STEP 1 聽對話，選出與問題最為符合的回答。 🎧 097

What position does Margaret have?
(A) General manager   (C) President
(B) Supervisor   (D) Secretary

STEP 2 確認正確答案及翻譯和解說。

M Hello Kelly. Did you hear the news that Margaret was promoted to general manager of our company?

W Yes, our supervisor told me yesterday. I think she's perfect for the job.

M Absolutely. The president made a great decision.

男：嗨，凱莉。瑪格莉特升任公司的總經理，妳聽說了嗎？

女：有啊，我的主管昨天跟我說過了。我覺得她很適合那個職位。

男：確實是。董事長英明。

What position does Margaret have?
(A) General manager
(B) Supervisor
(C) President
(D) Secretary

瑪格莉特擔任什麼職位？
(A) 總經理
(B) 主管
(C) 董事長
(D) 祕書

字彙

general manager 總經理   supervisor 主管

正確答案

(A) General manager

解說

對話開始男子說的第二句話，就提到瑪格莉特晉升總經理（general manager）了，所以選項(A)是正確答案。

聽對話，選出與問題最為符合的回答。🎧 098

Who is Harry?
(A) The former finance coordinator
(B) The former vice president
(C) The former president
(D) The former chairman

確認正確答案及翻譯和解說。

M Lauren, did you hear that Harry became vice president now that William has retired?	男：蘿倫，妳聽說了嗎？因為威廉退休，哈利繼任為副總裁的事？
W Really? That's great news. I think he is brilliant.	女：真的嗎？這是大好消息。我覺得他很優秀。
M I agree. Now I wonder who will replace him as our finance coordinator.	男：有同感。現在我在猜誰會遞補他空出來的財務專員職缺。
Who is Harry?	誰是哈利？
(A) The former finance coordinator	(A) 前任財務專員
(B) The former vice president	(B) 前任副總裁
(C) The former president	(C) 前任總裁
(D) The former chairman	(D) 前任主席

字彙

retire 退休　　former 前任的

正確答案

(A) The former finance coordinator

解說

如果注意聽提到關於職位的句子的「時態」，很快就能解題了。威廉退休（has retired）後哈利成了（became）副總裁。另外，男子的最後一句話提到，哈利當了副總裁後，不知道誰會來接替哈利以前的位置，來擔任財務專員（finance coordinator），所以可知哈利之前的職位是財務專員，正確答案是（A）。

2 命題分析

- 和上班有關的內容，一般來説，就是有關在辦公室完成的基本業務，以及和事務機器相關的事項。從會議時間表、工作截止日、編寫及發送文件、事務機器的操作狀況、必需品的準備，到僱用、晉升、退休等人事業務，資金的籌措，以及產品的生產及行銷。
- **試題類型**：詢問這段對話的**目的**或**主題**、**細節**，還有**推測**等題型。
- **解題戰略**：
  → 主題或目的題型的線索，會在**對話一開始的地方**出現
  → 細節型的題目，注意聽對話中和**題目 WH 疑問詞**相關的內容
  → 推測題型，正確答案的線索通常在**對話的最後面**出現。

STEP 1 聽對話，選出與問題最為符合的回答。🎧 099

1. Who most likely is the woman?
   (A) A technician
   (B) An artist
   (C) A curator
   (D) A philanthropist

2. What will the man be doing tomorrow?
   (A) Buying additional supplies
   (B) Finalizing a contract
   (C) Attending an event
   (D) Having lunch with Mr. Thompson

3. Why will the woman stop by around mid-afternoon?
   (A) The man has an appointment at lunchtime.
   (B) Inclement weather is expected.
   (C) A building will be closed at lunchtime.
   (D) There will be less traffic at that time.

M Hello, Ms. Thompson. This is Chris Rockman from Strengs Art Hall. I'm calling to see if you can stop by to discuss the details of your upcoming exhibition at our space.

男：您好，湯普森小姐。我是史雋斯藝廊的克里斯·洛克曼。我打來是要詢問您是否能過來一下，商討接下來您預計在我們場地舉辦的展覽會細節？

W Sure, I'd be happy to. What time should I come by?

女：當然，我很樂意。我該何時到？

M Well, tomorrow I have to attend a fundraising event here, so how about this Wednesday?

男：嗯，明天這裡有一場募款活動我必須參加，那麼，我們約星期三如何？

W Yeah, I have some time around lunchtime this Wednesday. Oh, but traffic is usually bad around that time, so I'll be there around mid-afternoon.

女：好啊，這個星期三午餐前後我有點時間。呃，不過那個時間多半都會塞車，所以我會在下午三點左右到。

字彙

stop by 順道拜訪　　upcoming 即將到來的　　fundraise 募款
mid-afternoon 下午三點左右　　technician 技術人員
finalize 最後確認

1. Who most likely is the woman?
(A) A technician
(B) An artist
(C) A curator
(D) A philanthropist

1.女子最有可能是誰？
(A) 技術人員
(B) 藝術家
(C) 策展人
(D) 慈善家

正確答案

(B) An artist

解說

本題要先掌握說話者之間的關係。男子表明自己在藝廊工作，並請女子到藝廊討論她即將開幕的展覽細節，所以可以知道，女子是開展覽的人。選項中最合適的是 (B)，所以 (B) 是正確答案。選項 (C) 的 curator 是策畫展覽的人，注意不要弄混了。

2. What will the man be doing tomorrow?

(A) Buying additional supplies

(B) Finalizing a contract

(C) Attending an event

(D) Having lunch with Mr. Thompson

2.男子明天將做什麼？

(A) 添購額外的日用品

(B) 完成簽約程序

(C) 參加一場活動

(D) 與湯普森先生共進午餐

PART
3

Chapter
01

短的對話

正確答案

(C) Attending an event

解說

男子説明天要參加一個 fundraising event（募款活動），所以選項 (C) 將之簡稱為 event 是正確答案。對話中出現的是湯普森小姐，所以選項 (D) 的湯普森先生是錯的。對話中也沒提到明天中午兩個人要見面簽約，所以 (B) 也不能選。

3. Why will the woman stop by around mid-afternoon?

(A) The man has an appointment at lunchtime.

(B) Inclement weather is expected.

(C) A building will be closed at lunchtime.

(D) There will be less traffic at that time.

3.為何女子要在下午三點左右才到？

(A) 男子有個午餐約會。

(B) 可能天候不佳。

(C) 有棟大樓將在午餐時間暫時關閉。

(D) 那時較不會塞車。

正確答案

(D) There will be less traffic at that time.

解說

女子在最後一句話中提到，因為中午的交通多半塞車（traffic is usually bad），所以她改成下午三點左右（mid-afternoon）到來，所以選項 (D) 是正確答案。

4. What does the woman ask about?
   (A) A job interview
   (B) A moving date
   (C) Office furniture
   (D) A new branch

5. What will the woman do today?
   (A) Hire a new employee
   (B) Share her work space
   (C) Rewrite a report
   (D) Cancel a meeting

6. What will the man probably do next?
   (A) Order a chair
   (B) Contact a new employee
   (C) Visit a storage space
   (D) Browse a website

W Good afternoon, Alex. Do you know if the new office desk and chair were delivered yesterday?

M No, I don't think so. The delivery person stopped by yesterday, but there weren't any large packages.

W That's a real disappointment. We have a new employee starting work today, and he will need some space to work. Maybe he and I will have to use the same desk.

M I'll check the supply room and see if we have at least a spare chair.

女：午安，艾力克斯。不知你知不知道新的辦公桌椅昨天送到了沒？

男：好像還沒有。送貨員昨天有來過，但沒看到任何大型包裹。

女：真令人失望。今天會有位新進員工開始上班，他會需要辦公空間。或許他和我必須共用一張桌子了。

男：我去倉庫看看，看我們是否至少還有一張多的椅子。

PART 3

Chapter 01

短的對話

字彙

stop by 過來一下　　spare 多餘的；備用的　　furniture 家具
work space 辦公空間

---

4. What does the woman ask about?
   (A) A job interview
   (B) A moving date
   (C) Office furniture
   (D) A new branch

4.女子詢問何事？
   (A) 工作面試
   (B) 搬遷日期
   (C) 辦公室家具
   (D) 新的分公司

正確答案

(C) Office furniture

解說

對話開頭女子就詢問男子辦公桌椅（office desk and chair）是否送過來了，所以(C)是正確答案。選項出現的全都是事物名，不是動詞，要注意這種類型的選項。

5. What will the woman do today?

(A) Hire a new employee

(B) Share her work space

(C) Rewrite a report

(D) Cancel a meeting

5.女子今天會做什麼？

(A) 僱用一名新員工

(B) 與人共享辦公空間

(C) 重寫一份報告

(D) 取消一場會議

(B) Share her work space

解説

整個對話的背景是，新進員工第一天上班，為他準備的辦公桌椅，昨天就應該送到，但今天仍還沒送到。女子説的最後一句話 maybe he and I will have to use the same desk，表示兩個人可能要共用辦公桌了。選項 (B) 是正確答案，它將 use the same desk 換成 share her work space，要注意這樣的改寫方式。新僱用的員工今天要上班了，所以 (A) 不能選。

6. What will the man probably do next?

(A) Order a chair

(B) Contact a new employee

(C) Visit a storage space

(D) Browse a website

6.男子接下來有可能做什麼？

(A) 訂購一張椅子

(B) 聯繫新員工

(C) 前往倉儲空間

(D) 瀏覽網頁

正確答案

(C) Visit a storage space

解説

男子説的最後一句話提到，要去倉庫找找看有沒有 spare chair。因為要去找椅子，不是訂購椅子，也不是上網查找，所以 (A) 和 (D) 都不對。選項 (C) 是正確答案，它將 supply room 換成倉儲空間（storage space）來表示。

3 實戰應用

聽對話，選出與問題最為符合的回答。🎧 101

1. Why is the man calling?
   (A) To schedule a meeting
   (B) To discuss an estimate
   (C) To explain a policy
   (D) To ask for help

2. Where do the speakers work?
   (A) At a software company
   (B) At a real estate agency
   (C) At a bank
   (D) At a hospital

3. What will the man do this afternoon?
   (A) Send a document
   (B) Receive training
   (C) Apply for a job
   (D) Attend a reception

4. What is the purpose of the man's visit?
   (A) To purchase a present
   (B) To apply for a job
   (C) To give a souvenir
   (D) To deliver some flowers

5. Why is the woman concerned?
   (A) The man will be late for a meeting.
   (B) The delivery will not arrive on time.
   (C) The shop will go out of business.
   (D) The item will not last very long.

6. What will the man do this Friday?
   (A) Contact another store
   (B) Celebrate an anniversary
   (C) Visit his wife at work
   (D) Open a new restaurant

Chapter 01

聽對話，選出與問題最為符合的回答。∩ 102

1. Who most likely is the man?
   (A) A mechanic
   (B) A receptionist
   (C) A patient
   (D) A taxi driver

2. What does the woman ask about?
   (A) Details of a medical procedure
   (B) Available appointment times
   (C) Directions to a location
   (D) The name of a doctor

3. What does the woman say she will do?
   (A) Drive to her home
   (B) Ask a favor of her parent
   (C) Reschedule an appointment
   (D) Call in sick

4. Who is the man?
   (A) A gardener
   (B) A courier
   (C) A store clerk
   (D) A telephone operator

5. Why was the woman unable to receive the man's call?
   (A) She was outside.
   (B) She was talking on the phone.
   (C) She was asleep.
   (D) She was running an errand.

6. What is the man concerned about?
   (A) Getting lost
   (B) Causing an accident
   (C) Being late for other deliveries
   (D) Looking for a gas station

Chapter 02 來回5句以上的長對話

1 題型暖身

STEP 1 聽對話，選出與問題最為符合的回答。🎧 103

1. What problem does the man have?
(A) He can't find the messaging program.
(B) He cannot send messages to his colleagues.
(C) He e-mailed the wrong list.
(D) His computer broke down.

2. What does the woman give to the man?
(A) The office phone number
(B) The department's contact list
(C) The messaging program
(D) An invitation

STEP 2 確認正確答案及翻譯和解說。

M Karen, can you help me? There's a problem with our department's messaging program.

W Sure, what's going on?

M Well, I tried to send out some instant messages to my colleagues today, and I kept getting an error notice that said "unable to deliver message."

W Maybe you haven't added them to your contact list. You can add each one as a new contact by pressing the "invite" button and entering the colleague's e-mail address.

M Oh, I see. I'll give that a try.

W Yes, and here's a list with our department staff's e-mail, addresses, and phone numbers. You can hold onto it.

男：凱倫，可以請妳幫個忙嗎？我們部門的內部通訊程式有點問題。

女：當然，怎麼回事？

男：嗯，今天我試著發送一些即時訊息給我的同事，但卻不斷收到系統的指令碼錯誤通知，說「訊息無法傳送」。

女：或許你還沒把他們加入你的聯絡人清單。你可以按下「邀請」鍵，把每一個同事加入新的聯絡人，然後再輸入同事的電子郵件地址。

男：喔，我了解了。我再試試。

女：好的，還有，這裡有張我們部門員工的通訊錄，上面有他們的電子郵件地址、居住地址以及連絡電話。你可以拿去用。

M Great! Thanks for your help. I sure hope this works—it's very frustrating!

男：太好了！謝謝妳的協助。希望這樣能行得通，一直沒發送成功真令人感到沮喪！

字彙

colleague 同事　　hold onto something 拿著；緊緊捉住
frustrating 令人沮喪的

---

1. What problem does the man have?
　(A) He can't find the messaging program.
　(B) He cannot send messages to his colleagues.
　(C) He e-mailed the wrong list.
　(D) His computer broke down.

1.男子遇到什麼問題？
　(A) 他無法找到通訊程式。
　(B) 他無法發送訊息給同事。
　(C) 他寄出了錯誤的名單。
　(D) 他的電腦當掉。

正確答案

(B) He cannot send messages to his colleagues.

解說

解題關鍵在於掌握男子向凱倫尋求什麼幫助，男子第二句話説，該部門內部通訊程式有問題，之後又説，寄給同事的訊息寄不出去，且一直收到系統的指令碼通知，所以正確答案是選項 (B)。

---

2. What does the woman give to the man?
　(A) The office phone number
　(B) The department's contact list
　(C) The messaging program
　(D) An invitation

2.女子交給男子什麼？
　(A) 辦公室的電話
　(B) 部門通訊錄
　(C) 通訊程式
　(D) 邀請函

正確答案

(B) The department's contact list

解說

要注意女子最後一句話 You can hold onto it 的 it 指的就是部門員工的通訊錄，也就是女子要給男子拿去用的名單，所以正確答案是選項 (B)。(A) 有談話者所在的 office，還有女子給的 phone numbers，是很容易讓人弄混的選項。hold on（要受話者等待）和 hold onto 表「拿著；緊緊捉住」音很相似，但不要搞混了。

聽對話，選出與問題最為符合的回答。🎧 104

3. What kind of event is the woman organizing?
- (A) An annual press conference
- (B) A department party
- (C) The yearly baseball match
- (D) A staff meeting

4. According to the man, why should they use H-Mart?
- (A) Because it has low shipping costs
- (B) Because it makes customized uniforms
- (C) Because it has vintage-style uniforms
- (D) Because it ships overseas

STEP 2 確認正確答案及翻譯和解說。

M Hello, This is Greg. I've been told that you're organizing the yearly baseball match this year. I'd like to help.	男：嗨，我是格雷格。我聽說你正在籌辦今年度的棒球比賽。我想盡一份力。
W That's right. Would you be able to put together a few things for me regarding uniforms?	女：沒錯。你能幫我處理關於制服的相關事宜嗎？
M Sure. I can check out the prices of the apparel we will need. It would be great to get some custom uniforms made. We should use H-Mart's website because they make customized uniforms at a pretty reasonable price. I bought something from them recently and was very happy with their service.	男：沒問題。我可以查一下制服的價格。如果可以買到訂做的制服就太棒了。我們可以使用 H 瑪特的網站，因為他們提供客製化制服，價格頗為合理。我最近才從他家買了些東西，很滿意他們的服務品質。
W Why don't we check out the website briefly together? We can scroll through their product list and see if there is anything suitable. Their shipping costs are a bit high, but if they can customize the jersey it would be worth it.	女：何不一起快速地查看一下他們的網站？我們可以瀏覽他們的商品清單，看看有沒有合適的衣服。他家的運費有點高，不過如果他們可以幫我們訂做運動衫，就值得了。

M I'd like to get some unique vintage-style uniforms.

W Ok, let's go check it out now, then.

M We could also try to get the players' names printed on the back of their jerseys.

男：我想選獨特、有復古風的制服。

女：好，那我們現在就來找找看。

男：我們也可以試著把球員的名字印在運動衫的背面。

字彙

organize 籌劃；組織　　yearly 年度的　　put together 整理
apparel 服裝　　custom (a.)按客戶要求的　　customize 客製化
reasonable 合理的　　check out 查看　　scroll through 瀏覽
shipping cost 運費　　unique 獨特的　　vintage 復古的

3. What kind of event is the woman organizing?

3.女子在籌辦什麼活動？

　(A) An annual press conference
　(B) A department party
　(C) The yearly baseball match
　(D) A staff meeting

　(A) 年度記者會
　(B) 部門派對
　(C) 年度棒球賽
　(D) 員工會議

正確答案

(C) The yearly baseball match

解説

透過男子第二句話中的關鍵字 organizing the yearly baseball match，可知女子籌辦今年度的棒球比賽，所以選項 (C) 是最合適的答案。

4. According to the man, why should they use H-Mart?

(A) Because it has low shipping costs
(B) Because it makes customized uniforms
(C) Because it has vintage-style uniforms
(D) Because it ships overseas

4.根據男子的說法,為何他們要使用 H 瑪特網站?

(A) 因為他們的運費低廉
(B) 因為他們提供客製化的制服
(C) 因為他們有復古風的制服
(D) 因為他們可以將貨物寄送至國外

正確答案

(B) Because it makes customized uniforms

解説

因為 H 瑪特網站在對話中只提到一次,所以不注意聽的話很容易錯過。對話中,男子提到可以訂做制服(custom uniforms),接著建議上 H 瑪特公司網站,因為該網站的客製化訂製(customized uniforms)價格很合理(reasonable price),由此可知上 H 瑪特公司網站的原因了,正確答案是選項(B)。

女子提到 H 瑪特時,說它們的運費(shipping cost)有點高,所以(A)不對。男子希望是復古風的制服,但無法判斷 H 瑪特有沒有,所以(C)不能選。對話沒有提到 H 瑪特是否能將貨物寄送海外,也不能選。

- Part 3 新增的題型，是以前來回不到 5 次的對話，現在增加到 5 次以上，連 6 次、7 次的長對話都出現了。
- 由於對話長，所以更要整理好聽到的訊息。
- **試題類型**：詢問對話的目的、細節，還有對話結束後**推測說話者的行動**。
- **解題戰略**：

→ 主題或目的題型的線索，會在**對話一開始的地方**出現

→ 細節型的題目，注意聽對話中和**題目 WH 疑問詞**相關的內容

→ 推測題型，正確答案的線索通常在**對話的最後面**出現

STEP 1 聽對話，選出與問題最為符合的回答。∩ 105

1. What does the man work as?
   (A) A florist
   (B) An artist
   (C) A wedding planner
   (D) A host

2. What did the man's clients like about the wedding?
   (A) The futuristic concept
   (B) The flowers
   (C) The food
   (D) The customers

3. What does the man ask the woman to do?
   (A) Get married
   (B) Find more florists
   (C) Find some dresses
   (D) Plan a wedding

W	James, you did a great job planning the wedding.	女：詹姆士，婚禮的籌畫工作你做得太棒了。
M	Thank you. The clients told me the guests loved the futuristic concept.	男：謝謝。客戶跟我說賓客們都很喜歡未來概念風格的婚禮。
W	I know. In fact, several customers asked for you.	女：我知道，事實上，許多客戶都指名要找你。
M	It looks like I'll be busy this winter.	男：看來今年冬天我會很忙碌。
W	Let me know if you need help with anything.	女：如果需要幫忙，儘管說。
M	Actually, can you find more florists for me?	男：正好，妳能幫我多找幾個花商嗎？

字彙

client 客戶　　guest 賓客　　futuristic 未來風格的
customer 顧客　　florist 花商　　bride 新娘　　get married 結婚

1.	What does the man work as?	1.男子的工作是？
	(A) A florist	(A) 花商
	(B) An artist	(B) 藝術家
	(C) A wedding planner	(C) 婚禮企劃
	(D) A host	(D) 主持人

正確答案

(C) A wedding planner

解說

對話中沒有直接提到男子的職業，因此要從對話情境推論出答案。對話一開始，女子就讚美男子婚禮籌畫得很棒，所以男子應該是婚禮企劃，(C) 是正確答案。(A) 是男子請女子幫忙找的花商，所以也不能選。婚禮企劃不是主持人，所以選項 (D) 不能選。籌畫婚禮不是創作藝術，所以 (B) 也不對。

2. What did the man's clients like about the wedding?

(A) The futuristic concept
(B) The flowers
(C) The food
(D) The customers

2.男子的客戶滿意婚禮的哪一部分？

(A) 未來概念
(B) 花藝
(C) 食物
(D) 顧客

(A) The futuristic concept

解說

本題要尋找對話中的細節。男子第二句話中提到，客戶喜歡未來概念（futuristic concept）風格的婚禮，因此正確答案是 (A)。

---

3. What does the man ask the woman to do?

(A) Get married
(B) Find more florists
(C) Find some dresses
(D) Plan a wedding

3.男子要求女子做什麼？

(A) 結婚
(B) 多找幾個花商
(C) 找些禮服
(D) 籌畫婚禮

正確答案

(B) Find more florists

解說

女子最後一句話跟男子說，如果需要幫忙，儘管說。接著男子說 actually，表示接下來要說出需要什麼幫助了，於是他問說：「可以多找幾個花商（florists）嗎？」，所以正確答案是 (B)。

4. What was the purpose of the call?

(A) To notify the man about checkout time

(B) To book a flight for his business trip

(C) To welcome him to the hotel

(D) To schedule a visit for his next stay

5. What does the man need to do before he leaves?

(A) Make a phone call

(B) Fax some paperwork

(C) Send some e-mail

(D) Print out some documents

6. What time does the man leave the hotel tomorrow?

(A) 5 a.m.

(B) 7 a.m.

(C) 10 a.m.

(D) 11 a.m.

PART 3

Chapter 02

來回5句以上的長對話

W Hello Mr. Choi. This is Julie from the front desk.	女：您好，崔先生，我是飯店的櫃台人員茉莉。
M Evening.	男：晚安。
W I'm just calling to remind you that your car service will leave for the airport at 11 a.m. The checkout time is 10 a.m. If you want a later checkout time, please notify us at any time. Also, you can relax in our complimentary VIP lounge while you wait.	女：我來電提醒您，您預約明天上午 11 點啟程前往機場的送機服務。退房的時間是上午 10 點，如果您想要晚一點退房，請隨時告知我們。還有，您可享用飯店的貴賓室等候司機前來，無須額外付費。
M Thank you, but I need to have a few documents faxed before I leave tomorrow. Where can I do this?	男：謝謝妳。但在我明天啟程前，還有一些文件需要傳真。哪裡可以讓我傳真？
W We have a business lounge on the 22nd floor with fax machines, computers, and printers for your use.	女：飯店 22 樓的商務室有傳真機、電腦，還有印表機可供您使用。
M OK. What time does it open and will there be a receptionist who can help me?	男：好的。商務室何時開放？有接待人員可以提供協助嗎？
W Yes, Miss Green can assist you with your work and the lounge opens at 5 a.m.	女：有的，葛林小姐可以協助您處理公務。飯店的商務室早上 5 點就會開放。
M Thank you. Can I get a wake-up call for 5 a.m.?	男：謝謝妳。那我可以預定明天早上 5 點的晨喚嗎？

字彙

front desk 飯店櫃檯　　remind 提醒　　notify 通知
complimentary 贈送的　　receptionist 接待員　　assist 協助
book 預訂　　book a flight 預訂機位　　schedule a visit 安排參訪

4. What was the purpose of the call?
- (A) To notify the man about checkout time
- (B) To book a flight for his business trip
- (C) To welcome him to the hotel
- (D) To schedule a visit for his next stay

4.來電的目的為何？
- (A) 通知男子退房時間
- (B) 幫他預訂出差機票
- (C) 在飯店迎接他
- (D) 為他下回入住飯店，安排參訪行程

正確答案

(A) To notify the man about checkout time

解説

來電目的，就是打電話的人要向接電話的人傳達的訊息。女子來電目的是要提醒男子，有關前往機場的送機服務，以及退房的時間。選項中，(A) 提到了通知退房時間，所以是正確答案。女子不是幫房客預約機票，所以 (B) 是錯的。她也不是打電話來歡迎男子，而是告知退房時間，所以 (C) 也不能選。(D) 無法從對話中確認。

5. What does the man need to do before he leaves?
- (A) Make a phone call
- (B) Fax some paperwork
- (C) Send some e-mail
- (D) Print out some documents

5.男子在離開之前需要做什麼？
- (A) 打個電話
- (B) 傳真文件
- (C) 寄送電子郵件
- (D) 列印一些文件

正確答案

(B) Fax some paperwork

解説

要掌握對話中的細節，才能答題。選項 (B) 是正確答案，它將含有被動意涵的 have a few documents faxed，改成主動語態的「傳真一些文件」（fax some paperwork）。不要被女子對話中的一連串電子設備弄混了男子的需求。

6. What time does the man leave the hotel tomorrow?

(A) 5 a.m.

(B) 7 a.m.

(C) 10 a.m.

(D) 11 a.m.

6.男子明天幾點離開飯店？

(A) 上午 5 點

(B) 上午 7 點

(C) 上午 10 點

(D) 上午 11 點

正確答案

(D) 11 a.m.

解説

清楚掌握對話中出現的每個時間訊息，就能解題。上午 5 點，是崔先生要使用的商務室開門的時間，11 點是前往機場的接駁車出發的時間，10 點是退房時間，女子有提到崔先生等車來之前，可以使用貴賓室，可以推知，從 10 點退房到 11 點車來，這段時間他會在貴賓室等，所以正確答案是車出發的 11 點，為選項 (D)。別將退房時間和「離開飯店的時間」弄混了。

3 實戰應用

聽對話，選出與問題最為符合的回答。🎧 107

1. What are the speakers discussing?
   (A) Teamwork among the new employees
   (B) Distributing instruction manuals
   (C) Appropriate integration of new employees
   (D) The new evaluation system

2. What does the woman imply when she says, "It would be bad for morale"?
   (A) Learning new systems is very easy.
   (B) People don't want to be evaluated.
   (C) Veteran employees will feel disrespected.
   (D) A vacation calendar has not been posted yet.

3. What does the woman plan to do?
   (A) Go through the training course
   (B) Learn the system herself and then teach it
   (C) Make everyone go into the training course
   (D) Write a new manual

4. What department do the speakers most likely work in?
   (A) Customer Support
   (B) Research and Development
   (C) Project Management
   (D) Financial Planning

5. What does the woman mean when she says, "It's been quite a while, you see"?
   (A) She has worked a long time for the company.
   (B) She forgot about a manager's request.
   (C) She has not led a training session in years.
   (D) She does not remember how to use a program.

6. What will the man probably do next?
   (A) Contact a department leader
   (B) Go over a contract
   (C) Use a new software program
   (D) Hold a staff training session

Chapter 02

聽對話，選出與問題最為符合的回答。🎧 108

1. What are the speakers discussing?
(A) Budget cuts
(B) Benefits of breakfast
(C) Company loans
(D) The employee cafeteria

2. What is implied about the company?
(A) The employees are paid well.
(B) It does not make enough money.
(C) It updated the equipment.
(D) It needs new facilities.

3. What would the speakers like employees to do?
(A) Have breakfast before work
(B) Buy coffee from the company
(C) Pay for their breakfast
(D) Get to work earlier

4. What is the conversation mainly about?
(A) Candidates at a job interview
(B) The personalities of employees
(C) The qualifications needed
(D) The questions asked at an interview

5. What does the man request from the woman?
(A) Her participation in the interview
(B) Her opinions about people
(C) Her submission of questions
(D) Her arrangement of a meeting

6. What will the man probably do next?
(A) Arrange a meeting
(B) Set up more interviews
(C) Post an advertisement
(D) Contact some people

Chapter

03 出現 3 個人的對話

1 題型暖身

STEP 1 聽對話，選出與問題最為符合的回答。🎧 109

1. Who most likely is Mrs. Park?
(A) A senior staff member
(B) A new employee
(C) The office manager
(D) A client

2. What does the man offer to do for Mrs. Park?
(A) To buy her some office supplies
(B) To show her where the supply room is
(C) To take her to his new office
(D) To introduce her to some new colleagues

STEP 2 確認正確答案及翻譯和解說。

W1	Hello, Mrs. Park. You have been with us now for three months. How are you settling in to your new role?	女1：嗨，帕克太太。妳已經入職三個月了。對於新工作適應得如何？
W2	I'm happy. I do need some more paper and office supplies for my desk. Do I have to buy my own or . . .	女2：很順心。但我的辦公桌需要多一點紙，還有一些辦公用品。我需要自己去買，還是……
W1	Oh, I'm sorry. There is a supply room on the third floor. I will have the office manager show you how to get there later on today.	女1：喔，真抱歉。三樓有用品供應室。晚一點我會請行政主管告訴妳怎麼去。
M	Hi, Mrs. Park. Nice to meet you. It's a pleasure to have you working with us at Smith and West. Would you like me to show you how to access the supply room?	男：嗨，帕克太太。很高興認識你。很開心妳能加入我們史密斯與衛斯特工作團隊。需要我告訴妳用品供應室怎麼去嗎？
W2	Yes, that would be great. Thank you.	女2：是的。太好了，謝謝。
M	Follow me this way, please.	男：請跟我來。

settle in 適應新環境　　role 角色　　office supply 辦公用品
supply room 用品供應室　　office manager 行政主管

---

1. Who most likely is Mrs. Park?

(A) A senior staff member

(B) A new employee

(C) The office manager

(D) A client

1.帕克太太最有可能是？

(A) 資深員工

(B) 新進員工

(C) 行政主管

(D) 客戶

正確答案

(B) A new employee

解說

帕克太太是第二位女性。對話中第一位女性說，帕克太太進來一起工作 3 個月了，所以可以知道帕克太太是新進人員。另外，告訴她到用品供應室的男子也說，很高興帕克太太能加入史密斯與衛斯特一起共事，可以知道正確答案是 (B)。(A) 的 senior 是隱含比較級的字，表示「更資深的」，所以跟進公司三個月的帕克太太不符。

---

2. What does the man offer to do for Mrs. Park?

(A) To buy her some office supplies

(B) To show her where the supply room is

(C) To take her to his new office

(D) To introduce her to some new colleagues

2.男子提議為帕克太太做什麼？

(A) 幫她買一些辦公用品

(B) 告訴她怎麼去用品供應室

(C) 帶她到他新的辦公室

(D) 介紹一些新同事給她認識

正確答案

(B) To show her where the supply room is

解說

第一位女性提到，下午請 office manager 告訴帕克太太怎麼去用品供應室，所以可以知道對話中的男子就是 office manager，因此 (B) 是正確的。帕克太太問同事說，辦公室用品要自己去買嗎，同事回答說三樓有用品供應室，間接回答不用買，從這點推知，男子不會為女子買辦公室用品，所以 (A) 是錯的。

STEP 1 聽對話，選出與問題最為符合的回答。🎧 110

3. What department does Bill need help from?
(A) Product Development
(B) Human Resources
(C) Accounting
(D) Research and Development

4. How can Jennifer Bradley help Bill?
(A) By finding a new payroll officer
(B) By redesigning a marketing poster
(C) By making connections in the marketing world
(D) By meeting some accountants

STEP 2 確認正確答案及翻譯和解說。

M	Hi, this is Bill Franklin. The accounting department plans to recruit a new payroll officer. Could you ask the human resources department to post an advertisement and start screening some candidates?	男：嗨，我是比爾・富蘭克林。會計部門計畫增聘一名出納。能否請妳讓人事部張貼徵人廣告，開始甄選應徵人員？
W1	Sure. If you could please e-mail a job description, we can begin the process.	女1：沒問題。能否請你寄電郵給我，告知職務內容，然後我們便可以開始招聘程序。
M	OK. Let me brainstorm the exact details and I'll get back to you.	男：好的。讓我好好想一想確切的需求，再把它寄給妳。
W1	Yes . . . and you should talk with Jennifer Bradley. She has some good connections that might be useful in filling the role.	女1：好……還有，你可以跟珍妮佛・布萊德莉談談。她有些好的人脈，或許對於找到合適的人選會有幫助。
M	OK. Ah, here she is. Hi . . . Jennifer?	男：好。啊，她正好過來。嗨，珍妮佛？
W2	Hi. How can I help you?	女2：嗨。需要幫忙嗎？

M Good news. We're hiring one more payroll officer. Could you organize a meeting with some of your connections in the field?

W2 Sure. I will make some phone calls and let you know the details later this afternoon.

男：好消息。我們想增聘一位出納。能否請妳邀集一些相關人脈，與他們談談？

女2：沒問題。我打幾通電話，今天下午晚一點再告知你相關細節。

字彙

accounting 會計　　payroll officer 出納

human resources 人力資源　　screen 甄選　　candidate 候選人

job description 職務說明　　brainstorm 腦力激盪

connection 人脈；關係　　fill 填補（職缺）　　organize 安排

field 領域

---

3. What department does Bill need help from?
   (A) Product Development
   (B) Human Resources
   (C) Accounting
   (D) Research and Development

3.比爾需要向哪一個部門尋求協助？
   (A) 產品研發部
   (B) 人事部
   (C) 會計部
   (D) 研發部

正確答案

(B) Human Resources

解說

對話中出現的部門有，人事部（human resources）和會計部（accounting department）。因為比爾的第三句話說，能否讓人事部張貼徵人廣告，所以可知比爾向人事部請求協助，正確答案是 (B)。因為部門名稱是只出現一次的細節，注意不要漏聽了。

4. How can Jennifer Bradley help Bill?

(A) By finding a new payroll officer
(B) By redesigning a marketing poster
(C) By making connections in the marketing world
(D) By meeting some accountants

4.珍妮佛‧布萊德莉可以怎麼幫比爾？

(A) 找一個新的出納
(B) 重新設計一幅新的行銷海報
(C) 串聯行銷界的人脈
(D) 與會計師會面

正確答案

(A) By finding a new payroll officer

解説

男子拜託第一位女性的事，是請她聯絡人事部登廣告（advertisement）並甄選（screen）應徵人員。接著第一位女性推薦了珍妮佛，要男子跟珍妮佛談談，因為珍妮佛認識很多可以擔任出納的人選，所以正確答案是(A)，珍妮佛可以幫男子找到一位新的出納。

珍妮佛有認識的人脈（connection），但並沒有要請她在行銷界創造新人脈，所以 (C) 不對。(B) 與對話內容無關。珍妮佛僅是聯繫相關人脈，沒有要直接和會計師見面，所以 (D) 不能選。

- 3 人對話是新多益的類型之一，由於對話人數增加，所以更要仔細聽每個人提及的訊息。
- 3 人對話大部分仍是和上班有關的內容，一般來說，就是有關在辦公室完成的基本業務，以及和操作事務機器相關的事項。
- **試題類型：詢問對話的目的、細節，還有對話結束後推測說話者的行動。**
- **解題戰略：**
  - ➜ 主題或目的題型的線索，會在**對話一開始的地方**出現
  - ➜ 細節型的題目，注意聽對話中和**題目 WH 疑問字詞**相關的內容
  - ➜ 推測題型，正確答案的線索通常在**對話的最後面**出現

STEP 1 聽對話，選出與問題最為符合的回答。♫ 111

1. What is the main problem?
   (A) The manager is away.
   (B) The supplier is away on vacation.
   (C) The man is not getting his supplies on time.
   (D) The man wants a discount on the supplies.

2. What does the man mention about the suppliers?
   (A) They have had a lot of strikes recently.
   (B) They haven't been getting products.
   (C) They didn't get a discount.
   (D) They were unhappy with the service.

3. What does the man say he needs from Rick?
   (A) The Sterling Project
   (B) The order number
   (C) The shipment of supplies
   (D) The number for Rick Franklin

M1 Hi, Stacey. This is Rick Franklin. I'm working on the Sterling Project in Utah. I'm having problems getting my shipments on time and it's really slowing down our progress.

W Oh, I'm sorry to hear that, sir. Let me put you through to our manager and you can talk with him.

M2 Hi, Rick? I'm sorry you've been having problems getting your shipments. Our supplier has had a lot of trouble with strikes lately. I will talk with our suppliers and ask them what is going on. In the meantime, I will give you 15% off your current order.

M1 OK. Please find out what's going on. I appreciate the discount.

M2 No problem. If you could please give me your order number, I can process the discount.

男1：嗨，史黛西。我是猶他州史特林工程的里克·富蘭克林。貨物無法準時送到，真的會延遲我們的進度。

女：喔，真是抱歉。讓我把您的電話轉給我們的經理，您直接與他談。

男2：嗨，里克？真抱歉無法讓您順利收到貨物。我們的供應商最近被罷工搞得焦頭爛額的。我會去電供應商，問問他們怎麼回事。同時，我也會給你這個訂單打個八五折。

男1：好吧。請查明到底怎麼回事，同時也感謝您提供的優惠。

男2：應該的。請給我您的訂單編號，讓我處理折扣事宜。

PART **3**

Chapter **03**

出現3個人的對話

字彙

slow down 減緩　　strike 罷工　　in the meantime 同時

1. What is the main problem?

(A) The manager is away.

(B) The supplier is away on vacation.

(C) The man is not getting his supplies on time.

(D) The man wants a discount on the supplies.

1.問題主要出在哪裡？

(A) 經理不在。

(B) 供應商休假去了。

(C) 男子無法準時收到供應物料。

(D) 他要求物料享優惠折扣。

正確答案

(C) The man is not getting his supplies on time.

解説

對話中第一位男子用 having problems getting my shipments on time，直接說出了「貨物晚到」這問題點，所以正確答案是 (C)。

---

2. What does the man mention about the suppliers?

(A) They have had a lot of strikes recently.

(B) They haven't been getting products.

(C) They didn't get a discount.

(D) They were unhappy with the service.

2.男子提到供應商怎麼了？

(A) 他們最近常有罷工。

(B) 他們沒收到貨物。

(C) 他們沒有享有折扣。

(D) 他們不滿意服務品質。

正確答案

(A) They have had a lot strikes recently.

解説

第二位男子說的話與貨物遲到的問題有關，他提到提供貨物的供應商（supplier）因為罷工而出現了很多問題，可以知道供應商的問題是罷工，所以正確答案是 (A)。

選項 (B) 說，沒收到貨物，這是第一位男子里克‧富蘭克林遇到的狀況，不是供應商的狀況。選項 (C) 提到的折扣是給富蘭克林先生的，不是給供應商，所以也錯。選項 (D) 說供應商對服務不滿，應該是第一位男子和富蘭克林先生對供應商不滿才對，所以 (D) 也錯。

3. What does the man say he needs from Rick?
(A) The Sterling Project
(B) The order number
(C) The shipment of supplies
(D) The number for Rick Franklin

3.男子需要里克提供什麼東西？
(A) 史特林工程
(B) 訂單編號
(C) 運送貨物
(D) 里克‧富蘭克林的電話

出現３個人的對話

正確答案

(B) The order number

解說

第一位男子里克‧富蘭克林遭受了不便，補償就是打折（discount）。最後一句話第二位男子提到 process the discount，process 當動詞使用時是「處理」，並説為了要處理打折，請里克提供他的訂單編號（order number），所以正確答案是 (B)。

4. Who is Ron Westwood?
   (A) Hillary's friend
   (B) Owner of the building
   (C) The building manager
   (D) The office manager

5. What does the man say about the Smithson building?
   (A) He does not really like it.
   (B) It has just had some renovations.
   (C) It has an insect problem.
   (D) The contract is ready.

6. Where does the man suggest they should go?
   (A) To the third floor
   (B) To the second floor
   (C) To the Smithson Hotel
   (D) To the office on the fifth floor

W Hi, Mr. Carpenter. I'm Hillary White. We spoke earlier during the week about taking over some office space in the Smithson building. Do you remember?

M1 Yes, of course. Good to see you again Hillary. Let me introduce you to the building manager, Ron Westwood. Ron will be able to take care of all your questions about the contract.

M2 Hi, Hillary. You have made a good choice with the Smithson Building. We actually just had the third floor renovated; I'm not surprised you are interested in it.

W Yes it is fantastic! I really liked the new design. However, I'd like to know more details about the contract.

M2 I suggest we go to the office on the fifth floor and I can go through all of the details. There are a few details we need to address before signing off on the contract.

女：嗨，卡本特先生。我是希拉蕊·懷特。這週稍早之前我們有聊到史密森大樓辦公空間的使用事宜。您還記得嗎？

男 1：哦，當然。很高興再次與妳見面，希拉蕊。讓我為妳引見大樓經理榮恩·韋斯特伍德。所有關於合約的問題，榮恩都能幫您處理。

男 2：嗨，希拉蕊，史密森大樓是您正確的選擇。事實上，我們的三樓才剛翻新過，您會對它有興趣我並不意外。

女：沒錯，真是美極了！我真的很喜歡新的裝潢設計。不過，我還想多多了解合約的相關細節。

男 2：何不到五樓的辦公室，我可向您逐條講解所有的細節。在合約簽訂之前，有一些細節必須詳細說明一下。

PART 3

Chapter 03

出現 3 個人的對話

字彙

take over 接管；借用 　　take care of 處理 　　renovate 翻新；整修

4. Who is Ron Westwood?

    (A) Hillary's friend

    (B) Owner of the building

    (C) The building manager

    (D) The office manager

4.榮恩‧韋斯特伍德是誰？

    (A) 希拉蕊的朋友

    (B) 大樓所有人

    (C) 大樓經理

    (D) 辦公室經理

正確答案

(C) The building manager

解說

第一位男性在介紹榮恩‧韋斯特伍時，提到他是大樓經理（ building manager ），所以正確答案是 (C)。

5. What does the man say about the Smithson Building?

    (A) He does not really like it.

    (B) It has just had some renovations.

    (C) It has an insect problem.

    (D) The contract is ready.

5.男子提到史密森大樓時，說了什麼？

    (A) 他並不真的喜歡它。

    (B) 大樓才剛剛做了一些翻新。

    (C) 大樓裡蚊蟲肆虐。

    (D) 合約已經備好了。

正確答案

(B) It has just had some renovations.

解說

選項 (A) 的個人意見，在對話中並沒有直接出現。但從第二位男子榮恩跟女子說「不意外您對它有興趣」，間接顯示，男子自己也對建築物的裝修很滿意，所以 (A) 和對話完全相反。選項 (C) 在對話中並沒有提到。兩個人要去另一個地方討論有關租賃合約的細節，從這裡可以知道，合約還沒有簽好，所以 (D) 也不對。

正確答案 (B) 可從榮恩跟女子說明的有關大樓的細節中找到「We actually just had the third floor renovated.」。

6. Where does the man suggest they should go?
(A) To the third floor
(B) To the second floor
(C) To the Smithson Hotel
(D) To the office on the fifth floor

6. 男子建議他們該前往何處？
(A) 去三樓
(B) 去二樓
(C) 去史密森飯店
(D) 去五樓的辦公室

正確答案

(D) To the office on the fifth floor

解說

本題掌握選項和場所相關的細節，就能解題。三樓是不久前剛進行裝潢工程的地方，但不是討論合約的樓層，所以 (A) 錯。(B) 的二樓和 (C) 的史密森飯店，對話中並沒有提到。

對話中最後一句話，男子建議為了逐條講解合約細節，要去五樓的辦公室 (the office on the fifth floor)，因此正確答案是 (D)。

聽對話，選出與問題最為符合的回答。🎧 113

1. What are the speakers mainly talking about?
- (A) Tips for saving money on travel
- (B) An upcoming business trip
- (C) Websites for reserving hotels
- (D) Presentations for the trade show

2. What problem do the speakers have?
- (A) Their room reservations are not complete.
- (B) Their client in New York cannot meet them.
- (C) Their transportation arrangements are for the wrong dates.
- (D) Their presentation date has changed.

3. What does the man suggest they do?
- (A) Reserve another car
- (B) Cancel a reservation
- (C) Search on the Internet
- (D) Prepare a sample

4. Where most likely is the conversation taking place?
- (A) In an airplane
- (B) In a café
- (C) In a conference room
- (D) In a break room

5. What does Caleb suggest about the coffee?
- (A) It comes with dessert.
- (B) It is too expensive.
- (C) It takes a long time to make.
- (D) It is high quality.

6. What does the woman say about the meeting?
- (A) It is mandatory for all employees.
- (B) It has already finished.
- (C) It will be in a different location.
- (D) It will be longer than usual.

Chapter 03

聽對話，選出與問題最為符合的回答。 🎧 114

1. What is the conversation mainly about?
   (A) An order for office equipment
   (B) A new sales strategy
   (C) An improved employee rest area
   (D) An alteration to a schedule

2. Why does the man say, "It's a real step up from the old one"?
   (A) He is satisfied with the change.
   (B) He would like an extra step.
   (C) He feels embarrassed.
   (D) He is critical of the plan.

3. What does the woman imply about the company?
   (A) It has hired more staff recently.
   (B) It treats its employees well.
   (C) It is having financial difficulties.
   (D) It has many employee lounges.

4. What does Mr. Rutherford ask for?
   (A) A list of speakers
   (B) Presentation materials
   (C) An e-mail address
   (D) Financial statements

5. What problem does the woman mention?
   (A) She left her laptop on a plane.
   (B) She did not send an e-mail.
   (C) She lost her hotel reservation.
   (D) She forgot to save a file.

6. Why does Mr. Rutherford ask to speak to Marcus after lunch?
   (A) To make a travel plan
   (B) To review a paper
   (C) To review a speech
   (D) To discuss a product

和圖表有關的對話

STEP 1　聽對話，選出與問題最為符合的回答。∩ 115

Marketing Firm	Contact
Omnipresent	Karen Jones
Y&G Inc.	Barret Lee
Ads Plus	Peter Ronson
Arbor Corp.	Kevin Kain

1. What did the woman do in Hong Kong?
- (A) Go sightseeing
- (B) Sell the latest model of robots
- (C) Look for marketing firms
- (D) Open a shop

2. Look at the chart. Which person did the woman go to college with?
- (A) Karen Jones
- (B) Barret Lee
- (C) Peter Ronson
- (D) Kevin Kain

M Nancy! Good to see you back. How was your trip to Hong Kong?	男：南西，真開心看到妳回來。香港行如何？
W Very productive. We sold several units of our latest model of robots. How were things here?	女：收穫豐富。我們賣了幾組最新型的機器人。這裡情況如何？
M Also productive. I received the list of marketing firms you wanted to see.	男：同樣大有斬獲。我收到了妳一直想要的行銷公司名單。
W Let me see. Wow, Kevin Kain? He was a classmate of mine in college.	女：讓我瞧瞧。哇，凱文·凱因？他是我的大學同學。

Marketing Firm	Contact
Omnipresent	Karen Jones
Y&G Inc.	Barret Lee
Ads Plus	Peter Ronson
Arbor Corp.	Kevin Kain

行銷公司名稱	聯絡人
歐米普振	凱倫·瓊斯
Y&G 有限公司	李貝瑞
廣告加	彼得·榮森
亞柏公司	凱文·凱因

字彙

productive 有生產力的

1. What did the woman do in Hong Kong?

(A) Go sightseeing

(B) Sell the latest model of robots

(C) Look for marketing firms

(D) Open a shop

1.女子在香港做什麼？

(A) 觀光

(B) 銷售最新型的機器人

(C) 尋找行銷公司

(D) 開店

正確答案

(B) Sell the latest model of robots

解説

從女子説的話「We sold several units of our latest model of robots.」，可知她在香港賣了幾組最新型的機器人，正確答案是 (B)。

2. Look at the chart. Which person did the woman go to college with?

(A) Karen Jones

(B) Barret Lee

(C) Peter Ronson

(D) Kevin Kain

2.請看表格。女子的大學同學是誰？

(A) 凱倫·瓊斯

(B) 李貝瑞

(C) 彼得·榮森

(D) 凱文·凱因

正確答案

(D) Kevin Kain

解説

因為對話中南西提到，凱文·凱因是她的大學同學，所以正確答案是 (D)。

Destination	Departure time
Kent Gardens	8:30 a.m.
Langley Lane	9:00 a.m.
Ridge Valley	10:00 a.m.
Mountain Valley	10:30 a.m.

3. Look at the graphic. What time will the speakers depart?
   (A) 8:30 a.m.
   (B) 9:00 a.m.
   (C) 10:00 a.m.
   (D) 10:30 a.m.

4. What does the woman want to do?
   (A) Wait for the next train to Mountain Valley
   (B) Take a bus to Kent Gardens
   (C) Visit the botanical gardens
   (D) Go to a restaurant

W Oh, no, we missed the eight o'clock train to Mountain Valley.	女：噢，不，我們沒趕上八點開往山谷的那班火車。
M That's alright, doesn't the train come every 30 minutes?	男：還好啦，不是每三十分鐘都有一班車？
W Unfortunately, not on holidays. We'll have to wait two hours for the next ride.	女：不幸的是，假日沒有。我們要等兩個小時，才能等到下一班車。
M How about this? I'll get tickets to Kent Gardens. We can take another train to Mountain Valley from there.	男：不如這樣。我去買前往肯特花園的車票。我們可以從那裡搭另一班前往山谷的車。
W Great idea! Meanwhile, I'd love to visit the botanical gardens while we're there.	女：好主意！到了那裡，我同時也想參觀一下那裡的植物園。

Destination	Departure time
Kent Gardens	8:30 a.m.
Langley Lane	9:00 a.m.
Ridge Valley	10:00 a.m.
Mountain Valley	10:30 a.m.

目的地	開車時間
肯特花園	上午 8：30
蘭里庭	上午 9：00
山脊谷	上午 10：00
山谷	上午 10：30

字彙

botanical garden 植物園

3. Look at the graphic. What time will the speakers depart?
(A) 8:30 a.m.
(B) 9:00 a.m.
(C) 10:00 a.m.
(D) 10:30 a.m.

3.請看圖表。對話者將在何時啟程？
(A) 上午 8：30
(B) 上午 9：00
(C) 上午 10：00
(D) 上午 10：30

正確答案

(A) 8:30 a.m.

解說

對話者現在對話的時間，如果不是假日的話，要去目的地山谷（Mountain Valley），可以搭乘 8 點 30 分的火車，如果是假日的話，火車的間隔時間就要變成 2 小時了。因為對話時是假日，所以要找替代方案。因為男子說的第二段第二句話，提到買去肯特花園的車票，所以可以知道他們要去的下一個地方是肯特花園，所以對照時刻表，時間是 8 點 30 分，正確答案是 (A)。

4. What does the woman want to do?
(A) Wait for the next train to Mountain Valley
(B) Take a bus to Kent Gardens
(C) Visit the botanical gardens
(D) Go to a restaurant

4.女子想做什麼？
(A) 等下一班前往山谷的火車
(B) 搭公車前往肯特花園
(C) 參觀植物園
(D) 去餐廳

正確答案

(C) Visit the botanical gardens

解說

本題詢問女子想做的事，女子說的最後一句話直接提到了想去看植物園（botanical gardens），所以正確答案是 (C)。因為去肯特花園的交通工具是火車，不是公車，所以 (B) 不對。

- 對話新類型之一，是在 13 組對話共 39 道題中，最後 3 組 9 道試題會出現圖表。
- 對話之外會出現一個和對話有關的圖表，可能是**條列式的表**、**圖示**、**日程表**、**時間表**、**飛機票價目表**、**菜單**等。
- 一般來說，3 道題中的第 2 道題會出類似這樣的問題：「Look at the graphic, what discount will the woman most likely receive . . . ?」。
- 聽的時候，要**一面聽一面看圖表**作答。

STEP 1　聽對話，選出最符合提問的選項。 ∩ 117

Mario's Lighting

Style	Price
Flush Mount	$ 150
Semi Flush	$ 200
Chandelier	$ 400
Pendants	$ 600

1. What does the woman say she is going to do?
(A) Remodel a house
(B) Buy a new apartment
(C) Upgrade her lighting
(D) Host a dinner party

2. Look at the graphic. What light will the woman buy?
(A) Flush Mount
(B) Semi Flush
(C) Chandelier
(D) Pendants

3. What does the man say he will do?
(A) Send her a letter
(B) Give her a discount
(C) Send a quote via email
(D) Install the lights today

M Good afternoon, this is Mario's Lighting. How may I help you?

W Hi. I'm remodeling a house at the moment and my friends told me that you have the best quality lights in town. I'd like you to install some light in my new place next month.

M OK. Do you know what style you would like?

W Well, I don't really like chandeliers. Money is not an issue, so just give me your most expensive products.

M OK, then. I recommend the pendants, which are very high quality. I will take your details down and then send you a quote for your total cost via e-mail.

男：午安，這裡是馬力歐燈飾。您需要什麼樣的服務？

女：嗨。我的家現在正在重新裝潢，聽朋友說你們有本市品質最好的燈飾。我想請你們下個月在我的新家安裝幾盞燈飾。

男：沒問題。您清楚自己想要什麼風格的燈飾嗎？

女：嗯，我並不是很喜歡枝形吊燈。錢不是問題，你只需要給我安裝最貴的燈飾就好。

男：那麼，好的。我建議這些吊燈，它們的品質非常好。我需要記下一些您新家的細節，再用電子郵件寄給您報價單。

Mario's Lighting	
Style	**Price**
Flush Mount	$ 150
Semi Flush	$ 200
Chandelier	$ 400
Pendants	$ 600

馬力歐燈飾	
種類	**價格**
吸頂燈	$ 150
半吸頂燈	$ 200
枝形吊燈	$ 400
吊燈	$ 600

字彙

chandelier 枝形吊燈　　not an issue 不構成問題　　quote 估價表

1. What does the woman say she is going to do?

(A) Remodel a house

(B) Buy a new apartment

(C) Upgrade her lighting

(D) Host a dinner party

1.女子說她將要做什麼？

(A) 裝潢房子

(B) 買一套公寓

(C) 改善家中燈飾

(D) 舉辦晚宴

正確答案

(A) Remodel a house

解說

試題問的是「女子說她要做什麼」，也就是來電目的，最合適的回答是「安裝燈飾」，但選項中沒有，所以再根據她一開始說的話，知道她現在正在重新裝潢房子，可以知道正確答案是 (A)。

因為女子重新裝潢，所以選項 (B) 不對。選項 (C) 的 upgrade 表「既有的東西再升級」，對話中女子說要安裝燈飾，但沒有說要升級舊有燈飾，所以也不對。選項 (D) 是對話中沒有出現的訊息。

---

2. Look at the graphic. What light will the woman buy?

(A) Flush Mount

(B) Semi Flush

(C) Chandelier

(D) Pendants

2.請看圖表。女子要買哪一種燈飾？

(A) 吸頂燈

(B) 半吸頂燈

(C) 枝形吊燈

(D) 吊燈

正確答案

(D) Pendants

解說

因為對話中女子說錢不是問題（money is not an issue），暗示了要用最貴的燈，又說自己不喜歡枝型吊燈，請男子介紹最貴的產品，接著男子介紹吊燈（pendant），確認了女子挑選的是吊燈，正確答案是選項 (D)。

3. What does the man say he will do?

(A) Send her a letter

(B) Give her a discount

(C) Send a quote via e-mail

(D) Install the lights today

3.男子說他會做什麼？

(A) 寄信給她

(B) 給她折扣

(C) 用電郵寄送報價單

(D) 今日安裝燈具

正確答案

(C) Send a quote via e-mail

解說

兩個人之後的聯絡方式，對話中只出現電郵，所以 (A) 不會是正確答案。選項 (B) 從對話中無法確認。女子拜託安裝燈飾是在下個月，不是今天，所以選項 (D) 也不對。quote 在這裡當作名詞使用，表「報價單」，所以正確答案是 (C)。

September	
Thursday	7
Friday	8
Saturday	9
Sunday	10
Monday	11

4. Where does the man work?
   (A) At a TV station
   (B) At a department store
   (C) At a salon
   (D) At a magazine company

5. What does the man mean by "takes the weekend off"?
   (A) Working only on the weekend
   (B) Being unavailable on the weekend
   (C) Not working on weekdays
   (D) Working on various days

6. Look at the graphic. What day will the customer schedule the appointment?
   (A) September 7
   (B) September 8
   (C) September 9
   (D) September 11

W Hi, I'd like to make an appointment with Jill to have my hair cut this weekend.

女：嗨，我想要預約吉兒幫我在這個週末剪個髮型。

M Oh, I'm sorry, Jill will be away for the next two weeks.

男：喔，真抱歉，吉兒下兩個禮拜都不在耶。

W Oh, may I ask why?

女：哦，可以知道為什麼嗎？

M She's gone to New York to take part in a workshop for hair stylists. Would you like to wait for her return?

男：她去紐約參加髮型設計師工作坊。您想要等她回來嗎？

W Actually, I need my hair done before my job interview on Monday. Can you recommend anyone? I love the way Jill styles my hair.

女：事實上，我需要在禮拜一面試之前弄好頭髮。你能幫我推薦設計師嗎？我喜歡吉兒幫我做的髮型。

M Yes, we have Brian who's actually trained with Jill. He'll do a great job, I promise. He takes the weekend off, however.

男：好的，其實布萊恩也是跟吉兒一起受訓的。他的手藝很棒，我保證。不過他週末都休息。

W Oh. Will he be in on Friday evening?

女：喔，那他星期五晚上會在嗎？

M Yes, I can squeeze you in at 7 p.m.

男：會的，我可以幫妳安插在晚上七點。

September	
Thursday	7
Friday	8
Saturday	9
Sunday	10
Monday	11

九月	
星期四	7
星期五	8
星期六	9
星期日	10
星期一	11

字彙

appointment 預約　　get someone's hair done 做髮型
be away 不在　　take part in 參加　　recommend 推薦
do a great job 表現很好　　take off 休假　　style (v.) 做造型
squeeze someone in (to) ... 安插某人進……

PART
3

Chapter
04

和圖表有關的對話

4. Where does the man work?

   (A) At a TV station

   (B) At a department store

   (C) At a salon

   (D) At a magazine company

4.男子在哪裡工作？

   (A) 電視台

   (B) 百貨公司

   (C) 美髮沙龍

   (D) 雜誌社

正確答案

(C) At a salon

解說

對話的大意是，女子要預約某人替她剪髮，男子說要幫女子安排，所以正確答案是 (C)。

5. What does the man mean by "takes the weekend off"?

   (A) Working only on the weekend

   (B) Being unavailable on the weekend

   (C) Not working on weekdays

   (D) Working on various days

5.男子說的「週末都休息」是指？

   (A) 只在週末工作

   (B) 週末不上班

   (C) 平常日不上班

   (D) 許多天都有上班

正確答案

(B) Being unavailable on the weekend

解說

「take . . . off」是「某天休息；不上班」的意思。要注意別弄混選項中的 weekend（週末）和 weekday（週間；平日）。因為男子提到布萊恩週末不上班，所以 (B) 是正確答案，選項 (B) 將「take . . . off」，換成用 unavailable（不能會面的）來表示，要注意這種改寫方式。

6. Look at the graphic. What day will the customer schedule the appointment?

(A) September 7

(B) September 8

(C) September 9

(D) September 11

6.請看圖表。該名顧客會預約哪一天？

(A) 九月七號

(B) 九月八號

(C) 九月九號

(D) 九月十一號

正確答案

(B) September 8

解説

男子在幫顧客敲定時間時，因為負責剪髮的布萊恩週末不上班，所以週末的選項 (C) 不能選。另外，女子問男子，布萊恩週五（在下週一面試之前）可不可以替她剪髮，男子表示週五晚上七點，也就是預約九月八號當天剪髮，正確答案是 (B)。

聽對話，選出與問題最為符合的回答。∩ 119

Discount Coupon
Computer Monitors

21-24"	$25 Value
25" and above	$50 Value

CompuTech
Expires 3/20

Name	Comment
1. Frank Brown	Rude teller
2. Eddy Su	No overdraft notice
3. Seung Hee Lee	Excessive maintenance fees
4. Jennifer Sinclair	Interest rate too low

1. What problem does the woman mention?
- (A) The monitor she purchased is defective.
- (B) The product she wants is not in stock.
- (C) She cannot find an item.
- (D) She cannot receive a discount.

2. What does the man say happened recently?
- (A) Monitors were placed in the same aisle.
- (B) A computer sale has ended.
- (C) Discount coupons were cancelled.
- (D) Products were relocated.

3. Look at the graphic. What discount will the woman most likely receive?
- (A) $3
- (B) $20
- (C) $25
- (D) $50

4. Where do the speakers most likely work?
- (A) At a department store
- (B) At a bank
- (C) At an airline company
- (D) At a post office

5. Look at the graphic. Which customer are the speakers discussing?
- (A) Frank Brown
- (B) Eddy Su
- (C) Seung Hee Lee
- (D) Jennifer Sinclair

6. What will the speakers do next?
- (A) Create an employee training program
- (B) Revise the penalty fee system
- (C) Update staffing schedules
- (D) Go over customer complaints

Chapter 04

聽對話，選出與問題最為符合的回答。 🎧 120

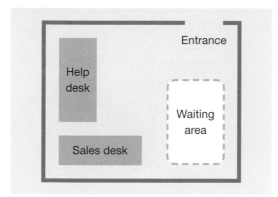

Electrical Repair Kit

1 x Circuit breaker

10 x Switches

2 x Electrical connector

5 x AC power plugs

1. What did the man recently do?
   (A) Go overseas for business
   (B) Have a business meeting
   (C) Go out for lunch
   (D) Move the sales desk

2. Why does the man want to move the sales desk?
   (A) So customers can leave quickly
   (B) To make the waiting area bigger
   (C) To adjust the temperature
   (D) To slow down sales

3. Look at the graphic. What is the man referring to as the "remaining area"?
   (A) Help desk
   (B) Entrance
   (C) Sales desk
   (D) Waiting area

4. What is the man doing?
   (A) Working at someone's house
   (B) Working in his house
   (C) Repairing a computer
   (D) Installing some pipes

5. Look at the graphic. What is the man missing?
   (A) A circuit breaker
   (B) Switches
   (C) AC power plugs
   (D) An electrical connector

6. What does the woman say she will do?
   (A) Deliver them by mail
   (B) Call her manager
   (C) Deliver them herself
   (D) Tell her worker to do it

聽對話，選出與問題最為符合的回答。 🎧 121

1. What does the woman imply when she says "A few of the people from the office are getting tickets for tonight's show"?

(A) She thinks the tickets for Broadway shows are expensive.

(B) She wants to do something for the man.

(C) She is inviting the man to join them.

(D) She bought a ticket for the man.

2. Why does the man have to stay late at work?

(A) He is due for a vacation.

(B) He had to update his computer.

(C) He has new software.

(D) He needs to finish some statements.

3. What solution does the man propose?

(A) That he won't join them

(B) Going to the show tomorrow

(C) That he will go alone

(D) Making some time to have a meal

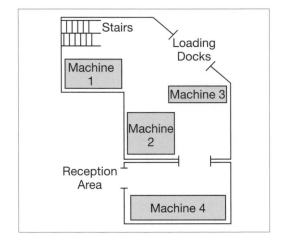

4. Why does the man need the machine fixed?

(A) Because his boss is upset

(B) To meet a quota

(C) So he can file a report

(D) To schedule an appointment

5. Look at the graphic. Which machine needs to be fixed?

(A) Machine 1

(B) Machine 2

(C) Machine 3

(D) Machine 4

6. What does the technician suggest?

(A) Keeping the machine on

(B) Upgrading the software

(C) Calling Human Resources

(D) Unplugging the machine

7. What field does Mr. Turner work in?

(A) Plumbing
(B) Painting
(C) Landscaping
(D) Carpentry

8. Why did the woman choose Mr. Turner?

(A) He offers the lowest prices.
(B) He has an established reputation in the area.
(C) He communicated well with her.
(D) He is available this month.

9. Why will the project start next month?

(A) Mr. Turner is overburdened.
(B) A special part must be ordered first.
(C) The woman asked him to do so.
(D) There are many things to prepare for the housewarming party.

10. Why did the woman make the call?

(A) To book a flight
(B) To cancel a flight
(C) To re-schedule a vacation
(D) To inform them about a mistake

11. What is the problem with the woman's itinerary?

(A) It is too expensive.
(B) It is a direct flight.
(C) It has layovers.
(D) It is booked on the wrong day.

12. What does the woman offer to give William?

(A) Her credit card number
(B) Her passport information
(C) Her booking number
(D) Her home address

PART

4

簡短獨白

Example   🎧 122

M   Hello, this is Michael Williams. I just received the computer that was shipped to my office. However, as I was setting everything up on my desk, I noticed that the keyboard is missing. I checked the box and it says that this model comes with everything, including the keyboard. Is there any way that a separate keyboard can be sent to my office? The sooner the better, of course. I need to use the computer by next week, which is when my clinic will be opened to patients. Please call me back as soon as you can.

1. What problem does the speaker mention?
(A) The product does not work
(B) The shipment is late
(C) An item is missing
(D) The wrong item was sent

2. What does the speaker request?
(A) Extra speakers
(B) A refund
(C) An exchange
(D) A call back

3. What kind of office does Michael Williams most likely work in?
(A) A corporate office
(B) A medical office
(C) A financial office
(D) A commercial office

1. C   2. D   3. B

▶ 先聽一個人說一段話，再看試題本上的試題和 (A)、(B)、(C)、(D) 選項，從四個選項中選擇最適合的答案。試題會印在試題本上，獨白與試題只播放一次。

Part 4 題型綜覽

- **題型概要**：聽一個人説一段話，這段獨白會是各式各樣不同類型的訊息，然後回答和它有關的三個問題。獨白只會播放一次，**而且不會印在試題本上**，會聽到試題錄音，試題也會在試題本上出現；選項則沒有錄音，只出現在試題本上。
- **獨白類型**：電話留言、宣布、通知、廣告、天氣預報、新聞播報、演説、見習、觀光導覽、人物介紹等。
- **試題類型**：
  → 有關**整篇內容**的問題：詢問**主題**或**目的**、**場所**或**人物**相關問題
  → 有關**細節**的問題：詢問**問題點**或**擔心的事**、**原因**或**方法**、找出**核心訊息**、**未來的事**、**建議**或**請求**
  → 詢問和各式**圖表**相關的問題

新制多益核心要點

- 試題數和舊制多益 Part 4 一樣，共 30 題。
- **新類型**：題目**圖表對應部分獨白內容**，考生須綜合分析後選出正確答案。
- **新類型**：從獨白內容中**找出談話者的意圖**，或回答**獨白含意**相關的問題。

新制多益準備策略

- 要仔細聽清楚獨白的**最前面**。
  獨白的主旨會在前半部出現，聽清楚主旨才能選出正確答案。
- 要熟記各試題類型常考的回答模式。
- 要事先知道固定的錯誤答案形式，例如：
  → 類似發音字
  → 同音異義字
  → 衍生字做成的錯誤答案
  → 聯想做成的錯誤答案
  → 時態的不一致做成的錯誤答案
  → 和試題無關的人稱做成的錯誤答案

Part 4 的考試說明（Directions）有 30 秒左右，要利用這段時間事先看一下這 30 道題。

1. 詢問獨白目的的試題，在獨白的**前半部分**會出現正確答案的**關鍵字**（keyword），時常第一句話就說明了**整篇獨白的主題或目的**。

2. 要特別注意聽在宣布、廣告、通知獨白中，出現的**時間**、**時期**、**數字**、**聯絡方法**，也就是 WH **疑問字**（who、when、where、how、what、why）之後出現的內容，要注意聽。

3. 題目出現的字彙，會**重複使用**獨白中的字彙，或經過**改寫**再使用。所以平時要熟悉題目常用的**改寫用語**，才能掌握改寫的部分。

4. 一般來說，試題會依**獨白展開的順序**來出題，所以可以一面聽，一面推論出正確答案。

5. 在獨白中出現的數字、星期、時間較少直接成為正確答案，多半都需要**經過計算**，才能得出正確答案。

6. 因為宣布類型的獨白常**指示人的行動**，因此正確答案時常會在
    Please, . . . ／You should . . . ／You are advised to . . .
    You are required to . . . ／You are asked to . . . 之後出現。

獨白類型

1. **留言**：主要是**電話留言**，題目會問來電留言的**目的**，聽留言的人和留下留言的人之間的**關係**，以及留言中的**重要訊息**等。

2. **宣布、通知與演說**：針對在特定時間和特定場所中的人，所傳達的宣布或通知，會以廣播播放出來，例如在飛機內、公共設施內、觀光巴士上、博物館裡、工廠見習、車站或機場等公共場所。題目會問**建築物施工與使用**、**辦公室搬遷**、**修理事項的說明**、**旅行或表演的時間表**、**時間表的變更**及其**原因**等。演說是在特定場合，由講者對一大群聽眾所做的發言，題目會問**演說的內容**、有關**演講者的資訊**、或**演講者和聽眾的互動**等。

3. **廣告**：產品或服務的廣告，題目會問產品及服務的**特徵**、**價格**、**折扣**、**銷售期間**、**日期**、**場所**、**優惠辦法**等。

4. **新聞或報導**：題目會問**播出時間**及**播出種類**、**事件內容**和**發生的時間**及**場所**、**結果**、**統計**、**展望**、**預測**等。

5. **觀光導覽**：主要是參觀觀光景點、展場、建築物時，導遊對**該景點與建築物的介紹**，題目會問導覽行程中，**關於時間及場所的內容**、**注意事項**等。

6. **介紹**：在特定的集會場合，介紹演說者或主要人物的獨白，題目會問被介紹人的**經歷**、**前職**、**現職**、**未來的工作**、**演說的主題**等。

試題類型

1. 聽整篇獨白才能作答的題型：詢問獨白**主題**的題目，以及**推測**的題型。

2. 聽部分獨白就能作答的題型：答題線索在 when、where、who、what、how、why 之後的題目，以及詢問其他細節的試題。

1 題型暖身

STEP 1 聽獨白，選出與問題最為符合的回答。🎧123

1. Why is the speaker calling?
   (A) To request assistance
   (B) To cancel an order
   (C) To answer an inquiry
   (D) To apply for a position

2. What is being expanded?
   (A) An office building
   (B) A break room
   (C) A parking lot
   (D) A meeting room

3. What does the speaker offer to do?
   (A) Reschedule a meeting
   (B) Write the listener's name on a list
   (C) Send an application
   (D) Wait for someone instead of the listener

確認正確答案及翻譯和解說。

W Hello, Mr. Miller. This is the building manager, Julie Thompson. (1) **I'm responding to your application for a designated parking space in the employee parking lot.** I'm sorry to have to tell you that at this time we have no vacant spaces. (2) **However, we are currently expanding the parking lot to accommodate more vehicles.** (3) **If you would like, I can put you on the waiting list for one of these new spaces.** The construction should be done by the end of the month. I'll contact you again at that time.

女：嗨，米勒先生。我是大樓經理茱莉‧湯普森。我是來回覆有關您申請員工停車場指定停車格的事。很抱歉，目前沒有空的停車位。不過，我們目前正在擴充停車空間，以容納更多的車輛。如果您有意願的話，我可以幫您安排在新車位的候補名單上。擴充工程應會在本月底前完成。屆時我會再與您聯繫。

字彙

application 申請　　designated 指定的　　vacant 空缺的
accommodate 容納

1. Why is the speaker calling?
   (A) To request assistance
   (B) To cancel an order
   (C) To answer an inquiry
   (D) To apply for a position

1.來電者的來電目的是？
   (A) 請求協助
   (B) 取消訂單
   (C) 答覆詢問
   (D) 應徵職務

正確答案

(C) To answer an inquiry

解說

說話者表明來電目的時用的動詞是 respond（回覆），所以可以從它後面的內容，找出正確答案。回覆的內容是 application for a designated parking space，所以可知米勒先生申請了停車位。正確答案是 (C)，它將回覆米勒先生的停車位申請，換成回覆詢問。application 在本獨白中是「（書面的）申請」，但它還可以依狀況解釋成求職申請書，或其他的申請書，所以要注意不要和選項 (D) 弄混了。

203

2. What is being expanded?　2.何者正在擴建？

   (A) An office building　(A) 辦公大樓

   (B) A break room　(B) 休息室

   (C) A parking lot　(C) 停車場

   (D) A meeting room　(D) 會議室

正確答案

(C) A parking lot

解說

說話者說明米勒先生申請的停車位沒有了，但之後又補充現在停車場正在進行擴充工程（expanding the parking lot），因此正確答案是 (C)。

3. What does the speaker offer to do?　3.來電者有什麼提議？

   (A) Reschedule a meeting　(A) 會議改期

   (B) Write the listener's name on a list　(B) 在名單上登記受話者的名字

   (C) Send an application　(C) 送交申請書

   (D) Wait for someone instead of the listener　(D) 放棄受話者，改等他人

正確答案

(B) Write the listener's name on a list

解說

米勒先生申請的員工停車場停車位沒有了，女子告知說擴建停車場的工程正在進行，可以先把米勒先生放到候補名單上（put you on the waiting list），等工程結束，有了新的停車位，就有機會分配到了，所以正確答案是 (B)。

4. What is the purpose of the message?
  (A) To cancel a reservation
  (B) To advertise a new service
  (C) To recall a defective product
  (D) To check the accuracy of an order

5. Which department does Ms. White work in?
  (A) Personnel
  (B) Marketing
  (C) Sales
  (D) Shipping

6. According to the speaker, why should Ms. White call him?
  (A) To solve a problem
  (B) To order some products
  (C) To explain how to make a reservation
  (D) To apply for an open position

PART 4

Chapter 01

電話留言

M Good afternoon. **(5) This is Harry Carter from the shipping department calling for Jen White from the sales department. (4) Ms. White, I would like to confirm an order before we ship it out to the customer.** I have an order here for a Carl Green. Your sales order says he ordered just one T-shirt. However, as you know, our company only sells T-shirts wholesale in orders of fifty or more. I'm wondering if this was a simple mistake. **(6) If you would like to correct this order, please call me before 4 p.m. today, as that's when shipments leave the warehouse.** My extension number is 2301. Thank you.

男：午安。我是貨運部的哈利‧卡特，想留言給業務部的珍‧懷特。懷特小姐，在將貨物送達顧客前，我想與妳確認一筆訂單。這是一筆寄給卡爾‧葛林的訂單。銷售訂單上顯示，他僅訂購一件T恤。不過，如妳所知，本公司只做批發生意，T恤的訂單是五十件以上起跳。我在想是否訂單哪裡出了錯。如果妳想要修改這張訂單，請於今日下午四點以前回電，因為之後倉庫就要出貨了。我的分機是2301，謝謝。

字彙

department 部門　　wholesale 批發的
extension number 分機號碼

---

4. What is the purpose of the message?

(A) To cancel a reservation

(B) To advertise a new service

(C) To recall a defective product

(D) To check the accuracy of an order

4.這則留言的目的是？

(A) 取消預訂

(B) 推銷新服務

(C) 回收瑕疵品

(D) 核對一筆訂單

正確答案

(D) To check the accuracy of an order

解說

說話者詢問懷特小姐，關於一張只訂購一件T恤的訂單。由於該公司只賣50件以上的批發商品，所以他想確認訂單是否有誤，故正確答案是 (D)。

5. Which department does Ms. White work in?

(A) Personnel

(B) Marketing

(C) Sales

(D) Shipping

5.懷特小姐在哪一個部門工作？

(A) 人事部

(B) 行銷部

(C) 業務部

(D) 貨運部

PART 4

Chapter 01

電話留言

正確答案

(C) Sales

解說

一開始哈利·卡特在介紹自己時，提到他來電給業務部的珍·懷特小姐，所以正確答案是 (C)。選項 (D) 是哈利·卡特工作的貨運部，不是珍·懷特的部門。

6. According to the speaker, why should Ms. White call him?

(A) To solve a problem

(B) To order some products

(C) To explain how to make a reservation

(D) To apply for an open position

6.根據來電者的說法，為什麼懷特小姐必須回電？

(A) 解決問題

(B) 訂購產品

(C) 說明如何預約

(D) 應徵職缺

正確答案

(A) To solve a problem

解說

談話者請懷特小姐確認訂單是不是有錯，而且請懷特小姐在出貨時間下午四點前聯絡他，顯示了談話者想解決問題，所以正確答案是 (A)。

> **留言**
>
> ● 主要是電話留言，會問**留言的目的**，聽留言的人和留下留言的人之間的**關係**，以及留言中的**重要訊息**等。
>
> **解題戰略**
>
> 1. 留言播放之前，先瀏覽並掌握試題問的是什麼：**主題、細節**還是**推測**。
>
> 2. 詢問主題的試題，要掌握留言**最前面的部分**；詢問細節的試題，要掌握留言中和 WH 疑問字詞相關的線索。別忘了正確答案常會**改寫**（paraphrase）！
>
> 3. 推測類的試題，要掌握留言的**最後面部分**。

STEP 1 聽獨白，選出與問題最為符合的回答。🎧 125

1. What is the speaker calling about?
   (A) A building improvement
   (B) A new employee
   (C) A system malfunction
   (D) A project proposal

2. What benefit does the speaker mention?
   (A) Improved performance
   (B) Increased profits
   (C) Utilities savings
   (D) Customer satisfaction

3. What does the speaker ask the listener to do?
   (A) Work late tonight
   (B) Accept a plan
   (C) Wait for a delivery
   (D) Replace a part

W Hello, this is Jane Nichols from the maintenance office calling for Ms. Hunt in the marketing department. (1) **Management has decided to replace all the incandescent bulbs in the building with fluorescent light bulbs.** Incandescent bulbs are outdated and wasteful. (2) **Although this change is initially somewhat expensive, it will reduce the company's monthly electricity bill in the long run.** Therefore, we will be replacing all the bulbs in your department tonight. I'm calling to make sure that no one will need to be working late tonight. We would like to begin around 7 p.m. (3) **I'll be waiting for your approval before we begin.**

女：嗨，我是維修室的珍‧尼可斯，想留言給行銷部的杭特小姐。管理階層決定要把大樓裡的白熾燈泡全都換成螢光節能燈泡。白熾燈泡過時又費電。雖然這項改變一開始的花費有點高昂，但長期來看，將能減少公司每個月的電費支出。因此，今晚我們預計會幫貴部門更換所有的燈泡。我之所以來電，是想確認貴部門今日是否有人需要加班到深夜。我們預計會在晚上七點左右開工。在取得您的同意後，我們才會開始動工。

PART

4

Chapter

01

電話留言

字彙

incandescent bulb 白熾燈泡
fluorescent light bulb 螢光（節能）燈泡　　outdated 過時的
initially 起初　　in the long run 從長遠來看　　approval 批准

1. What is the speaker calling about?

(A) A building improvement

(B) A new employee

(C) A system malfunction

(D) A project proposal

1.來電者來電是關於？
(A) 大樓裝修
(B) 新員工
(C) 系統故障
(D) 專案企劃書

正確答案

(A) A building improvement

解説

留言的第二句話提到 management，一般來説，它是公司或集團的管理或經營團隊。所以來電的目的就是要告知，經營團隊決定要換電燈泡。從結果來看，換了電燈泡會讓整個建築物更好，所以將「更好」用「更進步」（improvement）來表示，所以選項 (A) 是正確答案。

2. What benefit does the speaker mention?

(A) Improved health

(B) Increased profits

(C) Utilities savings

(D) Customer satisfaction

2.來電者提到何項好處？
(A) 改善的健康
(B) 增加收益
(C) 節省水電費
(D) 顧客滿意度

正確答案

(C) Utilities savings

解説

因為留言中提到要安裝的螢光節能燈泡（fluorescent light bulbs）有兩個特徵，所以聽留言時要特別注意這部分。第一個特徵是價格比原來的燈泡貴（initially expensive），第二個特徵是，長期來看能節省電費。選項 (C) 是正確答案，因為它將留言中的 electricity bill 換成 utilities（水電費）。

3. What does the speaker ask the listener to do?

(A) Work late tonight

(B) Accept a plan

(C) Wait for a delivery

(D) Replace a part

3. 來電者要求受話者做什麼？

(A) 加班到很晚

(B) 接受計劃

(C) 等待收件

(D) 替換零件

正確答案

(B) Accept a plan

解說

談話者請受話者做的事情有兩項，第一項是，更換電燈泡的當天晚上，所有在大樓行銷部辦公的員工都要離開；第二項是，在開始換燈泡的時間之前，也就是晚上 7 點之前，會等候杭特小姐的「等候同意」（will be waiting for your approval）。因此，選項 (A) 和談話者請求的事項完全相反。選項 (B) 將來電者的「等候同意」，換成用「接受計畫」（accept a plan）來表示，所以 (B) 是正確答案。

Order # 3870

Henderson Technologies

Item	Quantity
Juice bottles	20
Water bottles	30
Sandwich trays	2
Donuts	50

4. What type of event is being catered?

(A) An office party

(B) A business gathering

(C) A sales event

(D) A product launch

5. Look at the graphic. Which quantity on the original order form is no longer accurate?

(A) 20

(B) 30

(C) 2

(D) 50

6. What does the speaker ask the listener to do?

(A) Bring proper identification

(B) Pick up a security pass

(C) Email some information

(D) Provide a discount

W Hello, this is Elizabeth from Henderson Technologies. I'm calling about the catering order that I sent you about a week ago. (5) **We have almost 20 more people joining our conference meeting, so I would like to double the sandwich platter.** I think we may have enough of everything else though. Also I want to mention that you'll need security clearance to get through the building, so we'll have passes ready and (6) **please be sure to e-mail me the names of those who'll be delivering our order so that our security guards can clear them.**

女：嗨，我是韓德森科技公司的伊莉莎白。我來電是關於一個禮拜前我預訂的外燴服務。我們會再增加二十多名與會人員，所以我希望你們能將預計提供的三明治托盤份量加倍。至於其他的，我想我們的準備應該足夠了。另外，我想提一下，屆時你們可能需要通過安檢才能進入大樓，所以我們會幫你們準備通行證。請記得一定要寄給我們貴公司負責外燴配送的人員名單，這樣我們的保全人員才會放行。

Order # 3870

Henderson Technologies

Item	Quantity
Juice bottles	20
Water bottles	30
Sandwich trays	2
Donuts	50

訂單編號 # 3870

韓德森科技公司

品項	數量
果汁	20 瓶
礦泉水	30 瓶
三明治托盤	2 盤
甜甜圈	50 個

字彙

cater 供應伙食　　double (v.) 增加兩倍　　platter 大淺盤
security clearance 安全檢查　　clear 放行通過
gathering 集會　　launch 發表會

4. What type of event is being catered?

(A) An office party

(B) A business gathering

(C) A sales event

(D) A product launch

4.什麼樣的活動需要外燴？

(A) 辦公室派對

(B) 商業聚會

(C) 銷售活動

(D) 新品發表會

(B) A business gathering

解説

因為留言是給食物外燴公司，因為參加活動的人數增加，留言者要求追加食物，該活動的名稱是公司開會（conference meeting），留言者所屬的公司是她一開始介紹自己提到的韓德森科技，所以正確答案是 (B)。

5. Look at the graphic. Which quantity on the original order form is no longer accurate?

(A) 20

(B) 30

(C) 2

(D) 50

5.請見圖表。原始訂單上，哪個數量已不正確？

(A) 20

(B) 30

(C) 2

(D) 50

正確答案

(C) 2

解説

題目給的圖表是留言者原來訂購的食品以及數量，但本題要詢問的是留言中請求變更的食物是哪一個。留言者説因為參加活動的人增加了，所以三明治的盤數要增加兩倍（double the sandwich platter），之後又説其他食物（everything else）都足夠，所以三明治的數量不對，圖表中三明治的數量是兩盤，所以要選選項 (C)。

6. What does the speaker ask the listener to do?

(A) Bring proper identification

(B) Pick up a security pass

(C) E-mail some information

(D) Provide a discount

6.來電者要求受話者做什麼？

(A) 攜帶個人身分證件

(B) 取得通行證

(C) 電郵一些資料

(D) 提供折扣

正確答案

(C) E-mail some information

解說

留言後半提到因大樓安檢的緣故，必須先將外燴公司食物配送員的通行證先交給外燴公司，申請通行證需要配送人員的姓名，所以留言者請對方先將配送人員的姓名名單電郵過來，人員的姓名也算是一種訊息（information），所以 (C) 是正確答案。配送人員雖然需要通行證，但通行證還沒做好，所以選項 (B) 是錯的。

1. Who most likely is the speaker?
(A) An author
(B) A librarian
(C) A banker
(D) A customer

2. Why does the speaker apologize?
(A) A sale has ended earlier than scheduled.
(B) A shipment has been delayed.
(C) An item is out of stock.
(D) The listener was charged incorrectly.

3. What is the listener asked to bring with him?
(A) A credit card
(B) A receipt
(C) A library card
(D) An overdue book

4. What problem does the speaker mention?
(A) Some luggage was misplaced.
(B) A flight was postponed.
(C) All tickets are sold out.
(D) A passenger missed a flight.

5. What does the speaker suggest?
(A) Buying flight insurance
(B) Visiting an office in Denver
(C) Utilizing an online service
(D) Becoming a frequent flyer member

6. What does the speaker say she will do?
(A) Arrange for a delivery
(B) Waive a late fee
(C) Send a booking reminder
(D) Provide a baggage claim number

宣布、通知與演說

Chapter 02

1 題型暖身

STEP 1 聽獨白，選出與問題最為符合的回答。🎧 128

1. Who most likely is the speaker?
   (A) A market researcher
   (B) A make-up artist
   (C) A graphic designer
   (D) A magazine editor

2. What does the speaker say about her company's new product line?
   (A) It is reasonably priced.
   (B) It is for a specific age group.
   (C) It is sold at department stores.
   (D) It is for both men and women.

3. What will the speaker do next?
   (A) Introduce a keynote speaker
   (B) Perform a demonstration
   (C) Distribute free samples
   (D) Share research results

W Hello, I'm honored to be given the opportunity to speak to you all today here at the 4th Annual Cosmetics Research Conference. (1) **My name is Amy Marsh and I'm a senior researcher at Your Beauty Cosmetics.** (2) **This month we are launching a new product line specifically for older women.** As you know, most cosmetics are targeted at the younger demographic, so there are very few products for this group. However, our research has found that many older women want products tailored to their needs. Particularly, they want cosmetics that help moisturize dry skin and protect it from further sun damage. (3) **Now, I'd like to tell you about this research and explain how our company is taking advantage of this untapped market.**

女：大家好，本人很榮幸今天能在第四屆美妝研究會議上向各位發表演說。我的名字叫艾咪·馬希，是優爾美妝公司的高級研究員。本公司在這個月發表了一系列專為年長女性設計的新產品。眾所周知，大多數的美妝品都以年輕族群作為銷售目標，所以市面上少有針對年長族群設計的產品。然而，我們的研究卻發現，許多年長的女性希望能有特別針對她們的需求所設計的產品。她們尤其需要可以滋潤乾燥肌膚、保護肌膚免受過多紫外線傷害的美妝品。現在，我想與各位分享我們的研究成果，並說明本公司在此一未開發的市場上，如何取得致勝先機。

 字彙

senior 資深的　　demographic（顧客）族群　　untapped 未開發的

1. Who most likely is the speaker?	1.發言者最有可能是？
(A) A market researcher	(A) 市調研究員
(B) A make-up artist	(B) 彩妝師
(C) A graphic designer	(C) 平面設計師
(D) A magazine editor	(D) 雜誌編輯

(A) A market researcher

因為演說者介紹自己時，提到她是化妝品公司的資深研究員（**senior researcher**），並提到了公司新的產品線及有關研究，所以 (**A**) 是最合適的答案。

2. What does the speaker say about her company's new product line?

(A) It is reasonably priced.
(B) It is for a specific age group.

(C) It is sold at department stores.
(D) It is for both men and women.

2.對於公司的新產品線，講者說了什麼？

(A) 定價合理。
(B) 針對特殊年齡族群設計。

(C) 於百貨公司販售。
(D) 男女皆適用。

(B) It is for a specific age group.

演說者介紹公司的新產品線，是特別為年長女性（**specifically for older women**）而開發的，所以正確答案是 (**B**)。

3. What will the speaker do next?
(A) Introduce a keynote speaker
(B) Perform a demonstration
(C) Distribute free samples
(D) Share research results

3.發言者接下來會做何事？
(A) 介紹主講人
(B) 進行展示
(C) 發送免費試用包
(D) 分享研究成果

(D) Share research results

最後演說者說，將告訴大家有關他們做的研究成果（**tell you about this research**），所以正確答案是 (**D**)。

4. What type of company does the speaker most likely work for?
(A) An entertainment agency
(B) A film organization
(C) An event planning company
(D) A catering business

5. What is the purpose of the talk?
(A) To reschedule an opening date
(B) To negotiate a contract
(C) To prepare a report
(D) To designate responsibilities

6. Who has the speaker met with?
(A) An event planner
(B) A film director
(C) An award recipient
(D) A leading actor

M Good morning, everyone. Please listen to me carefully. **(4) We have been contracted to cater the opening party for this year's Fenton Film Awards in November.** Therefore, we are going to be extremely busy and will need to be well prepared. **(5) I'd like to take this time to outline our work schedule and determine who will be doing what tasks. (6) I have met with the organizer of the awards ceremony, and I'm sure this is going to be our biggest project ever.** Now, please look at this screen.

男：早安，各位。請專心聽我說。我們已簽定合約，要為今年 11 月的芬頓電影獎開幕派對提供外燴服務。因此，接下來我們會非常忙碌，也必須好好預做準備。我想趁此機會簡要地說明一下我們的工作時程，並分派每個人屆時的負責工作。我已經與頒獎典禮的主辦單位見過面了，相信這將是本公司有史以來最大的案子。現在，請看螢幕。

字彙

outline 概述　　organizer 主辦者　　leading actor 主角

4. What type of company does the speaker most likely work for?
   (A) An entertainment agency
   (B) A film organization
   (C) An event planning company
   (D) A catering business

4.發言者最有可能為何種公司工作？
   (A) 經紀公司
   (B) 電影協會
   (C) 活動企劃公司
   (D) 外燴服務公司

正確答案

(D) A catering business

解說

從整個上下文來看，談話者正在對員工談話，因為提到簽約的內容是，為某活動的開幕派對負責提供餐點（cater the opening party），所以可以知道提供外燴餐點（catering）是他們公司主要的業務，因此正確答案是選項 (D)。

5. What is the purpose of the talk?

    (A) To reschedule an opening date

    (B) To negotiate a contract

    (C) To prepare a report

    (D) To designate responsibilities

5.談話的目的是什麼？

    (A) 更改開幕日期

    (B) 協商合約

    (C) 撰擬報告

    (D) 指派任務

正確答案

(D) To designate responsibilities

解說

談話者真正的意圖，在 I'd like to take this time to . . . 之後出現，可以知道要完成的工作有兩項，第一項是 outline work schedule，第二項是 determine who will be doing what tasks，選項中提到這兩項或其中一項，就會是正確答案。選項 (D) 說「指派任務」，所以是正確答案。選項 (B) 不對，因為合約是已經簽好的狀態（We have been contracted to cater . . .）。

6. Who has the speaker met with?

    (A) An event planner

    (B) A film director

    (C) An award recipient

    (D) A leading actor

6.發言者已經見過誰了？

    (A) 活動策畫

    (B) 電影導演

    (C) 得獎人

    (D) 主角

正確答案

(A) An event planner

解說

宣布中用動詞 meet 的過去式表示「已經見過面」，之後直接接 organizer of the awards ceremony，表示已經和「頒獎典禮的主辦單位」見過面，所以 (A) 是正確答案。選項 (B)、(C)、(D) 雖然和電影獎相關，但都不是談話者接觸的人。

2 命題分析

宣布、通知與演說

- 針對在特定時間和特定場所中的人所傳達的宣布或通知，會以廣播播放出來，像在飛機內、公共設施內、觀光巴士上、博物館裡、工廠見習、車站或機場等公共場所。題目會問**建築物施工與使用**、**辦公室搬遷**、**修理事項的說明**、**旅行或表演的時間表**、**時間表的變更**、**變更的原因**等。演說是在特定場合，由講者對一大群聽眾所做的發言，題目會問**演說的內容**、有關**演講者的資訊**、或**演講者和聽眾的互動**等。

解題戰略

1. 宣布、通知或演說的獨白播放前，先瀏覽並掌握試題問的是什麼：**主題**、**細節**還是**推測**。

2. 詢問主題的試題，要掌握宣布、通知或演說**最前面的部分**；詢問細節的試題，要掌握獨白中和 **WH 疑問字詞**相關的線索，別忘了正確答案常會**改寫**（paraphrase）。

3. 推測類的試題，要掌握宣布、通知或演說**最後面部分**。

STEP 1　聽獨白，選出與問題最為符合的回答。🎧 130

1. What is the purpose of the meeting?
   (A) To decide on a curriculum
   (B) To approve an annual budget
   (C) To choose an architectural design
   (D) To vote on a new policy

2. What does Sarah Hart do?
   (A) She designs book covers.
   (B) She teaches at a university.
   (C) She runs a construction firm.
   (D) She edits a fashion magazine.

3. What will listeners most likely do next?
   (A) Attend a design class
   (B) Go to a library
   (C) Watch a presentation
   (D) Create a work of art

M Welcome, members of the city council. **(1) We are here today to select one of the many design proposals being considered for the building of the new local library.** As you know, many architects have submitted their designs to our competition. Our first contestant is Sarah Hart. **(2) She is a professor at the local university and teaches classes on sculpture and design.** Her designs are innovative and often praised for their very modern styles. **(3) She will now give a short presentation explaining the concept behind her library design.** Please welcome her.

男：歡迎諸位市議員出席本會。今日邀集諸位在此，是要為本地興建新的圖書館，挑選出一個最優的設計提案。如諸位所知，此次評比有眾多建築師提交設計圖參賽。我們的第一位參賽者是莎菈·哈特。她是本地的大學教授，教授雕塑及設計課程。她的設計新穎，摩登的風格也常為人所稱道。現在她將做個簡短的報告，說明她設計圖書館背後的理念。我們歡迎她。

字彙

proposal 提案　　competition 競賽　　contestant 參賽者
sculpture 雕塑　　innovative 新穎的
be praised for 因……獲得讚揚　　modern 現代的

---

1. What is the purpose of the meeting?
(A) To decide on a curriculum
(B) To approve an annual budget
(C) To choose an architectural design
(D) To vote on a new policy

1.開會的目的是？
(A) 決定課程規劃
(B) 批准年度預算
(C) 挑選建築設計
(D) 表決一項新政策

正確答案

(C) To choose an architectural design

解說

詢問主題的題型，要掌握宣布最前面的部分。第二句話「我們今天在這裡是為了要挑選新圖書館的設計提案」（we are here today to select . . . new local library），所以選項 (C) 是正確答案，因為圖書館尚未蓋好，所以將它說成建築設計（architectural design）也沒錯。(A)、(B)、(D) 則和宣布內容無關。

2. What does Sarah Hart do?

    (A) She designs book covers.

    (B) She teaches at a university.

    (C) She runs a construction firm.

    (D) She edits a fashion magazine.

2.莎菈‧哈特從事什麼工作？

    (A) 設計書籍封面。

    (B) 在大學任教。

    (C) 經營建設公司。

    (D) 編輯時尚雜誌。

正確答案

(B) She teaches at a university.

解説

宣布的中段提及莎菈‧哈特的部分，她是當地大學的教授，教授雕塑及設計，因此選項 (B) 是正確答案，注意它將教授（**professor**）改說成在大學任教（**teach at a university**）是合理的。介紹人還提及莎菈‧哈特的設計很創新，很受好評，但沒有提到書封設計、經營公司、時尚雜誌編輯等，所以 (A)、(C)、(D) 都不對。

---

3. What will listeners most likely do next?

    (A) Attend a design class

    (B) Go to a library

    (C) Watch a presentation

    (D) Create a work of art

3.聽眾接下來最有可能做什麼？

    (A) 上設計課程

    (B) 去圖書館

    (C) 看一段簡報

    (D) 進行藝術創作

正確答案

(C) Watch a presentation

解説

介紹人介紹了莎菈‧哈特之後，直接說她將做個簡短報告（**a short presentation**）。題目的主詞是聽眾，也就是現在和介紹人在一起的市議會議員們，因此以他們的角度就是「看」一個簡報，所以正確答案是 (C)。

	0 - poor 5 - excellent
Website Design and Navigation	4
Services Provided	5
Accommodations	4
Prices and Fees	2

4. Where does the speaker most likely work?

   (A) At a hotel

   (B) At an airport

   (C) At a restaurant

   (D) At a department store

5. Look at the graphic. What does the speaker want the listeners to discuss?

   (A) Website design and navigation

   (B) Services provided

   (C) Accommodations

   (D) Prices and fees

6. What will probably happen next?

   (A) The meeting will end.

   (B) Others will speak.

   (C) Customers will be contacted.

   (D) A report will be filed.

M We're going to start off this meeting by looking at this chart here. These are the results of the customer feedback survey we took last month. As you can see here, our customers seem generally happy about their stay with us. (5) **But, if you notice the last item on the chart, the reviews were unusually low. We need to come up with some solutions, since we have so many competitors around us and there is the construction of an affordable inn just a few blocks from us.** We need to find ways to stay competitive. I'd like to hear some of your ideas. Would anyone like to start?

男：會議一開始，讓我們先來看一下這個圖表。這是我們上個月所進行的顧客意見回饋調查結果。大家可以明顯看出，我們的顧客似乎大致上都頗滿意入住期間所享受的服務。但如果你們注意到圖表的最後一個項目，評分意見通常都頗低。因為強敵環伺，且附近幾個街區外正有一家平價旅館正在興建，所以我們需要對此想出解決方案。我們必須尋找維持我們競爭優勢的方法，希望你們能發表一些意見。哪一位想先開始？

0 - poor 5 - excellent	
Website Design and Navigation	4
Services Provided	5
Accommodations	4
Prices and Fees	2

0 - 表現差勁 5 - 表現優異	
網頁設計及操作便利性	4
旅館提供的服務	5
旅館設施	4
定價及收費	2

字彙

affordable 負擔得起的　　inn（小）旅館
competitive 具有競爭力的；競爭的

4. Where does the speaker most likely work?

(A) At a hotel

(B) At an airport

(C) At a restaurant

(D) At a department store

4.說話者最有可能在哪裡工作？

(A) 旅館

(B) 機場

(C) 餐廳

(D) 百貨公司

正確答案

(A) At a hotel

解説

説話者在和員工開會的時候，提到了同為競爭對手的旅館（inn），圖表裡也是和旅館有關的事項，所以正確答案是(A)。

5. Look at the graphic. What does the speaker want the listeners to discuss?

(A) Website design and navigation

(B) Services provided

(C) Accommodations

(D) Prices and fees

5.請看圖表。說話者希望聽眾討論何事？

(A) 網頁設計及操作便利性

(B) 旅館提供的服務

(C) 旅館設施

(D) 定價及收費

正確答案

(D) Prices and fees

解説

談話者要員工看圖表，並提到顧客最不滿的地方是圖表中的定價及收費（the last item on the chart = prices and fees），並説想找出解決方法，請大家發表一些意見，所以正確答案是(D)。

6. What will probably happen next?

(A) The meeting will end.
(B) Others will speak.
(C) Customers will be contacted.
(D) A report will be filed.

6.接下來最有可能發生何事？

(A) 會議將結束。
(B) 他人將發言。
(C) 與顧客取得聯繫。
(D) 提交一份報告。

正確答案

(B) Others will speak.

解說

說話者的最後一句話是，要聽聽大家的意見，並問誰要先講？所以正確答案是選項 (B)。既然要大家發表意見，會議將不會結束，所以選項 (A) 不能選。會議並未提到和顧客連繫或是報告，故選項 (C) 與 (D) 也錯。

1. What will Invent XM be used for?
   (A) Collecting client information
   (B) Backing up important data
   (C) Tracking warehouse items
   (D) Managing investments

2. Why is the training session being held in the conference room?
   (A) To provide enough seats
   (B) To use audio-visual materials
   (C) To conduct a group survey
   (D) To present some awards

3. What are listeners asked to do?
   (A) Take notes
   (B) Submit a questionnaire
   (C) Report malfunctions
   (D) Ask questions

Greenfood Anniversary Discounts	
Free Range Eggs	50%
Organic Yogurt	40%
Whole Wheat Bread	30%
Organic Vanilla Ice Cream	25%

4. Why is the store discounting some of the products?
   (A) Because they are close to the expiry date
   (B) Because they are celebrating an anniversary
   (C) Because they are losing business
   (D) Because they are having a grand opening

5. Look at the graphic. What is the discount on the item that is almost sold out?
   (A) 50%
   (B) 40%
   (C) 30%
   (D) 25%

6. Where can customers see the list of discounts?
   (A) Near the produce section
   (B) On a chalkboard
   (C) At the meat section
   (D) Close to the dairy aisle

Chapter

03 廣告

1 題型暖身

STEP 1 聽獨白，選出與問題最為符合的回答。🎧 133

1. According to the speaker, how can customers receive a discount?
   (A) By mentioning an advertisement
   (B) By presenting a coupon
   (C) By applying for membership
   (D) By bringing a customer

2. What is available for customers?
   (A) Wireless Internet connection
   (B) A personal consultation
   (C) Free refreshments
   (D) A virtual experience service

3. What does the speaker suggest doing?
   (A) Updating a software program
   (B) Comparing prices
   (C) Arranging an appointment
   (D) Reading a flyer

W Looking to change your style? This week at Jay's Hairdressing, we are offering a special deal. (1) **If you bring someone with you to get a haircut, each of you will get 20 % off the regular price of a haircut.** (2) **You can use our state-of-the-art three-dimensional visualization software in order to find a look that is right for you.** You can also browse our large selection of hairstyle magazines and catalogs. (3) **We are expecting a lot of customers this week, so we recommend that you make an appointment by calling at 657-555-6842.** We look forward to helping you find a new style at Jay's Hairdressing.

女：想要改變您的造型嗎？本週傑斯髮型設計將提供特別的優惠方案。如果兩人同行，則每個人都可獲得剪髮八折的優惠折扣。我們還提供最先進的 3D 影像模擬軟體，讓您找出最適合自己的髮型。同時，您也可以瀏覽我們系列豐富的髮型雜誌及型錄。預計本週我們會有眾多顧客前來消費，所以建議您先預約，撥打我們的預約電話：657-555-6842。傑斯髮型設計期待能幫您找到新造型。

字彙

state-of-the-art 最先進的　　three-dimensional 3D 立體的
visualization 影像化　　browse 瀏覽

1. According to the speaker, how can customers receive a discount?
(A) By mentioning an advertisement
(B) By presenting a coupon
(C) By applying for membership
(D) By bringing a customer

1.根據說話者，顧客如何才能取得優惠折扣？
(A) 提及一則廣告
(B) 出示折價券
(C) 申請會員資格
(D) 引進一名顧客

正確答案

(D) By bringing a customer

廣告中先提到 a special deal，接著說帶一個人來剪髮（bring someone with you）兩個人都可享八折優惠（20 % off），所以選項 (D) 是正確答案。(A)、(B)、(C) 都沒有在廣告中提及，所以錯誤。

2. What is available for customers?

(A) Wireless Internet connection

(B) A personal consultation

(C) Free refreshments

(D) A virtual experience service

2.顧客可以享有什麼服務？

(A) 無線網路

(B) 個人諮詢

(C) 免費點心

(D) 體驗虛擬服務

正確答案

(D) A virtual experience service

解説

廣告講完優惠方案後，接著介紹店裡最先進的 3D 影像模擬軟體（state-of-the-art three-dimensional visualization software），幫客戶找出最適合自己的髮型。visualization（影像化）這名詞感覺有點難，它是由形容詞 visual（視覺的）而來的。這種 3D 影像化軟體，是將一般從雜誌或書籍中看到的髮型，透過 3D 影像，讓人能更明確知道自己適合哪種髮型。將這種功能說成是「虛擬體驗」（virtual experience）也可以，所以選項 (D) 是正確答案。(A)、(B)、(C) 在廣告中都沒有出現。

3. What does the speaker suggest doing?

(A) Updating a software program

(B) Comparing prices

(C) Arranging an appointment

(D) Reading a flyer

3.說話者提出什麼建議？

(A) 更新軟體程式

(B) 比價

(C) 預約

(D) 閱讀宣傳單

正確答案

(C) Arranging an appointment

解説

廣告的最後面建議打電話預約剪髮（make an appointment by calling at 657-555-6842），所以選項 (C) 是正確答案。

聽獨白，選出與問題最為符合的回答。🎧 134

4. What kind of business is being advertised?
   (A) A travel agency
   (B) A vacation resort
   (C) A catering company
   (D) A real estate agency

5. What did the television show recently say about the business?
   (A) It has expanded its parking lot.
   (B) It was founded by a local entrepreneur.
   (C) It features superb facilities.
   (D) It is offering discount prices to children.

6. According to the speaker, how can listeners receive a promotional offer?
   (A) By booking online
   (B) By applying for membership
   (C) By contacting a television station
   (D) By mentioning an advertisement

STEP 2 確認正確答案及翻譯和解說。

M Looking for a perfect vacation spot for you and your family this summer? **(4) Look no further than the White Sands Resort in Newport Beach, California. (5) The television show *Happy Traveler* recently reviewed our resort and praised it for the quality and diversity of our recreational facilities.** We offer swimming, golf, tennis, dining, and much more. Book now and you can receive an extra day for free. **(6) All you have to do is call now and mention this radio advertisement.** So why wait? Give us a call at 555-8945!

男：正在找尋今夏家族度假的最佳地點嗎？別再找了，就是它了，加州新港灘的白沙休閒度假中心。電視節目《樂遊者》最近對本度假中心做了評鑑，針對本中心遊樂設施的高品質及豐富多樣性，多所讚揚。本中心設有各式各樣的娛樂設施，游泳池、高爾夫球場、網球場，以及餐飲設施。現在預約，您就可獲得免費多住一日的優惠。您只需要馬上撥打電話，並提及這則電台廣告。還在等什麼？快撥打電話555-8945！

字彙

look no further than . . . 想要的就在眼前　　praise 讚揚

recreational facility 娛樂設施　　book 預訂　　mention 提及

---

4. What kind of business is being advertised?

(A) A travel agency

(B) A vacation resort

(C) A catering company

(D) A real estate agency

4.哪種企業在做廣告？

(A) 旅行社

(B) 休閒度假中心

(C) 外燴公司

(D) 房地產仲介公司

正確答案

(B) A vacation resort

解説

這是要掌握整個廣告才能作答的題目。廣告宣傳的對象是度假中心 (White Sands Resort)，且它擁有各式各樣娛樂設施（游泳池、高爾夫球場、網球場、以及餐飲設施等），可以知道它應該是提供多種設施的旅館業者，所以正確答案是選項 (B)。題目問的是被宣傳的對象，而被宣傳的對象不是旅行社，故 (A) 錯。廣告內容和不動產、外燴無關，所以選項 (C)、(D) 也不對。

---

5. What did the television show recently say about the business?

(A) It has expanded its parking lot.

(B) It was founded by a local entrepreneur.

(C) It features superb facilities.

(D) It is offering discount prices to children.

5.近期的電視節目對該度假中心有何評論？

(A) 其停車場已擴建。

(B) 它是由本地的企業家所創辦。

(C) 一流的活動設施是其主打特色。

(D) 它讓兒童享優惠價格。

(C) It features superb facilities.

廣告中提及的電視節目是《樂遊者》(*Happy Traveler*),題目要找出該節目參訪後給了什麼評價,屬於詢問細節的試題。praised for . . . 是「因……而讚美」,該片語後接讚美的原因,也就是 quality and diversity of our recreational facilities(品質高,娛樂設施多樣),所以選項 (C)「一流的活動設施是其主打特色」,是正確答案。

---

6. According to the speaker, how can listeners receive a promotional offer?

   (A) By booking online
   (B) By applying for membership
   (C) By contacting a television station
   (D) By mentioning an advertisement

6.據說話者所言,聽眾如何能取得促銷優惠?

   (A) 線上預訂
   (B) 申請會員
   (C) 聯繫電視台
   (D) 提及廣告內容

(D) By mentioning an advertisement

試題詢問的 promotional offer,也就是廣告中提到的 an extra day for free,要得到「免費多住一日的優惠」有兩個條件,第一是現在就要預訂(book now),第二是預約時要提到本廣告(mention this radio advertisement)。提到這兩項或其中一項,就是正確答案,所以正確答案是提到第二項條件的選項 (D)。

播出這個廣告的媒體可能是電視台或電台,但是廣告給的電話號碼是休閒度假中心的電話,不是電視台的電話,所以 (C) 不對。(A) 說線上預約,但廣告中是打電話預約,所以也不對。選項 (B) 廣告中沒有提到。

2 命題分析

廣告

● 產品或服務的廣告，會問產品及服務的**特徵**、**價格**、**打折**、**銷售期間**、**日期**、**場所**、**打折優惠辦法**等。

解題戰略

1. 廣告類的獨白播放前，先瀏覽並掌握試題問的是什麼：**主題**、**細節**還是**推測**。

2. 詢問主題的試題，要掌握廣告**最前面的部分**；詢問細節的試題，要掌握廣告中和 WH **疑問字詞**相關的線索，別忘了正確答案常會**改寫**（paraphrase）！

3. 推測類的試題，要掌握廣告的**最後面部分**。

STEP 1　聽獨白，選出與問題最為符合的回答。𝄞 135

1. What is being advertised?
(A) A sporting contest
(B) A fundraiser
(C) A community event
(D) A literary festival

2. Who is Hal Johnson?
(A) An organizer
(B) A novelist
(C) A musician
(D) An athlete

3. Why would some listeners call Tom Keller?
(A) To purchase a ticket
(B) To reserve a location
(C) To inquire about a product
(D) To apply for a construction permit

W **(1) Tickets for the annual Clinton County Fair went on sale today.** Enjoy thrilling carnival rides and tasty food and have a good time with family and friends. The fair will take place over the weekend from May 4 to May 6. **(2) This year, popular country singer Hal Johnson will be performing on the main stage.** You can watch the show just by purchasing the general ticket to enter the fairgrounds.

(3) And remember, if you are a craft vendor and want to apply for a spot inside the vendors' tent, you can do so by calling Tom Keller at 555-3221.

女：柯林頓郡一年一度的園遊會門票今天開賣了。有刺激的遊樂設施，還有美食，讓你與家人朋友一同狂歡作樂。時間是在這個週末，五月四日至五月六日。今年的表演節目，將由眾所喜愛的鄉村歌手霍爾‧強森負責擔綱。只要購買園遊會的門票，就可以進入遊樂場內觀賞表演。

還有，如果您是手工藝品攤商，想申請租賃攤位，可撥打電話 555-3221，向湯姆‧凱勒洽詢相關事宜。

字彙

rides（遊樂園裡）供人乘坐的遊樂裝置　　fair 園遊會
perform 表演　　general ticket 門票　　fairground 露天遊樂場
craft vendor 手工藝品攤商

---

1. What is being advertised?

(A) A sporting contest

(B) A fundraiser

(C) A community event

(D) A literary festival

1.本文在為什麼做廣告？

(A) 運動賽事

(B) 募款活動

(C) 社區活動

(D) 文學季

正確答案

(C) A community event

解說

廣告中出現的票是柯林頓郡園遊會的票，這裡的 county 是比州小的「郡」。也就是廣告推廣的活動，是柯林頓郡舉辦的園遊會，(C) 是正確答案，它將郡改寫成 community（社區）也很合理。選項 (D) 用 festival（慶典）來指稱該活動也可以，不過園遊會的內容和文學是無關的，所以選項 (D) 不對。

2. Who is Hal Johnson?

(A) An organizer

(B) A novelist

(C) A musician

(D) An athlete

2. 霍爾‧強森是誰？

(A) 主辦者

(B) 小說家

(C) 音樂家

(D) 運動員

正確答案

(C) A musician

解說

廣告中提到霍爾‧強森時，對他的形容是 popular country singer（眾所喜愛的鄉村歌手），所以選項(C)是正確答案，它將 singer 改寫成 musician（音樂家）。

3. Why would some listeners call Tom Keller?

(A) To purchase a ticket

(B) To reserve a location

(C) To inquire about a product

(D) To apply for a construction permit

3. 為何有些聽眾會要打電話給湯姆‧凱勒？

(A) 為了購買門票

(B) 為了預訂攤位

(C) 為了諮詢產品

(D) 為了申請施工執照

正確答案

(B) To reserve a location

解說

題目詢問為何有些聽眾要打電話給湯姆‧凱勒，提到湯姆‧凱勒的前一句話是，如果聽眾是手工藝品攤商（if you are a craft vendor），想申請租賃攤位販賣商品（apply for a spot inside the vendors' tent），就要打電話給湯姆‧凱勒，所以選項(B)正確。廣告中沒有提及跟湯姆‧凱勒購票或訂購商品、申請施工執照，所以(A)、(C)、(D)都錯。

NEWSPAPER COUPON

Zafron's Furniture Grand Opening SALE!
This coupon is good for one free ice cream on the day of the grand opening only.
Redeem this with Ralph or Lizzie Zafron, and you will be given a raffle ticket and entered in our drawing. The drawing will be held at eight o'clock sharp. If the owner of the winning ticket is not present within 3 minutes of the drawing, it will be forfeited and another ticket will be drawn.

---

4. What is indicated about Zafron's Furniture?

(A) They have a range of household electronics.

(B) They are offering incentives to bring people into their store.

(C) They specialize in home repair.

(D) This is their final sale.

5. Look at the graphic. What can you infer about Zafron's Furniture?

(A) They will be open until 8 p.m.

(B) They expect a lot of people to attend the raffle.

(C) Zafron's Furniture is a family owned business.

(D) There are too many orders for the delivery service.

6. What service does Zafron's Furniture offer to today's customers?

(A) Free shipping on all orders

(B) Free shipping on orders over $200

(C) Home installation on orders over $200

(D) Wall papering services

M Welcome to Zafron's Furniture Grand Opening! (6) **It's our first day of business, and we're offering free shipping to every customer in the greater Blithe area on purchases of $200 or more!** This bargain ends at midnight, so get down here as soon as you can! Additionally, there are special deals on everything in our store, including our handcrafted dining room tables and chairs. When you factor in the savings you will receive from the free delivery, it would be a bargain at twice our prices! Get a copy of today's *Blithe Journal* and look for our coupon. Every customer who brings in a coupon will enjoy a free ice cream cone and be entered in our raffle!

男：歡迎蒞臨柴弗龍家具店盛大開幕式！今天是本公司第一天營運，只要是購物金額達 200 美元以上的大布利茲地區的顧客，皆可享免運費服務。這個特惠活動只到今晚午夜為止，所以，動作要快！此外，本店的每個商品都有特別的優惠，包含手工打造的餐桌椅。如果再算上減免運費所省下的錢，等於是我們的商品打了對折！趕快去買份今日的《布利茲日報》，裡面附有本公司的折價券。每位出示折價券的顧客，皆可免費享用一支冰淇淋甜筒，同時加入我們的摸彩抽獎活動！

NEWSPAPER COUPON

Zafron's Furniture Grand Opening SALE!

This coupon is good for one free ice cream on the day of the grand opening only.

Redeem this with Ralph or Lizzie Zafron, and you will be given a raffle ticket and entered in our drawing. The drawing will be held at eight o'clock sharp. If the owner of the winning ticket is not present within 3 minutes of the drawing, it will be forfeited and another ticket will be drawn.

報紙折價券

柴弗龍家具店盛大開幕特賣會！

出示本折價券，可免費獲贈一支冰淇淋甜筒。僅適用於開幕當天。

拿著本券與雷夫・柴弗龍或麗姿・柴弗龍兌換摸彩券，參加我們的抽獎活動。摸彩儀式將在八點準時舉行，如果屆時得獎者並未在場，逾時三分鐘，則該次抽獎作廢，將再另行抽出另一得主。

purchase (n.) 購買　　bargain 協議　　raffle 摸彩

---

4. What is indicated about Zafron's Furniture?

(A) They have a range of household electronics.

(B) They are offering incentives to bring people into their store.

(C) They specialize in home repair.

(D) This is their final sale.

4.關於柴弗龍家具店，本文提到何事？

(A) 供應一系列家用電器。

(B) 做促銷吸引顧客上門。

(C) 專門做居家維修。

(D) 正舉行最終折扣。

正確答案

(B) They are offering incentives to bring people into their store.

解說

柴弗龍家具店今天開幕，為了吸引顧客上門，提供了折價券、摸彩抽獎、打折等優惠。這些手段都是為了吸引顧客，所以選項 (B) 是正確答案。廣告沒有提及家具店販售家用電器或提供家居維修，所以 (A)、(C) 錯誤。廣告說這是柴弗龍家具店第一天營運，所以也不是舉辦最終折扣，(D) 也不能選。

---

5. Look at the graphic. What can you infer about Zafron's Furniture?

(A) They will be open until 8 p.m.

(B) They expect a lot of people to attend the raffle.

(C) Zafron's Furniture is a family owned business.

(D) There are too many orders for the delivery service.

5.請看報紙折價券。由此可推知柴弗龍家具店？

(A) 營業至晚上八點。

(B) 預期很多人會參加抽獎。

(C) 是一個家族企業。

(D) 有太多訂單需要配送服務。

(C) Zafron's Furniture is a family owned business.

看到報紙折價券，要將折價券交給雷夫‧柴弗龍或麗姿‧柴弗龍，可以知道他們兩個是員工，而且他們都姓柴弗龍，也就是家具商店名，所以可以推知，該商店是家族經營的商店，所以正確答案是 (C)。廣告中提到的八點（eight o'clock）是摸彩舉辦的時間，所以可以推論家具店八點之後還開著，故 (A) 錯。

6. What service does Zafron's Furniture offer to today's customers?
   (A) Free shipping on all orders
   (B) Free shipping on orders over $200
   (C) Home installation on orders over $200
   (D) Wall papering services

6. 柴弗龍家具店為今日的顧客提供什麼服務？
   (A) 所有訂單都免收運費
   (B) 購物金額達 200 美元以上的訂單可免運費
   (C) 購物金額達 200 美元以上的訂單可享到府安裝服務
   (D) 壁紙工程服務

(B) Free shipping on orders over $200

廣告說，買超過 200 元就免費提供配送（free shipping . . . on purchases of $200 or more），所以正確答案是選項 (B)。

1. What is the subject of the exhibition?
   (A) Ancient fossils
   (B) Native artifacts
   (C) Astronomical discoveries
   (D) French history

2. Who is Ferdinand Martin?
   (A) A Native American
   (B) A curator
   (C) A documentary director
   (D) A scholar

3. What are listeners invited to do?
   (A) Read a brochure
   (B) Watch a performance
   (C) Visit a website
   (D) Purchase a ticket in advance

4. What type of business is being advertised?
   (A) A toy store
   (B) A library
   (C) A gift shop
   (D) A bookstore

5. Who is Michael Richardson?
   (A) The manager of the store
   (B) A writer
   (C) A customer
   (D) The owner

6. What does the speaker encourage listeners to do?
   (A) Buy a best-seller
   (B) Come later
   (C) Read more books
   (D) Visit the library

Chapter

04 新聞報導

1 題型暖身

STEP 1 聽獨白，選出與問題最為符合的回答。🎧 138

1. What is the purpose of this broadcast?
   - (A) To advertise the opening of a new shop
   - (B) To announce the new changes to a facility
   - (C) To report the closure of a program
   - (D) To reveal the news concerning a sports team

2. What will listeners probably hear next?
   - (A) Financial news
   - (B) Local news stories
   - (C) The weather forecast
   - (D) A commercial

W In local news today, the Brentwood Public Sports Center has officially re-opened its doors after a months-long renovation effort. A new wing has been added to the building. It houses a new indoor rock-climbing wall and four indoor tennis courts. The gyms have brand new exercise equipment and now offer professional yoga, Pilates, and aerobics classes. The swimming center is accepting registrations for swimming lessons this summer, and finally a senior center has been set up to help senior citizens with their individual exercise needs. For more information, you can visit the website at www.brentwoodsportscenter.com. (2) **And now we turn to the weather.**

女：本地新聞。布蘭伍德公共運動中心在經過長達多個月的翻新之後，今日正式重新開放。主建物旁新增建了一幢側樓，內有嶄新的室內攀岩牆以及四座室內網球場。健身中心增添新的健身器材，且現有開設專業的瑜伽課程、皮拉提斯以及有氧運動課程。游泳中心將於今夏開辦的暑期游泳班，現在也正開放報名。而年長者，也終於盼來一座老人活動中心以滿足他們的個別運動需求。想知道更多相關資訊，請上運動中心官網：www.brentwoodsportscenter.com。現在播報氣象。

字彙

house (v.) 容納　　brand new 嶄新的　　registration 註冊
needs 需求　　facility 設施　　closure 終止　　forecast 預報

1. What is the purpose of this broadcast?

(A) To advertise the opening of a new shop

(B) To announce the new changes to a facility

(C) To report the closure of a program

(D) To reveal the news concerning a sports team

1.播報這則新聞的目的是？

(A) 為一家商店的開幕做廣告

(B) 宣布一項設施的新改變

(C) 報導一項計畫的終止

(D) 揭露運動隊伍的相關消息

正確答案

(B) To announce the new changes to a facility

解説

新聞報導的主題是布蘭伍德公共運動中心的擴建，在一個月的施工後，運動中心主建物旁新增建了一幢側樓，側樓內增加了許多設備。因此，選項 (B) 說一個設施（facility = 布蘭伍德公共運動中心）有了新的改變是合理的，所以選項 (B) 是正確答案。重新開幕的是公共運動中心，不是商店開幕，所以 (A) 不能選。

2. What will listeners probably hear next?

(A) Financial news

(B) Local news stories

(C) The weather forecast

(D) A commercial

2.聽眾接下來有可能聽到什麼？

(A) 財金新聞

(B) 本地新聞

(C) 氣象預報

(D) 廣告

正確答案

(C) The weather forecast

解説

電視或廣播媒體的新聞報導，一般狀況是在最後播報氣象報告，但解題關鍵是報導的最後一句話提到 turn to the weather，明顯指出接下來會報導氣象，所以正確答案是 (C)。本篇報導一開始就說是 local news（當地新聞），所以選項 (B) 不能選。

聽獨白，選出與問題最為符合的回答。∩ 139

1. Parkwood Elementary School
2. Parkwood Church
3. Parkwood Community Center
4. Paid Public Parking

3. Look at the graphic. What area does the speaker suggest drivers avoid parking at?

(A) 1   (B) 3   (C) 2   (D) 4

確認正確答案及翻譯和解說。

W This Saturday is the 10th annual Parkwood Community Summer Festival. The festivities will take place at the Parkwood Community Center and the surrounding field, so traffic will be heavier than usual, with hundreds expected to attend. (3) **Please avoid parking at the community center.** Extra parking will be available at Parkwood Elementary school and Parkwood Church. The Parkwood public parking lot will also be open to visitors of the festival at no extra charge. Festivalgoers will need to present tickets in order to receive free parking.

女：本週六是第十屆帕克伍德年度社區夏日嘉年華會。嘉年華活動的地點，將在帕克伍德社區中心以及鄰近的場地。預期屆時會有數以百計的民眾參加，所以周邊的交通會較往常擁擠，請民眾不要將車停在社區中心。帕克伍德小學以及帕克伍德教堂有額外的停車位可供應。而帕克伍德公共停車場也會開放給參加此次嘉年華的遊客停車，不會額外收費。遊客僅需出示嘉年華門票，即可免費停車。

1. Parkwood Elementary School	1. 帕克伍德小學
2. Parkwood Church	2. 帕克伍德教堂
3. Parkwood Community Center	3. 帕克伍德社區中心
4. Paid Public Parking	4. 付費公共停車場

take place at（某地）舉辦　　festivity 歡慶活動
attend 參加　　festivalgoer 嘉年華會參與者

---

3. Look at the graphic. What area does the speaker suggest drivers avoid parking at?

(A) 1

(B) 3

(C) 2

(D) 4

3.請見圖表。說話者建議駕駛避免在哪一個區域停車？

(A) 1

(B) 3

(C) 2

(D) 4

正確答案

(B) 3

解說

本題是要找出報導的細節，所以要一一掌握報導中提到有關停車的地方。因為數以百計的民眾參加，會造成交通壅塞，所以不要將車停在帕克伍德社區中心，而是可以使用帕克伍德小學和帕克伍德教會的停車空間；帕克伍德公共停車場（public parking lot）也免費開放給遊客。題目這 4 個停車空間中，說話者建議因交通壅塞而要避開的是圖表中的第 3 項 Parkwood Community Center，所以選項 (B) 是正確答案。

> **新聞報導**
>
> ● 新聞報導會問**播出時間及播出種類、事件內容和發生的時間及場所、確認、結果、統計、展望、預測**等。
>
> **解題戰略**
>
> 1. 新聞報導的獨白播放前,先瀏覽並掌握試題問的是什麼:**主題、細節**還是**推測**。
>
> 2. 詢問主題的試題,要掌握新聞報導**最前面的部分**;詢問細節的試題,要掌握新聞報導中和 **WH 疑問字詞**相關的線索,別忘了正確答案常會**改寫**(paraphrase)!
>
> 3. 推測類的試題,要掌握新聞報導的**最後面部分**。

STEP 1 聽獨白,選出與問題最為符合的回答。🎧 140

1. Who most likely is the speaker?
   (A) A radio host
   (B) A professional athlete
   (C) A business owner
   (D) A city official

2. According to the speaker, what is a negative effect of high temperatures?
   (A) The number of tourists will diminish.
   (B) Environmental damage will occur.
   (C) Melting snow will flood city streets.
   (D) Some resorts will open later.

3. What will Mr. Bolton most likely discuss?
   (A) Next week's weather forecast
   (B) Nice places to visit in winter
   (C) Promotional offers
   (D) Climate change

W Good morning. ⁽¹⁾ **You're listening to the weather report for Aspen, Colorado, on Radio 95.5.** The temperatures this week are exceptionally high for another week in a row. This means conditions at the ski hills are going to be less than desirable. ⁽²⁾ **For a city that relies heavily on winter sports tourism, these high temperatures are adversely affecting tourism profits.** However, at the end of the month, we will hopefully start seeing some significant snowfall. Next, we'll be talking with Jason Bolton, president of the Resort Owners' Association here in Aspen. ⁽³⁾ **He'll be telling us about the discounted ski pass prices many local resorts are offering in order to encourage skiers to hit the slopes.** Welcome, Mr. Bolton.

女：早安。您現在正在收聽 95.5 廣播電台，現在播報科羅拉多州亞斯本氣象預報。本周將延續前一週，出現異常高溫。這表示滑雪場地的狀況恐不甚理想。對一個重度仰賴冬季運動觀光的城市來說，連續的高溫將會衝擊本地的觀光收益。不過，在本月底，我們將有希望迎來幾場大雪。接下來，我們將與亞斯本度假中心協會理事長傑森‧波頓對談，他將與我們分享本地許多度假中心業者，為招徠更多滑雪者前往滑雪，現正提供滑雪入場券優惠的消息。波頓先生，歡迎你來。

字彙

temperature 溫度　　exceptionally 異常地　　in a row 連續的
less than desirable 未達期望的　　rely on 依賴　　tourism 旅遊業
significant 重大的　　snowfall 降雪　　climate 氣候

1. Who most likely is the speaker?

(A) A radio host

(B) A professional athlete

(C) A business owner

(D) A city official

1.說話者最有可能是？

(A) 廣播節目主持人

(B) 職業運動員

(C) 公司老闆

(D) 市政官員

正確答案

(A) A radio host

解說

這是推測類的題型，說話者一開始就說出了現在收聽的廣播頻道（95.5.）以及廣播的節目內容——天氣狀況，之後又訪談一位與節目內容相關的人士，談論相關話題。所以可以推知說話者是節目主持人（host），所以正確答案是 (A)。

2. According to the speaker, what is a negative effect of high temperatures?

(A) The number of tourists will diminish.

(B) Environmental damage will occur.

(C) Melting snow will flood city streets.

(D) Some resorts will open later.

2.根據說話者，高溫帶來的負面影響是？

(A) 遊客將會減少。

(B) 會對環境造成傷害。

(C) 融雪會淹沒城市街道。

(D) 一些度假中心將會延遲開業。

正確答案

(A) The number of tourists will diminish.

解說

說話者在氣象報告中提到，本週又將是異常地高溫，這樣的氣溫將對觀光收入有不利的影響（adversely affecting tourism profits），而收入減少一定是觀光客人數減少了，因此正確答案是 (A)。和度假中心（resort）有關的內容，只提到滑雪入場券優惠，和選項 (D) 的營業時間沒有關係。

3. What will Mr. Bolton most likely discuss?

(A) Next week's weather forecast

(B) Nice places to visit in winter

(C) Promotional offers

(D) Climate change

3.波頓先生最有可能談論什麼？

(A) 下一週的氣象預報

(B) 冬季推薦的度假地點

(C) 促銷活動

(D) 氣候變遷

正確答案

(C) Promotional offers

解説

説話者介紹波頓先生後，説波頓先生將談談有關滑雪入場券優惠的消息（discounted ski pass prices），選項 (C) 將優惠改寫成 promotional offers（促銷活動）也合理，所以是正確答案。選項 (D) 氣候變遷，説話者在報導一開始時已經講過，所以不會是波頓先生等一下要講的內容。

4. What has recently happened at Bowen Elementary School?

(A) Its curriculum has been redesigned.

(B) A new gymnasium has been built.

(C) The number of students has increased.

(D) Its sports team won a championship.

5. According to the news report, what has led to the influx of families to Bowen?

(A) A new factory

(B) A low property tax

(C) A TV documentary

(D) An award

6. What will the city do this summer?

(A) Hold a film festival

(B) Approve a development plan

(C) Build public facilities

(D) Raise income taxes

M Good morning, everyone. This is Chris Gibson. (4) **In today's morning news, Bowen Elementary School reported a sharp rise in new students this year.** (5) **The increase has been attributed to the city of Bowen winning the "Most Livable City" award last year. The attention the city has received has been bringing over new families, who are attracted by the renowned education system and beautiful natural surroundings.** Additionally, these families have tended to be wealthier than previous citizens, meaning the city of Bowen has seen a large increase in property tax revenue. (6) **The city plans to spend this extra revenue this summer by building a public swimming pool for its residents.**

男：大家早安。我是克里斯·吉布森。今日晨間新聞，波恩小學今年的入學新生激增。會出現這樣的現象，導因於波恩市去年榮獲「最宜居城市」獎。獲獎為該城市贏得關注，也吸引許多著眼於其著名的教育體系，及美麗的自然環境的家庭遷居於此。此外，這些新遷入的家庭，似乎較當地的區民更為富裕，也意味著波恩市的財產稅收出現大幅度的增加。市府也計畫於今夏運用此筆新增收入，為市民興建一座公共游泳池。

字彙

attribute . . . to 將……歸因於　　renowned 著名的
property tax 財產稅；房地產稅　　revenue 稅收

4. What has recently happened at Bowen Elementary School?
 (A) Its curriculum has been redesigned.
 (B) A new gymnasium has been built.
 (C) The number of students has increased.
 (D) Its sports team won a championship.

4.波恩小學最近發生何事？
 (A) 課程已重新規劃。
 (B) 已興建新的體育館。
 (C) 入學新生人數增加。
 (D) 體育隊贏得冠軍。

(C) The number of students has increased.

説話者一開始就提到，波恩小學說今年學生人數暴增（a sharp rise in new students），之後報導就一直在探討會發生這情形的原因，所以正確答案是(C)。

---

5. According to the news report, what has led to the influx of families to Bowen?

(A) A new factory

(B) A low property tax

(C) A TV documentary

(D) An award

5.根據新聞報導，是什麼原因導致眾多家庭大量湧入波恩市？

(A) 新工廠

(B) 財產稅徵收低廉

(C) 電視紀錄片

(D) 獲獎

(D) An award

報導中提到，因為波恩市獲得最宜居城市獎（"Most Livable City" award），因此吸引了許多家庭來此定居，同時學生人數也增加了，所以正確答案是選項(D)。

---

6. What will the city do this summer?

(A) Hold a film festival

(B) Approve a development plan

(C) Build public facilities

(D) Raise income taxes

6.該市今夏預計做何事？

(A) 舉辦電影節

(B) 批准一項發展計畫

(C) 興建公共設施

(D) 提高所得稅收

(C) Build public facilities

在報導的最後提到，因為新遷入的家庭較為富裕，波恩市財產稅收入也增加了，於是市政府計畫要為市民蓋一座公共游泳池（building a public swimming pool），所以正確答案是(C)，它將 swimming pool 改成設施（facilities）。

1. What is the broadcast about?
   (A) A weather update
   (B) A film festival
   (C) A local election
   (D) A music festival

2. What benefit does the speaker mention?
   (A) Economic stimulation
   (B) Discounted ticket prices
   (C) Educational opportunities
   (D) Increased publicity

3. What will listeners most likely hear next?
   (A) A speech
   (B) An interview
   (C) A weather report
   (D) An emergency announcement

4. What type of event is being announced?
   (A) A competition
   (B) A fundraising event
   (C) A symphonic concert
   (D) A musical

5. Why should listeners visit the website?
   (A) To get information
   (B) To purchase tickets
   (C) To join the orchestra
   (D) To download music

6. According to the speaker, why is money being raised?
   (A) To fund the library
   (B) To buy new instruments
   (C) To repair the classrooms
   (D) To pay for a trip

1 題型暖身

STEP 1　聽獨白，選出與問題最為符合的回答。∩ 143

1. Who most likely are the listeners?
(A) Faculty members
(B) Facility managers
(C) Local residents
(D) Prospective students

2. What regulation does the speaker mention?
(A) A time to return
(B) An age requirement
(C) A speed limit
(D) A building code

3. What will the listeners do next?
(A) Attend a class
(B) Prepare a presentation
(C) Tour a residence hall
(D) Have a meal

STEP 2 確認正確答案及翻譯和解說。

W Here is the next stop on our campus tour. **(1) If you do decide to attend our college, this is where you would be living.** Our residence halls were built just last year, and the facilities are clean and modern. **(2) However, students who live in the residence hall have to be back in their rooms by midnight, when the gates will be closed.** **(3) Next we'll be heading to the cafeteria, where everyone will be able to enjoy a free lunch.**

女：現在到了我們校園巡禮的下一站。如果你們真的決定就讀本校，這裡將是你們的宿舍。我們的學生宿舍是去年才蓋好的，所有的設施都是乾淨又現代化。不過，住在學生宿舍裡的學生，門禁時間是午夜十二點，屆時大門就會關閉。下一站，我們將前往自助餐廳，在那裡所有人將可以免費享用午餐。

字彙

attend 就讀　　residence hall 學生宿舍　　facility 設施
midnight 午夜　　cafeteria 自助餐廳

1. Who most likely are the listeners?

(A) Faculty members

(B) Facility managers

(C) Local residents

(D) Prospective students

1.聽眾最有可能是誰？

(A) 大學教職員

(B) 設備主管

(C) 當地居民

(D) 未來的學生

正確答案

(D) Prospective students

解說

說話者在跟聽眾介紹大學宿舍時，提到如果你們決定就讀本校，這裡將是你們的宿舍，所以可以推知，聽眾是未來可能會讀這所大學的學生。因此選項 (D) prospective students（有可能入學的學生），是正確答案。

2. What regulation does the speaker mention?

    (A) A time to return

    (B) An age requirement

    (C) A speed limit

    (D) A building code

2.說話者提到何項規定？

    (A) 回宿舍的時間

    (B) 年齡限制

    (C) 速限

    (D) 建築法規

正確答案

(A) A time to return

解説

導覽中沒有直接提到限制的字眼，像 restriction 或 limitation 等，不過在說明宿舍規定時，提到了住宿生必須在午夜 12 點前回宿舍（to be back in their rooms by midnight），因為 12 點宿舍會關大門（when the gates will be closed），所以正確答案是有「回宿舍時間」的選項 (A)。導覽中並沒有提到年齡或限速，雖有提到建築物，不過是建築物關門的時間，不是建築物的代碼。

3. What will the listeners do next?

    (A) Attend a class

    (B) Prepare a presentation

    (C) Tour a residence hall

    (D) Have a meal

3.聽眾接下來會做什麼？

    (A) 上課

    (B) 準備做簡報

    (C) 參觀學生宿舍

    (D) 用餐

正確答案

(D) Have a meal

解説

聽簡短獨白時，要注意提示字 next 或 now，因為它們提示接下來的活動。head 當動詞時是「朝向……方向走」，要去的地方是自助餐廳（cafeteria）並享用免費午餐，所以選項 (D) 是正確答案。(C) 的參觀宿舍已經完成了，不是接下來要做的活動。

4. Where is the talk taking place?
(A) In a national museum
(B) In a children's hospital
(C) In a historic house
(D) In a laboratory

5. What can listeners purchase?
(A) A book
(B) A lock
(C) A computer program
(D) A picture

6. What does the speaker remind listeners to do?
(A) Sign up for a class
(B) Wear protective gear
(C) Pay attention to the tour guide
(D) Retrieve personal possessions

PART
4

Chapter
05

觀光導覽

M ⁽⁴⁾ **This concludes the tour of this historic birthplace of inventor James Winston. We hope this tour of his childhood home has given you meaningful insights.** ⁽⁵⁾ **We remind you that a biography of James Winston is available for purchase at the entrance on your way out.** Half of the proceeds are donated to educational programs for children. ⁽⁶⁾ **Also, please don't forget to retrieve any belongings that you may have placed in a locker at the beginning of the tour.** Thank you for choosing Clarkson History Tour.

男：到這裡，我們將結束發明家詹姆士・溫士頓的出生故居導覽。希望這趟參觀他幼時居所的行程能讓諸位深受啟發。提醒各位，出口處有詹姆士・溫士頓的生平傳記可供選購，其中一半的收益將會捐助給兒童教育相關課程。此外，請別忘記取回您放置在儲物櫃的隨身物品。感謝您參加克萊克森古蹟遊覽。

字彙

conclude 結束　　birthplace 出生地　　inventor 發明家
insight 啟發；洞察力　　biography 傳記　　retrieve 取回

---

4. Where is the talk taking place?
　(A) In a national museum
　(B) In a children's hospital
　(C) In a historic house
　(D) In a laboratory

4.談話的地點位在何處？
　(A) 國家博物館
　(B) 兒童醫院
　(C) 古蹟宅邸
　(D) 實驗室

正確答案

(C) In a historic house

解說

本題詢問導覽進行的場所，透過 this historic birthplace of inventor James Winston 可知，導覽員正在介紹發明家詹姆士・溫士頓的出生故居，所以正確答案是 (C)。選項 (B) 是利用獨白中出現 children 而做成的錯誤答案，導覽的場所不是兒童醫院。

5. What can listeners purchase?

(A) A book

(B) A lock

(C) A computer program

(D) A picture

5.聽眾可以購買何物？

(A) 書籍

(B) 鎖

(C) 電腦程式

(D) 圖畫

正確答案

(A) A book

解説

在導覽的中間部分，導覽員提到可以購買詹姆士・溫士頓的傳記（biography）。傳記，換句話說是書，因此選項 (A) 是正確答案。

6. What does the speaker remind listeners to do?

(A) Sign up for a class

(B) Wear protective gear

(C) Pay attention to the tour guide

(D) Retrieve personal possessions

6.說話者提醒聽眾做何事？

(A) 報名課程

(B) 穿戴防護配備

(C) 注意聆聽導覽

(D) 拿回私人物品

正確答案

(D) Retrieve personal possessions

解説

在導覽的最後面部分，導覽員要聽眾不要忘記取回放置在儲物櫃的隨身物品，所以正確答案是選項 (D)。

> **觀光導覽**
>
> ● 觀光導覽的內容，主要是參觀觀光景點、展場、建築物時，導遊對**該景點與建築物的介紹**，或**說明行程、注意事項**等。要集中注意力聽依時間及場所排定的行程，因為這是主要的出題方向。
>
> **解題戰略**
>
> 1. 觀光導覽的獨白播放前，先瀏覽並掌握試題問的是什麼：**主題、細節**還是**推測**。
>
> 2. 詢問主題的試題，要掌握觀光導覽**最前面的部分**；詢問細節的試題，要掌握觀光導覽中和 **WH 疑問字詞**相關的線索，別忘了正確答案常會**改寫**（paraphrase）！
>
> 3. 推測類的試題，要掌握觀光導覽的**最後面部分**。

STEP 1 聽獨白，選出與問題最為符合的回答。 🎧 145

1. According to the speaker, what is true about the factory?
   (A) It has been in operation since last year.
   (B) It was built by a foreign company.
   (C) It was opened by a well-known musician.
   (D) It is the biggest in the domestic field.

2. What does the speaker warn against?
   (A) Leaving children unattended
   (B) Using a camera
   (C) Disturbing workers
   (D) Making noise

3. What are listeners asked to do?
   (A) Complete a form
   (B) Submit an application
   (C) Visit a gift shop
   (D) Purchase a product

W Welcome to the Davis Guitar Company factory tour. Davis guitars are praised around the world for their superior quality and craftsmanship. **(1) This is the largest factory of musical instruments in the country, and it is continually growing.** First, we will be visiting the factory floor, where I will show you how guitars come to life through the hands of the craftsmen. **(2) We would like to remind you that no photography is allowed on the factory floor. (3) After the tour, we encourage you to fill out a survey to help us improve visitors' experiences.** If you have any questions, just let me know.

女：歡迎參加戴維斯吉他公司工廠導覽。戴維斯吉他因為卓越的品質及工藝技術，享譽全球。這裡是全國最大的樂器生產工廠，且規模仍持續增長。首先，我們將參觀廠區，在那裡大家可以看到工藝師的巧手如何賦予吉他生命。但要提醒各位，廠區內不得拍照攝影。而導覽結束後，歡迎各位幫我們填寫問卷，以改善我們的導覽品質。如果有任何疑問，請隨時提出。

PART 4
Chapter 05
觀光導覽

字彙

superior 優越的　　craftsmanship 工藝　　factory floor 廠區
craftsman 工藝師

1. According to the speaker, what is true about the factory?
   (A) It has been in operation since last year.
   (B) It was built by a foreign company.
   (C) It was opened by a well-known musician.
   (D) It is the biggest in the domestic field.

1.根據說話者，下列何項關於工廠的敘述是正確的？
   (A) 自去年開始營運。
   (B) 由外國公司出資籌建。
   (C) 由著名的音樂家所創立。
   (D) 是國內最大的樂器工廠。

正確答案

(D) It is the biggest in the domestic field.

本題要在有關工廠的敘述中找答案，第三句話用 this 指稱 Davis Guitar Company，說它是全國最大的樂器生產工廠（the largest factory of musical instruments in the country）選項 (D) 將 in the country 換成 domestic（國內的）也可以，所以是正確答案。

2. What does the speaker warn against?

(A) Leaving children unattended
(B) Using a camera
(C) Disturbing workers
(D) Making noise

2.說話者對何事提出警告？

(A) 放任小孩
(B) 使用相機
(C) 干擾工作者
(D) 發出噪音

正確答案

(B) Using a camera

解說

導覽中沒有直接表禁止或限制的句子，而是用了較客氣的說法 We would like to remind you that no photography is allowed on the factory floor.（提醒各位，廠區內不得拍照攝影。），所以正確答案是選項 (B)。

3. What are listeners asked to do?

(A) Complete a form
(B) Submit an application
(C) Visit a gift shop
(D) Purchase a product

3.聽眾被要求做何事？

(A) 填寫表格
(B) 提出申請
(C) 造訪禮品專賣店
(D) 購買產品

正確答案

(A) Complete a form

解說

導覽員在最後鼓勵參觀者填寫問卷（fill out a survey），以改善導覽品質，所以選項若符合上述，就是正確答案。因為填問卷也可以說是填表，所以選項 (A) 是正確答案。選項 (B) 的 application 是申請（書），例如到某些地方觀光時，旅客要填寫申請書，但導覽中沒有提到這部分。選項 (C) 和 (D) 也在導覽中沒有提到。

Duty Free Shopping

Item	Price
Crown Whiskey	$ 230
Gourmet Chocolates	$ 60
Diamond Perfume	$ 120
Stedman Cologne	$ 95

4. What does the speaker ask the passengers to do?
   (A) Purchase duty free items
   (B) Turn off their electronic devices
   (C) Set their seats to the upright position
   (D) Fasten their seatbelts

5. Look at the graphic. Which item can't be purchased during the flight?
   (A) Crown Whiskey
   (B) Gourmet Chocolates
   (C) Diamond Perfume
   (D) Stedman Cologne

6. What does the speaker say will be available to customers for free?
   (A) Duty free shopping
   (B) Beverages
   (C) In-flight meals
   (D) Internet use

PART
4

Chapter
05

觀光導覽

M Welcome aboard Northern Air Flight 007. The current temperature is 15 degrees Celsius and it's clear and sunny outside. The time is 3:45 p.m. Our destination is Toronto, Canada. The flight will take approximately four hours. We ask that all passengers keep all bags and other personal items stored safely in the overhead bins or under the seat in front of you.[4] **Please keep your seatbelts fastened whenever the seatbelt sign lights up.** Today passengers will also have a chance to shop for exclusive duty free items during the flight, so please check our duty-free magazine.
[5] **Unfortunately we are sold out of liquors, but the other items are still available for purchase.**
[6] **Once we reach cruising altitude, our cabin crew will come around with complimentary beverages.**

男：歡迎搭乘北方航空 007 號班機。目前外面的氣溫是攝氏 15 度，晴朗無雲。時間是下午三點四十五分。我們即將飛往加拿大多倫多。飛行時間預計是四個小時。請各位乘客將所有行李及其他個人物品安置在頭頂的置物櫃內，或座位下的前方踏腳處。當安全帶警示燈亮起時，請繫好您的安全帶。今日航班售有獨家免稅商品，乘客可翻閱免稅商品雜誌。酒類商品業已售罄，不過仍有其他品項可供選購。當飛機到達巡航高度，我們的機組人員將會為您送上免費飲料。

Duty Free Shopping

Item	Price
Crown Whiskey	$ 230
Gourmet Chocolates	$ 60
Diamond Perfume	$ 120
Stedman Cologne	$ 95

免稅商品購物品項

品項	價格
皇冠威士忌	$ 230
精選巧克力	$ 60
璀璨香水	$ 120
斯特德曼古龍水	$ 95

字彙

Celsius 攝氏　　　complimentary 免費贈送的　　　cologne 古龍水

4. What does the speaker ask the passengers to do?

(A) Purchase duty free items

(B) Turn off their electronic devices

(C) Set their seats to the upright position

(D) Fasten their seatbelts

4.說話者要求乘客做何事？

(A) 購買免稅商品

(B) 關掉電子用品

(C) 豎直椅背

(D) 繫好安全帶

正確答案

(D) Fasten their seatbelts

解説

說話者要求乘客在安全帶警示燈亮的時候，要繫上安全帶，所以正確答案是選項 (D)。說話者提到免稅商品的販售服務，但這不是要求乘客去做的事，所以 (A) 不能選。

---

5. Look at the graphic. Which item can't be purchased during the flight?

(A) Crown Whiskey

(B) Gourmet Chocolates

(C) Diamond Perfume

(D) Stedman Cologne

5.請看圖表。乘客無法在此次航程中購買何項物品？

(A) 皇冠威士忌

(B) 精選巧克力

(C) 璀璨香水

(D) 斯特德曼古龍水

正確答案

(A) Crown Whiskey

解説

說話者提到酒類已經賣完了，所以乘客不能購買酒類，選項中只有 (A) 是酒類，所以正確答案是 (A)。

6. What does the speaker say will be available to customers for free?

(A) Duty free shopping

(B) Beverages

(C) In-flight meals

(D) Internet use

6. 說話者提到顧客可以免費享用何物？

(A) 選購免稅品

(B) 飲品

(C) 飛機餐點

(D) 網路連線

正確答案

(B) Beverages

解說

説話者最後提到，機組人員會送上免費飲料（complimentary beverages），所以正確答案是選項 (B)。

1. Who most likely is the speaker?
   (A) A film director
   (B) An event organizer
   (C) An award winner
   (D) A theater owner

2. According to the speaker, what makes the event special?
   (A) It features famous directors and actors.
   (B) Its guests can enter free of charge.
   (C) It marks a 50th anniversary.
   (D) Its proceeds will be donated to charity.

3. What are listeners asked to do?
   (A) Fill out a survey
   (B) Buy a ticket
   (C) Pick up a program
   (D) Make a donation

4. According to the speaker what is happening?
   (A) A building is being renovated.
   (B) A new product is being released.
   (C) A festival is being celebrated.
   (D) A structure is being opened to the public.

5. What does the speaker mean when he says "hard to miss?"
   (A) The building looks similar to surrounding buildings.
   (B) The building is difficult to get to.
   (C) The building is easy to spot.
   (D) The building is still unfinished.

6. According to the speaker, what is the building's most important feature?
   (A) The volume and variety of books and videos
   (B) Its small size
   (C) Its membership
   (D) The location

1 題型暖身

STEP 1 聽獨白，選出與問題最為符合的回答。🎧 148

1. Where is the talk being given?
   (A) At a job fair
   (B) At a sports arena
   (C) At a school
   (D) At a business event

2. What did Ms. Sawyer do after she retired?
   (A) She earned a college degree.
   (B) She started a new job.
   (C) She founded a charity.
   (D) She moved to a different country.

3. What will Ms. Sawyer discuss?
   (A) Long-term investment strategies
   (B) Crisis management
   (C) Successful communication
   (D) The sports business world

M Tonight's guest speaker is athlete Debra Sawyer. **(1) Although a business conference may be a strange place for a soccer player to give a talk, I think what Ms. Sawyer has to say about teamwork on the soccer field applies to the workplace as well. (2) After Ms. Sawyer retired from professional women's soccer last year, she became a professional motivational speaker.** She has visited a lot of companies and schools in the country to spread her message of teamwork. **(3) Today she is going to share some methods for communicating effectively in the business world.** Now, please join me in welcoming Debra Sawyer.

男：今晚邀請到的客座講者是運動員黛博拉·索耶。雖然一名足球員在商業會議中發表演說看似突兀，但我相信索耶小姐將與我們分享的足球場上的團隊合作方式，同樣也可運用到職場上。索耶小姐自去年從女子職業足球退休之後，現已成為一名勵志演說家。她在國內諸多企業及學校發表演說，傳遞其關於團隊合作的心得。今日，她將與我們分享商業界的效率溝通方式。現在讓我們一同歡迎黛博拉·索耶。

字彙

give a talk 發表演說　　retire 退休　　motivational 激勵的
degree 學位　　investment 投資　　crisis 危機

---

1. Where is the talk being given?
(A) At a job fair
(B) At a sports arena
(C) At a school
(D) At a business event

1.演講在何處舉行？
(A) 工作博覽會
(B) 運動場
(C) 學校
(D) 商業活動場合

正確答案

(D) At a business event

介紹者一開始提到，演講者是運動員，接著又說足球員在商業會議
（business conference）發表演說，所以可知演講的地方是「商業會
議」。選項 (D) 將「商業會議」說成是「商業活動」也合理，所以是正確
答案。

2. What did Ms. Sawyer do after she retired?

(A) She earned a college degree.

(B) She started a new job.

(C) She founded a charity.

(D) She moved to a different country.

2.索耶小姐退休之後從事何事？

(A) 取得大學學位。

(B) 展開新工作。

(C) 成立慈善事業。

(D) 移居他國。

(B) She started a new job.

介紹者說，索耶女士去年退休後成了專業的勵志演說家（a professional
motivational speaker），所以可知，她從足球員職涯轉換了跑道。選項
(B) 將轉換職涯跑道，說成是展開新工作，所以是正確答案。介紹中有提
到，索耶女士演說的場所都在國內（in the country），並沒有搬到國外，
所以選項 (D) 和獨白的內容完全相反。

3. What will Ms. Sawyer discuss?

(A) Long-term investment strategies

(B) Crisis management

(C) Successful communication

(D) The sports business world

3.索耶小姐將要探討的主題是？

(A) 長期投資策略

(B) 危機處理

(C) 成功的溝通

(D) 運動商業界

(C) Successful communication

介紹者提到，他認為索耶女士演説的內容——在足球場上的團隊合作（team work），可運用到職場上。介紹的最後又提到一個小主題，就是效率溝通方式（methods for communicating effectively），選項若表達前述兩點或其中一點的，就是正確答案，因此最合適的是選項 (C)。

STEP 1 聽獨白，選出與問題最為符合的回答。🎧 149

4. What is the purpose of the announcement?
   (A) To introduce a new client
   (B) To announce a job opening
   (C) To welcome a new employee
   (D) To promote a sale

5. How does the speaker know Vince Tang?
   (A) They attended the same university.
   (B) They met at an awards ceremony.
   (C) They had a job interview on the same day.
   (D) They worked together previously.

6. According to the speaker, what is Vince Tang skilled at doing?
   (A) Solving technological issues
   (B) Running workshops
   (C) Assisting clients
   (D) Managing employees

M (4) **Next, I'd like to introduce our newest member of the Bailey Logistics team, Vince Tang.** (5) **I first met Mr. Tang when we both worked in the sales department at a different international logistics company.** Now I'm happy to work with him again at our company. (6) **Mr. Tang is a software expert and computer technician, and has always been able to fix any problem thrown his way.** Please join me in giving a warm welcome to Mr. Tang.

男：接下來，讓我來為大家介紹「貝禮物流團隊」的新成員，唐文斯。我認識唐先生的時候，我倆正在另一家國際物流公司的業務部任職。現在我很高興能再度與他在本公司共事。唐先生是軟體專家，也是電腦技師，所有的疑難雜症在他這總能迎刃而解。讓我們一起熱烈歡迎唐先生的加入。

字彙

logistics 物流　　expert 專家

4. What is the purpose of the announcement?

(A) To introduce a new client
(B) To announce a job opening
(C) To welcome a new employee
(D) To promote a sale

4.這個宣布的目的是？

(A) 介紹一名新客戶
(B) 宣告職務出缺
(C) 歡迎新進員工
(D) 促銷

正確答案

(C) To welcome a new employee

解說

說話者一開始說接下來（next），表示他要開始說下一個主題，也就是介紹一位新成員（newest member of the . . . team），所以正確答案是（C），它將 newest member 換成新員工（new employee）也是合理的。

5. How does the speaker know Vince Tang?

    (A) They attended the same university.

    (B) They met at an awards ceremony.

    (C) They had a job interview on the same day.

    (D) They worked together previously.

5.說話者如何認識唐文斯？

    (A) 他們上同一所大學。

    (B) 他們在一場頒獎典禮上見過。

    (C) 他們在同一天參加工作面試。

    (D) 他們以前共事過。

正確答案

(D) They worked together previously.

解說

題目問「怎麼認識某人」（how does someone know . . .），也就是問最初是在怎樣的情況下見面並認識的，這是詢問人物之間的關係時常見的題型。介紹人說他認識唐文斯的時候，他倆正在同一個部門（I first met . . . both worked in the sales department）工作，所以正確答案是選項(D)。

6. According to the speaker, what is Vince Tang skilled at doing?

    (A) Solving technological issues

    (B) Running workshops

    (C) Assisting clients

    (D) Managing employees

6.根據說話者，唐文斯的專長是？

    (A) 解決技術性問題

    (B) 舉辦研討會

    (C) 客戶協助

    (D) 管理員工

正確答案

(A) Solving technological issues

解說

在介紹的後段，談話者提到唐文斯是軟體專家與電腦技師（a software expert and computer technician），任何問題都能解決。所以選項(A)說「解決技術性問題」是正確的。

介紹

● 介紹類型的獨白,是在特定的集會場合,介紹演説者或主要人物。會問被介紹的人的**經歷**、**前職**、**現職**、**未來的工作**、**演說的主題**等。

解題戰略

1. 介紹播放之前,先瀏覽並掌握試題問的是什麼:**主題**、**細節**還是**推測**

2. 詢問主題的試題,要掌握介紹**最前面的部分**;詢問細節的試題,要掌握介紹中和 WH **疑問字詞**相關的線索,別忘了正確答案常會**改寫**(paraphrase)!

3. 推測類的試題,要掌握介紹的**最後面部分**。

STEP 1 聽獨白,選出與問題最為符合的回答。 ∩ 150

1. What is the purpose of the talk?
- (A) To explain a budget proposal
- (B) To decide on a new policy
- (C) To introduce a new employee
- (D) To announce an official event

2. What department do the listeners most likely belong to?
- (A) Sales
- (B) Accounting
- (C) Marketing
- (D) Personnel

3. What does the speaker say she wants to avoid?
- (A) Project delays
- (B) Customer complaints
- (C) Scheduling errors
- (D) Excessive expenditure

W Good morning, everyone. (1) **I would like to start off today's staff meeting by introducing you to our newest team member, Janet Price. (2) Ms. Price has been transferred from the marketing department and I think she is going to be a huge asset for us in the personnel department.** She also has previous experience working in the sales department of a different company. She will be in charge of taking care of employee paychecks and our department's budget. (3) **I am hoping that with her help we can avoid exceeding our allotted budget each month.** If you don't know her yet, I suggest you say hello after this meeting. Now, let's give Ms. Price a warm welcome.

女：大家早。今天部門會議一開始，我想向各位介紹我們的最新成員珍娜特·普萊斯。普萊斯小姐調自行銷部，將會是我們人資部重要的資產。她過去也曾待過另一家公司的業務部門；如今，她將掌管員工薪資以及本部的部門預算。希望藉由她的協助，能讓我們避免每個月的部門預算超支。如果你們還不認識她，我建議開完會後，大家可以跟她寒暄一下。現在，讓我們熱烈歡迎普萊斯小姐。

字彙

transfer 轉調　　asset 資產　　personnel department 人事部
budget 預算　　exceed 超出（額度）　　allotted 分配的

1. What is the purpose of the talk?
   (A) To explain a budget proposal
   (B) To decide on a new policy
   (C) To introduce a new employee
   (D) To announce an official event

1.這個談話的目的是？
   (A) 說明預算案
   (B) 裁決新政策
   (C) 引見新員工
   (D) 宣告官方活動

正確答案

(C) To introduce a new employee

説話者一開始就説明了她談話的目的，介紹一位新員工（I . . . introducing you to our newest team member），所以目的是「介紹新員工」，因此正確答案是 (C)。選項 (D) 將介紹員工説成是「官方活動」，是不對的。在這介紹中也沒談到關於政策的主題，所以選項 (B) 不對。

2. What department do the listeners most likely belong to?

(A) Sales

(B) Accounting

(C) Marketing

(D) Personnel

2.聽眾最有可能是屬於哪個部門？

(A) 業務部

(B) 會計部

(C) 行銷部

(D) 人事部

正確答案

(D) Personnel

解説

題目問聽眾工作的部門，這點要注意。在介紹普萊斯小姐時，介紹者説她從行銷部（marketing department）轉到我們人事部（. . . for us in the personnel department），所以正確答案是 (D)。這題細節題頗有難度，因為介紹者説了普萊斯小姐以前的經歷以及未來的工作，她之前曾在另一家公司的業務部工作，又説今後她要管理員工薪資及預算等，許多職務名稱很容易讓人弄混。

3. What does the speaker say she wants to avoid?

(A) Project delays

(B) Customer complaints

(C) Scheduling errors

(D) Excessive expenditure

3.説話者説她想要避免什麼事？

(A) 計畫延遲

(B) 顧客投訴

(C) 時程安排出錯

(D) 超額支出

正確答案

(D) Excessive expenditure

介紹者説，希望在普萊斯小姐的幫助下，避免每個月的部門預算超支（avoid exceeding our allotted budget each month），所以選項（D）將 exceed . . . budget 改説成 excessive expenditure（超額支出），是正確答案。

STEP 1　聽獨白，選出與問題最為符合的回答。🎧 151

4. What field does Casey Harper work in?
   (A) Marketing
   (B) Advertising
   (C) News
   (D) Medicine

5. According to Casey Harper, what is true about American teenagers?
   (A) Boys drink more soda than girls on average.
   (B) Boys exercise more regularly than girls.
   (C) Girls prefer drinking milk instead of soda.
   (D) Girls spend more money on snacks than boys.

6. What will the speaker probably do next?
   (A) Introduce a host
   (B) Discuss a certain study with a guest
   (C) Answer some questions
   (D) Try a new soda

W Welcome to *Sunday Review*. I'm your host, Mary O'Neil. Today our guest is Dr. Casey Harper. **(4)(6) She'll be discussing the findings of her new research on the effect of soft drinks on the health of teenagers. (5) The most shocking finding is that the average American teenage boy drinks an average of one can of soda every day. In contrast, teenage girls only drink an average of three cans of soda per week.** Dr. Harper says it is important to talk to your children about limiting soda consumption because it is a major contributing factor to the development of diabetes. Now, let's welcome Dr. Harper.

女：歡迎收聽《週日評論》。我是主持人瑪麗・歐尼爾。今天邀請到的來賓是凱西・哈珀博士。她最近正就飲料對青少年的健康造成的影響進行研究，今日將與我們討論其新的研究發現。其中最驚人的發現是，美國青少年平均每天喝下一罐蘇打汽水。相對地，青少女每週平均喝下三罐汽水。哈珀博士提到，告誡孩子減少汽水的攝取量非常重要，因為它是糖尿病的主要成因。現在，讓我們歡迎哈珀博士。

字彙

host 主持人　　findings 調查結果　　soft drink （不含酒精的）飲料
teenage 十幾歲的　　an average of 平均　　consumption 攝取
contributing factor 形成原因　　diabetes 糖尿病

---

4. What field does Casey Harper work in?

(A) Marketing

(B) Advertising

(C) News

(D) Medicine

4.凱西・哈珀研究的領域是？

(A) 行銷

(B) 廣告

(C) 新聞

(D) 醫學

正確答案

(D) Medicine

主持人在介紹凱西・哈珀博士時，沒有直接提到她從事的工作，所以只能由她在節目討論的主題推論她的工作。哈珀博士要討論的是美國青少年男女飲料的攝取量，並說攝取飲料和糖尿病有直接的關係。由此來推測她工作的領域，應該是和醫學有關，所以正確答案是選項 (D)。

5. According to Casey Harper, what is true about American teenagers?

(A) Boys drink more soda than girls on average.

(B) Boys exercise more regularly than girls.

(C) Girls prefer drinking milk instead of soda.

(D) Girls spend more money on snacks than boys.

5.根據凱西・哈珀，關於美國青少年，下列何者為真？

(A) 男孩平均比女孩喝下更多的汽水。

(B) 男孩較女孩更常做運動。

(C) 比起汽水，女孩更喜歡喝牛奶。

(D) 女孩比男孩花更多的錢購買零食。

正確答案

(A) Boys drink more soda than girls on average.

解説

在介紹研究結果的地方，將青少年區分成青少年和青少女，這部分要仔細聽清楚。青少年平均每天攝取一罐蘇打汽水，青少女平均每週攝取三罐蘇打汽水，因此青少年攝取蘇打汽水的量多於青少女，所以選項 (A) 是正確答案。要注意表對照的片語 in contrast（與……相比；相對地），常常是考點所在。介紹中並沒有提到運動、牛奶、零食等，所以 (B)、(C)、(D) 都錯。

6. What will the speaker probably do next?

 (A) Introduce a host

 (B) Discuss a certain study with a guest

 (C) Answer some questions

 (D) Try a new soda

6.說話者接下來最有可能做何事？

 (A) 介紹主持人

 (B) 與來賓探討某項研究

 (C) 回答提問

 (D) 試飲新款蘇打汽水

正確答案

(B) Discuss a certain study with a guest

解說

主持人開始介紹哈珀博士時，提到博士將討論有關她新研究的發現（discussing the findings of her new research），所以正確答案是選項(B)。主持人是介紹來賓，不是介紹主持人本身，所以(A) 錯。

1. Where is the introduction taking place?
- (A) At an awards ceremony
- (B) At a training session
- (C) At a university lecture
- (D) At a business event

2. Who is Mr. Cameron?
- (A) A consumer
- (B) A professor
- (C) An executive
- (D) An inventor

3. According to the speaker, what will happen after Mr. Cameron's talk?
- (A) A lecturer will be introduced.
- (B) A product will be revealed.
- (C) A meal will be served.
- (D) A prize winner will be announced.

4. Who is Kathy Hill?
- (A) An artist
- (B) A florist
- (C) An art critic
- (D) A radio host

5. According to the speaker, what did Kathy Hill do in China?
- (A) She learned the Chinese language.
- (B) She researched local traditions.
- (C) She engaged in creative activities.
- (D) She held an exhibition.

6. What are listeners encouraged to do?
- (A) Purchase a vase
- (B) Secure a ticket
- (C) Attend a class
- (D) Arrive early

聽獨白，選出與問題最為符合的回答。∩ 153

1. In what field does the speaker most likely work?
   (A) Banking
   (B) Advertising
   (C) Finance
   (D) Manufacturing

2. What is the purpose of the message?
   (A) To hire a model
   (B) To reschedule a meeting
   (C) To order a product
   (D) To introduce an agent

3. What does the speaker ask the listener to do?
   (A) Return a phone call
   (B) Submit an annual report
   (C) Expedite shipping
   (D) Provide some information

4. Where will the event take place?
   (A) At a park
   (B) At a museum
   (C) At a theater
   (D) At a school

5. What will happen after the talk?
   (A) A video will be shown.
   (B) A question-and-answer session will be held.
   (C) A film critic will be introduced.
   (D) A document will be handed out.

6. What is said about the event?
   (A) It is scheduled on a weekend.
   (B) It is open to professors at no charge.
   (C) It will be broadcast on television.
   (D) It will be held outdoors.

BATTLE OF THE BANDS BALLOT

Band Name	Lyrics 10	Performance 10	Percussion 10	Rhythm 10
Princely Fire	7	7	6	7
Road Blues	6	8	7	7
Singing Sisters	6	9	9	10
Lonely Roy	9	5	5	10

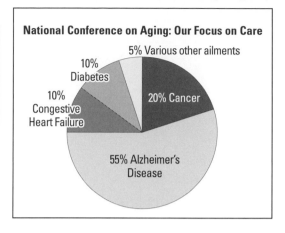

7. Who is likely giving the talk?
- (A) The Battle of the Bands coordinator
- (B) The Battle of the Bands volunteer engineer
- (C) The local radio host
- (D) A newspaper reporter

8. Look at the graphic. What could you predict about Singing Sisters?
- (A) They will be successful.
- (B) They will sell a lot of T-shirts.
- (C) Next year they will participate again.
- (D) They will record an album at Wonderlix Studios.

9. What will likely change about the Battle of the Bands next year?
- (A) There will be more bands.
- (B) There will be a lot of newspaper articles.
- (C) There will be T-shirts and more sponsors.
- (D) The winner will record an album at Wonderlix Studios.

10. What topic would the audience at this conference be interested in?
- (A) Elderly care
- (B) Teenage life
- (C) Birth control
- (D) New medicine to treat cancer

11. Look at the graphic. Which disease probably concerns the audience the most?
- (A) Diabetes
- (B) Alzheimer's disease
- (C) Congestive heart failure
- (D) Cancer

12. According to the speaker, what is true about Lauren James?
- (A) She will be giving a speech with another keynote speaker.
- (B) She will be giving a speech on work ethics.
- (C) She has worked closely with Jerry Sighburgh.
- (D) She is not a famous expert.

MEMO

中譯＋解析

1. B   2. D   3. C   4. B   5. A   6. D

1.

(A) The man is assisting a shopper.
(B) The man is reaching for an item.
(C) The man is folding up an apron.
(D) The man is sharpening a tool.

翻譯 (A) 男子正協助顧客購物。
(B) 男子正伸手拿取物品。
(C) 男子正在折疊圍裙。
(D) 男子正磨銳工具。

解說 reach for 這個片語雖然沒有手（hand）這單字在裡面，但它表示「手伸出去拿東西」的意思，這點要注意。所以正確答案是選項 (B)。(C) 的主詞和受詞圍裙（apron）都有出現在照片中，但是並沒有折疊（folding）的動作，所以是錯誤答案。

字彙 assist 協助　fold 折疊
sharpen 使銳利

2.

(A) A man is examining some wooden planks.
(B) Some boards are being loaded onto a truck.
(C) A construction site is being cleared.
(D) Some building materials are stacked up.

翻譯 (A) 男子正在檢視木板。
(B) 一些木板正被裝上貨車。
(C) 建築工地正被清空。
(D) 一些建材成堆疊放。

解說 每個選項中的主詞、受詞、動詞都不一樣，很容易弄混，要特別注意。(A) 的主詞 a man 和正在檢查（examine）的動作，都有在照片中出現，不過受詞不是木板，所以不能選。
選項 (B) 的卡車（truck）和木板（board）都有看到，不過正在承載（are being loaded）這個動作沒辦法確認，所以也是錯的。正確答案是沒有說明人物，只說明照片中某一部分事物狀態的選項 (D)。

字彙 examine 檢查　board 木板
construction site 建築工地
building material 建築材料

3.

(A) He's making a sandwich.

(B) He's watching a TV program.

(C) He's wearing a suit.

(D) He's adjusting his necktie.

翻譯 (A) 他正在做三明治。

　　(B) 他正在收看電視節目。

　　(C) 他穿著一套西裝。

　　(D) 他在調整領帶。

解說 (A)、(B)、(D) 都是在說明照片中人物的動作，而選項 (C) 和這些相反，它用 is wearing 表示目前男子穿著的狀態，也就是在描述人物的外貌，這點要注意。(A)、(B)、(D) 的動作都無法從照片中確認，所以選項 (C) 是正確答案。

字彙 adjust 調整

4.

(A) The man is exiting the laboratory.

(B) The man has goggles on.

(C) The man is taking off his gloves.

(D) The man is stacking glass containers.

翻譯 (A) 男子正走出實驗室。

　　(B) 男子有戴護目鏡。

　　(C) 男子正把手套脫掉。

　　(D) 男子正在疊放玻璃容器。

解說 本題要掌握動詞和後方受詞的關係。因為 exit、stack 的動作沒辦法從照片中確認，所以 (A)、(D) 不能選。take off 表示「脫掉穿或戴的衣物」，(C) 的手套，男子正戴在手上，並沒有脫掉的動作，所以也不對。正確答案是選項 (B)。

字彙 take off 脫掉　stack 堆疊

5.

(A) He's leaning over the engine.

(B) He's dialing a phone number.

(C) He's opening the vehicle's hood.

(D) He's filling the car with gas.

翻譯 (A) 他正俯身向著引擎。

　　(B) 他正在打電話。

　　(C) 他正打開車子的引擎蓋。

　　(D) 他正在替車子加油。

解說 選項的主詞都一樣，動詞都是現在進行式，所以正確掌握男子正在進行的動作，就能立刻解題。(D) 加汽油，從男子的手部動作來看，不像在加油，所以是錯的。而撥電話號碼（dialing a phone number）這動作，男子的手必須正在按電話鍵盤才對。另外，車廂蓋已經打開了，所以選項 (B)、(C) 也都不對。正確答案是選項 (A)。

字彙 dial 撥打　lean over 俯身向前

6.

(A) She's typing on the keyboard.

(B) She's turning on a computer monitor.

(C) She's examining a seating chart.

(D) She's sipping from a cup.

翻譯 (A) 她正在鍵盤上打字。

　　(B) 她正替電腦螢幕開機。

　　(C) 她正在檢視座位表。

　　(D) 她正啜飲杯中物。

解說 本題只要正確掌握人物的動作，就能解題。照片均出現鍵盤和螢幕，不過和照片中人的動作沒有連結，所以 (A) 和 (B) 是錯的。女子正在看的東西不像是座位表（seating chart），所以 (C) 也是錯的。一般來說，和醫療有關的圖表或資

料，會用 chart 來表示，要特別注意，不要弄混了。正確答案是選項 (D)。

字彙 seating chart 座位表

Mini Test **Chapter 02** p. 033
以 **2** 人以上為中心的照片

---

1. D　2. C　3. B　4. C　5. A　6. D

1.

(A) A man is writing on a clipboard.
(B) Both of the men are talking on radios.
(C) A man is rolling up some documents.
(D) One of the men is wearing glasses.

翻譯 (A) 一名男子正在寫字板上書寫。
　　　(B) 兩名男子都在使用無線對講機說話。
　　　(C) 一名男子正捲起一些文件。
　　　(D) 其中一名男子戴著眼鏡。

解說 這是主詞和動詞容易混淆的題目。照片中的兩個男子，都沒有出現寫（writing）的動作，所以 (A) 是錯的。用對講機講話的男子只有左邊這一位，所以 (B) 也是錯的。選項 (D) 說，其中一名男子戴著眼鏡，正確描述了右邊男子的外貌，所以 (D) 是正確答案。

字彙 clipboard 寫字夾板　roll up 捲起

2.

(A) Some folders are being collected from the people.
(B) There are some documents under the table.
(C) One of the men is gesturing to the other man.
(D) One of the women is giving a presentation.

翻譯 (A) 人們手裡的文件夾正被收回。
　　　(B) 桌子下有一些文件。
　　　(C) 其中一名男子正對另一名男子做手勢。
　　　(D) 其中一名女子正在做簡報。

解說 注意照片中的人和事物就能解題。選項 (B) 提到了照片中的桌子和文件，不仔細看很容易選錯，因為文件是在桌子上面，不是在下面，所以選項 (B) 是錯的。(A) 和 (D) 都沒辦法從照片中確認。選項 (C) 是正確答案，因為它正確描述左邊男子的動作。

字彙 gesture 做手勢

3.

(A) They are signing a contract.
(B) Two men are shaking hands.
(C) Both of the men are facing the window.
(D) A man is greeting some customers.

翻譯 (A) 他們正在簽約。
　　　(B) 兩名男子正在握手。
　　　(C) 兩名男子都面對著窗戶。
　　　(D) 一名男子正在招呼顧客。

解說 因為圖片中兩名男子正在握手，所以 (B) 正確。(A) 和 (C) 的動作沒有出現在照片中。(D) 也是錯的，因為和其中一名男子（a man）打招呼的顧客們（customers）並未出現於照片中。

字彙 shake hands 握手　greet 迎接

4.

(A) One of the women is opening a notepad.
(B) One of the men is passing out some documents.
(C) One of the women is resting her arms on the table.
(D) One of the men is pouring coffee into cups.

翻譯 (A) 其中一名女子正打開記事本。
　　 (B) 其中一名男子正在分發文件。
　　 (C) 其中一名女子將手臂擱放在桌上。
　　 (D) 其中一名男子正將咖啡倒入杯中。

解說 本題解題關鍵，在於能區分已經完成的事和正在進行的事。女子的記事本已經打開了，所以選項 (A) 用現在進行式 is opening 是錯的。(B) 是沒有發生的事。(C) 的 resting her arms on the table，其中的 rest 在這裡不是「休息」，而是表「擱放」，要特別注意，正確答案是 (C)。

字彙 rest arms on 手臂擱放在
pass out 分發　pour 倒入

5.

(A) They're looking at a screen.
(B) They're standing by a door.
(C) They're putting a laptop into a case.
(D) They're exiting the meeting room.

翻譯 (A) 他們正看著電腦螢幕。
　　 (B) 他們正站在門邊。
　　 (C) 他們正把手提電腦收進提套裡。
　　 (D) 他們正走出會議室。

解說 選項 (C) 的筆電（laptop），照片中有出現，不過並沒有放進提套裡，所以是錯的。(B) 與 (D) 是沒有發生的事，正確答案是 (A)。

字彙 exit 離開

6.

(A) One of the men is pointing at a toolbox.
(B) Both of the men are using tools.
(C) One man is handing a screw to another.
(D) One man is bending over under the hood.

翻譯 (A) 其中一名男子正指著工具箱。
　　 (B) 兩名男子都正在使用工具。
　　 (C) 其中一名男子正把螺絲遞給另一名男子。
　　 (D) 其中一名男子正彎身在引擎蓋下。

解說 掌握兩名男子各自的動作，立刻就能解題。(A) 說其中一名男子正在指某物品，這個動作可以在照片中看到，不過並不是在指工具箱，所以 (A) 不對。因為正在使用工具的男子只有一名，所以 (B) 也不對。(C) 是沒有發生的事。正確答案是選項 (D)。

字彙 toolbox 工具箱　tool 工具
screw 螺絲　hood 引擎蓋

1. C 2. B 3. B 4. C 5. B 6. D

1.

(A) Some customers are looking at a menu.
(B) One of the men is carrying a laptop.
(C) The server is standing by the table.
(D) One of the women is clearing some dishes.

翻譯 (A) 一些顧客正在看菜單。
(B) 其中一名男子正拿著手提電腦。
(C) 服務生正站在桌子旁。
(D) 其中一名女子正在清理碗盤。

解說 先觀察照片中出現的事物，然後聽選項，就很容易解題了。照片中只有一位女子在看菜單，且沒有出現盤子，所以 (A) 和 (D) 不對。(B) 用了動詞 carry，也就是正在「搬運；帶著某物移動」的意思，但照片中沒有出現這動作，所以也不對。正確答案是選項 (C)，它正確描述出服務生與物品之間的關係。

字彙 server 服務生；侍者

2.

(A) The men are sorting some building materials.
(B) One of the men is holding a steering wheel.
(C) One of the men is pointing to himself.
(D) The men are riding to a construction site.

翻譯 (A) 這群男子正在為建材分類。
(B) 其中一名男子正手握方向盤。
(C) 其中一名男子正指著自己。
(D) 這些男子正乘車前往建築工地。

解說 正確掌握各選項主詞和動詞的關係，就能立刻解題。選項 (A) sort（分類）的動作沒有在照片中出現，所以是錯的。選項 (B)、(C)、(D) 的動詞都有在照片中出現，照片中有看到男子正在「指」（point）的動作，不過不是在「指」他自己，所以 (C) 是錯誤答案。
ride to 表示「騎乘交通工具前往某處」，但目的地是否為建築工地（construction site）則無法從照片中確認，所以 (D) 也是錯的。正確答案是選項 (B)，它正確描述出最左側男子手握方向盤的動作。

字彙 sort 分類整理
steering wheel 方向盤

3.

(A) Some paintings are being hung on the wall.
(B) People are walking past some artwork.
(C) Lights are suspended from the ceiling.
(D) A tour group has gathered at an aquarium.

翻譯 (A) 幾幅畫作正被懸掛在牆上。
(B) 人們正從藝術品前走過。
(C) 電燈自天花板懸掛著。
(D) 一個旅遊團體在水族館集合。

解說 解題關鍵在動詞的時態上。選項 (A) are being hung 以「現在進行被動語態」，表示「正被掛在……」，因為牆壁上已經掛著畫了，所以 (A) 是錯的。(C) 的 suspended from，是表空間中懸掛著某物的狀態，因為燈是固定安裝在畫作的上方，不是懸掛著的，所以 (C) 也不對。正確答案是選項 (B)，請注意，painting（畫作）也可説成是 artwork（藝術品）。

字彙 artwork 藝術品   aquarium 水族館

4.

(A) The table has been covered with a cloth.
(B) They're glancing out the window.
(C) One of the chairs is unoccupied.
(D) Beverages are being served from a teapot.

翻譯 (A) 桌子上已鋪了桌巾。
　　(B) 他們正瞥向窗外。
　　(C) 其中一個椅子沒有人坐。
　　(D) 飲品正從茶壺中倒出端上。

解說 掌握好照片中人和事物的細節，就能解題。照片中的桌子並沒有被布蓋著，所以 (A) 是錯誤答案。(B) 也不對，因為照片中的兩個人，沒有一個人是向窗外看的。選項 (D) 的 being served 是直接從茶壺 (teapot) 將飲品倒到杯子裡的動作，但照片中沒有這動作，所以也是錯的。正確答案是選項 (C)。

字彙 glance 匆匆瞥看
　　unoccupied 未被佔用的

5.

(A) One of the men is folding some papers.
(B) One of the women is holding a notepad.
(C) People are leaving a meeting room.
(D) Some physicians are examining a patient.

翻譯 (A) 其中一名男子正在折疊一些報告。
　　(B) 其中一名女子手裡正拿著記事本。
　　(C) 人們正離開會議室。
　　(D) 一些醫生正在為病人做檢查。

解說 注意每個選項的主詞以及人物的動作，就能解題。(A) 和 (C) 的動作沒辦法從照片中確認。選項 (D) 的主詞 physicians，不一定只是指「醫生」，也可以指「醫療人員」，不過 (D) 所描述的情形和照片不一致，所以選項 (D) 也是錯的。examine 和 patient 搭配使用時，表「診斷」。正確答案是選項 (B)。

字彙 physician 醫生；醫療人員
　　examine 檢查

6.

(A) A walkway has been blocked.
(B) Some lampposts are being replaced.
(C) People are strolling in a meadow.
(D) Shadows are being cast on the ground.

翻譯 (A) 通道被封閉了。
　　(B) 一些路燈柱正被置換。
　　(C) 人們在草地上散步。
　　(D) 陰影正被投射到地面上。

解說 各選項的主詞都有出現在照片中，所以要仔細聽，掌握細節，就能解題。道路並沒有被封閉，路燈柱也沒有正在被置換 (are being replaced)，所以 (A) 和 (B) 都不對。(C) 的 meadow，是指一片草地，但照片中沒有草地。正確答案是選項 (D)，它關注在照片中的細節——影子 (shadow)。cast 有很多意思，跟影子搭配使用時，是「投射」的意思，要注意。

字彙 meadow 草地
　　cast shadow on 在……上投下陰影

1. A   2. B   3. C   4. C   5. D   6. C

1.

(A) Various objects have been placed on the furniture.
(B) Broken pots have been left on the floor.
(C) Some pottery has been packed into containers.
(D) Some vases have been filled with flowers.

翻譯 (A) 各種物品被擺放在家具上。
　　(B) 破罐子被遺留在地上。
　　(C) 有些陶器被裝進箱子。
　　(D) 有些花瓶插著花。

解說 觀察照片物品的細節就能解題。選項 (C) 說一些陶器裝在箱子裡（has been packed into containers），在照片中並沒有看到箱子，所以是錯誤答案。選項 (D) 的花（flowers）也沒有出現在照片中。正確答案是選項 (A)，它將瓶瓶罐罐描述成物品（objects），然後用「家具」表達物品放置的地方。這種把同類事物，用概括的字詞表達的選項，要特別注意。

字彙 various 各種的　pot 瓶罐
　　pottery 陶器

2.

(A) Lines are being painted on the street.
(B) Flags are hanging from some poles.
(C) Trees are being planted along a road.
(D) Vehicles are stopped at an intersection.

翻譯 (A) 路面上正漆著車道線。
　　(B) 旗子正從旗桿上懸掛而下。
　　(C) 行道樹正被沿路栽種。
　　(D) 車輛被擋在在十字路口。

解說 (A) 的 line 是車道線，照片中並沒有正在畫車道線，所以是錯的。選項 (B) 是正確答案，它正確地用複數形表現照片中出現的國旗和旗桿。

字彙 flag 旗子　pole 杆子
　　intersection 十字路口

3.

(A) Some windmills are being erected.
(B) Waves are crashing on the shore.
(C) Ducks are floating on the water.
(D) A bridge passes over a waterway.

翻譯 (A) 風車正被建造起來。
　　(B) 海浪正衝擊著海岸。
　　(C) 鴨子漂游在水面上。
　　(D) 橋梁橫跨在河道上。

解說 erect 是動詞，表示「豎立」或「建立」，照片中的風車已經建造完成了，所以 (A) 是錯的。本題的考點不是照片中心的風車，而是照片的細節——鴨子，(C) 正確描述鴨子漂游在水面上，所以是正確答案。

字彙 windmill 風車　shore 海岸
　　　 float 漂浮

4.

(A) A road leads to a forest.
(B) A shutter is being closed.
(C) A vehicle is parked in a garage.
(D) A driveway has been resurfaced.

翻譯 (A) 道路通往森林。
　　 (B) 鐵捲門正被拉下來。
　　 (C) 一輛車停在車庫裡。
　　 (D) 車道路面已翻新。

解說 本題正確掌握動詞，就能解題。(A) 無
　　 法從照片中確認。選項 (B) 的正被拉
　　 下（is being closed），和照片右方已
　　 被拉下的鐵捲門不符合。正確答案是
　　 選項 (C)。選項 (D) 用現在完成被動
　　 語態，描述車道已經重鋪（has been
　　 resurfaced），也很難從照片中確認，
　　 故為錯誤答案。

字彙 shutter 捲簾鐵門；百葉窗
　　　 driveway 車道　resurface 重鋪路面

5.

(A) The walkway in the plaza is being
    replaced.
(B) Umbrellas have been set up on the
    beach.
(C) A crowd has gathered at an outdoor
    arena.
(D) Railings run along the exterior of the
    building.

翻譯 (A) 廣場上的走道正在修整。
　　 (B) 遮陽傘被豎立在海灘上。
　　 (C) 人群聚集在戶外表演場地。
　　 (D) 欄杆沿著大樓外牆架設。

解說 正確答案是選項 (D)，其中 run along
　　 照字面解釋，是「沿著……跑」，不過在
　　 這裡是「沿著……分布」的意思，要特
　　 別注意。選項 (B) umbrella 設置的地
　　 方不是海灘（beach），所以不對。選項
　　 (C) 的群眾（crowd），照片中有出現，不
　　 過並沒有看到表演場地（arena），所以
　　 也不對。

字彙 walkway 走道　umbrella 雨傘
　　　 arena 表演或競技場所　railing 欄杆
　　　 run along 沿著……分布

6.

(A) Buttons are being pressed on a device.
(B) A screen is being installed on the
    equipment.
(C) A credit card is being inserted into a
    machine.
(D) An ID card is being presented to a
    clerk.

翻譯 (A) 裝置上的按鍵正被按下。
　　 (B) 設備的螢幕正在進行安裝。
　　 (C) 信用卡正被放進機器中。
　　 (D) 身分證被出示給職員看。

解說 選項的動詞全都是「現在進行被動語
　　 態」，因此解題的關鍵，要特別注意正
　　 在進行的動作。正確答案是選項 (C)，
　　 其中卡片（card）是動作的承受者，動
　　 詞用 is being inserted，正確表達信
　　 用卡正被放入的動作。選項 (D) 是錯
　　 的，因為照片中沒有出現身分證（ID
　　 card），也沒出現職員（clerk）。(A) 和
　　 (B) 都是照片中沒有出現的動作。

字彙 device 裝置　screen 螢幕
　　　 credit card 信用卡　ID card 身分證
　　　 present 出示

1. C 2. D 3. A 4. C 5. C 6. A

1.

(A) She's talking on the phone.
(B) She's installing some equipment.
(C) She's gazing ahead.
(D) She's repairing a headset.

翻譯 (A) 她正在講電話。
(B) 她正在安裝某種設備。
(C) 她正盯著前方。
(D) 她正在修理頭戴式耳機。

解說 可用刪除法來解題，觀察人物的動作，刪除錯誤的答案。照片中的人並沒有談話；有戴耳機，但並沒有修理（repairing）的動作，所以 (A) 和 (D) 都不對。(B) 的動作並沒有在照片中出現。gaze 是「盯著、凝視」的意思，所以 (C) 是正確答案。

字彙 gaze 盯著；凝視

2.

(A) One of the men is sweeping the hallway.
(B) The men are greeting each other.
(C) One of the men is selling a newspaper.
(D) Some windows line the corridor.

翻譯 (A) 其中一名男子正在打掃走廊。
(B) 男子正互相打招呼。
(C) 其中一名男子正在販售報紙。
(D) 窗戶沿著走廊裝設。

解說 確認了選項中的動詞，就能解題。sweep 是「拿著掃帚清掃」，所以 (A) 不對。照片中的男子並沒有在賣報紙，所以 (C) 也不對。照片中的兩個人都一邊看報紙一邊走路，並沒有在打招

呼（greet），選項 (B) 錯。選項 (D) 中，line 當動詞使用時是「沿著……排成一列」，用來描述照片中窗戶的狀態，所以 (D) 是正確答案。

字彙 sweep 打掃　greet 打招呼
line (v.) 沿著……排成一列

3.

(A) The buildings have more than one story.
(B) Pedestrians are passing through a narrow walkway.
(C) Potted plants have been arranged on some steps.
(D) The entrance of the street is under construction.

翻譯 (A) 建築物不只有一層樓。
(B) 行人正穿行在狹窄的通道中。
(C) 盆栽被擺放在階梯上。
(D) 街道的入口正在施工。

解說 觀察照片的內容和各選項主詞之間的關係，就能解題。選項 (B) 的行人，在照片中並沒有出現。選項 (C)，照片中的花盆是被擺放好了（have been arranged），但不是放在階梯上，所以 (C) 也不對。正確答案是 (A)。

字彙 story 樓層　walkway 通道；走道
entrance 入口

4.

(A) A light is being turned on.
(B) Gloves are being distributed to workers.
(C) Some equipment is being operated.
(D) Boxes are being moved into a building.

翻譯 (A) 燈正開著。
　　　(B) 手套正被分發給工人們。
　　　(C) 某個設備正在運作。
　　　(D) 箱子正被搬進一棟建築物內。

解說 選項的動詞全都是「現在進行被動語態」，所以要好好掌握照片裡的動作。(A) 的動作在照片中並沒有出現，所以不對。選項 (B)，照片中只出現一個人，而且已經戴著手套了，所以和照片中的狀況不符。正確答案是 (C)。選項 (D) 說正在移動的物品是盒子（box），而且是要移到建築物裡，這些從照片中都無法確認，所以選項 (D) 也不能選。

字彙 distribute 分發　operate 運作；操作

5.

(A) A plant is being trimmed.
(B) Some gardening tools are being sharpened.
(C) A hole is being dug in the ground.
(D) The man is washing a shovel.

翻譯 (A) 植物的枝葉正被修剪。
　　　(B) 園藝工具正被磨利。
　　　(C) 地面正被開挖出一個洞。
　　　(D) 男子正在清洗鐵鏟。

解說 trim 和植物搭配使用，是修剪枝葉的意思，和照片中的情況不同，所以 (A) 是錯的。正確答案是選項 (C)，為了種植物，地面正被開挖出一個洞。選項 (C) 的主詞不是人，而是人挖的洞（hole），這點要注意。

字彙 trim 修剪　gardening 園藝
　　　sharpen 磨鋒利　shovel 鐵鏟

6.

(A) Two sections of the bridge have been raised.
(B) Boats are floating near a cliff.
(C) People are swimming toward a sailboat.
(D) A canal is flowing past a forest.

翻譯 (A) 橋的兩段已被拉起。
　　　(B) 船隻漂行在峭壁附近。
　　　(C) 人們正往帆船方向游去。
　　　(D) 運河流經一座森林。

解說 (A) 的 section 是「部分；片段」，也可當作劃分出來的土地或地區，這點要注意。選項 (B) 和 (C) 沒辦法從照片中確認。選項 (D) 的 forest 並沒有在照片中出現。所以正確答案是 (A)。

字彙 section 部分；片段　cliff 峭壁
　　　sailboat 帆船　canal 運河

Chapter 01 p. 094

WH 疑問句

1. C	2. B	3. A	4. A	5. C
6. C	7. B	8. B	9. B	10. A
11. B	12. B	13. C	14. A	15. A

1. Who should I ask about updating the software on the office computers?
(A) I'm updating my wardrobe soon.
(B) My computer software is working fine.
(C) You should call the technical department.

翻譯　辦公室電腦的軟體要升級，我應該向誰詢問？
　　　(A) 我的衣櫃很快就要換季了。
　　　(B) 我的電腦軟體運作尚可。
　　　(C) 你應該打電話給技術部門。

解說　本題詢問辦公室電腦的軟體要升級的話，要詢問誰。選項 (C) 回答說，打電話去問技術部門，是最合適的回答。

字彙　wardrobe 衣櫃

2. Who chose the wallpaper for the apartment?
(A) I spilt juice on my wallpaper.
(B) My wife picked it out.
(C) We had better get a new apartment.

翻譯　公寓的壁紙是誰選的？
　　　(A) 我把果汁灑到壁紙上了。
　　　(B) 我妻子選的。
　　　(C) 我們最好買間新公寓。

解說　問話者詢問公寓的壁紙是誰選的。選項 (B) 回答說，是我太太挑的，是最合適的回答。

字彙　wallpaper 壁紙　spill 使灑出；使濺出

3. Who'd like to help me out with this new project I'm working on?
(A) I'd like to be involved.
(B) This project is going well.
(C) Six months ago I did a project.

翻譯　誰願意幫忙我正在進行的新計畫？
　　　(A) 我願意參與。
　　　(B) 這個計畫進行得順利。
　　　(C) 六個月前我執行了一個計畫。

解說　問話者詢問誰要來幫忙新計畫。選項 (A) 回答說，我願意參與，是最合適的回答。

字彙　involve 使參與

4. Where'd you find that beautiful sweater?
(A) I bought it from a small boutique.
(B) I always wear beautiful sweaters.
(C) I found your sweater.

翻譯　你是在哪裡找到那件漂亮的毛衣的？
　　　(A) 我在一家精品小店買的。
　　　(B) 我總是穿著漂亮的毛衣。
　　　(C) 我找到你的毛衣了。

解說　本題問美麗的毛衣是在哪裡買的。選項 (A) 回答說，在精品小店買的，是最合適的回答。

字彙　boutique 精品店

5. Where did you book our hotel?
(A) Alex said to go to the hotel.
(B) I booked it for ten thirty.
(C) I thought you booked it.

翻譯 你是在哪裡訂旅館的？
　　(A) 艾力克斯說要去旅館。
　　(B) 我訂的是十點半。
　　(C) 我以為你已訂了。

解說 問話者詢問，在哪裡訂旅館的？一般而言，正確選項應表示在哪裡訂旅館，但本題沒有直接回答，所以難度較高，選項 (C) 而是回説：「我以為你已訂了。」是最合適的回答。

字彙 book 預訂

6. Where's the closest place to get a drink around here?
(A) The closest post office is on George Street.
(B) I had a drink at my place last night.
(C) Go across the street and turn left.

翻譯 離這兒最近、可以喝一杯的地方在哪？
　　(A) 最近的郵局在喬治街上。
　　(B) 我昨晚在家裡喝過了。
　　(C) 過街後左轉。

解說 本題詢問，距離最近的喝酒的地方在哪裡。選項 (C) 直接説明該場所如何去，是正確答案。

字彙 post office 郵局

7. When are the building designs due?
(A) The designs look pretty good.
(B) On September 1st.
(C) We can start building right away.

翻譯 建築設計圖何時完成？
　　(A) 設計看來很美。
　　(B) 九月一日。
　　(C) 我們可以馬上動工。

解說 問話者問，建築物設計圖什麼時候完成。選項 (B) 表示了具體的時間，是最合適的回答。

字彙 due 到期的

8. When can you have your presentation ready for Mr. Porter?
(A) Yesterday I did a presentation.
(B) By Wednesday afternoon at the latest.
(C) Mr. Porter isn't here.

翻譯 要給波特先生做的簡報，何時可以準備好？
　　(A) 我昨天做了一場簡報。
　　(B) 最晚星期三下午前。
　　(C) 波特先生不在這。

解說 問話者詢問，為波特先生做的簡報何時能準備好。選項 (B) 回答了具體的時間也就是最晚星期三下午前，是最合適的回答。

字彙 at the latest 最晚

9. When do you think that the crew will arrive?
(A) The crew is well dressed.
(B) Probably around six o'clock tonight.
(C) I know the crew well.

翻譯 你覺得全體工作人員何時會到？
　　(A) 全體工作人員的穿著都很體面。
　　(B) 大概今晚六點左右。
　　(C) 我與全體工作人員都很熟。

解說 詢問全體工作人員什麼時候抵達。選項 (B) 回答了具體的時間——今晚六點左右，是最合適的回答。

字彙 crew 全體工作人員

10. What's the cost of parking in the underground car park?

(A) I think it's free for employees or visitors.

(B) We need to pay for the parking ticket.

(C) The cost of parking is rising.

翻譯 地下停車場的停車費是多少？
(A) 員工或是訪客應該是免費。
(B) 我們必須付違規停車罰單。
(C) 停車的費用不斷提高。

解說 本題詢問，在地下停車場停車要花多少錢。選項 (A) 回答説，員工或訪客免費，是最合適的回答。

字彙 cost 價錢　underground car park 地下停車場　employee 員工
visitor 訪客
parking ticket 違規停車罰單

---

11. What was that delivery that arrived today?

(A) I think it arrived three weeks ago.

(B) I think it's the new office chairs.

(C) Let's get delivery for dinner tonight.

翻譯 今天送來的貨品是什麼？
(A) 應該是三個禮拜前就送來了。
(B) 應該是新的辦公椅。
(C) 今天晚餐叫外送好了。

解說 問話者詢問，今天送來的貨品是什麼。選項 (B) 回答説，應該是新的辦公椅，是正確答案。

字彙 delivery 運送（的物品）

---

12. What would be a nice place to take a client on the weekend?

(A) I always have pasta for lunch.

(B) The city zoo and garden are great places to visit.

(C) Actually I'll just call you later.

翻譯 週末要接待客戶，帶往何處較佳？
(A) 我午餐都吃義大利麵。
(B) 市立動物園及植物園都是很棒的參觀地點。
(C) 事實上，我晚一點再打給你。

解說 題目詢問，週末要帶客戶去哪裡比較好。選項 (B) 推薦市立動物園和植物園，是最合適的回答。

字彙 client 客戶

---

13. Why did they book such a small gallery for the exhibition?

(A) The exhibition was a success.

(B) I lived next door to a small gallery.

(C) We weren't sure how many people would come.

翻譯 為何他們會訂這麼小間的畫廊舉辦展覽？
(A) 展覽非常成功。
(B) 我家隔壁有一家小型畫廊。
(C) 我們不確定有多少人會來。

解說 問話者問，為什麼會訂一間小畫廊辦展覽。選項 (C) 説明，因為不確定會有多少人來看展覽，是最合適的回答。

字彙 gallery 畫廊　exhibition 展覽

---

14. Why are all the computers piled up in the storage room?

(A) The tech crew put them there because we are upgrading.

(B) The computers are all in good condition.

(C) Jack said he wanted to use your computer.

翻譯 為何所有的電腦都堆放在儲藏室裡？
(A) 技術人員把電腦堆放在那裡，因為我們的電腦正要升級。
(B) 這些電腦的狀態都很好。
(C) 傑克說他想用你的電腦。

解說 本題詢問，為什麼所有電腦都堆放在儲藏室。選項 (A) 説明，因為電腦要升級，所以技術人員把它們搬到了那裡，是最合適的回答。

字彙 pile up 堆放
storage room 儲藏室；倉庫
condition 狀況

15. Why is the exhibition hall being cleared early?

(A) We need to prepare for the next product display.

(B) The exhibition hall is next to the museum.

(C) It is around the corner.

翻譯 為何展覽廳這麼早就在清空？
　　(A) 我們需要為下一場產品展示會準備。
　　(B) 展覽廳就在博物館旁邊。
　　(C) 就在附近。

解說 問話者詢問，為什麼這麼早就在清空展覽廳。選項 (A) 說明，為了準備下一場展示會，是最合適的回答。

字彙 exhibition hall 展覽廳
　　around the corner 就在附近

Actual Test　　p. 120

p. 120

1. A	2. A	3. B	4. B	5. A
6. B	7. C	8. A	9. C	10. A
11. B	12. B	13. C	14. B	15. B
16. C	17. A	18. C	19. A	20. B
21. B	22. A	23. B	24. C	25. A

1. Did you get my message?

(A) Oh, sorry, my battery was out.

(B) Yes, I'd like that very much.

(C) No, I think I cancelled it.

翻譯 你收到我的訊息了嗎？
　　(A) 喔，抱歉，我的電池沒電。
　　(B) 沒錯，我想那會很棒。
　　(C) 不，我應該已經取消了。

解說 題目詢問有沒有收到手機訊息。選項 (A) 回答說，（手機）電池沒電了，所以沒收到，是最合適的回答。

字彙 cancel 取消

---

2. Haven't you traded in your old device yet?

(A) Actually, I've been so busy.

(B) I want to buy a new tablet.

(C) I've been using this smartphone for five years.

翻譯 你還沒賣掉舊的設備嗎？
　　(A) 其實，我一直很忙。
　　(B) 我想買一台新的平板。
　　(C) 這支智慧型手機我已經用了五年了。

解說 問話者問，舊設備還沒賣嗎。選項 (A) 回答說，因為很忙，暗指還沒有時間處理這件事，故 (A) 是最合適的回答。

字彙 trade in 以……折價換購
　　device 設備

3. When did he last place his order?

(A) I talked with him already.

(B) Two weeks ago.

(C) We haven't seen him.

翻譯 他最後下訂單是在何時？

(A) 我已經跟他談過了。

(B) 兩週前。

(C) 我們還未見到他。

解說 題目問說，他最後下訂單是在何時。選項 (B) 回答說兩週前，是最合適的回答。

字彙 last 最後　place an order 下訂單

---

4. The meeting is at 3 p.m., isn't it?

(A) You could be wrong.

(B) Actually it was cancelled.

(C) We need to discuss a few important matters.

翻譯 會議是在下午三點召開，不是嗎？

(A) 你不一定對。

(B) 其實會議被取消了。

(C) 我們需要討論幾件重要事項。

解說 問話者問，會議是下午三點召開，對嗎？選項 (B) 回答，會議已經取消了，是最合適的回答。

字彙 cancel 取消　discuss 討論
　　 matter 事情

---

5. We'd appreciate it if you called us as soon as possible.

(A) That won't be a problem.

(B) Thanks for getting back to me.

(C) I have your e-mail address.

翻譯 如果你能盡快回電，我們會很感激。

(A) 沒問題。

(B) 謝謝您的回電。

(C) 我有你們的電子郵件信箱。

解說 敘述句說，能盡快回電的話，我們會很感謝。選項 (A) 回答「沒問題」，是正確答案。

字彙 appreciate 感謝
　　 as soon as possible 盡快
　　 get back 回電話；回電子郵件

---

6. Which payment method will you be using?

(A) I have a few loyalty cards.

(B) Is credit card OK?

(C) I left my cash at home.

翻譯 你要用何種方式付款？

(A) 我有幾張會員卡。

(B) 可以使用信用卡嗎？

(C) 我沒帶現金。

解說 本題問說，要選擇哪種付款方式。選項 (B) 反問說，用信用卡支付可以嗎，是最合適的回答。

字彙 payment 付款　method 方式
　　 loyalty card 會員卡
　　 credit card 信用卡　cash 現金

---

7. I can't find your name on the list.

(A) I'll sign it here.

(B) Can I borrow a pen?

(C) Did you check the first page?

翻譯 名單上找不到你的名字。

(A) 我把名字簽在這裡。

(B) 可以借我一支筆嗎？

(C) 第一頁查過了嗎？

解說 敘述句說，名單上找不到你的名字。選項 (C) 反問說，第一頁查過了嗎，是最合適的回答。

字彙 sign 簽名　borrow 借

8. Who will be heading the new design team?

(A) We haven't decided yet.

(B) The group is very talented.

(C) We have the prototype here.

> 翻譯 誰將領導新的設計團隊？
> (A) 我們尚未決定。
> (B) 這個團隊才華洋溢。
> (C) 樣品已經出來了。

> 解說 問話者問，誰將領導新的設計團隊。選項 (A) 回答說，我們尚未決定，是最合適的回答。

> 字彙 head 領導　talented 有才華的
> prototype 樣品

---

9. How long does it take you to get to work?

(A) I drive every day.

(B) I usually take the bus.

(C) By subway around 30 minutes.

> 翻譯 你上班通勤要花多久時間？
> (A) 我每天開車。
> (B) 我通常都搭公車。
> (C) 搭地鐵的話大概 30 分鐘。

> 解說 本題詢問上班通勤要花多少時間。選項 (C) 回答了搭乘的交通工具以及所需時間，故為正確答案。

> 字彙 around 大約

---

10. Will they have the meeting in the conference room or the main office?

(A) The larger room is preferable.

(B) It's at noon sharp.

(C) I haven't forgotten the meeting.

> 翻譯 他們要在會議室開會，還是要在總部辦公室開會？
> (A) 大一點的空間比較合適。
> (B) 中午十二點整開始。
> (C) 我沒忘記要開會。

> 解說 本題問說，他們會在會議室還是在總部辦公室開會。選項 (A) 雖然沒有直接做出選擇，但回答大一點的空間比較好，也是合適的回答。選項 (B) 與 (C) 雖提到 meeting，但和題目所問的開會場所無關，是錯誤答案。

> 字彙 conference room 會議室
> main office 總部辦公室
> preferable 更合適的

---

11. Could we hire a few more interns?

(A) I like these candidates.

(B) I'll see if our budget can allow it.

(C) I'll change the schedule.

> 翻譯 我們能多僱幾名實習生嗎？
> (A) 我喜歡這些人選。
> (B) 要看預算夠不夠。
> (C) 我會更改行程。

> 解說 問話者問，能再多僱一些實習生嗎。選項 (B) 回答說，看看預算是否許可，是最合適的回答。

> 字彙 hire 僱用　candidate 候選人
> budget 預算

---

12. Did you order the supplies I asked for?

(A) I'm checking the time.

(B) I will after I finish these.

(C) These are on sale.

> 翻譯 我要的日用品你訂購了嗎？
> (A) 我正在查看時間。
> (B) 我做完這些就會去訂。
> (C) 這些東西在打折。

> 解說 本題詢問日用品是否已訂購。選項 (B) 回答說，做完這些就會去訂，是最合適的回答。

> 字彙 order 訂購　supply 日用品

13. Why didn't my credit card work?
(A) Cash is preferable.
(B) I have a debit card.
(C) Maybe it isn't activated.

翻譯 為何我的信用卡不能刷？
(A) 更建議使用現金。
(B) 我有一張簽帳金融卡。
(C) 或許是還沒開卡。

解說 問話者問，為什麼信用卡不能使用。選項 (C) 推測說，可能是還沒開卡，是最合適的回答。

字彙 credit card 信用卡　cash 現金
preferable 更合適的；更好的
debit card 簽帳金融卡
activate 啟動；啟用

---

14. Should we take a taxi or go by bus?
(A) My car needs to be repaired.
(B) Taxi will be faster.
(C) I take the bus to work.

翻譯 我們要搭計程車，還是公車？
(A) 我的車需要維修了。
(B) 計程車比較快。
(C) 我搭公車上班。

解說 本題詢問要搭乘計程車還是公車。選項 (B) 回答說，計程車比較快，意思就是要搭計程車，所以是正確答案。

字彙 repair 維修；修理

---

15. How did you get VIP tickets?
(A) I had to ask for permission.
(B) I paid an extra fee.
(C) You won't believe them.

翻譯 你是如何取得貴賓票的？
(A) 我必須申請許可。
(B) 我多付了一些費用。
(C) 你不會相信他們的。

解說 問話者問，是用什麼方法買到貴賓票。選項 (B) 回答說，付了額外的費用才買到，是最合適的回答。

字彙 permission 許可

---

16. Let's try to finish this report before the deadline.
(A) You won't regret it.
(B) I need to work on it.
(C) I doubt that's possible, but we can try.

翻譯 讓我們試著在期限前完成這份報告。
(A) 你不會後悔的。
(B) 我需要好好下功夫了。
(C) 不確定可不可行，但我們可以試試。

解說 直述句說，讓我們試著在截止時間前完成報告。選項 (C) 回答說，能不能完成不知道，但會盡力，是最合適的回答。

字彙 deadline 截止時間

---

17. Can you arrange the meeting for tomorrow?
(A) Absolutely.
(B) No, I can make it.
(C) Yes, I was there.

翻譯 你能不能安排明天的會議呢？
(A) 沒問題。
(B) 不，我可以的。
(C) 是的，我當時在場。

解說 題目問能否安排明天的會議。選項 (A) 說當然，表示可以、沒問題，所以是正確答案。

字彙 arrange 安排

---

18. Who wrote the script to that play?
(A) I never watched it.
(B) He's quite entertaining.
(C) My nephew.

翻譯 這齣戲的劇本是誰寫的？
(A) 我從沒看過這齣戲。
(B) 他蠻風趣的。
(C) 我外甥。

解說 問話者詢問寫劇本的人是誰。選項 (C) 直接回答說，我外甥，表示是他寫的，所以是正確答案。

字彙 script 劇本　play 戲劇
entertaining 風趣的；有趣的
nephew 外甥

19. We've been planning our office party.

(A) How's it going so far?

(B) I can't wait until the end.

(C) Hasn't it been a long time?

翻譯　我們一直在計畫辦公室派對。

(A) 目前進行得如何了？

(B) 我等不及了。

(C) 過了好長一段時間了吧？

解說　敘述句內容是，我們一直在計畫辦公室派對。選項 (A) 反問說，現在派對進行得如何了，是最合適的回答。

字彙　so far 到目前為止

---

20. Don't you want to try on the dress first?

(A) I don't have enough money.

(B) It's OK; I can always return it.

(C) I really like it.

翻譯　不想先試試這套洋裝嗎？

(A) 我錢不夠。

(B) 沒關係的，可以隨時退回去。

(C) 我真的很喜歡。

解說　問話者問，不先試洋裝嗎。選項 (B) 回答說，沒關係，以後隨時可以退回，是最合適的回答。

字彙　try on 試穿　return 退還

---

21. This computer is still under warranty, isn't it?

(A) I'm sorry but we can't fix it.

(B) Unfortunately, it isn't.

(C) Yes, it was.

翻譯　電腦還在保固期間吧，不是嗎？

(A) 很抱歉，但我們沒法修理。

(B) 很遺憾，它已過保固期了。

(C) 是的，曾經是。

解說　問話者詢問，電腦還在保固期間，不是嗎。選項 (B) 回答說，很遺憾，不在保固期間了，是最合適的回答。

字彙　under warranty 在保固期間
unfortunately 遺憾地

---

22. I just postponed our meeting.

(A) Great. That will give us time to finish this.

(B) Are you going home?

(C) Great! I'll be there.

翻譯　我剛把會議時間延期了。

(A) 很好，這樣我們就有時間做完這個了。

(B) 你正要返家嗎？

(C) 太好了，我會到。

解說　敘述句內容是，我剛把會議時間延期了。選項 (A) 回答說，很好，這樣我們就有時間做完這個了，是最合適的回答。

字彙　postpone 使延期

---

23. Can I get a catalogue for next season?

(A) The products are unbelievable.

(B) Oh, we just ran out.

(C) I will give you my card.

翻譯　能給我一份下一季的目錄嗎？

(A) 這些產品實在太棒了。

(B) 喔，我們才剛發完。

(C) 我會給你我的卡。

解說　問話者詢問，可以給我一份下一季的目錄嗎。選項 (B) 回答說，剛發完了，是最合適的回答。選項 (A) 提到產品的品質，沒有回答是否給問話者目錄，是錯誤答案。選項 (C) 提到的卡（card）和目錄無關，也是錯誤的選項。

字彙　catalogue 目錄
unbelievable 難以置信的
run out 耗盡

24. Which tablet would best fit in this pouch?

(A) That is a great selection.

(B) I think it suits you.

(C) The smaller one.

翻譯 哪種平板電腦的大小最適合放進這個提袋裡？

(A) 選得好。

(B) 我覺得它很適合你。

(C) 小一點的平板電腦。

解說 本題詢問哪種大小的平板電腦最適合放進這提袋裡。選項 (C) 回答說，小一點的平板電腦，是最合適的回答。選項 (A) 與 (B) 都沒有回答到問題，所以是錯誤的。

字彙 fit in 相合；相配　pouch 袋 selection 選擇 suit (v.) 適合

---

25. The intern will come by with sample sizes for you.

(A) I can't wait to see them.

(B) The clothes are beautiful.

(C) I interned once.

翻譯 實習生會把樣品帶來給你。

(A) 真讓人迫不及待。

(B) 衣服很漂亮。

(C) 我有過一次實習經驗。

解說 敘述句內容是，實習生會帶樣品給你。選項 (A) 回答說，我等不及要看樣品了，是最合適的回答。和衣服漂亮與否、有沒有實習經驗無關，所以 (B) 與 (C) 是錯的。

字彙 intern 實習生　size 尺寸

實戰
應用 **Chapter 01** p. 138

1 和日常生活有關的內容

---

1. D 2. A 3. D 4. B 5. B 6. C

Questions 1-3 refer to the following conversation.

M Hello. ^Q1 I'm the director of the play you just watched. One of my actors mentioned that you wanted to speak with me. How can I help you?

W Hi, Mr. Heller. My name is Ann Walker. First, I'd like to say I really enjoyed this production. I write for the Arts and Entertainment section for the Chester Times and I'm going to write a review of your play. ^Q2 I was wondering if we could sit down somewhere so I could ask you a few questions.

M Sure. ^Q3 Because our theater's two publicists recently quit their jobs, we have been experiencing difficulty promoting our play. I think this could be a great opportunity to attract more publicity.

男：嗨，我是妳剛欣賞過的那齣戲的導演。有個演員跟我提到妳想與我聊聊。請問有哪裡我可以效勞的地方？

女：嗨，海勒先生。我是安·沃克。首先，我想說我真的很喜歡這齣劇。我在為《雀斯特時報》的藝文專欄寫稿，打算為您的戲寫一篇評論。我在想，我們是否可以找個地方坐下來，讓我向您提幾個問題？

男：沒問題。我們劇場的兩名公關最近剛好離職，所以我們正遭遇無法宣傳戲劇的窘境。我想這會是我們吸引媒體關注的大好機會。

字彙 production （影片）製作
publicist 公關　publicity 關注；宣傳

1. 這名男子是誰？

(A) 記者　(B) 演員　(C) 編輯　(D) 導演

解說 男子對話一開始就提到 I'm the director of the play，所以正確答案是選項 (D)。

2. 女子說她想要做何事？

(A) 進行採訪
(B) 購買門票
(C) 照相
(D) 索取親筆簽名

解說 女子的談話在最後面提到，「是否可以找個地方坐下來，讓我向您提幾個問題」，所以可知是要「採訪」，正確答案是 (A)。

3. 男子提到劇院何事？

(A) 正在施工。
(B) 週末不營業。
(C) 是城裡唯一的劇院。
(D) 正缺少人手。

解說 男子第二段第二句話提到，「我們劇場的兩名公關最近剛好離職」，所以選項 (D) 說「正缺少人手」是正確答案。

Questions 4-6 refer to the following conversation.

M Q4 Hi, I'm a member here at the gym. I came to do some weight training today, but I forgot my combination code for my locker in the locker room.

W Oh, I see. Q5 If you show me a valid form of photo identification, I can let you reset your combination code.

M Thank you. Also, I forgot to bring a towel. Is it possible to borrow one?

W Of course. Q6 Actually, they are provided free of charge by the gym. Just wait here and I'll get you one immediately.

男： 嗨，我是健身房的會員。我今天來做點重量訓練，但我忘了更衣室裡我的寄物櫃密碼。

女： 喔，我了解了。如果你能出示有效且附照片的身分證照，我可以讓你重新設定密碼。

男： 謝謝。我也忘了帶毛巾，有可能借我一條嗎？

女： 當然。其實，健身房有提供免費毛巾。在這裡等著，我馬上拿一條給你。

字彙 combination code 密碼　valid 有效的 photo identification 有照片的證件 complimentary 免費贈送的

4. 對話者人在何處？
(A) 在電腦室　　　(B) 健身房
(C) 培訓研討會　　(D) 電器行

解說 男子一開始打招呼後，就說「我是這個健身房的會員」，所以選項 (B) 是正確答案。

5. 女子要求男子提供什麼？
(A) 他寄物櫃的密碼
(B) 身分證件
(C) 會員費用
(D) 電腦密碼

解說 男子說他忘了寄物櫃密碼，女子回答說，「出示有效且附照片的身分證照，我可以讓你重新設定密碼」，所以可知正確答案是選項 (B)。

6. 女子說會拿什麼給男子？
(A) 折價券
(B) 宣傳手冊
(C) 免費物品
(D) 設施簡介

解說 男子問可以借一條毛巾嗎，女子回答說，「其實，健身房有提供免費毛巾，在這裡等著，我馬上拿一條給你」，所以選項 (C) 的 complimentary（免費物品）是正確答案。

實戰應用 **Chapter 01** p. 147
2 和上班有關的內容

1. D　2. C　3. B　4. A　5. D　6. B

Questions 1-3 refer to the following conversation.

M Hello, Stephanie. This is James. Can I talk to you for a minute? I'm having trouble using this new software. Q1 Could you come to my office to give me a hand?

W Hello, James. Q3 Actually, there is going to be a training session for my team this afternoon. Q2 Some of my team members are having similar difficulties after our bank introduced the new accounting software, so we're having a special training session. You're welcome to attend it.

M Oh, really? Q3 I'll definitely attend it. I could use some assistance. How can I do that?

W Just come to my office at 3 p.m. today. You can bring your team members if they want to attend, too.

男：嗨，史蒂芬妮。我是詹姆士。可以給我一分鐘嗎？我用新軟體的時候，有點問題，能否請妳到我的辦公室幫個忙？

女：嗨，詹姆士。事實上，今天下午我的工作團隊會有個訓練課程。在本行引進新的會計軟體後，我的幾名同事也遇到類似的問題，所以我們下午才會特別開一個訓練課程。歡迎你參加。

男：喔，真的嗎？我絕對會出席。這樣我就可以得到一點協助了。我該怎麼做？

女：只要在今天下午三點來我的辦公室就可以了。你也可以把你的工作夥伴帶來，如果他們也想參加的話。

字彙 definitely 絕對　estimate 預算
reception 歡迎會

1. 男子來電的原因是？

(A) 安排會議時程

(B) 討論預算

(C) 說明一項政策

(D) 請求協助

解說 男子說使用新軟體時有點問題，「能否請妳到我的辦公室幫個忙？」，所以正確答案是選項 (D)。

2. 對話者在哪裡工作？

(A) 軟體公司

(B) 房地產仲介公司

(C) 銀行

(D) 醫院

解說 女子說，「在本行引進新的會計軟體後……也遇到類似的問題」，所以可知談話者是在銀行工作。正確答案是選項 (C)。

3. 男子這個下午會做何事？

(A) 送文件

(B) 受訓

(C) 應徵職務

(D) 參加歡迎會

解說 女子的談話一開始就提到，今天下午有訓練課程；男子也說絕對會出席訓練，所以正確答案是選項 (B)。

Questions 4-6 refer to the following conversation.

W Hello, and welcome to Martha's Flower Shop. What can I help you with?

M Q4 I'm looking for a pretty bouquet to give to my wife. Q6 This Friday is our 2nd wedding anniversary. She'll be coming from Denver to visit me then.

W Oh, congratulations. However, if you plan to give her the flowers this Friday, I suggest you don't buy them today. Q5 They could start to turn brown by then. We could deliver the flowers to your wife in Denver.

M No, thank you. I would rather give her the flowers in person. Q6 I'll pick them up before our restaurant reservation on Friday night.

女：您好，歡迎光臨瑪莎花店。有哪裡我可以效勞的？

男：我想送妻子一束美麗的鮮花。這個星期五是我們結婚兩週年紀念，到時她會從丹佛來找我。

女：喔，恭喜。不過，如果您計畫要在星期五送花給她，建議不要在今天就買。可能不到那時，花就開始枯萎了。我們可以幫您送花到丹佛給您的妻子。

男：不了，謝謝妳。我比較想要親自送花給她。我會在星期五晚上，赴預定的餐廳用餐前，再過來買。

字彙 in person 親自　apply 申請
last 持續　celebrate 慶祝

4. 男子光臨花店的目的是？

(A) 購買禮物

(B) 應徵職務

(C) 贈送紀念品

(D) 運送花朵

解說 因為男子第一句就說，正在找一束漂亮的花（a pretty bouquet）送給太太，所以選項 (A)「購買禮物」是正確答案。選項 (C) 的 souvenir，是因為參觀一個特別的場所而買的紀念品。對話中，男子要買的是送給太太慶祝結婚紀念日的花束，和紀念品不同，所以不能選。

5. 為何女子會有疑慮？

    (A) 男子開會會遲到。

    (B) 配送可能無法準時抵達。

    (C) 商店恐會歇業。

    (D) 該品項無法維持太久時間。

解說 本題比較難解，因為女子並沒有直接表示擔心或煩惱。細節在於，女子建議男子今天不要買，因為到週五花會變成褐色了，也就是女子擔心男子現在買花，到星期五時花已經開始枯了。選項 (D) 是正確答案，它用 item 表示花。因為男子說不用配送，所以選項 (B) 不用考慮。(A) 和 (C) 都無法從對話中確認。

6. 這個星期五男子會做什麼？

    (A) 聯繫另一家商店

    (B) 慶祝週年紀念

    (C) 赴太太工作處探班

    (D) 開新餐廳

解說 男子第二句話說，星期五是他和太太的結婚兩週年紀念日，最後又說，會在星期五晚上，赴預定的餐廳用餐前，再過來買花。所以可以推知，送花和去餐廳吃飯，都是為了要慶祝結婚紀念日，所以正確答案是選項 (B)。星期五和太太見面吃飯，不是去太太工作處探班，所以 (C) 不對。(A) 和 (D) 並沒有在對話中出現。

Mini Test
Chapter 01   p. 148
短的對話

1. B   2. A   3. B   4. B   5. A   6. C

Questions 1-3 refer to the following conversation.

W Hello, this is Barbra Fletcher. Q1 I'm coming in to see Dr. Lewis on Monday to get a dental treatment. Q2 I was wondering if I will be able to drive after the operation, or if I will need someone to pick me up.

M We will be using some special medication to alleviate the pain. You might be sleepy and dizzy for a few hours. Therefore, I'm afraid you cannot drive a car after the operation. Q1 If you can't have someone pick you up, we can arrange a taxi to pick you up.

W Thanks, but that won't be necessary. Q3 I will just ask my father to do it.

M Oh, I see. Then, I'll see you on Monday.

女：嗨，我是芭芭拉·費萊查。我來是預約路易斯醫師幫我在星期一看牙。我想知道在手術過後，我是否還能開車，或者需要別人來接我。

男：我們會用特殊的藥物減輕您的疼痛，可能在幾個小時內妳會感到昏昏欲睡。因此，恐怕妳在手術之後無法開車。如果妳無法找到人來接，我們可以安排計程車來接妳。

女：謝了，應該不需要。我會請我父親來接我。

男：喔，我明白了。那麼，就星期一見了。

字彙 alleviate 減輕（痛苦）   dizzy 暈眩的
operation 手術   necessary 必要的
receptionist 接待員   procedure 程序
ask a favor of 請求幫忙
call in sick 打電話請病假

1. 男子最有可能是誰？

    (A) 技工

    (B) 接待人員

    (C) 病患

    (D) 計程車司機

解說 女子一開始對話就提到，週一要見醫師，所以可以知道她是患者；而男子提到了各式各樣有關醫療的事項，並說需要的話可以安排計程車送她回家，所以可以知道男子是負責協助處理醫療事務的人員。選項 (B) 接待人員是最合適的答案。

2. 女子詢問何事？

    (A) 療程的細節

    (B) 可預約的時間

    (C) 到某處的路徑

    (D) 醫師姓名

解說 女子問手術後能不能開車，所以正確
選項應和醫療程序相關。對話中女子
就診時間已確定，也沒提到該如何去
某處，所以選項 (B) 和 (C) 不用考慮。
女子一開始就提到醫生的名字是路易
斯醫生（Dr. Lewis），所以選項 (D) 也
不對。正確答案是選項 (A)，它將手術
（operation）替 換 成 療 程（medical
procedure）。

3. 女子說她將做何事？

(A) 開車回家

(B) 要求父親協助

(C) 預約改期

(D) 打電話請病假

解說 對話的脈絡是，女子問男子術後是否能
開車，男子回答，手術後不能開車，接
著表示，如果沒有人來接女子回家，可
以替女子安排計程車。最後女子說，會
請她爸爸來接「ask my father to do it
（drive me home）」，所以選項 (B) 是
最適當的答案。

**Questions 4-6 refer to the following
conversation.**

M Hello, Ms. Palmer. ᴼ⁴ This is the
delivery person for Swift Services. I
have been looking for your house for
the past 30 minutes, but I can't find
your address. I'm relieved you finally
answered the phone.

W I'm sorry. ᴼ⁵ I was in the garden
when you called before. Did you see
the Quick Stop gas station? I live
across the street from there.

M Oh, I actually passed that a while
ago. ᴼ⁶ I'm worried that if I go back
I'll get behind schedule today. I'll
have to make your delivery tomorrow
instead. I'm really sorry about that.

W I understand. I'll make sure to be
near my phone tomorrow.

男：喂，帕瑪小姐。我是快捷服務的貨運人
員。我找妳家已經找了三十分鐘了，還是
找不到。電話終於接通讓我鬆了一口氣。

女：抱歉。你之前來電的時候，我人在花
園。你看到快克加油站了嗎？過馬路對
面就是我家。

男：噢，我車已經過加油站了，離你家有一
段距離。我擔心如果我掉頭回去，我今
天的貨會送不完。妳的貨我必須改到明
天再送。真的很抱歉。

女：我了解了。明天我會注意待在電話旁邊
的。

字彙 relieved 放心的
get behind something 落後
courier 快遞員　clerk 職員
run an errand 出外辦事

4. 男子是誰？

(A) 園丁

(B) 快遞員

(C) 店員

(D) 電話接線生

解說 男子一開始就介紹他自己是快捷服務
公司的貨運人員，所以正確答案是選項
(B)。

5. 女子為何不能接聽男子的電話？

(A) 她人在外面。

(B) 她正在講電話。

(C) 她睡著了。

(D) 她外出辦事了。

解說 女子的第二句話說，男子之前來電
的時候，她人在花園（I was in the
garden），所以這就是她沒接電話的原
因。說女子正在打電話或正在睡覺，都
不對，所以選項 (B) 和 (C) 可以刪除。
選項 (D) 的 run an errand 是「出外辦
事」，這和「在花園」的意思不一樣，所
以也不能選。正確答案是選項 (A)，它把
「在花園」改成「在外面」。

6. 男子擔心何事？

(A) 迷路

(B) 肇禍

(C) 延遲其他貨物的遞送

(D) 尋找加油站

解說 本題理解男子在擔心什麼，就可以解題
了。女子告訴男子來她家的方法後，男
子說他開過頭了，再開回去會耽誤他的
送貨行程（get behind schedule），也
就是說，接下來要送的東西都會延遲送
達，這是他擔心的。所以正確答案是選
項 (C)。

1. D　2. C　3. B　4. B　5. D　6. A

Questions 1-3 refer to the following conversation.

M Hello, Jessica. As you know, the new evaluation system is currently being integrated into our training program. The new employees are already being trained.

W Yes, well, the rest of us are still having difficulty adjusting to it. It is more complicated than it looks.

M Yes, but there is an instruction manual.

W I know, but it is a bit hard to understand.

M Would you like to go through the training course with the new employees?

W I don't think that's appropriate. It would be bad for morale. Q3 Why don't you have the trainer show me how to do it step by step, and then I will go through it with everyone else?

男： 嗨，潔西卡。妳知道，我們的培訓課程現在也納入新的評鑑系統，新進員工都正在受訓了。

女： 嗯，不過，我們其他人適應上還是有困難。實際使用後，它困難得多。

男： 沒錯，不過有操作說明書啊。

女： 我知道，但有點難懂。

男： 那你們想要與新進員工一同受訓嗎？

女： 我覺得不合適，這樣會有損士氣。你何不先請訓練講師循序漸進地教我一遍，然後我再仔細教導其他的同仁？

字彙 currently 現在　integrate 使併入
adjust 適應
instruction manual 操作說明書
morale 士氣

1. 對話者在討論何事？
   (A) 新進員工的團隊合作
   (B) 分發操作說明書
   (C) 適度納入新進員工
   (D) 新的評鑑系統

解說 男子提到，新員工正在學新的評鑑系統；女子提到，其他人都不太適應這個新的系統。由此可知他們在討論的是「新的評鑑系統」，故 (D) 正確。

2. 當女子說到「這會有損士氣」，她暗指的是？
   (A) 學習新的系統很簡單。
   (B) 人們不想要被評價。
   (C) 資深員工會覺得不受尊重。
   (D) 機關行事曆還未張貼。

解說 男子建議說，要不要跟新員工一同受訓，女子回答說，和新員工一起上課，會傷害到員工的士氣，女子說的「員工」，從情境上推論是已經在公司工作的員工了。選項 (C) 說，資深員工會感覺不受尊重，這和女子的意思最接近。

3. 女子打算怎麼做？
   (A) 參加受訓課程
   (B) 自己學好後，再教其他人
   (C) 讓每一個人都去受訓
   (D) 撰寫新的說明書

解說 女子說，請講師過來教她，告訴她操作的步驟，然後她再教其他人。這跟選項 (B) 說的一樣，她自己先學然後再教別人。

Questions 4-6 refer to the following conversation.

M Did you hear, Priyanka? We're finally going to be using the CSF-5 system. It's that project management system.

W That's great news. Q4 It'll be a big help for us in the research and development department. You know, the financial planning office uses it, so it'll help us communicate more efficiently with them.

M Oh, that's right. So you must already be familiar with the program, seeing as how you used to use it.

W Ah, it's been quite a while, you see.

M Q6 Then maybe we can ask the financial department manager Hank to show us how to use it.

W Good thinking. Let's do it!

男：琵艷卡，妳聽說了嗎？我們終於要使用CSF-5系統了，就是那個專案管理系統。

女：太好了，它將會為我們研發部門帶來很大的助益。你知道嗎，財務規劃室用的就是這個系統，所以我們雙方的溝通將會更有效率。

男：喔，沒錯。所以妳一定已經很熟這個軟體了，既然是妳過去慣用的。

女：呃，你要知道，我已經有一段時間沒用了。

男：那麼，或許我們可以請財務部經理漢克教我們如何使用。

女：好主意。就這麼辦！

字彙 financial 財務的　go over 仔細檢查

4. 對話者最有可能在哪個部門工作？
(A) 客戶支援
(B) 研發
(C) 專案管理
(D) 財務規劃

解說 男子說，要使用專案管理系統了，女子接著說，對我們研發部會有很大的幫助（it'll be a big help for us in the research and development department），所以可以知道，談話者在研發部工作，所以 (B) 正確。

5. 當女子說到「已經有一段時間了」，她指的是？
(A) 她已經在公司服務很久了。
(B) 她忘了經理的要求。
(C) 她已經數年沒帶過訓練課程了。
(D) 她不記得如何使用軟體。

解說 男子說，女子以前就用過這個軟體，對它應該很熟悉；女子回答說，已經有一段時間沒用了，意思就是選項 (D) 所說的，她不記得如何使用了。

6. 男子接下來最有可能做何事？
(A) 聯繫部門主管
(B) 仔細檢視合約
(C) 使用新的電腦軟體
(D) 舉辦員工訓練課程

解說 男子最後說，請財務部經理漢克來教我們如何使用新系統，女子也同意，所以男子等一下會去連絡部門主管，正確答案是選項 (A)。

Mini Test **Chapter 02** p. 162
來回 5 句以上的長對話

1. A　2. C　3. C　4. A　5. B　6. D

Questions 1-3 refer to the following conversation.

W Thanks for meeting me in such short notice.

M No problem. What did you need my input on?

W We're over budget because of the new equipment installations. We need to cut back on some of the costs.

M I see. Well, the company deli provides free breakfasts, but only about half of the employees take advantage of it. It still costs the company quite a lot.

W Alright. Q3 Maybe we can just provide free coffee and have employees pay for breakfast if they choose.

M That sounds good. Do we need to make more cuts?

W No, I think based on my rough estimates that may be enough.

M Great!

女： 這麼臨時通知，謝謝你還能來見我。

男： 沒什麼。妳需要我給妳什麼意見？

女： 因為安裝新的設備，我們超支了。我們需要縮減開支。

男： 我懂了。嗯，公司的餐廳有提供免費早餐，大約只有一半的員工有善加利用這項福利。不過這仍花了公司許多經費。

女： 好。或許我們可以只提供免費咖啡，然後讓選擇吃早餐的員工自付餐費。

男： 聽起來不錯。我們還需要再刪減開支嗎？

女： 不，根據我粗略的估計，我想這樣應該夠了。

男： 太好了！

字彙 short notice 臨時通知　input 意見
over budget 超過預算
cut back 削減　rough 粗略的
estimate 估計

1. 對話者在討論何事？

(A) 刪減預算

(B) 早餐的益處

(C) 公司貸款

(D) 員工自助餐廳

解說 女子說，因為安裝新設備而使預算超過，所以要刪減部分費用。所以可以知道他們在討論有關「刪除預算」的事，正確答案是選項 (A)。

2. 對話暗示該公司何事？

(A) 員工薪資很高。

(B) 獲利不足。

(C) 更新設備。

(D) 需要新的設施。

解說 女子說，因為安裝新設備而使預算超過，由此可知公司安裝了新的設備。選項 (C) 說「更新設備」，是正確答案。

3. 對話者想要員工做何事？

(A) 上班前吃早餐　(C) 付費買早餐

(B) 在公司買咖啡　(D) 早一點上班

解說 男子說，公司提供免費早餐花了很多錢。接著女子建議，可以免費提供咖啡，但早餐要員工自己付費。所以可知正確答案是 (C)，要員工自己付費買早餐。

Questions 4-6 refer to the following conversation.

M Hello, Rachel. Thanks for meeting with me. We cut down the list of applicants to these five candidates. Q5 What was your impression of them as they waited for their interview?

W Hmm, I thought the first guy and this woman seemed really friendly and open. I was comfortable speaking with them.

M Yes, we think John and Linda have great potential. What about the others?

W I can't say I had any particular impressions of these two here. They just sat quietly for the most part.

M Hm, Harry and Gina do seem a little introverted, but they have excellent qualifications and good recommendations from previous employers. So which two did you like best?

W John and Linda. Who are you thinking of hiring?

M John and Linda. We need people whom others feel comfortable talking to for the positions. Thank you Rachel. Q6 Now I'm going to make some calls.

男： 嗨，瑞秋。謝謝妳來。我們把應徵者篩選到剩下五名。在他們等待面試的時候，妳對他們的印象如何？

女： 嗯，我認為第一位男子還有這名女子看起來似乎非常友善大方。跟他倆談話很舒服。

男： 沒錯，我們也覺得約翰及琳達兩人很有潛力。那其他人呢？

女： 對於這兩位，我沒辦法說我有任何特殊的印象。在大部分的時間裡，他們只是靜靜地坐著。

男： 嗯，哈利和吉娜看起來確實有點內向，但他們條件優異，且前任僱主對他們讚譽有加。那麼，妳最喜歡哪兩位？

女： 約翰及琳達。你考慮僱用誰？

男： 約翰及琳達。這個職位需要能讓他人覺得談話愉悅的人來擔任。瑞秋謝謝妳。現在我要打幾通電話。

字彙 candidate 候選人　impression 印象
potential 潛力　qualification 資格
opinion 看法　submission 提交
arrangement 安排

4. 對話的主題是？

　(A) 應徵職務的候選人

　(B) 員工的個性

　(C) 需求的資格能力

　(D) 面試中提出的問題

解說 男子詢問女子說，對應徵者（applicants）印象如何，女子回答了對其中兩位應徵者個性方面的印象，所以很容易選成了選項 (B)，而且選項 (B) 稱呼應徵者為員工（employee）也不對，因為他們在討論的是應徵者，不是已經在公司工作的員工。內文雖提到理想人選應具備的個性，但不是對話主要談論的主題，故選項 (C) 不能選。選項 (D) 並沒有在對話中提到。選項 (A) 是正確答案，注意它將應徵者（applicants）換成說是候選人（candidates）。

5. 男子要求女子何事？

　(A) 參與面試

　(B) 提供對人的看法

　(C) 提出疑問

　(D) 安排會議

解說 男子在對話開始就問女子說，在應徵者等待面試的時候，對他們的印象（impression）如何，所以正確答案是選項 (B)，它將印象（impression）換成是看法（opinions）。

6. 男子接下來最有可能做何事？

　(A) 安排會議

　(B) 敲定更多面試

　(C) 張貼廣告

　(D) 聯繫一些人

解說 男子最後一句話說，要「打幾通電話」（make some calls），這是會話中常見的說法。選項 (D) 是正確答案，它把打幾通電話（make some calls）換成說是「聯絡一些人」（contact some people）。

1. B　2. A　3. C　4. B　5. D　6. C

Questions 1-3 refer to the following conversation with three speakers.

W1 The New York trade show is just around the corner.

M I know. It should be good for our business with all those major companies there. Our transportation is squared away, right?

W2 Well, I've already booked our plane tickets and reserved a rental car, and you arranged the hotel accommodations for us, didn't you Allison?

W1 Q2 Oh no! I completely forgot to reserve the hotel room! I've been so busy getting my trade show presentation ready!

W2 OK. We're going to be there in three days—it might be nearly impossible to get a room now!

M Let's not overreact. I've always been able to get a room in New York. Q3 Let's look online now and see what we find.

女1：快要舉辦紐約貿易展了。

男　：我知道。有了那些大公司的參與，將會對我們的生意有所幫助。我們的交通都搞定了，對吧？

女2：嗯，我已經訂好機票，也預約了租車。而妳負責為我們安排飯店住宿，對嗎，艾莉森？

女1：喔不！我完全忘了要訂飯店！我一直都在忙著準備我的貿易展簡報！

女2：好吧。我們再三天就要到那裡了，現在要訂到住宿幾乎不太可能了！

男　：別反應過度。我總是能在紐約找到住處。我們現在上網看看可以找到什麼。

around the corner 即將來臨
square away 把一切搞定
accommodation 住所

1. 對話者談論的主題是？

(A) 省錢旅遊的訣竅

(B) 即將到來的商務旅行

(C) 預訂飯店的網站

(D) 貿易展的簡報

解說 對話者在談論，出差前往紐約貿易展的行前準備工作，所以選項 (B) 是正確答案。

2. 對話者遭遇什麼問題？

(A) 尚未預訂飯店房間。

(B) 無法與紐約的客戶碰面。

(C) 交通運輸的日期安排錯誤。

(D) 上台簡報的時間改期。

解說 對話中艾莉森說忙著準備貿易展簡報，忘記訂旅館了（Oh no! I completely forgot to reserve the hotel room!）所以可以知道，出現的問題是沒有訂旅館，選項 (A) 是正確答案。

3. 男子建議做何事？

(A) 預訂另一輛車　　(C) 上網搜尋

(B) 取消預約　　　　(D) 備妥樣品

解說 男子最後說，上網找找看（Let's look online now and see what we find.），所以可以知道，男子建議上網搜尋可以預約的旅館，選項 (C) 是正確答案。

Questions 4-6 refer to the following conversation with three speakers.

M1 So Caleb, what did you order?

M2 Q5 I got a Dutch coffee. It's fantastic here. Have you tried it?

M1 No, I'm not crazy about coffee, but I do like their other drinks.

M2 Yeah, they have lots of types of coffee, juices, and desserts.

M1 Right, and the prices are reasonable, too. Oh, hi, Rebecca. Do you want to join us?

W Hey, guys. I would love to, but I have a meeting in 20 minutes. Aren't you going, too?

M2 Oh, right. I almost forgot about it.

W It's a good thing I bumped into you, then. Q6 Remember we're meeting in Conference Room 3 today, not Room 1 like usual.

M1 OK, thanks for letting us know. I guess we'd better have our drinks to go.

男 1：那麼迦勒，你點了什麼？

男 2：我點了冰滴咖啡。這裡的冰滴咖啡太棒了，你喝過沒？

男 1：沒，我不是很愛喝咖啡，但我很喜歡他家其他的飲品。

男 2：對，他們提供各式各樣的咖啡、果汁以及甜點。

男 1：沒錯，而且價格也很公道。喔，嗨，蕾貝卡。妳想加入我們嗎？

女　：嘿，大夥。我是很想加入，但 20 分鐘後我有個會要開。你們不也要參加嗎？

男 2：噢，對喔。我幾乎都忘了。

女　：那還好我碰巧遇見你們。要記得我們是在三號會議室開會，不是平常的一號會議室。

男 1：好的，謝謝告知。我想我們最好外帶咖啡吧。

reasonable 合理的
bump into 碰巧遇到
mandatory 強制的

4. 對話最有可能發生在何處？

(A) 飛機上

(B) 咖啡館

(C) 會議室

(D) 休息室

解說 一開始男子問迦勒要點什麼飲料，迦勒回答說，要點冰滴咖啡，所以可以知道，他們是在咖啡店，答案是 (B)。

5. 迦勒暗示咖啡怎樣？

(A) 常附上甜點。

(B) 太貴了。

(C) 需要長時間的煮咖啡。

(D) 品質很棒。

解說 從迦勒説，我點了冰滴咖啡，這裡的冰滴咖啡非常好喝（I got a Dutch coffee. It's fantastic here.），可以知道他的冰滴咖啡品質非常棒，所以正確答案是選項 (D)。

6. 關於會議，女子提到？

　(A) 所有員工都須參加。
　(B) 已經開完了。
　(C) 開會地點有變。
　(D) 會比往常耗時。

解說 女子提到説，記住今天開會的地方是在三號會議室，不是平常的一號會議室（Remember we're meeting in Conference Room 3 today, not Room 1 like usual.），所以可以知道，會議會在和平常不同的地方召開，選項 (C) 是正確答案。

Mini Test **Chapter 03** p. 177

出現 **3** 個人的對話

---

1. C　2. A　3. B　4. B　5. D　6. C

Questions 1-3 refer to the following conversation with three speakers.

M1	Did you see the work on the new employee lounge? It's fantastic!
M2	Yeah, I checked it out this morning. It's a real step up from the old one.
W	I'm curious when it will be ready.
M2	Bill told me it should be done this week.
M1	That's right. They just have to finish installing the TVs.
M2	I guess the company wants to reward us for making a record profit last quarter.
W	For sure. Our sales were far beyond the projections. I'm just happy that the company values our contributions so much.
M1	I couldn't agree with you more.

男1：看過新的員工休息室的工程了嗎？真是棒極了！
男2：有啊，我今早看過了。跟舊的相比真是好太多了。
女　：我很好奇何時會完工。
男2：比爾説這個禮拜應該會完工。
男1：沒錯。他們只需要將電視機安裝完畢。
男2：我猜，這是公司為了要犒賞我們上一季的盈利打破紀錄。
女　：那當然。我們的銷售額遠超過預期。我只是很開心公司如此看重我們的貢獻。
男1：完全同意。

字彙 record 記錄　quarter 一季
　　　projection 預測　alteration 更改

1. 對話的主題是？

　(A) 訂購辦公室設備
　(B) 新的銷售策略
　(C) 改建後的員工休息區
　(D) 行程更改

解說 男子一開始就説，看過新的員工休息室的工程了嗎，好棒啊（Did you see the work on the new employee lounge? It's fantastic!），所以可以知道，他們是在談「改建後的員工休息區」，選項 (C) 是正確答案。

2. 為何男子説「比舊的更好了」？

　(A) 他滿意這個改變。
　(B) 他想要更進一步。
　(C) 他感到不好意思。
　(D) 他挑剔計畫。

解說 男子説，它比以前的更好了（It's a real step up from the old one.），表示他對新的休息室很滿意，所以選項 (A) 是正確答案。

3. 女子暗示公司何事？

　(A) 近來增僱員工。
　(B) 員工待遇很好。
　(C) 遭遇財務困境。
　(D) 有許多員工休息室。

女子在她説的最後一句話中提到，我很開心公司如此看重我們的貢獻 (I'm just happy that the company values our contributions so much.)，可知公司對員工很好，選項 (B) 是正確答案。

Questions 4-6 refer to the following conversation with three speakers.

M1 Marcus, I was looking through your e-mail about today's meeting.

M2 Q4 And you noticed that the presentation was not attached?

M1 Q4 Exactly. When do you expect to send it?

M2 I think Tori should explain that.

W Sorry, Mr. Rutherford. Q5 I forgot to save the presentation when I was working on it last night. I've been remaking it all morning.

M1 Alright. When will it be done?

W I've only got a couple more slides to go, so maybe in an hour?

M1 OK. Send it as soon as possible. Q6 And Marcus, I wanted to ask you about your speaking points for the meeting. Let's talk about them after lunch.

男1：馬庫斯，我剛正在看你傳送的有關今天會議的電子郵件。

男2：而你注意到簡報資料忘了附上？

男1：正是。你打算何時寄來？

男2：這得問多莉。

女　：抱歉，盧瑟福先生。我昨晚在做簡報資料時忘了存檔。我這個早上都在重作。

男1：好吧。何時會好？

女　：只剩幾張幻燈片了，或許一個小時內會好？

男1：好，盡快寄來。還有，馬庫斯，我想要看看你在會議中報告的講綱。午餐後我們來討論一下。

字彙 a couple (of) 幾個
　　 as soon as possible 盡快

4. 盧瑟福先生想要什麼？
(A) 講者名單
(B) 簡報資料
(C) 電子郵件信箱
(D) 財務報表

解說 盧瑟福先生看了電子郵件後，發現沒有附上簡報資料，並問什麼時候會寄來（When do you expect to send it?），所以正確答案是選項 (B)。

5. 女子提到什麼問題？
(A) 她把手提電腦遺留在飛機上。
(B) 她沒寄送電子郵件。
(C) 她沒訂到飯店。
(D) 她忘了存檔。

解說 女子説，昨天晚上做簡報資料時忘了存檔（I forgot to save the presentation when I was working on it last night.），所以可以知道，她忘記存檔了，正確答案是選項 (D)。

6. 為何午餐後，盧瑟福先生要找馬庫斯談話？
(A) 擬定旅行計畫
(B) 審視報告
(C) 檢視發言資料
(D) 討論產品

解說 盧瑟福先生最後説，他想問馬庫斯關於會議的事（And Marcus, I wanted to ask you about your speaking points for the meeting.），所以正確答案是和會議報告有關的選項 (C)。

實戰應用 Chapter 04

和圖表有關的對話

p. 192

1. C　2. D　3. D　4. B　5. B　6. D

Questions 1-3 refer to the following conversation and coupon.

W Q1 Q3Excuse me, I'm looking for a 27-inch computer monitor, but I only see 21- and 24-inch monitors. Do you have larger monitors in stock?

M Q2 Yes. The monitors used to all be together, but we recently moved the larger displays to a separate aisle. I'll show you where they are.

W OK, thanks a lot. I have this discount coupon for CompuTech. Is it valid for your store, too?

M Yes, we accept our competitor's coupon. Just show it to the cashier when you check out to receive your discount.

女：不好意思，我在找 27 吋的電腦螢幕，但我只看到 21 吋及 24 吋的螢幕。你們店裡有較大的螢幕嗎？

男：有的。以前螢幕都擺在一起，不過最近我們把較大的螢幕搬到另一個走道。我告訴妳它們放哪。

女：好的。多謝。我有這張康普科技的折價券，在你們的店裡也可以用嗎？

男：可以，我們也接受競爭對手的折價券。只要在結帳時，向收銀員出示折價券，妳就可以享有折扣。

折價券
電腦螢幕

21-24 吋	25 美元折價金
25 吋以上	50 美元折價金

康普科技
3 月 20 日到期

字彙 in stock 有庫存的　aisle 走道
defective 有瑕疵的

---

1. 女子提到什麼問題？
   (A) 她買到的螢幕有瑕疵。
   (B) 她想要的產品沒有庫存。
   (C) 她找不到物品。
   (D) 她無法享有折扣。

解說 女子一開始就說，正在找 27 吋的電腦螢幕，但是只看到 21 吋及 24 吋的，接著問，庫存有更大的螢幕嗎。所以可以知道，她找不到她想要的產品，選項 (C) 是正確答案。

2. 男子說最近發生何事？
   (A) 螢幕過去都擺放在同一走道。
   (B) 電腦特賣中止了。
   (C) 折價券被取消。
   (D) 產品被移動位置。

解說 男子說，以前螢幕都擺在一起，但最近將較大的螢幕搬到另一個走道。所以可以知道，最近產品的位置移動了，選項 (D) 是正確答案。

3. 請看圖表。女子最有可能享有多少折扣？
   (A) 3 元
   (B) 20 元
   (C) 25 元
   (D) 50 元

解說 女子要購買的電腦螢幕是 27 吋的，圖表顯示 25 吋以上便宜 50 美元，所以正確答案是選項 (D)。

Questions 4-6 refer to the following conversation and card.

W We've received a lot of customer complaints lately.

M Unfortunately, you're right. I was just dealing with an unhappy client a moment ago.

W Uh-oh. What was the problem?

M He was extremely upset. Q5 His checking account was overdrawn, but he did not receive a notice from us. He had to pay two overdraft fees because of this.

W Alright. I think we should reconsider some of parts of our penalty fee system. I think it might be affecting our customer satisfaction more than we realized.

M I agree. There are some other issues we have to consider as well. ^{Q6}Look at the rest of these comments— let's figure out what to do.

女：最近我們收到很多顧客投訴。
男：遺憾的是，妳說得對。我前一刻還在應付一名不滿的客戶。
女：喔喔。什麼問題？
男：他超生氣的。因為他的支票存款帳戶透支了，但卻沒收到我們的通知。為此，他必須支付兩筆透支手續費。
女：難怪。我覺得我們應該重新審視部分的罰款制度。或許它對於我們顧客滿意度的影響，這超過我們所能想像。
男：有同感。我們也同時需要考量其他問題。看看其餘的評價，我們來想想該做什麼。

姓名	評價
1. 法蘭克·布朗	行員態度惡劣
2. 蘇艾迪	帳戶透支未通知
3. 李承熙	管理費過高
4. 珍妮佛·聖克萊	利率太低

字彙 complaint 抱怨
checking account 支票存款帳戶
overdrawn 透支的　overdraft 透支

4. 對話者最有可能在何處工作？
　(A) 百貨公司
　(B) 銀行
　(C) 航空公司
　(D) 郵局

解說 男子第二段第二句話說，一位客戶的支票存款帳戶透支了，但沒收到通知，因此這位客戶要被罰款兩次。對話者在討論帳戶事宜，所以可以知道，他們是在銀行工作，答案是 (B)。

5. 請看圖表。對話者討論的客戶是哪一位？
　(A) 法蘭克·布朗
　(B) 蘇艾迪
　(C) 李承熙
　(D) 珍妮佛·聖克萊

解說 對話者在討論該名客戶不滿的原因，是因為他的支票存款帳戶透支了，卻沒收到通知，所以對照圖表可知他是蘇艾迪，正確答案為 (B)。

6. 對話者接下來會做何事？
　(A) 創設員工訓練課程
　(B) 修訂罰款制度
　(C) 更新人員進度表
　(D) 仔細檢視顧客投訴

解說 男子最後一句話說，Look at the rest of these comments—let's figure out what to do.（讓我們看看其他評價，再看看該怎麼做），所以選項 (D)「仔細檢視顧客投訴」是正確答案。

Mini Test　Chapter 04　p. 193
和圖表有關的對話

1. B　2. A　3. D　4. A　5. B　6. C

Questions 1-3 refer to the following conversation and map.

W ^{Q1}Did the business meeting go well?

M Very well. We agreed to do business together under certain conditions.

W Oh really? What did he say?

M He said the help desk is much bigger than the sales desk, ^{Q2}and the sales desk should be closer to the entrance, so customers can leave straight after purchasing.

W I agree. I suggest we make those changes and the remaining area will be closer to the help desk.

M Sounds great. I'll inform the staff to start changing the store structure as soon as possible.

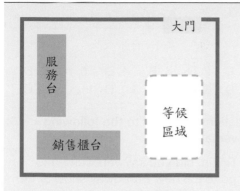

女：商務會議進行得順利嗎？

男：很順利。雙方同意在特定的條件下進行合作。

女：喔，真的嗎？他怎麼說？

男：他說服務台怎麼這比銷售櫃台大，而銷售櫃台應該要更靠近門口，這樣顧客在購買完畢後就可以直接離去。

女：有同感。我建議我們做些調整，這樣服務台旁就會有留有較大的區域。

男：聽起來很棒。我會通知員工盡快開始調整店內的擺設。

字彙 certain 某些　condition 狀況
as soon as possible 盡快

1. 男子最近從事何事？

(A) 到國外出差
(B) 開商務會議
(C) 外出午餐
(D) 移動銷售櫃台

解說 女子第一句話問說，商務會議開得順利嗎（Did the business meeting go well？），所以可以知道男子最近開商務會議，答案是 (B)。

2. 為何男子想要移動銷售櫃台？

(A) 顧客可以快速離開
(B) 擴增等候區域
(C) 調整溫度
(D) 減緩銷量

解說 男子說，銷售櫃檯靠近門口，顧客結完帳就可以離開了，所以可以知道，是為了讓顧客買完東西能快點離去，答案為 (A)。

3. 請看圖表。男子所說的「剩餘區域」是指？

(A) 服務台
(B) 門口
(C) 銷售櫃台
(D) 等候區域

解說 從圖上可以看出，銷售櫃台移靠近門口的話，等候區域就能更靠近服務台，所以正確答案是「等候區域」，答案為 (D)。

Questions 4-6 refer to the following conversation and list.

M Hi, I bought an electrical repair kit for a house I'm installing electrical wiring in, but I think there are some missing pieces. Q4 I'm supposed to finish the job today, so I really need them or the client will be upset.

W I see. What exactly is the problem?

M Q5 Well, everything works fine but there are only seven switches, so the whole system won't work properly.

W Ah, I see what the problem is. Q6 We have four people in the shop today, so I can drive over to your location and bring them to you if you'd like.

M That's great! Hold on, I'll just get the address of where I am so you can write it down.

電器維修工具組

斷路器 1 組
轉換器 10 個
電子連接器 2 個
AC 電源插頭 5 個

男：嗨，我要為屋子安裝電線，所以買了一組電器維修工具組，不過我想或許少了一些零件。我必須要在今天完工，所以我真的需要這些零件，否則客戶會不高興。

女：我了解。實際的問題是什麼？

男：嗯，其他一切都還好，就是工具組內只有七個轉換器，所以整個電線系統無法順利運作。

女：啊，我了解問題在哪了。今天店裡有四名人手，所以如果你願意，我可以開車到你的所在地，把東西帶給你。

男：太好了！別掛電話，我去要這裡的地址，讓妳可以拿筆記下來。

字彙 kit 成套工具

4. 男子正在做何事？

(A) 在某處人家中工作

(B) 在家工作

(C) 維修電腦

(D) 安裝管道

解說 男子說他正在安裝電線，並說今天要完工，否則客戶會不高興。所以可以知道，男子正在某個客戶家工作，答案是 (A)。

5. 請看圖表。男子少了什麼？

(A) 斷路器

(B) 轉換器

(C) AC 電源插頭

(D) 電子連接器

解說 男子說，工具組一切都好，卻只有七個轉換器（everything works fine but there are only seven switches）。看圖表可以知道，應該要有 10 個轉換器，所以轉換器少了，答案是 (B)。

6. 女子說要做何事？

(A) 用郵寄方式寄送所缺零件

(B) 打給她的經理

(C) 親自送去

(D) 請她的員工送去

解說 女子說，店裡有四個人，所以她可以開車送過去，所以可以知道，女子會親自將零件送過去，答案是 (C)。

Actual Test	p. 194

1. C	2. D	3. B	4. B	5. A	6. D
7. D	8. C	9. A	10. D	11. C	12. C

Questions 1-3 refer to the following conversation.

W Robin, did you say you wanted to go to the new Broadway show at the Golden Theater?

M Yes. I did actually.

W A few of the people from the office are getting tickets for tonight's show.

M Oh really? What time does it start? Q2 I'm struggling to finish my cash flow statements for August. I will probably be working until after 9 p.m.

W The show starts at 9 p.m. Maybe you can try and get your work finished by eight?

M I don't think that's possible. Q3 Can we go tomorrow night? I could definitely make it then.

W OK, sure. I'll let the others know and we will book tickets for tomorrow night at 9 p.m.

女：羅賓，你是不是說過你想去黃金劇院看新上演的百老匯的秀？

男：是啊，我確實想去。

女：辦公室裡幾個同事在訂今天晚上的票。

男：喔，真的嗎？秀何時開始？我現在正忙著要將八月的現金流量表趕出來。我很可能要加班到晚上九點之後。

女：秀在晚上九點開始。或許你可以試著在八點以前把工作做完？

男：我覺得不太可能。我們能不能明晚再去？我一定可以在那之前完工。

女：當然好啊。我會跟其他人說訂明晚九點的秀。

字彙 struggle to 努力做……
cash flow statement 現金流量表
due for 理應有的

1. 女子所說「幾個同事在訂今天晚上的票」，是在暗示何事？

(A) 她覺得百老匯的票很貴。

(B) 她想為男子做點事。

(C) 她在邀請男子一起看戲。

(D) 她為男子買了張票。

解說 本題要從女子的話，推測出她沒有直接講明的意思。如果單就從她表面所說的話，會認為她只是在傳達「某人買了票」，但對話一開始，女子問男子說，你不是說想去看百老匯的秀嗎，可以知道女子的目的是想邀男子一起去看，所以正確答案是 (C)。對話的最後一句，出現了訂票（book）這動詞，也可能會誤選選項 (D)。

2. 男子為何得加班？

(A) 他理應休假。

(B) 他必須更新電腦。

(C) 他灌了新的軟體。

(D) 他必須完成幾份財務報表。

解說 struggle to 是「為了……而努力奮鬥」，statement 除了表「說明」、「陳述」，在財務方面也有「報表」的意思。男子說正在努力將八月的現金流量表趕出來，要工作到很晚，所以可以知道正確答案是選項 (D)。

3. 男子提議何種解決方案？

(A) 他將不會加入他們

(B) 明天再去看秀

(C) 自己去

(D) 排開時間用餐

解說 掌握男子最後說的那段話，就能解題了。男子說可不可以明天晚上去（go tomorrow night），到那時報表一定能做完（make it），所以正確答案是 (B)。make it 有「在時間內參加」或「成功」的意思，要依據上下文來做最適當的解釋。

Questions 4-6 refer to the following conversation and map.

M1 Hello, this is Jim Smith from the 3rd Floor. Is this the maintenance technician?

M2 Yes, how can I help you?

M1 One of our machines has stopped working. There is a burning smell in the room, so I think something happened to the electronics. Q4 We need to get it fixed because we have to meet a quota by this evening or the boss will be very upset.

M2 Which machine is it?

M1 I'm not sure what it's called, Q5 but it is right next to the stairs.

M2 Ah, I know that machine. We have been having problems with it for a while now. I'm repairing something on the fifth floor; when I finish I will come and help you. Q6 I suggest you unplug the machine until I arrive.

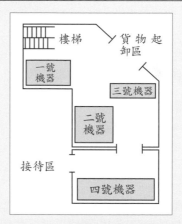

男 1：嗨，我是三樓的吉姆·史密斯。請問是維修技工嗎？

男 2：我是，需要我做什麼？

男 1：我們的一部機器壞了。房間裡有一股燒焦味，所以我想是電器出了點問題。我們必須把它修好，才能在今天晚上完成預定的工作額度，否則老闆會很生氣。

男 2：是哪一部機器？

男 1：我不知道它叫什麼，但它就放在樓梯旁。

男2： 啊，我知道那部機器。它出問題已有一陣子了。我現在正在五樓修東西，修完後就會去幫你。建議你在我到之前，先把機器的插頭拔掉。

字彙 maintenance technician 維修技師
meet a quota 完成限額

4. 為何男子要叫人修機器？

(A) 因為他的老闆不高興
(B) 為了要完成工作限額
(C) 他才能提交報告
(D) 安排約會

解說 解題關鍵是 We need to get it fixed because we have to meet a quota by this evening（我們必須把機器修好，才能在今天晚上完成預定的工作額度），所以正確答案是 (B)。

5. 請看圖表。哪台機器需要修理？

(A) 一號機器
(B) 二號機器
(C) 三號機器
(D) 四號機器

解說 男子說，不確定是幾號機器，但知道它在樓梯旁邊，圖中樓梯旁的是一號機器，所以正確答案是選項 (A)。

6. 維修技工建議何事？

(A) 讓機器保持運作
(B) 更新軟體
(C) 接洽人資部
(D) 拔掉機器插頭

解說 最後一句話男子（維修技工）建議說，在我到達前，先將機器插頭拔掉，所以正確答案是選項 (D)。

Questions 7-9 refer to the following conversation.

M Q7 Linda, did you decide which carpenter you'll hire to install new cupboards in your kitchen?

W Q7 Yeah, I signed a work contract with someone called Donald Turner. I called several carpenters in the area and left messages. Q8 His response was very quick and informative, so I hired him.

M Oh, great. So will the new cupboards be ready in time for your housewarming party next week?

W Q9 No, he said he has a lot of work to do this month and couldn't start the project until next month.

男： 琳達，決定好要僱用哪一位木匠幫妳的廚房安裝新的櫥櫃了嗎？

女： 決定好了，我與一位名叫唐諾・透納的木匠簽了工作合約了。我給幾個本地的木匠打了電話，也留了訊息。他的回覆快速又詳盡，所以我決定僱用他。

男： 喔，太好了。那麼新的櫥櫃會在妳下週舉辦喬遷派對之前就裝好嗎？

女： 不會，他說他這個月有很多工作，要到下個月才能開工。

字彙 carpenter 木匠
informative 提供資訊的
housewarming party 喬遷派對
plumbing 水管裝置
landscaping 景觀設計
carpentry 木工手藝
establish reputation 建立名聲

7. 透納先生在哪個領域工作？

(A) 水管裝置
(B) 繪畫
(C) 景觀設計
(D) 木工手藝

解說 對話一開始，男子就問女子決定好要僱用哪一位木匠（carpenter）安裝櫥櫃？之後女子又說跟透納先生簽訂工作合約，可知透納先生的工作領域是木工相關，正確答案是選項 (D)。

8. 為何女子選擇透納先生？

(A) 他的報價最低。
(B) 他在當地頗負盛名。
(C) 他與她溝通良好。
(D) 他這個月有空。

解說 關於女子僱用（hire）透納先生的原因，因為女子提到透納的回覆最快最好（quick and informative），所以就僱用他了，這就是原因。將回覆得最快最好，改成說溝通得良好，也沒錯，所以選項 (C) 是正確答案。

9. 為何工程會在下個月才開始？

  (A) 透納先生的工作量太大。

  (B) 必須先預訂特殊的零件。

  (C) 應女子要求。

  (D) 舉辦喬遷派對有太多東西要準備。

解說 女子最後一句話說明了她僱用的木匠透納，本月有很多工作要做（a lot of work to do this month），所以要從下個月開始，所以選項 (A) 正確。選項 (B) 和 (C) 對話中並沒有提到。喬遷派對和木匠做櫥櫃的時間延後，沒有直接的關係，所以選項 (D) 也是錯的。

Questions 10-12 refer to the following conversation with three speakers.

M1 Hello, Dream Travels, this is Jake speaking. How can I help you?

W Hello, Jake. Q10 Q11This is Janet Lee, I just received my itinerary, and I noticed that my flight has two layovers, but I booked a direct flight.

M1 I'm sorry, do you know who processed your request?

W It was William Banks.

M1 Hold on a second, I will transfer you to William.

W OK, thank you.

M2 Hello, William speaking. What can I do for you?

W Hello, William. My name is Janet Lee. I called you a week ago and booked a direct flight to New York, but there are two layovers on my itinerary. Q12Hold on, I'll give you my booking number.

男1：理想旅行社您好，我是傑克，我能為您提供什麼服務嗎？

女：嗨，傑克，我是李珍娜。我剛剛收到我的班機行程表，發現我的班機要轉機兩次，可是我訂的是直航班機。

男1：很抱歉，請問您知道是哪一位處理您的行程表嗎？

女：是威廉·班克斯。

男1：請您稍等一下，我幫您轉接威廉。

女：好，謝謝你。

男2：您好，我是威廉。我能為您做些什麼？

女：嗨，威廉。我是李珍娜，一週前我打來請你預訂前往紐約的直航班機，可是我的班機行程卻要轉機兩次。你等等，我去拿我的航班訂位號碼。

字彙 itinerary 班機行程表
layover（尤指飛行途中的）短暫停留

10. 女子為何來電？

  (A) 預訂航班

  (B) 取消航班

  (C) 度假改期

  (D) 告知哪裡出錯

解說 女子打電話給旅行社說，剛收到班機行程表，她訂購的是直航機票（a direct flight），結果行程表上寫要轉機兩次，所以可知，女子告知旅行社員工行程表有錯，選項 (D) 是正確答案。

11. 女子的班機行程表有何問題？

  (A) 價錢太貴。

  (B) 是直航班機。

  (C) 要轉機。

  (D) 訂錯班機日期。

解說 女子說她的行程表有兩次轉機（two layovers），但她訂的是直航機票，所以問題出在「有轉機」，故 (C) 正確。

12. 女子主動提供給威廉什麼？

  (A) 她的信用卡號

  (B) 她的護照資料

  (C) 她的航班訂位號碼

  (D) 她家地址

解說 女子最後說，我把我的訂位號碼（booking number）給你，所以可以知道，正確答案是選項 (C)。

1. B　2. D　3. C　4. A　5. C　6. A

Questions 1-3 refer to the following phone message.

M Hello, Mr. Holmes. ^{Q1} This is James Hood at the Milford Public Library. I noticed you e-mailed us about some late fees that you were confused about. ^{Q2} After reviewing your account, I've determined that you are right and you were wrongly charged for late fees on your most recently returned books. I am so sorry about that. If you stop by the library sometime this week, we will reimburse you for those incorrect late fees. ^{Q3} Please just make sure to bring your library card with you at that time. Again, we apologize for the mistake and hope to see you again soon.

男： 您好，福爾摩斯先生。我是米佛公共圖書館的詹姆士・胡德。我看到您發電郵告知我們您對幾筆書籍逾期費有點疑問。在查過您的帳戶後，我發現您是對的，我們扣錯了您近期歸還書籍的逾期費。真的很抱歉。如果您在這個禮拜路過圖書館，我們將會退還給您算錯的逾期費用。請記得屆時一定要帶您的圖書證。對於扣款出錯，我們再次表示歉意，希望能盡快再次與您見面。

字彙 notice 看到　late fees 逾期費
account 帳戶
charged for 被……收費
incorrect 錯誤的　reimburse 退還

1. 來電者最有可能是誰？
(A) 作家　　　(C) 銀行家
(B) 圖書館員　(D) 顧客

解說 留言者一開始介紹自己是圖書館的詹姆士・胡德。留言內容是關於受話者福爾摩斯先生的逾期費問題。所以留言者應該是在圖書館管理讀者逾期費事宜的人。正確答案是選項 (B)。

2. 為何來電者要道歉？
(A) 特賣在預定時間前結束。
(B) 貨運延誤。
(C) 某個物品沒有現貨。
(D) 受話者被錯誤扣款。

解說 留言者道歉的地方，是在留言中段的 I am so sorry about that 這句，這句話的 that 是指上一句的 wrongly charged for late fees。從上下文來看，之前收到了受話者對逾期金表疑問的電郵，經查證發現收錯了逾期金，所以來電說明並道歉。正確答案是選項 (D)。其他選項的特賣、貨運、庫存，都跟道歉無關，所以都是錯的。

3. 受話者被要求要攜帶何物？
(A) 信用卡　　(C) 圖書證
(B) 收據　　　(D) 逾期未還的書

解說 留言的最後出現了「make sure to ＋原形動詞」的片語，是請求對方「務必一定要做……」的意思，要記住這類表請求的片語。詹姆士・胡德請福爾摩斯先生帶圖書證（library card）來，所以正確答案是 (C)。雖然談話中出現很多次逾期金（late fees），但實際上福爾摩斯先生逾期金已被錯誤扣款，所以和選項 (A) 繳費用的信用卡無關。福爾摩斯先生已歸還書（recently returned books），所以 (D) 也是錯的。

Questions 4-6 refer to the following phone message.

W Hello, Mr. Hoffman. My name is Ellen Cooper and I'm a customer service representative at Globe Airlines. I'm sorry to have to tell you that we have located your lost luggage, but it has still not arrived in New York. Q4 It seems that it was mistakenly placed on a plane to Denver. Q5 In the meantime, if you log on to our website and input your baggage claim number, you will be able to receive updates concerning the location of your luggage. Q6 Because you are one of our frequent flyer members, as soon as your luggage arrives I will have it delivered to your hotel free of charge with a small gift as a token of our apology. Thank you for your patronage.

女： 您好，霍夫曼先生。我是全球航空公司客服代表艾琳・庫柏。很抱歉我必須通知您我們找到您遺失的行李了，不過我們還未將它送抵紐約。它似乎被錯掛到前往丹佛的航班上。同時，如果您登入我們的官網，輸入您的行李提領號碼，您將可取得行李當下位置的最新消息。因為您是本航空公司的常飛會員，所以當您的行李一抵達紐約，我會隨即免費幫您送至您的下榻旅館，並附贈一個小禮品以示本公司的歉意。感謝您的搭乘。

字彙 representative 代表
mistakenly 錯誤地
frequent flyer 飛行常客　token 象徵
patronage 惠顧　waive 省免

4. 來電者提到何問題？
(A) 行李錯掛了。
(B) 班機延誤。
(C) 所有機票都賣光了。
(D) 一名旅客錯過航班。

解說 留言者提到，霍夫曼先生的行李被誤送上了往丹佛（Denver）的班機，所以行李現在還沒送到紐約，故正確答案是 (A)。

5. 來電者提議何事？
(A) 購買旅遊平安保險
(B) 前往位於丹佛的辦事處
(C) 使用網路服務
(D) 成為飛行常客會員

解說 留言者建議霍夫曼先生，登錄航空公司的網站（log on to our website），輸入行李提領號碼。所以可知，留言者建議利用網路服務。正確答案是選項 (C)。

6. 來電者說她將做何事？
(A) 安排寄送
(B) 免收逾期金
(C) 電郵提醒預約時間
(D) 提供行李提領號碼

解說 留言者最後說，行李一到，立刻和小禮物一起寄送到旅館。所以可以知道，她會去準備寄送事宜，正確答案是選項 (A)。

Mini Test **Chapter 02** p. 230
宣布、通知與演說

---

1. C　2. B　3. D　4. B　5. A　6. B

Questions 1-3 refer to the following excerpt from a meeting.

W I'd like to welcome all of the warehouse workers to today's special training session. We will be introducing you to new software called Invent XM. Q1 The software will help the company keep track of inventory and improve operation efficiency in the warehouse. Q2 We are holding this training session in the conference room so that we can first show you a training video. After watching the video, Chris Hunter from the information technology department will explain how to utilize Invent XM. Q3 If you have any questions, please ask them after his talk so that they can be answered by Mr. Hunter and his coworkers. Thank you.

女： 歡迎各位倉管員工參加今日的特別培
訓課程。我們今天向各位介紹新的軟
體 Invent XM。這個軟體將有助公司
掌握倉庫存貨，改善倉庫的作業效率。
特訓課程將在會議室舉辦，以便播放
訓練影片。等各位看完影片後，資訊科
技部的克里斯・杭特將會解說如何使
用 Invent XM。如果各位有任何疑問，
請在他解說完畢之後提出，以便杭特
先生及他的同事進行答覆。謝謝。

字彙 warehouse 倉庫　inventory 存貨
investment 投資　submit 提交
questionnaire 問卷

1. Invent XM 將被用來做何事？
(A) 收集客戶資料
(B) 備份重要資料
(C) 追蹤倉庫品項
(D) 管理投資案

解說 宣布中提到，這個軟體將有助公司掌握
倉庫存貨，改善倉庫的作業效率。所以
可以知道，Invent XM 是用在管理倉庫
物品上的，正確答案是選項 (C)。

2. 為何培訓課程會在會議室舉辦？
(A) 才有足夠的座位
(B) 需使用視聽資料
(C) 以進行團體調查
(D) 以進行頒獎

解說 宣布中提到，為了要先看訓練影片
（training video），所以特別培訓課
程要在會議室舉行，正確答案是選項
(B)。

3. 聽眾被要求做何事？
(A) 記筆記
(B) 繳回問卷
(C) 提報故障
(D) 提出問題

解說 宣布類型的獨白，時常指示人的行動。
宣布最後面提到，如果員工有任何疑
問，在杭特先生說明完後，可以請教他
和他的同事，由此可知說話者是請聽眾
問問題，正確答案是 (D)。

Questions 4-6 refer to the following announcement.

M Welcome, Greenfood shoppers. Q4 Today we're celebrating 10 years of bringing organic and environmentally friendly products to our customers. Without your support, we wouldn't have been able to expand to over 100 shops around the country, and we're continuing to grow. Q5 To celebrate this event we are holding sales on some of our most popular products, including our free range eggs, which are selling out fast. Q6 The list of items on sale is in our flyers, which are available at the front entrance and written on the chalkboard near the cashiers. Thank you for your continued support.

男： 歡迎來到綠色食物商品店。今天我們將
歡慶我們引進有機及環境友善產品的
第十週年紀念。沒有您的支持，我們無
法在全國拓展超過一百多家分店，而且
業績還在持續成長。為了盛大慶祝，本
店針對數種最熱門的產品舉辦特賣，包
括很快就銷售一空的放山雞蛋。前門入
口處可取得本店的廣告傳單，內有特賣
品項的詳細清單；而收銀台附近的黑板
上也有寫明特賣品項。感謝您長期的惠
顧。

綠色食物週年慶優惠	
放山雞蛋	5 折
有機優酪乳	6 折
全麥麵包	7 折
有機香草冰淇淋	75 折

字彙 free range egg 放山雞蛋
expiry date 保存期限
produce 農產品　dairy 乳製品

4. 為何商店針對某些品項做折扣？
(A) 因為這些品項快過期
(B) 因為在慶祝週年慶
(C) 因為業績下滑
(D) 因為盛大開幕

解說 詢問主題的題型，要掌握宣布最前面的部分。說話者一開始提到，他們將歡慶引進有機及環境友善產品的第十週年紀念，又在宣布中段提到「To celebrate this event we are holding sales on some of our most popular products.」，所以可以知道，是為了慶祝銷售十週年，所以有些商品要打折，正確答案是選項 (B)。

5. 請看圖表。常銷售一空的品項打幾折？

(A) 5 折

(B) 6 折

(C) 7 折

(D) 75 折

解說 宣布中提到，放山雞蛋銷售最快（our free range eggs, which are selling out fast）。所以看到圖表，放山雞蛋是50%，因此正確答案是選項 (A)。

6. 顧客可以在何處看到特賣品清單？

(A) 在農產品區

(B) 在黑板上

(C) 肉類區

(D) 靠近乳製品走道

解說 在宣布的最後面提到，打折產品的清單可在入口處拿，收銀台附近的黑板上也有寫出特賣品項，所以選項中 (B) 是正確答案。

Mini Test　Chapter 03　p. 244

廣告

1. B　2. D　3. C　4. D　5. B　6. A

Questions 1-3 refer to the following advertisement.

W Q1 All this month at the Santiago History Museum, there will be an exhibition featuring the hunting tools used by Ojibwe Native Americans over 200 years ago. Q2 These artifacts were discovered by French archaeologist Ferdinand Martin last year during an archaeological dig in the Midwest. Along with a display of artifacts such as bows, arrows, and spears, museum guests will have the opportunity to view a documentary about the lives of contemporary Ojibwe people. Q3 Please visit our website to watch a preview of the film and learn more about the exhibition.

女：這一整個月，聖地牙哥歷史博物館，將以兩百年前美國原住民毆吉維族所使用的狩獵工具為題，舉辦特展。這些原始工具是由去年在中西部進行考古挖掘的法國考古學家費迪南・馬丁所挖掘而出。除了展出一系列諸如弓、箭、矛等等的狩獵工具外，參觀民眾也將有機會觀賞現代毆吉維族人的生活紀錄片。民眾可上我們的官網觀賞該紀錄片的預告，並獲知更多展覽的相關訊息。

字彙 exhibition 展覽　feature 以……為特色　archaeologist 考古學家　artifact（有歷史價值）的文物　contemporary 現代的；當代的　preview 預告片

1. 展覽的主題是？

(A) 古代化石

(B) 原住民的原始工具

(C) 天文新發現

(D) 法國歷史

解說 詢問主題的試題，要掌握廣告最前面的部分。廣告中的第一句話提到，有一個展覽（exhibition），展示美國某部落的狩獵工具，所以答案為 (B)。feature 當動詞表「以……為特色」，要注意這個字的用法。選項 (A) 的化石（fossil），是生活在古代的生物遺骸，和展覽主題無關。(C) 的天文新發現，在廣告中並沒有提到。古時候的狩獵工具也可以視為是一種歷史，不過這些狩獵工具是北美原住民（Native Americans）的遺物，不是法國的，所以選項 (D) 也不對。

2. 費迪南・馬丁是誰？

(A) 美國原住民

(B) 策展人

(C) 紀錄片導演

(D) 學者

解說 廣告提到費迪南・馬丁的地方，說他是找到這些狩獵工具的考古學家，所以選項 (D) 是正確答案，它將考古學家（archaeologist）改稱為學者（scholar）。

3. 廣告邀請聽眾做何事？

(A) 閱讀手冊

(B) 觀賞表演

(C) 瀏覽網站

(D) 預先購票

解說 廣告的最後一句話，請民眾上官網觀賞該紀錄片的預告（Please visit our website to watch a preview of the film.），所以正確答案是選項 (C)。

Questions 4-6 refer to the following advertisement.

M Q4 Grandview Mega Bookstore has opened at its new location on Grandview and 52nd Avenue. This giant store boasts 5 stories filled with tens of thousands of books from all genres and from all over the world. Q5 Best-selling author Michael Richardson will be at the weekend opening blitz to sign books. Q6 Only the first 30 people through the door will have the opportunity to have their picture taken with him, so be sure to get there early. Q6 Plus all best-selling books will be 20% off during this weekend only. The bookstore features couches and coffee tables all over the store as well as coffee, gift, toy, and stationary shops. There is something for everyone in the family. Come check out the Grandview Mega Bookstore.

男： 格朗維大型書店已經在 52 大道的新址開幕了。這家大型圖書商店自詡擁有五個樓層，販售來自全球各地、數以萬計的各類圖書。暢銷書作家麥可・理察森將會在本週末的快閃開幕式中，舉辦簽書活動。只有進入書店的前三十名民眾才有機會與他合照，所以記得要提早到場。此外，本店舉辦所有暢銷書皆享八折的優惠活動，特惠期間僅限這個週末。書店的招牌特色，是店內各個角落充斥著躺椅及咖啡桌；同時，本店亦附設有咖啡館、禮品店、玩具店以及文具店。是個全家大小老少咸宜的好去處。快來逛逛格朗維大型書店吧！

字彙 boast 以⋯⋯而自豪

feature (v.) 使⋯⋯成為特色

4. 廣告中所宣傳的是哪一類的商店？

(A) 玩具店　　(B) 圖書館

(C) 禮品店　　(D) 書店

解說 廣告開始就提到，格朗維書店在新的地點開幕了，所以選項 (D) 正確。選項 (A)、(C) 都是附屬在格朗維書店內，要注意這種重複獨白用字的錯誤答案。

5. 誰是麥可・理察森？

(A) 書店經理　　(C) 顧客

(B) 作家　　　 (D) 書店老闆

解說 在廣告中段提到，麥可・理察森是暢銷書作家（best-selling author），並提到他會參加週末的快閃開幕式簽書，所以正確答案是選項 (B)。

6. 説話者鼓勵聽眾做何事？

(A) 購買暢銷書

(B) 晚點抵達

(C) 多多閱讀

(D) 上圖書館

解說 在廣告中段提到，最早進場的 30 名客人，可以和麥可・理察森合影，所以請大家盡早到場；之後又提到，暢銷書打八折（best-selling books will be 20% off），所以可以知道廣告鼓勵大家購買暢銷書，正確答案是選項 (A)。

Mini Test | Chapter 04
p. 257

新聞報導

---

1. D　2. A　3. B　4. B　5. A　6. D

Questions 1-3 refer to the following broadcast.

W This is Morning Update on radio TZX. Q1 **Today marks the beginning of the seventh annual Salem Blues Festival.** The festival has been growing every year, and this year promises to be the largest yet. Q2 **As a result, local businesses have been reporting increased traffic and sales.** It seems that over 25,000 town visitors will come to see the festival this time. Q3 And now, we will be interviewing Robert Stam, one of the musicians who will be performing today. As many of you know, Mr. Stam is a world-famous blues guitarist.

女：　這裡是 TZX 廣播頻道的晨間新聞。今天是第七屆薩勒姆藍調音樂節的第一天。該音樂盛事的規模每年持續增長，預計今年將會是史上規模最大的一場。因此，本地的商家皆反映來客量及銷售量有顯著提升。今年預計會有超過兩萬五千名的城鎮居民前來參與本次盛會。而現在，我們將訪問即將於今日登台表演的音樂家之一，羅伯特·史坦。可能大部分的聽眾都知道，史坦先生是一名享譽全球的藍調吉他手。

字彙　annual 年度的　traffic 客流量
perform 表演

1. 廣播的內容關於？
(A) 氣象狀況更新
(B) 電影節
(C) 本地選舉
(D) 音樂節

解說　報導的第二句話說，今天是第七屆薩勒姆藍調音樂節（seventh annual Salem Blues Festival）的第一天，所以可以知道新聞廣播的主題和音樂節有關，選項 (D) 將藍調（blues）說成是 music festival（音樂節）也合理，因為藍調也是音樂的一種，所以選項 (D) 是正確答案。報導中的 mark 除了表「做標記」，還有「紀念特定事物」的意思。

2. 說話者提到有何利益？
(A) 刺激經濟
(B) 有優惠門票
(C) 教育機會
(D) 增加曝光率

解說　報導中段提及因為音樂節，當地的商家或行號，交易增加、銷售增加（local businesses have been reporting increased traffic and sales.），所以選項 (A) 用刺激經濟（economic stimulation）換句話說音樂節刺激了經濟，意思是對的，所以是正確答案。報導中的 traffic，一般是「交通」或是「交通流量」，但在商業和網路的領域，它時常當作「客流量、交易量、來訪量」。因為音樂節訪客增加，同時現在有新聞廣播為它作宣傳，所以可能會誤認為好處是選項 (D)「增加曝光率」，這點要小心。因為題目問的是「音樂節帶來的好處」，如果舉辦音樂節是為了獲得增加曝光率的話，那這篇新聞廣播，就要提到大眾的反應是如何，或其他媒體是否爭相報導，所以選項 (D) 不對。

3. 聽眾接下來最有可能聽到？
(A) 演說
(B) 專訪
(C) 氣象報告
(D) 緊急消息宣布

解說　廣播的最後面提到，將訪問今日出場表演的音樂家羅伯特·史坦，所以會聽到訪問，正確答案是選項 (B)。

Questions 4-6 refer to the following announcement.

M ^{Q4 Q6} Now, a JRFM community announcement: Cloverdale Junior High is holding a bake sale to raise money for their orchestra group trip to Vienna, Austria. The Cloverdale Junior High Orchestra has won the municipal, city, and state contests. They hope to raise enough money to enter the international contest in Vienna, where over 200 schools from around the world will be competing next fall. Come out and support Cloverdale Junior High. They are currently accepting donations from the community. They have raised over $5,000 so far. They hope to raise another $3,000. ^{Q5} For more information, visit the school website at www.cloverdalejhigh.com/orchestra.

男： 現在播報 JRFM 社區消息：克羅弗戴爾國中正舉辦烘焙義賣會，為了替該校的管弦樂團籌措前往奧地利維也納的旅行經費。克羅弗戴爾國中管弦樂團迄今已贏得市級、城級、以及州級的音樂競賽。他們此次募款，是為了參加在維也納舉辦的國際比賽，預計將有來自全球各地、超過兩百所的學校於明年秋天進行比賽。請大家快來支持克羅弗戴爾國中。他們現在正接受地區居民的捐款，目前已募得了大約五千元美金，但他們希望能再多募得三千元。想知道更多相關資訊，可上學校的官網 www.cloverdalejhigh.com/orchestra 了解更多。

字彙 municipal 市立的 fundraising 募款 symphonic 交響樂團的

4. 廣播宣告的活動是哪一類型？
(A) 一項競賽
(B) 募款活動
(C) 交響音樂會
(D) 音樂劇

解說 報導一開始就提到，克羅弗戴爾國中正舉辦烘焙義賣會，為該校的管弦樂團籌措出國比賽的旅行經費（... raise money for their orchestra group trip）。所以可以知道是募款活動，正確答案是選項 (B)，它將 raise money 用 fundraising 來表示也可以。

5. 聽眾為何要瀏覽網站？
(A) 取得資訊
(B) 購買門票
(C) 加入管弦樂團
(D) 下載音樂

解說 報導的最後一句話說「For more information, visit the school website at ...」，所以可以知道，上網是為了要獲取更多訊息，正確答案是選項 (A)。

6. 根據說話者所言，為何要募款？
(A) 為資助圖書館
(B) 為添購新樂器
(C) 為修建教室
(D) 為了旅費

解說 報導一開始就提到，克羅弗戴爾國中正舉辦烘焙義賣會，為了替該校的管弦樂團籌措去維也納參賽的旅費，所以正確答案是選項 (D)。

Mini Test **Chapter 05** p. 271
觀光導覽

1. B　2. C　3. C　4. D　5. C　6. A

Questions 1-3 refer to the following speech.

W ^{Q1} Welcome, everyone, to the opening night of the Auburn Independent Film Festival. This year has been a huge success, with all of our tickets having sold out during the first weekend of sales. ^{Q1 Q2} This year's film festival is an extremely momentous occasion because it is the 50th year since it started.

While the very first festival was only one day long, now it is an entire week. Today's festival also features filmmaking workshops and various interviews and talks. We would like to thank all of you for supporting this festival for such a long time. Q1 Q3 After the opening ceremony, please take a festival program on your way out of the theater. It contains the detailed history of the festival and brief information about famous directors and actors from the festival.

女：歡迎諸位今晚蒞臨奧本獨立電影節的開幕晚會。今年電影節的門票，在開賣首週即銷售一空，盛況空前。今年的電影節，因為是自其開辦以來的第五十屆，所以是重大的盛會。電影節開辦之初，僅為期一日；但現在已發展成持續一週的活動。而今天的電影節活動，特別的是同時會舉辦電影製作工作坊，以及各式各樣的專訪及座談。在此我們要感謝諸位對電影節長期以來的支持。在開幕式結束後，請各位在走出劇院前順手拿取一份電影節節目單，其中包含電影節詳細的歷史沿革，及歷屆知名導演及演員的相關簡介。

字彙 sold out 售罄　momentous 重大的
entire 全部的　various 各式各樣的
support (n.) 支持
opening ceremony 開幕式
festival program 典禮節目單
detailed history 詳細的歷史
brief 簡短的

1. 說話者最有可能是？
(A) 電影導演
(B) 活動企劃
(C) 得獎人
(D) 劇院老闆

解說 獨白一開始，說話者並沒有告知她身分或屬於什麼公司，所以要從她所說的內容，來推測她的身分。說話者一開始說，歡迎大家來參加電影節，接著就開始說明電影節的歷史、期間、特色等，所以可以知道她是對活動非常關心的人。

另外，她還請聽眾在開幕式之後，帶著電影節的節目單離開劇院，由此可知選項 (B) 活動企劃（an event organizer）是最符合說話者身分的選項。

2. 根據說話者的說法，這個活動的特別之處在於？
(A) 它以知名導演及演員為號召。
(B) 來賓可以免費進場。
(C) 是第五十週年紀念。
(D) 它的收益將捐作慈善。

解說 題目中的 special 表「特別的」。若掌握今年召開的電影節和其他年度的電影節，有什麼不同之處，就能解題。第三句話，說話者在說明今年的電影節時，用了重大的（momentous）這個形容詞，這就是試題所問的特別的（special）地方；她說今年是電影節開幕以來的第 50 年，所以說選項 (C)「是第五十週年紀念」是正確答案。說話者只說電影節的節目單，有知名導演及演員的相關簡介，而非電影節是主打知名導演和演員，所以選項 (A) 不對。

3. 聽眾被要求做何事？
(A) 填寫調查表　(C) 拿一份節目單
(B) 購買門票　　(D) 捐款

解說 說話者在介紹了電影節的歷史、特色、期間等等後，請（來參加電影節的）聽眾，帶著節目單（take a festival program）走出劇院。program 可當作「電腦程式」、「電視節目」，也可當作辦活動時的「節目單」，所以正確答案是選項 (C)。

Questions 4-6 refer to the following speech.

M Q4 This is Robert Lee at the grand opening of Rivervalley's public library. Q5 The massive structure located next to the city's courthouse and theater hall is hard to miss with its distinctive design and unique structural features. The architect behind the structure is Johan Jermain, who also designed the famed Rivervalley Art Museum and the Renaissance Building in the downtown financial core. There is a large crowd of locals and tourists here who are taking pictures of the various sculptures around the library lobby. Dozens of residents have already signed up for a membership card with many more waiting in line. Q6 Inside there are tables, desks, and couches and most important of all, tens of thousands of books and videos from all fields and subjects. This is Rivervalley's largest public building.

男： 我是羅伯特・李，歡迎諸位蒞臨河谷市公共圖書館盛大開幕式。這座巨型建築坐落於本市法院以及戲劇廳旁，其特殊的設計及獨特的建築特色，令人過目難忘。背後操刀的建築師，約翰・謝美，同時也是設計本市金融中心兩座著名建築物——河谷市藝術博物館及文藝復興大樓的建築師。圖書館大廳擺設著各式雕塑，常見有大批當地民眾及觀光客到此拍照留念。許多居民已註冊申請本館的會員圖書證，還有更多的民眾排隊等著申請加入。圖書館內設有桌子、書桌、以及沙發，更重要的是，有數以萬計，各個領域、學門的書籍及影帶供民眾閱覽，是河谷市最大的公共建築物。

字彙 distinctive 獨特的
financial core 金融中心
sculpture 雕塑

4. 根據説話者所言，何事正在進行？
(A) 建築物正在翻新。
(B) 正發表一項新產品。
(C) 正在慶祝節日。
(D) 一幢建築物對民眾開放中。

解説 在獨白一開始就提到，市立圖書館盛大開幕(the grand opening of Rivervalley's public library)，所以可知答案是 (D)，圖書館建築物對民眾開放中。

5. 發言者所説「難以忽略」，指的是？
(A) 此建築外觀與周邊建築物相似。
(B) 此建築不好找。
(C) 此建築很顯眼。
(D) 此建築尚未完工。

解説 第二句話提到，圖書館坐落於法院以及戲劇廳旁，其特殊的設計及獨特的建築特色，令人過目難忘。令人過目難忘換句話説，就是圖書館建築很顯眼，正確答案是選項 (C)。

6. 根據説話者所言，此幢建築物最重要的特色是？
(A) 書籍、影片藏量的規模及豐富性
(B) 規模小
(C) 會員圖書證
(D) 地點

解説 獨白的倒數第二句出現了 most important of all 這片語，表「最重要的是」，用這片語強調圖書館擁有各個領域、學門且數量眾多的書籍及影帶，所以正確答案是選項 (A)。

Mini Test
Chapter 06　　p. 285
人物介紹

1. D　2. C　3. B　4. A　5. C　6. B

Questions 1-3 refer to the following speech.

W Q1 Welcome to the 37th Annual Consumer Electronics Expo here in Tokyo, Japan. Q2 To kick off our opening ceremony, I would like to introduce Roy Cameron, the CEO of the consumer electronics company Surge. Mr. Cameron has been a leading figure in the field for decades, pioneering some of the most important developments in home computing. Q3 At the end of the talk, Mr. Cameron will be unveiling a solar-powered smartphone, Solar X.

It's Surge's newest innovation that will be available on the market next month. Now, let's give a warm welcome to Mr. Cameron.

女： 歡迎蒞臨日本東京第 37 屆消費電子產品展。開幕儀式的一開始，我想為大家介紹賽爾吉消費電子公司的執行長羅伊・卡麥隆。卡麥隆先生數十年來始終為業界的指標性人物，開創數個家用電腦的重大性發展。在談話結束後，卡麥隆先生將公開發表一款由太陽能發電的智慧型手機，Solar X。它是賽爾吉公司即將於下個月推出的最新創新性產品。現在，讓我們熱烈歡迎卡麥隆先生。

字彙 kick off 開始
leading figure 指標性人物　field 領域
decade 十年　pioneer (v.) 開創
home computing 家用電腦
solar-powered 太陽能發電的
unveil 發表；展示　innovation 創新

1. 這段介紹發生的地點在哪？
(A) 頒獎典禮上
(B) 訓練研習會中
(C) 大學講座
(D) 商業活動中

解說 介紹人的第一句說，活動名稱是第 37 屆消費電子產品展（37th Annual Consumer Electronics Expo），所以談話的場所就是在展覽會場裡，選項 (D) 將展覽會場改說成在一個商業活動上，也很合理，所以是正確答案。

2. 卡麥隆先生是誰？
(A) 消費者
(B) 教授
(C) 高級行政主管
(D) 發明家

解說 介紹人在介紹卡麥隆時，說他是賽爾吉（Surge）的執行長，選項 (C) 將公司的執行長說成是高級行政主管（executive）也可以，所以選項 (C) 是正確答案。來參加展覽的人一定也有很多消費者，但一般而言不會特別介紹消費者，文中也未提及，所以 (A) 不對。

3. 根據說話者，卡麥隆先生談話結束後，會有何事發生？
(A) 會引介一名講者出場。
(B) 發表一項產品。
(C) 會開始供餐。
(D) 將公布得獎人。

解說 介紹的後半部，提到卡麥隆演講後將發表（unveil）太陽能智慧型手機。unveil 原表「掀開」，引申為「產品首次公諸於世」。所以說選項 (B)「發表一項產品」是正確答案。

Questions 4-6 refer to the following broadcast.

W You're listening to *Art Watch* on your local public radio station. Q4 After the commercial break, we will be talking with Kathy Hill about her current exhibition at the Clinton Exhibition Hall. Ms. Hill works in the medium of ceramics, and will be displaying a series of large painted vases in this exhibition. Q5 She made the vases while living for five years in China. She said her deep relationships with locals are what inspired her to create the series of vases. Q6 Since this exhibition is very popular, you should buy tickets in advance online. By doing so, you can also receive 20 percent off the original price. Now, let's welcome Ms. Hill.

女： 您現在正在收聽的是本地公共廣播電台的《藝術前哨站》。在廣告之後，我們將與凱西・希爾聊聊她現正在柯林頓展覽館展出的作品。希爾小姐以陶土為創作素材，將於此次展覽展出一系列大型彩繪花瓶。這些花瓶是她旅居中國五年期間所創作的作品。根據她的說法，她與當地居民的深厚情誼，是促成她創作這一系列花瓶的靈感來源。因為這個展覽非常轟動，有興趣的民眾，最好事先上網訂票。網路訂票同時也可以享有八折的門票優惠價。現在，讓我們歡迎希爾小姐。

4. 凱西·希爾是誰？

(A) 藝術家

(B) 花藝師

(C) 藝評家

(D) 廣播節目主持人

解說 介紹中並沒有直接說出凱西·希爾的職業，不過有提到要和她談談關於她的展覽（exhibition），所以可以推知，她是辦展覽的藝術家，選項 (A) 是正確答案。之後主持人又提到她創作素材是陶土，展覽的作品是彩繪花瓶（painted vases），再次確認了她是藝術家沒錯。選項 (D) 廣播主持人，是本段獨白正在談話的人，小心不要弄錯了。

5. 根據說話者，凱西·希爾在中國做何事？

(A) 學習中文。

(B) 研究當地傳統。

(C) 從事創作。

(D) 舉辦展覽。

解說 在介紹凱西·希爾的展覽時，主持人提到她住在中國五年製作花瓶（She made the vases while living for five years in China.），所以選項 (C) 將「製作花瓶」，換成說是「從事創作」也對，是正確答案。介紹中雖提及她與當地人的深厚情誼，而創造出了這些作品，但是沒有提到她學中文、研究當地的傳統或在中國辦展，所以 (A)、(B) 與 (D) 是錯的。

6. 聽眾被鼓勵做何事？

(A) 購買花瓶

(B) 搶門票

(C) 上課

(D) 提早抵達

解說 由於展覽非常受歡迎，所以主持人向想來參觀展覽的聽眾建議，要事先在網路上購票（buy tickets in advance online），也就是選項 (B) 所說的「搶門票」。

Actual Test p. 286

> 1. B 2. A 3. D 4. D
> 5. A 6. B 7. A 8. D
> 9. C 10. A 11. B 12. C

Questions 1-3 refer to the following phone message.

W Q1 Good afternoon, my name is Janice Decker and I'm currently producing a commercial for QX Apparel, the world-famous sporting apparel company. Q2 I'm calling your agency because I'm looking for a woman between the ages of 40 and 60 to appear in the commercial. The model needs to be physically fit and have a slim body build. Q3 If you have such a model available, please e-mail me her résumé and photos. My e-mail address is janicedecker@qxgroup.com and my phone number is 555-6512. Thank you.

女： 午安，我是詹妮絲·戴珂，正在為全球知名的體育服飾公司 QX 服飾拍攝廣告。我打電話給貴經紀公司，是因為我想找一名年齡介於 40 歲到 60 歲之間的女性，來參與廣告演出。模特兒必須外型健康，且有纖細的體格。如果貴公司有這樣條件的模特兒，請電郵寄給我她的履歷及照片。我的電子信箱是 janicedecker@qxgroup.com，我的電話是 555-6512。感謝您。

字彙 commercial 商業廣告
world-famous 全球知名的
physically fit 身體健康
slim 纖細的　body build 體格

1. 來電者最有可能在哪一領域工作？

(A) 銀行業

(B) 廣告業

(C) 金融業

(D) 製造業

解說 留言者一開始就說，她正在為特定對象拍商業廣告（producing a commercial for . . .），所以可以說她是在廣告業工作，選項 (B) 是正確答案。produce 表「製造」，考生會因為聽到這字，誤以為是在製造業（manufacturing）工作，要小心。

2. 留言的目的為何？

(A) 僱用模特兒

(B) 會議改期

(C) 訂購商品

(D) 引介經紀人

解說 留言者為了製作一支廣告，正在向聽話者所屬的模特兒經紀公司，請他們提供一位特定年齡的模特兒參與廣告的演出（I'm looking for a woman . . . appear in the commercial）。所以可以說，她留言的目的是要僱用模特兒，正確答案是選項 (A)。留言者不是要經紀公司提供其他的模特兒仲介，所以選項 (D) 是錯的。另外，留言者要找的是人，不是物品，所以選項 (C) 也是錯的。

3. 來電者要求受話者做何事？

(A) 回電

(B) 提交年度報告

(C) 加速貨物運送

(D) 提供資訊

解說 留言者在留言的後半部提到，請受話者將合適的模特兒的履歷和照片，電郵給留言者（please e-mail me her résumé and photos），選項 (D) 將「履歷和照片」換成是訊息（information），也很合理，所以是正確答案。雖然談話者提供了她的電話號碼當作連絡方式之一，但並沒有要聽話者回電，所以選項 (A) 是錯的。

Questions 4-6 refer to the following announcement.

M Q4 This Thursday at 7 p.m. at the Milton College auditorium archeologist John Baker will be giving a special talk. His talk will focus on his research on the ancient monument Stonehenge, located in Wiltshire, England. Q5 After the talk, a short film documenting the history of this ancient site will be screened. Q6 Students, faculty, and staff will be granted free entrance to this event. Therefore, no prior purchase of tickets is necessary. Come and enjoy this informative talk.

男： 星期四晚上七點，考古學家約翰‧貝克將在米爾頓大學的禮堂，發表一場特殊的演說。演說將聚焦於他在英格蘭威爾特郡古蹟「巨石陣」的研究上。在演說結束後，將會播映一部簡短的紀錄片，講述此古蹟遺址的歷史沿革。本校的學生、教職員皆可免費入場聆聽演講。因此，不需事先購票。請大家記得來聆賞這場極具知識性的演講。

字彙 auditorium 禮堂
monument 歷史遺跡
document （影片等）紀實記錄
screen 把……放映在銀幕上
grant 許可 prior 事先的
informative 提供資訊的

4. 活動將在何處舉行？

(A) 公園

(B) 博物館

(C) 劇院

(D) 學校

解說 宣布的第一句話就說明了演說的日期、時間和地點，用表場所的介系詞 at，引導出了具體的地點米爾頓大學禮堂（Milton College auditorium）。因為是某學校的禮堂，所以是「學校」或是「禮堂」的選項，都可以是正確答案。正確答案是選項 (D)。

5. 演說結束後，會發生何事？

    (A) 播映影片。

    (B) 舉辦 Q & A 座談會。

    (C) 將引介影評人入場。

    (D) 分發文件。

解說 在宣布的中段出現了 after the talk，表示說話者將公布約翰·貝克演說之後的流程，所以要非常注意聽。介紹人說在演說結束後，將會播映一部簡短的紀錄片（a short film . . . will be screened）。screen 在這用被動語態，表示「被播放出來」。所以正確答案是 (A)，它將「短片」改成說是「錄影」（video）也是對的。

6. 關於活動，下列何者為是？

    (A) 將在週末舉辦。

    (B) 教授可免費入場。

    (C) 將在電視上轉播。

    (D) 將在戶外舉辦。

解說 最後倒數第三句說，學生、教職員免費進場（Students, faculty, and staff will be granted free entrance . . .），所以選項 (B) 說教授免費是合理的。faculty 表「教職員」，包含了教授、助教等所有和教學有關的人。集合的日期是星期四，所以 (A) 不對。另外，舉行的地點是禮堂（auditorium），所以 (D) 也不對。

Questions 7-9 refer to the following speech.

W Alright everyone, congratulations on the successful completion of this year's Battle of the Bands. We had a great turnout this year, and the coverage that we got on the local radio station has been very strong. Q9 Next year I hope to coordinate even more with local sponsors, and try to get into some T-shirt merchandising as well. Just like in previous years, the winners of the Battle of the Bands will receive free studio time from Wonderlix Studios here in town, with the goal of producing an album. Wonderlix has promised that they will even distribute the winning band's album through their regional outlets. All we have to do now is decide on who should win. You have all seen the bands perform over the last several days, so cast your vote on the form provided.

女： 好了，各位，恭喜今年的樂團大競技圓滿落幕。今年的報名非常踴躍，本地廣播電台也對本活動的消息不斷強力放送。明年，我希望能與更多的本地贊助商配合，請他們贊助，也會試著同時推銷販售一些 T 恤。如同往年一樣，樂團大競技的獲勝隊伍將獲得本市旺得立克斯錄音室的免費錄音時間，以便錄製專輯。旺得立克斯也承諾將在其地區性的銷售通路上，為冠軍樂團的專輯鋪貨。現在，我們所需要做的，就是決定誰該贏得冠軍。過去這幾天，你們都已觀賞過各個樂團的演出，所以，請在所提供的表格上，投下你神聖的一票吧。

樂團大競技投票表決

團名	歌詞（滿分 10 分）	表演（滿分 10 分）	打擊樂（滿分 10 分）	節奏（滿分 10 分）
壯麗火焰	7	7	6	7
藍調之路	6	8	7	7
歡唱姊妹	6	9	9	10
寂寞羅伊	9	5	5	10

字彙 turnout 參加者　coverage 新聞報導　coordinate 配合　regional outlet 地區性的銷售通路　merchandise 推銷

7. 說話者最有可能是誰？

    (A) 樂團大競技的統籌者

    (B) 樂團大競技的志工工程師

    (C) 本地廣播節目主持人

    (D) 報紙記者

解說 本題可由説話者宣布的內容與説話的
對象，來推論説話者的身分。説話者都
在談有關樂團大競技（Battle of the
Bands）的事，包括未來比賽籌備的改
進方向（I hope to coordinate even
more with local sponsors）、合作的
錄音室，最後請大家投票，具有這能
力的人，只有選項 (A) 中的協調者、統
籌者（coordinator）或選項 (C) 主持人
（host）了。不過，選項 (C) 是廣播主持
人，現在是不是正在廣播，無法確定，所
以正確答案是選項 (A)。

8. 請看圖表。關於「歡唱姊妹」可以預期的
是？

(A) 她們會成功。

(B) 她們會賣出很多 T 恤。

(C) 明年還會參賽。

(D) 她們將會在旺得立克斯錄音室錄製專
輯。

解說 看到圖表，四隊中「歡唱姊妹」是分數
加總最高的，所以可知它是優勝樂團。
然後要再注意，宣布中關於優勝者可以
獲得的獎勵，這樣就能找到正確答案。
説話者提到，優勝者可以獲得錄音室免
費使用錄音間、錄製及專輯販賣，所以
正確答案是選項 (D)。販賣 T 恤是明年
度的計畫，且和獲勝樂團的獎勵無關，
所以選項 (B) 不對。另外，宣布中也沒
有説「歡唱姊妹」很成功，所以選項 (A)
也不對。

9. 明年的樂團大競技，可能有何改變？

(A) 會有更多樂團參賽。

(B) 會有更多的新聞報導。

(C) 會有更多的贊助商及 T 恤。

(D) 冠軍隊伍將會在旺得立克斯工作室錄
製專輯。

解說 説話者提到關於明年的事時，出現了
more local sponsors 和 try to get
into some T-shirt merchandising，
選項 (C) 提到了這兩項，所以是正確答
案。本地廣播電台對此活動的強力放
送，是今年樂團大競技成功的原因之
一，但無法由宣布內容來推論明年報導
的狀況如何，所以選項 (B) 不能選。題

目問的是明年會變更的事，選項 (D) 的
錄音室錄專輯，是每個年度優勝者都
會有的獎勵，不是變更事項，所以也不
對。

Questions 10-12 refer to the following announcement.

W Q10 Hello everyone, my name is
Pamela Greer, and I would like to
welcome you all to the National
Conference on Aging. We regret
to inform you that our keynote
speaker, Jerry Sighburgh, could
not be with us this evening, but we
have an astounding replacement,
Professor Lauren James. Q12
Professor James is a world-
renowned expert on end-of-life
issues and has written numerous
articles on the ethics of long-term
care for the terminally ill, especially
those with Alzheimer's disease. Q10
Q12 In addition, Professor James
has worked intimately with Jerry
Sighburgh on his campaign for
elder care reform, so we are
confident that you will receive
the information that drew you to
our conference in the first place.
Please welcome Professor Lauren
James!

女： 各位好，我是潘蜜拉·葛瑞爾，歡迎各
位參加全國老化議題會議。很遺憾通
知各位，我們原定的主講人傑瑞·賽博
格，今晚無法出席演講。不過，我們另
外為各位請到令人驚喜的講者，羅倫·
詹姆士教授。詹姆士教授是全球知名
的臨終議題專家，以重症臨終者的長
照醫療道德標準為題，尤其是阿茲海
默症患者，撰寫過無數論述。此外，他
與傑瑞·賽博格在老年照護的改革上，
是合作無間的戰友，因此，我們深信諸
位絕對能獲得原先所預期從會議中取
得的所有知識。現在，讓我們來歡迎羅
倫·詹姆士教授！

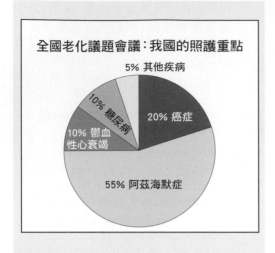

全國老化議題會議：我國的照護重點

5% 其他疾病
10% 糖尿病
10% 鬱血性心衰竭
20% 癌症
55% 阿茲海默症

字彙 keynote 主要演說的　expert 專家
congestive 充血的

10. 會議的聽眾會對何種主題感興趣？

　　(A)　老年照護
　　(B)　青少年生活
　　(C)　生育控制
　　(D)　治療癌症的新藥物

解說 介紹的第一句話就說，歡迎各位參加全國老化議題會議（on aging），在中後段又提及傑瑞·賽博格和詹姆士教授在老年照護的改革（elder care reform）上，是合作無間的戰友，相信與會聽眾能獲取他們想知道的知識，所以正確答案是選項 (A)。

11. 請看圖表。哪一種疾病最可能引起聽眾關注？

　　(A)　糖尿病
　　(B)　阿茲海默症
　　(C)　鬱血性心衰竭
　　(D)　癌症

解說 介紹的中段提及羅倫·詹姆士教授曾撰述多篇重症臨終者的長照醫療道德標準，特別是阿茲海默症，且依據圖表資料，照護重點有 55% 是阿茲海默症患者，所以該疾病最可能引起聽眾關注，正確答案是選項 (B)。

12. 根據說話者所言，關於羅倫·詹姆士的敘述何者為真？

　　(A)　他將與另一個主講人一同發表演說。
　　(B)　他的演說主題是工作倫理。
　　(C)　他曾與傑瑞·賽博格密切合作。
　　(D)　他不是一位知名學者。

解說 介紹者說，演說者傑瑞·賽博格不能來，換成由羅倫·詹姆士博士來演講，所以選項 (A) 錯。會議一開始就說演講主題是老化議題，因此工作倫理不是羅倫·詹姆士的演講主題，(B) 也不能選。要注意選項利用獨白中出現的 ethics（倫理）做成的錯誤答案。介紹者提到傑瑞·賽博格和詹姆士教授在老年照護的改革，曾密切合作（. . . has worked intimately . . .），選項 (C) 將 intimately 換成 closely 也可以，所以是正確答案。介紹者也說詹姆士教授是全球知名的專家（world-renowned expert），所以 (D) 錯。